MW00560324

THE
PHALANX
CODE

ALSO BY A. J. TATA

Total Empire

Chasing the Lion

Double Crossfire

Dark Winter

Direct Fire

Besieged

Three Minutes to Midnight

Foreign and Domestic

Reaper: Drone Strike (with Nicholas Irving)

Reaper: Threat Zero (with Nicholas Irving)

Reaper: Ghost Target (with Nicholas Irving)

Mortal Threat

Hidden Threat

Rogue Threat

Sudden Threat

THE PHALANX CODE

A. J. TATA

ST. MARTIN'S PRESS
NEW YORK

This is a work of fiction. All of the characters, organizations, and events portrayed in this novel are either products of the author's imagination or are used fictitiously.

First published in the United States by St. Martin's Press, an imprint of St. Martin's Publishing Group

Printed in the United States of America. For information, address St. Martin's Publishing Group, 120 Broadway, New York, NY 10271.

www.stmartins.com

Library of Congress Cataloging-in-Publication Data

Names: Tata, A. J. (Anthony J.), 1959– author.
Title: The Phalanx code / A. J. Tata.
Description: First edition. | New York : St. Martin's Press, 2024. | Series: Garrett Sinclair ; 3
Identifiers: LCCN 2023038139 | ISBN 9781250281463 (hardcover) | ISBN 9781250281470 (ebook)
Subjects: LCGFT: Thrillers (Fiction) | Novels.
Classification: LCC PS3620.A87 P43 2024 | DDC 813/.6—dc23/eng/20230825
LC record available at https://lccn.loc.gov/2023038139

First Edition: 2024

10 9 8 7 6 5 4 3 2 1

For Laura with all my love, and to my grandchildren Allison Kate and Leonardo Anthony, may you live full and productive lives worthy of the sacrifices made by the Garrett Sinclairs and Team Daggers of this country.

THE
PHALANX
CODE

JUNE 7, 1944

NEARLY TWO DAYS INTO the D-Day invasion of Normandy Beach, newly promoted Army Ranger Major Garrett "Coop" Sinclair stood atop Pointe du Hoc with the sun setting behind an American flag snapping in the stiff breeze.

Coop's youthful face was smeared with mud and camouflage on top of three days of beard stubble. His tired eyes stared into the horizon of the undulating Normandy Peninsula as a line of German prisoners, hands laced over their Stahlhelm helmets, walked under guard just beyond the casement Coop's Rangers had captured.

Second Ranger Battalion Commander Lieutenant Colonel James Rudder approached with a young Frenchman in tow.

"The 505th paras are having a hard go of it a few miles from here," Rudder said. "This is Marius. He's with a resistance group that was tasked with guiding us, but he says there're some women and children in trouble up the road. Take five men and go see what's happening. Then come back or we'll come to you, whichever makes sense."

The eager-eyed Frenchman was maybe sixteen years old. He was wearing a black beret and gray herringbone coat. His leather shoes looked ill-suited for the task of guiding Rangers through German defenses. When Marius pointed west, a rhombus-shaped black tattoo flashed inside the wrist of his right hand. It was the same insignia turned on its side, like an elongated baseball diamond, that Coop and the other Rangers wore on the sleeve of their uniforms. The Rangers had been briefed they would be linking up with resistance members and that they should look for the Ranger rhombus-shaped tattoos that signaled they were talking to bona fide allies.

"Rapide! Rapide!" the man said.

"Cool it, Frenchy," Coop said, then to Rudder: "Sir, we're barely hanging on here. If I take five of my men things will get even more dicey."

As if to emphasize Coop's point, machine-gun fire chattered nearby, snapping overhead with white arcs of German tracers etching against the muted purple hues of dusk. Waves of Allied troops continued to pour onto Utah and Omaha beaches below Coop's position.

"We've got this, Coop. If we can't save women and children, what's the point? Now get moving," Rudder said.

"Roger that, Colonel," Coop replied. He'd made his protest and now would follow his commander's orders.

Explosions from the naval artillery blanketing the coastline rumbled. The ground shook. Someone yelled, "Incoming!" and Coop grabbed Marius and dove to the ground, shrapnel whizzing like angry hornets.

"Can't show us the way if you're dead," Coop grumbled.

"Je suis pierre-tranchant," Marius said, holding up his wrist with the tattoo and pointing at the small black rhombus. *"La pierre est tranchant."*

"Rudder said you're good to go, but thanks for that. Yes, the stone is sharp," Coop said in reply to Marius' offering of bona fides. The planning in Titchfield, England, had called for French resistance members to etch a small Ranger rhombus henna tattoo on the inside of their right wrist and use the phrase "The stone is sharp" when linking up with the Rangers.

The French liaison suggested this because the Ranger insignia looked like a "sharp stone."

Coop pulled Marius by his trench coat the way a coach tugs a quarterback into a sideline huddle. He eyed his gaggle of twenty men and gathered his five nearest Rangers, who were cleaning their M1 Garand rifles and licking the inside of combat ration cans, commonly known as "c-rats."

"Special mission, men, let's go," he said. They reassembled their weapons and grabbed their gear without complaint. They had survived the climb up Pointe du Hoc and most likely considered themselves invincible or lucky or both. Coop tucked in behind Marius, who hurried them along a trail that kept the assault on Utah Beach to their immediate rear and right flank. Marius' shoes didn't seem to be an impediment as Coop and his men began running to keep up with the worried Frenchman.

"Rapide! Rapide!" Marius whispered over his shoulder, loud enough for the men to hear.

It was the second night of the invasion. Coop and his men had been operating continuously. Artillery rained down. Naval ships bombed the coast without precision. Machine-gun fire chattered. Lead pinged off thousands of landing craft in Seine Bay, which fronted Normandy Beach, sounding like a symphony from hell.

Following a drainage gulley from north to south, Marius led Coop and his team to a small shelter. Stemming from the outbuilding was a worn path to the town. By now, Coop could hear shrieks louder than any artillery explosion or rifle fire. The plaintive cries of women and children became his beacon in the night.

Coop grabbed Marius by the shoulder and said, "We've got it from here."

Marius pointed at a group of German soldiers herding women and children into the basement of a French farmhouse situated on a sloping ridge. The box frame of the house fronted the high ground while the back side offered a generous bottom level dug into the terrain. One of the Germans near the cellar door was holding a jerry can filled with gasoline.

"Follow me, men," Coop said to his Rangers.

Coop and his men charged the German troops, who were shouting, *"Tod durch feurer! Tod durch feurer!"* Death by fire! Death by fire!

Coop fired his M1 Garand rifle until he ran out of ammunition. His teammates provided cover for one another as they took turns charging the Germans. Coop led the assault and stuck his bayonet in the man by the basement door. Another German soldier held the petrol can and a lighter, which he tossed into the doorway leading to the basement just as Coop rammed the butt of his rifle into the man's face.

The flame ignited, burning red and yellow against the angry black sky.

Screams pierced the night as Coop ran into the blazing inferno toward the prisoners inside.

PRESENT DAY

I CLOSED MY GRANDFATHER'S World War II combat diary, the ink diffused by tears, the pages covered in dark stains I took to be blood. I ran my finger across the worn cover where he had drawn in pencil the Ranger patch rhombus, a square turned on a point. The pencil had traced and retraced the four sides, as if he had been deep in thought when sketching.

Holding the leather-bound tome in my manacled hands, as if in prayer, I looked up when the guard rattled her baton between the bars of my cell.

"Let's go Sinclair," Sergeant Robin Calles said. "Going to see the big guy."

I slid the diary beneath my mattress and walked with Calles' baton in my back through the byzantine maze of new and old construction until I was standing in the warden's office, looking through his panoptic window.

The winter sun hung low behind the khaki-colored cornfields, stalks severed and broken; a metaphor for something, I thought. Perhaps the state of the country or even the world. The warden's view looked down upon the prison yard, the razor wire stretching between the guard towers and the bluffs of the Missouri River. The sun's muted, fading hues cast a diminishing glow across the acres of frozen penitentiary land the inmates tended in the spring under the watchful eyes of snipers.

"Inmate Sinclair, why do you think you're still under my charge?" Warden Phillip Smyth asked me.

Smyth was an active-duty full bird colonel. His hair was gelled back Gordon Gekko style. His throwback Army olive-and-tan uniform bulged at all the seams. Tall and thickset, Smyth was a military police officer charged with operating the Fort Leavenworth Disciplinary Barracks, known in the military as "the DB." The DB was a maximum-security prison that held everything from death row inmates who would receive lethal injections to felons who cheated the military supply system by stealing blankets. And then there was me with pending murder charges, among other lesser allegations, to the best of my knowledge. No one had told me. Normally a prisoner was afforded protections of due process but given the atmospherics around my arrest, I'd yet to be charged with a crime.

Smyth stood profile to me, gazing out the same window as if he were posing for a Grant Wood portrait. Instead of the pitchfork of *American Gothic* fame, he held a gnarled and lacquered walking stick in his fleshy right fist, its shiny tip appearing unblemished and pristine. I shifted my gaze from beyond the walls of the prison to Smyth's narrow eyes, which refused to meet mine. His typically arrogant countenance was replaced by something I hadn't seen before. Perhaps, worry?

I had been in this office only once before and that was a year ago when the FBI had delivered me here fresh from an FBI ambush on Figure Eight Island, North Carolina, perhaps baited by the president of the United States herself.

"Warden, I don't know what day it is, much less why I'm in your facility," I replied.

"It's Thursday. President's Day weekend is coming up. A holiday," he said, as if that mattered to me. Finally, he turned and looked at me. "I've been instructed to give you two pieces of information."

He paused, but I said nothing.

"First, your lawyer was found dead yesterday," Smyth said.

My "lawyer" was Charles Green, a family friend of my late grandfather, General Garrett "Coop" Sinclair. Green was a garden-variety attorney who handled everything imaginable in Fayetteville, North Carolina. Before writing a dozen letters to the president and chief of staff of the army about my confinement, to no avail, his most important duty had been handling Coop's estate when my grandfather had passed a few years ago. Coop was a genuine World War II legend, having scaled the cliffs of Pointe du Hoc on D-Day during the Normandy Invasion with the Second Ranger Battalion. Green had smuggled my grandfather's combat diary inside a leather-bound Bible during his one and only visit a year ago.

I shrugged. I had liked Green and knew him mostly from when I was a kid helping Coop work on his cars.

"Our communications department tells me he sent a package for you, which you can have tomorrow," Smyth said.

"Why can't I have it today?" I didn't really care, but I was mildly curious.

He coughed and said, "That's the second piece of information. I've been instructed to release you. Tomorrow, you'll be officially discharged from my facility and the army. The inspector general's office has completed their investigation and made their recommendations to the secretary of defense, who has reported the findings to the president. The president, evidently, showed mercy and granted you a pardon, which allows you to maintain your rank. Your discharge is effective at noon tomorrow. Behave until then and you're free, a retired three-star general. Give me one reason . . . one reason . . . to keep you here, and I will. Understand?"

I stood there motionless. His words were artificial. They didn't resonate. They couldn't be real.

"You're gone tomorrow," Smyth said again. "Discharged. Full pension. Not my choice, but the president is in charge."

I remained motionless and said nothing.

"Sinclair. Do you hear me, inmate Sinclair?"

The volume of his voice cracked the veneer of my protective shield. In prison I felt nothing, believed very little, and said even less.

"One more time, Sinclair. Do you understand me?!"

I didn't respond then, either, but a sense of sorrow washed over me. I'd had nearly a year to contemplate my situation and the likelihood that my career was over, but that didn't make this news any easier to accept. I had never expected a gold watch or farewell party, not even before I'd been secreted to the shadowy confines of the DB. But I had thought this mistake would have been rectified, that they would have cleared my name when I was released. At the very least, I wanted the opportunity to thank my troops and say goodbye to a few friends. Instead, I was being shamefully ushered into the cold winter of Kansas. The finality was incomprehensible.

A year ago, the FBI had swarmed across the sand dunes of Figure Eight Island, North Carolina, and snatched Sergeants Major Joe Hobart, Randy Van Dreeves, and me when we were debriefing the Eye of Africa mission with President Campbell. Somehow my former team member Jake Mahegan had avoided capture. Last I saw, he had a federal agent in a hammerlock as they wrestled on the beach. My money had been on Mahegan, though I had never learned the outcome.

Once a college roommate of my wife and a theoretical friend to me, President Campbell was now trying to salvage what was left of her term and consolidate her political power. Her cabinet had secretly enhanced ties with the Chinese government and some tech moguls, but only she and her team knew their part in the endgame in that relationship. Once someone who had been read on to every special access, code word program in the United States government, I was now just another prisoner and, evidently, a soon-to-be discharged veteran. No charges filed. No trial date set. And now released and retired? I didn't believe what Smyth was saying.

"I'm calling the guards unless you acknowledge that you understand what I just said, inmate Sinclair."

"I do," I said, but I didn't. There was no way it was over, just like that. Either I was being ambushed when I left tomorrow, or I would find an untimely demise this evening in my cell.

"Nothing to say? Your career is over and you're speechless?"

"No farewell party?" I quipped.

Smyth's eyes got distant, and the faintest hint of a smirk turned on his lips.

"I'm sure your peers will think of something," he said. "Golden handcuffs might be fitting, don't you think?"

I caught the flash of a police strobe outside on Route 73, which bordered the military reservation. A gaggle of black-and-white police cars had gathered about a mile away. A spider of intuition crawled along my spine.

I nodded. "Sure. I'd like to notify my kids."

"Tomorrow morning you will be allowed to make one phone call prior to your departure. In the meantime, Sergeant Calles will escort you to dinner and then back to your cell. And remember, Sinclair, you're still just another inmate doing time while you're in my facility."

"Roger that," I replied.

"Let's go, Sinclair," Sergeant Calles said.

Calles was a big woman with inch-long blond hair on top that was tapered with shears on the sides and back. One day several months ago while working the mail room, I'd overheard her complaining to another guard that she had failed out of the army's challenging Ranger School. Originally from Nebraska, she had chosen military police as her career field, and Fort Leavenworth as her first assignment to be near her home.

I respected her straightforward approach to her job and her inmates, but her wanton use of the baton had grown tiresome. In her block, I was just another prisoner, as it should be, though she must have recognized the pressure of housing a three-star general in pretrial confinement.

Prison had not required much of an adjustment for me. I had never taken comfort in the trappings of rank. Having led from the front lines, much to the criticism of some of my peers who saw career progression as a pathway out of danger, I didn't see a wide chasm between a foxhole and a prison cell. Three hots and a cot, as they say. Many had it worse. Who was I to bitch?

With Calles' baton in my back, we departed the command wing of the prison with its big windows full of daylight, shiny floors, and executive furniture. We transitioned back into the dark, depressing catacombs of muted cinder block walls and hydraulic barred doors. I shuffled along until the heavy metal door opened with a hiss and I was standing in the cafeteria line with my fellow inmates.

"General," Private First-Class Johnnie Hooper said. Hooper had been convicted for distributing fentanyl from his barracks room in Fort Hood, Texas.

"Hoop," I replied.

"No talking!" Calles shouted. Her baton plowed into my kidney. I nodded at her as the forty or so prisoners turned and looked at her with hard eyes. I might have been an inmate, but they knew I was an active-duty general. More to the point, I was *their* general. An odd respect emanated from my status and my reputation as a combat warrior.

Not a day went by where there wasn't some rumor about me and my status, especially in relation to the Eye of Africa battle last year. My Dagger team had risked it all to stop China from releasing four or five nuclear hypersonic glide vehicles on the United States and maybe several European cities. The irony was that there had been online traffic, surely fabricated, that implicated my team and me in the Chinese scheme to launch nukes at the United States. The media had portrayed me as the ringleader of the nuclear threat against America. It was preposterous, but the power of the corporate media had half the world believing it to be true. I had transitioned from a shadow warrior leading our nation's finest to support and defend our Constitution, to an infamous prisoner mysteriously held in contravention of that very document.

Because I took no part in social media, I didn't see the volumes of information people told me were being spewed across all the platforms such as Twitter, Facebook, Instagram, billionaire Mitch Drewson's newest app called Shoutter, and LanxPro, tech mogul Aurelius Blanc's app. My fellow inmates tried to keep me up to date with the latest musings about my fate.

A broken man, I was barely interested.

I shuffled forward in the line for food, Calles still at my back. Hooper got his glop, then I held up my tray. With his white hairnet and apron, Private Sam McWhorley looked like a fry cook at McDonald's. Grease-stained white apron. Stringy mustache and beard. Tattoo sleeves on both arms. Hateful sneer on his face. He leaned over and let a long stringy loogie slip between his lips and sucked it back in before it hit the ladle in his hand. He had been a mechanic at Fort Campbell in Kentucky and was here for sexual assault of a fellow soldier. I had been the court-martial convening authority at the time and gave him the maximum punishment. I figured no chow was better than something mixed with his bodily fluids, so I kept shuffling ahead. If there was an inside job to hit me this evening, McWhorley would gladly be the ringleader.

Handing out the sweet tea in plastic cups was Corporal Sonny Jones, a big African American from New Orleans and relatively recent addition to the Disciplinary Barracks population. He put a cup of iced tea on my tray and slid a cheeseburger from who knows where next to it.

"General," he said with a nod. "Hearing news."

"Sonny," I said.

He smiled. A few weeks ago, Jones told me he had posted a long rant about the Eye of Africa battle and how my former Dagger team had saved the country, maybe the world. He said that it was trending on social media and he had used the hashtags #EAB #garrettsinclair #savingamerica.

I sat down and listened to the sounds of chains scraping, men slurping gravy, and guard boots tapping the linoleum floor. The place smelled of decaying meat and disinfectant. I lifted the bun of my cheeseburger after spying a white hair on it. The hair turned out to be a piece of paper with a message:

8 pm tonight. Stay in bed!

I looked at the clock on the wall, which read 7:04 P.M. The clock was circular like we had in Fayetteville Public Schools some forty years ago. It was battery powered and high up on the wall so no one could reach in and use the second hand as a shiv.

In my periphery, I saw McWhorley's hand flash with a kitchen knife. A small group of unfamiliar prisoners gathered maybe twenty meters away near the kitchen entrance. In the opposite direction I noticed Smyth ascend the steps to a small sally port bridge that looked like a church choir balcony. He stared in my direction as the group near the kitchen began walking toward me like a blocking wedge for a kick-off returner on the football field.

I rotated my neck and rolled my shoulders. I ate the cheeseburger and the piece of paper, which went down smoothly with the warm, diluted tea. Was it poisoned? I pushed away from my table and began to stand to confront the aggressors.

"What's that?" Calles demanded. She moved between me and McWhorley's wedge; McWhorley stopped, eyes curious, when Calles inserted herself in the equation. Without her, the battlefield geometry was five to one. After a year of lifting weights, I put my meager prison bank account on me, despite my fifty-two years.

I continued to stand. That was the protocol. If a guard addressed you, standing to pay respects was expected. I was six feet two inches tall, and she was every bit of six feet in her jackboots.

"Cheeseburger, Sergeant," I said. McWhorley's group inched forward, some casting their eyes upward at the bridge where Smyth stood.

"The white thing," she snapped.

"Oh, mayonnaise, I guess. Or maggots. I don't look at it. I just eat it. Like in Ranger school," I said.

Importantly, the inmate chatter claimed that Calles had played college softball at the University of Nebraska. The Ranger School comment was probably unnecessary and resulted in a swing for the fences into my kidneys. I would be pissing blood tonight for sure. Was she the artillery to soften up the target for McWhorley and team?

"You're out of line, Sinclair," she barked in my face. Then she turned to the halted wedge and said through clenched teeth, "Stand down!"

The entire cafeteria had gone silent. The clock ticked loudly. Time froze. McWhorley's wedge was conspicuously motionless, maybe stunned by her intervention.

"Yes, Sergeant," I said.

I was thankful for the interruption, though I wouldn't have minded a good fight right now. Emotionally processing an abrupt halt to a lifetime of service was already challenging, especially from the confines of a maximum-security prison. So, goddamnit, bring it on. Make me a convict and I'll act like one.

As I stood there watching the motionless cafeteria like a narrator walking through a three-dimensional movie freeze-frame, I reverted to my observation training as an army Ranger and special mission unit operator.

McWhorley's knife was a forked garden tool with a wooden handle and tips honed to razor points. The lead man in the attack had a shaved head and tattoos crawling up his neck. He was jacked and the look in his eyes told me he was high on meth. He stood there flexing like a weight lifter who had just bounced a personal best snatch-and-clean on the floor.

The two men on either flank of McWhorley were equally muscled. Why they had left the task to the smallest guy in the foursome, McWhorley, was a mystery, but I could guess it was revenge for my sentencing of his rape charge.

I thought of my dead wife, Melissa, and my daughter, Reagan, anger rising again at his crime. Maybe now I could give him an even more proper sentence.

The freeze-frame went from motionless to fast-forward.

The man leading the wedge barreled toward me. Calles attempted to block him but was tossed aside with the flick of the man's left arm. His demonic eyes sparked red with evil. The two flankers protected McWhorley. The thing about fighting someone doped up on amphetamines is that they are all energy and no coordination. The army had transitioned to a respectable hand-to-hand combat training regimen about twenty years before in special mission units; we practiced combative techniques almost daily. As the commander, I did "man in the middle" drills where my men would come at me one at a time from a different direction as I stood in the center of the circle they formed.

It was rare that I lost.

My mind roared. *Make me a convict and I'll act like one.*

I let the wedge leader into my personal space, where I immediately clinched him and landed four debilitating knee strikes into his ribs then used his momentum to trip him forward. I spun to find the right-side flanker dueling with Calles, who had rejoined the fray. McWhorley was pushing the left-side flanker with his right hand. I jabbed the left flanker twice as he broke his focus when McWhorley tried to hide behind him. A roundhouse kick snapped his neck to the left, causing him to stand up straight. I used that opening to land two straight kicks to his larynx with my prison boots. As he clasped his neck with both hands, I put the toe of my boot squarely in his crotch. He doubled over, whereupon I laced my fingers and pulled his head down with my hands and drove my knee into his face, breaking his nose, blood spraying everywhere.

With the wedge breaker and flankers preoccupied, McWhorley skittered haplessly toward me with his modified garden tool. As the wiry, skinny meth head and rapist lunged at me, my hand was like a rattlesnake, latching onto his wrist and twisting his arm upward. I did a sweeping back kick, landing him on the table where I had been eating. Drinks and food exploded onto the chairs and floor. I wrapped my hand like a vise around his left fist holding the weapon and slowly arced it toward his face. The two shiny, sharpened prongs were closing with his eyes. His breath smelled like a dead rat in a week-old garbage pail of rotting food. Piss spread on his orange jumpsuit, and I smelled feces.

I was laser focused on his scared pupils flitting about, looking for help. By now the entire cafeteria full of convicts was chanting, "Sinclair! Sinclair! Sinclair! Sinclair!"

As I slowly lowered his resisting fist toward his face, I whispered into the noise, "Come at me you little bitch? I'm not some fourteen-year-old girl."

Calles shouted, "Sinclair stand down!" Two guards pulled at me with the weapon scraping McWhorley's cheek. "Stand down! Stand down!"

As two beefy military police prison guards muscled me away from McWhorley, I released his fist that had been resisting. The weapon shot forward and scraped my biceps as the guards held me in place, almost as if they wanted to do the wedge breaker's job and make me a target. Calles intervened and flung McWhorley up against the wall where two more military police guards secured him and the garden tool.

"Sinclair, you're headed to solitary!" Calles shouted as she pushed me through the crowd.

Smyth bellowed from the bridge, "Sinclair! You couldn't even behave for an hour?" Then, "Sergeant Calles, make sure inmate Sinclair is properly treated in solitary."

"Roger that, sir," she said. Another demonstrative thud with the baton drew a thin-lipped smile from Smyth. Pain rocketed through my back into my shoulder blades and up my spine into the base of my skull.

"You're clearly a danger, Sinclair. I'll be making a report post haste," Smyth said. There was satisfaction in his voice. I wasn't sure if he wanted me dead or mixed up in a fight so he could try to overturn my release. Ankles chained and wrists handcuffed, I shuffled along with Calles, who was shouting down each corridor, "Solitary coming through!"

We arrived in the solitary wing where a guard I had never seen before opened the door and shoved me in, but not before Calles' baton landed one more blow on my bruised back. She tossed a bottle of Betadine and some gauze on the concrete slab that passed for a bed.

"Get on the bed and don't move other than patching yourself up. Understand?" Calles said.

I nodded.

"I asked you a question, inmate. Do you understand that for the next thirty minutes you are confined to that bed?"

As if solitary wasn't enough, now she wanted me in a specific location in a cell isolated from the rest of the prison.

"Yes, Sergeant," I said as if I was a young lieutenant attending basic training.

The heavy door closed with a metallic clank, the lock snapping with a hydraulic whisper.

I had no wristwatch, phone, or wall clock. The solitary room was simple, but bigger than I expected. It was maybe twenty-five feet wide. A concrete slab on the left was covered with a threadbare blanket and thin feather pillow dotted with the cavity drool of hundreds of previous inmates. There was a concrete divider maybe three feet wide at the head of the bed. A toilet on the right. No lid. No seat. Just a hole.

I sat on the bed, leaned against the cinder block wall, and thought about the note on my cheeseburger.

8 pm tonight. Stay in bed!

The clock in my head told me I had twenty-two minutes to go.

Whatever was supposed to happen at 8:00 P.M., I was in a different location than anyone might expect me to be. It could have been that Smyth preferred I be assassinated here in solitary since the attempt in the dining facility had not panned out. Or it may have been a warning from a friend to protect me from some violent act that was happening at the prison that night. Or it might have been something random, like a gathering to discuss potential informal inmate leadership moves, rule changes, or the latest social media screed about me.

I was breathing rapidly from the exertion and checked myself the way I would do after any airborne or combat operation. Feet, legs, torso, face, neck, skull. Check. Right arm bleeding but not terribly. My back was hurting from Calles' baseball swings, but there was nothing I could do about that. My lungs were burning from the aerobic exercise, but that felt good. Other than my arm and back, I was fine. I picked up the Betadine and checked the laceration. I peeled away the jumpsuit as best I could, revealing two parallel gashes across my right biceps muscle. Blood was seeping. I dabbed at it with the gauze, then poured the purple disinfectant all over my arm. Once the stinging subsided, I poured more, then wrapped my arm in gauze, which quickly soaked up the blood and medicine.

I used my teeth and cuffed hands to tie the gauze, then lay down on the bed, curious why Calles had instructed me to be in that one spot. My primal defenses were on high alert after the fight and Smyth's obvious manipulation. Was there a bomb under the bed? Cage fight with another inmate? What was the play?

A small camera was situated in the top right-hand corner of the cell, its smoky gray globe concealing the actual lens. Was it off or "malfunctioning"? If everything was on the level, I figured I should probably stay where I was unless I wanted more shots to the kidneys.

After twenty minutes of reflection about Sally McCool, Joe Hobart, and Randy Van Dreeves, the heart of my Dagger team, my head shot up.

Three knocks on the outer wall, not the door, preceded a blast in the far opposite corner of the cell, blowing inward. Smoke and debris ricocheted around the cell, the concrete divider at my head absorbing some of the blast. A hole the size of a car was left in its wake. Alarms sounded. Lights flashed. Sprinklers sprayed.

Through the smoke and haze, Jake Mahegan stepped into the opening wearing night vision goggles and carrying enough weapons for both of us.

He used a set of bolt cutters to snap my ankle chains and handcuffs, handed me a Beretta pistol, and said, “Follow me, boss.”

I FOLLOWED MAHEGAN THROUGH a tunnel until we were walking through frozen mud along the banks of the Missouri River.

We angled north. Neither of us had spoken a word. We had caromed through an earthen limestone shaft that zigged and zagged until we were in the biting winds howling along the river valley, the patter of feet echoing pursuit behind us. After about a mile of moving north, Mahegan dragged a small Zodiac with an electric motor from the deadwood along the shore. As we sped across the river, I was thankful that we didn't have to swim. A big, lumbering kid from the Outer Banks of North Carolina, Mahegan was a waterman who built his strength by fighting the fabled currents of the Graveyard of the Atlantic off the coast of Cape Hatteras.

We emerged on the far side after some slight drift. The water had huge chunks of ice in it, and as it was, we had to disembark and wade chest deep through the icy muck on the eastern shore where the water moved more slowly and froze more quickly. We cracked ice with the butts of our pistols and Mahegan tossed his phone in the boat and let it drift south as we trudged onto dry land. Soon after plodding another half mile north, we found an old cabin where he said, "Here. Quick," which was a major conversation for Mahegan, who like Sergeant Major Joe Hobart, was sparse with his words when in full execute mode.

Inside the barren shack, Mahegan had pre-positioned a change of clothes, food, water, medical supplies, communications gear, ammunition, and weapons. He powered up two new phones, checked them, then shut them off.

"Change, kit up, and let's go," he said.

I nodded. In less than five minutes we both had discarded our wet clothes and changed. I applied some ointment to the gashes on my arm and bandaged it again. Mahegan tossed the river-soaked clothing into a burn barrel in the ground, poured some gas on them and flipped a lit match inside. The gas burned brightly, blue and orange flames licking upward. It felt good to have the heat stinging my face after even a short period of time in the freezing water.

"Could be tracking devices in your clothes," he said. "Smart dust."

"Smart dust?"

"Blanc and his Phalanx company have weaponized microchips the size of a grain of sand that can track you."

"Roger," I said, adjusting the new clothes Mahegan had stashed for me: black cargo pants, black polypropylene long sleeve T-shirt, loose fitting jacket, Oakley Light Assault boots, and black outer tactical vest. "Where to next?" I asked. We both took a long drink of water, the sweat quickly pouring through my skin as the fuel burned in the barrel and my racing heart slammed against my chest.

"Link up with Randy and Joe," Mahegan said.

"You mean to get them out?" I asked. "They're in prison, too, I heard."

"Negative. Patch Owens and Zion Black walked them out last night from the Navy Brig in San Diego. Mitch Drewson apparently intervened. That's all I know."

"The tech billionaire? The Shoutter app guy?"

"Roger." He shrugged. "Not sure why, but he wanted you all out. I didn't need any more explanation."

I nodded. I was glad and wasn't going to look a gift horse in the mouth just yet. Patch Owens was an operator who served as a unit medic. He and Mahegan had left the service at about the same time, and both had worked various odd jobs in North Carolina. Zion Black was a former professional football defensive end who was as big as Mahegan at six foot five inches and pushing 280 pounds. He had been with me during the Eye of Africa mission as part of my personal security detail. As were all my crew, they were teammates.

"What's Drewson's angle here?" I asked. I wasn't a social media fan, but something was scratching at the back of my mind. Jake had to blow a shape charge through the wall of the DB to get me out, but Hobart and Van Dreeves just walked through the front gate of the Navy brig?

"All I know is that he's funding this," Mahegan said. "I was minding my own business in Cape Hatteras when I got a random visit from him personally. Flew into Manteo from Kinston on a private jet and pulled up in a four-wheel on the beach where I was surfing with some other locals. It's where all this gear came from," he said.

He waved his hand around the dilapidated shack.

"Go on," I said.

"He asked if I was interested in getting you and the others out of jail. I packed my shit and flew with him to Colorado. Called Patch and Zion en route and here we are."

"Nothing else?" I asked.

He shrugged. "He's a talkative guy, so yeah, he mentioned an assload of stuff but nothing relevant." After a brief pause, Mahegan said, "He did mention your grandfather. Something to do with Evelyn Champollion and your grandfather."

"Coop?"

"Yes, sir," Mahegan said.

I nodded and turned my eyes to the fractured ceiling at the sound of a helicopter chopping through the sky. It became louder before it faded away. Louder again before fading again. The whipping blades echoed along the Missouri River Valley, blunted off and on by a whistling north wind.

"Cloverleaf search pattern. Let's put this fire out and get moving," I said.

"We've got wheels a mile up the river," Mahegan said. "It's going to be tight."

We stepped into the frigid air. The dry clothes were welcome. Movement was swift with Mahegan leading. I had never met a better navigator than Mahegan and he had us handrailing along the military crest, that area just below the backbone of the ridgeline that kept us from being silhouetted against the night sky. The moon was a dim sliver of pale light.

Up ahead and across the river, blue lights flashed. Police cars raced toward Fort Leavenworth, now several miles to our southwest. Mahegan slowed as we dipped into a small tributary creek running into the Missouri River.

Another helicopter raced low along the river, no doubt using thermal imaging to locate our warm bodies against the cold terrain.

"Croatan," Mahegan whispered.

"Dare," Joe Hobart's unmistakable voice replied through the throat microphone and earpiece set Mahegan had provided in the cabin.

With bona fides exchanged we crested a small hillock dotted with some hardwoods. The underbrush was thick with thorny vines that clawed against my pant legs. Mahegan powered through, so I followed his path and we reappeared next to an idling black-and-white Chevrolet Suburban with a roof rack of lights switched off for the moment. Stenciled on the doors was: CLINTON COUNTY SHERIFF'S OFFICE. Clinton County was part of the greater Kansas City metropolitan area about thirty miles south of Leavenworth. Beside the car I spotted Sergeant Major Randy Van Dreeves on one knee aiming a long rifle across the river.

"Boss," he said when I passed him, as if we had just spoken a few hours ago when it had been more than a year since the FBI raid that had cornered my team. A lump caught in my throat when I thought about Van Dreeves' one true love, Lieutenant Colonel Sally McCool, who had perished in my arms during the Eye of Africa fight.

Hobart was behind the wheel, and I knew from the sirens, the helicopter blades, and the flashing lights that we had no time to waste on nostalgia or emotions. These three men were the core of my team, and we were like a championship basketball team that hadn't practiced in the last year. We were rusty, but we knew the plays and could execute.

As we were transitioning to the SUV, Van Dreeves shouted, "Halt!"

We turned and looked as he aimed his rifle at a figure that came crashing through the same thorny underbrush we had traversed. Dressed in a military uniform and larger than average, the pursuer stumbled onto the ground where Mahegan moved swiftly and put a knee in the person's back.

"I'm Sergeant Calles! The insider! I helped!" she shouted far louder than any of us preferred.

Calles. My guard. She was soaking wet and shivering.

"Throw her in the back," I said.

"Could be tracked," Mahegan said.

"We're all going to be tracked if we don't hurry. She helped us, I think. Had to know something. She put me in that cell. Let's go," I said, remembering her instructions to stay on the bed for the "next thirty minutes."

Mahegan and Van Dreeves disarmed her, tossed her baton into the brush, checked her for communications devices or transmitters the best they could, found my Ziploc bag containing my grandfather's diary in her pocket, and then hog-tied her before raising the rear door of the SUV.

"How the hell did you get across the river, Sergeant?" Van Dreeves asked. Mahegan handed me the diary.

"Your boat got hung up in some debris," she said, breathing hard and probably on the edge of hypothermia. I swam to it and took it across."

Mahegan asked, "What was in the boat?"

"I found a phone in the bottom, yes. Tossed it in the river," she said.

Her story seemed to track. As they were escorting her to the back hatch, Calles nodded at the bag in my hand.

"That's for the general," she said. "His grandfather's diary and something his lawyer just sent."

I looked at the bag. In the bottom was a silver triangular device.

"Let's go," I said.

Calles continued, "Smyth was trying to have his IT team decipher it, but it was encrypted, and it looks like it's only half of something. They called it a 'package.' Looks like a flash drive."

"Roger that," I said. I stowed the diary in my cargo pocket and the small triangular "package" in an interior zipper in my tactical boot.

"The warden did say they had something for me," I said.

"Could be a tracking device," Mahegan said.

"I'll risk it," I said.

They lifted Calles into the cargo hatch of the SUV. I slipped into the back seat on the passenger's side as Mahegan racked his left rear seat behind Hobart all the way back. Van Dreeves slid into the front passenger seat, and we were a whole unit again, almost. Sally's noticeable absence, I imagined, and hoped, would be with us forever. I looked over my shoulder at the Sergeant Calles, roles reversed, then leaned forward.

"Patch? Zion?" I asked.

"They're at Drewson's compound," Van Dreeves said.

"What's Drewson's angle here?"

"The two tech giants Mitch Drewson and Aurelius Blanc are going at it like the old US and Soviet Union days," Van Dreeves said.

"Blanc as in founder of LanxPro? Why do we care about two billionaires going at each other?"

"All I can say is that we got in last night, and before launching us to get you, Drewson gave us a briefing about his Project Optimus. Something about how Blanc's Phalanx Corporation is imposing technofascism on our country and the world and he, Drewson, is trying to stop that."

Hobart was racing the SUV to nearly a hundred miles per hour. We hit a large pothole that threw Mahegan's head into the ceiling of the SUV.

"Sorry, Jake," Hobart said.

Next to me, Mahegan said nothing. He just kept scanning the rolling hills and split rail fences looking for threats to us and our mission.

The forever chatty Van Dreeves said from the front seat, "What I read is that Blanc has programmed Phalanx's algorithms to constantly update random facial image captures, which lead to a scan of Facebook, Instagram, Twitter, LinkedIn, TikTok, Snapchat, Shoutter, Truth Social, Gettr, or LanxPro," Van Dreeves said. "Like worldwide surveillance."

"I don't follow that bullshit," I said.

"Elon Musk has Twitter. Drewson has his Shoutter app. And Blanc has LanxPro where Phalanx coders connect it all. One app to access your business profile, microblog, family pictures, political discourse, et cetera. Their software accesses the public images and words from all the user content, combines it with what is on the internet, and instantly creates a profile of everything ever posted by or about a person. Drewson says Blanc is using all that to create a global security state."

Mahegan and I said nothing. As we rounded the bend in the road to gain access to the interstate heading north, a police barricade was blocking the entrance ramps.

"Randy did a lot of reading in the Navy brig," Hobart said.

"True that," Van Dreeves said.

Hobart flipped on the lights on the roof rack briefly to show he was "friendly." He slowed enough to wave his arms outside the window, as if we were just another cop car racing to find the escapee. The police officers looked at each other, shrugged and nodded at the one in the wrecker, who backed up enough for Hobart to thread through the extensive blockade. Hobart stopped to chat with the heavyset cop who was carrying an AR-15 at a lazy port arms.

"Y'all looking for the jailbreak?" Hobart asked.

"Army general. Traitor. Good as dead if I see him," one of the cops said.

"Where'd you hear he was a traitor?"

"Right here on my OptiPhone." He held up an OptiPhone, Drewson's competitor to the iPhone, Droid, and LanxPro smartphones. The picture was of me in a gray prison uniform. My face still looked pretty much the same, a year later. Mahegan was directing an infrared laser pointer at the cop, who squinted without realizing his vision was being disrupted by the invisible beam. I turned slightly so that the officer would not have a full profile view of my face, but I didn't want to bring any attention to Calles in the back. It was a major test of her true loyalties to see if she remained quiet.

"I'm betting I get him first," Hobart said.

"You guys don't look like normal cops," he said.

"Sheriff's department down in KC," Hobart said. "When the break happened, we scrambled from our homes. Moving into position."

"Wasting time," Van Dreeves said, impatiently.

"Yeah, yeah, sorry. You guys must be SWAT," the cop said. "We've been waiting for you. Wait a minute."

I held my breath as the cop stared at his phone and said, "Hold on, guys."

"We gotta run," Van Dreeves said.

The cop turned his phone and showed it to us. "Says they've got him. False alarm. Back in captivity. You boys can head back to Clinton County."

After a pause, Van Dreeves said, "Well, that's good news. Hear that team?"

"Roger that," Hobart replied, and then gunned the Suburban through the slalom of dragon's teeth obstacles and onto the interstate north.

As we got up to cruising speed, Van Dreeves said, "See that? Phalanx Alert. Instant information cross-checked across billions of images. Then hits every phone with your picture, boss, and then some bullshit about how you were back in jail. Everything was fine."

"Thought you guys had erased all that," I said.

"Blanc's tech easily defeats our home-cooked eraser app. I can probably counter it, but, you know, boss, we've been in jail, too. It's not like they let me program there."

Van Dreeves had developed programming skills and had created an app that immediately found and erased any picture of any Dagger team member from the internet. Given Moore's law of technology capabilities doubling every eighteen months, it was understandable that our web-crawling code had not kept pace with Blanc's.

"But clearly, I'm back in," I said. "What do you guys make of that?"

"My guess is that Blanc wants you all to himself. He's erasing everything so he can come after you with his Phalanx teams. Only thing it can mean," Van Dreeves said. "He wants the locals out of the picture."

I nodded. "But why me?"

Hobart kept the lights on and rocketed north.

"Well, not sure how to say this, boss," Van Dreeves said.

"Not like you," I quipped.

"Something to do with your grandfather," Van Dreeves mumbled.

"Coop? How so? What makes you say that?"

He looked over the rear seat at me and said, "Evelyn Champollion says so."

"Evelyn?" I stuttered.

"Yes. She said she must warn you about a connection between your grandfather and Blanc."

EVELYN CHAMPOLLION WAS AN archeologist and cryptologist, which was consistent with her family lineage. Her great-great-grandfather had interpreted the Rosetta Stone and was a famed Egyptologist. She might also be a French DGSE operative, but that was uncertain. I had come to like her for her wit and cunning during the Eye of Africa battle. I was curious about what she was doing in Drewson's compound, what she knew about Coop, and what she wanted to discuss with me.

Hobart turned off the highway, onto a secondary road, and finally swerved into a tight, tree-lined dirt two-track path that led to a crop duster airfield where recently retired Air Force pilot Lieutenant Colonel Jeremy West waited with a CASA 212 cargo short-take-off-and-landing airplane, its propellers spinning.

Mahegan had Calles change out of her clothes on the apron and don an olive pilot's jumpsuit.

"Smart dust," he said. "Hurry."

Once in the cargo bay, I put on a headset and strapped into the webbing that ran along the interior skin of the aircraft. Two pallets filled with weapons, ammunition, cases of water bottles, combat rations, and communications gear sat in the middle of the bay. Drewson was serious about whatever endeavor he was funding.

Hobart, Van Dreeves, and I poured into the aircraft. Mahegan had his vise grip wrapped around Calles' biceps as he guided her into the seat next to him. He had not replaced the restraints around her ankles but had retied her hands after making her change.

"Good to see you, jailbird," West said through the headset. He looked over his shoulder and grinned, then throttled forward and lifted the aircraft into the sky, banking low to the west barely above the treetops.

"Thought you'd be flying for JetBlue by now," I shot back.

West had rescued us from the Eye of Africa using Sally McCool's MH-60 Black Hawk. He was qualified and rated on every aircraft in the air force inventory and many that weren't. He was of the Chuck Yeager "Right Stuff" gene pool, a natural stick-and-rudder pilot.

"Wouldn't have me," he joked. "Passengers didn't appreciate a good barrel roll."

Most likely he had retired and signed on with a private air freight carrier that performed clandestine missions for secret agencies. "By the way, got Matt Garrett up here in the co-pilot's seat."

"General," Garrett said.

"Hey, Matt. Been a while," I said.

"Where have you been hiding, General?" he quipped.

"No slack from you guys," I said.

Matt Garrett was the former head of the CIA's Special Operations Group. He retired not long after his niece, Amanda Garrett, and brother, Zach Garrett, saved a natural vaccine that cured several illnesses caused by a variety of sub-Saharan viruses. Amanda had developed the medical regimen in the Serengeti and saved it from the maniacal clutches of big pharmaceutical companies that employed assassins to prevent the drug from coming to market. During that mission, Hobart and Van Dreeves had been working with Zach Garrett, who was one of my unit commanders.

"Where we headed?" I asked.

Van Dreeves said, "Boss, we've got people chasing us. Misha says that there was smart dust on your prison uniform, so they tracked you until you changed at the cabin. We have to hop from airfield to airfield and get to Wyoming."

"Misha Constance?" I asked.

"Yes," Jake said. Mahegan had rescued Misha after she blocked the Iranians from deploying the swarming code she developed. Somewhere deep on the autism scale, Misha was a brilliant and humorous eleven-year-old girl who had a difficult time communicating. She had formed a connection with Mahegan, who had saved her life on an earlier mission. Afterward, operational necessity compelled me to redeploy Mahegan immediately. That day on Wrightsville Beach, North Carolina, I pulled him away from everything he cared about to send him on the next mission. In hindsight, that might explain the tension between Jake and me that had followed. It may even have been why he left the Dagger team.

"She's in a makeshift command center in Atlantic City," Van Dreeves said. "Wyoming, this. It's about forty miles southeast of Jackson. Some two hundred miles of gold and silver mines are there. Drewson claims Phalanx has penetrated all levels of the government, so Jake set us up underground in Drewson's headquarters for the time being."

"Why drag an eleven-year-old kid into this mess?" I asked.

"She's eighteen," Mahegan replied, as if that explained everything.

"Drewson and his Project Optimus are holed up there. Expecting a big showdown with Blanc and Phalanx," Van Dreeves said.

"What's that got to do with Misha?" I asked.

We banked hard and hit some turbulence. My stomach flew into my throat.

"Didn't see that coming," West said. He didn't explain what he had avoided, but we were still alive, so I didn't ask.

"Misha joined Drewson's team about six months ago. She wrote most of the code for Drewson's public square app, Shoutter. Was working remote in Wilmington, North Carolina until Drewson began picking up signal traffic that Phalanx was either going to try to steal her away or . . . something worse. So, her dad moved out to Jackson and took up an IT job there."

"A lot to catch up on," I said.

"Hopefully, Corporal 'Sonny Jones' kept you in the loop," Van Dreeves said, using air quotes for Jones' name.

"Not an inmate?"

"Not there for a crime," Van Dreeves replied. "According to Drewson."

We landed at a remote airfield in the darkness, rolled to a stop, and switched personnel and cargo to a UH-60 helicopter. The process took us twenty minutes, and we were powering forward to the Wyoming high plains south of the Grand Tetons and Jackson Hole ski resort. After an hour, the helicopter slowed and began a hovering descent into a small valley. In the darkness I only saw my thin and haggard reflection in the door windows. The rotor wash kicked up blinding snow as West crept the aircraft into the landing zone. We had no running lights and no landing lights to aid in navigation of the approach. West was a pro and went by the call sign "Falcon Six."

As the wheels touched lightly into the snowbank, someone came jogging from the side of a ridgeline toward the aircraft. Hobart and Van Dreeves jumped out, weapons at the ready. The suspected interloper was one of Drewson's security guys.

"Follow me!" he shouted.

"Jeremy, where are you going?" I asked West.

"Just going to reposition the ride and I'll join you guys," he replied.

"Roger that. See you in a few," I said.

"In a few."

I followed Hobart and Van Dreeves beneath the whipping rotor blades into the side of the mountain. Mahegan followed me, watching to the rear and pulling Calles with him. We passed through two heavy metal doors, both with armed guards holding M4A1 long rifles with suppressors and scopes, including night optics. The sentries were wearing night vision goggles and Ops-Core Future Assault Shell Technology helmets. These FAST helmets were common among my Special Operations troops, and I wondered if any of my former soldiers were behind the equipment.

The guard who had jogged to the helicopter flipped up his goggles and stood before an eye scanner. After a few seconds, a metallic hiss preceded the opening of two doors. We stepped into a brightly lit white-paneled room with shiny floors and ceilings with an array of lights and cameras pointing at us from all directions. The guard pointed at Calles and made her stay with another sentry while we stepped into a sleek, futuristic rail car that felt like it was levitating with small, controlled vibrations beneath our feet.

"Hyperloop," Mahegan said.

The doors snapped shut and we were strapped into standing positions not unlike an amusement park ride. A red light at the far end of the car flashed to yellow, then green. Inside the pod were ventilation systems and tanks that said OXYGEN on them. Like an airplane, this thing was probably pressurized, or the oxygen might have been to assist passengers in case of an accident underground deep in the mine shafts. The car shot at seven hundred miles per hour through the mountainside, and a few minutes later we stopped just as abruptly as we had started. My math told me that seven hundred miles per hour was eleven point five miles per minute. We probably traveled between thirty and forty miles underground. This was a huge complex.

We unsnapped from our harnesses and walked through the open doors into another well-lit foyer where the guide was eye scanned again. We were greeted by a tall blond man with broad shoulders. He looked like he might have been a college athlete thirty years ago. Maybe a baseball pitcher with long arms and lanky legs.

"Hi, General, I'm Mitch Drewson," he said.

"Garrett Sinclair," I said.

"Just so you know, General, while you were in my south station anteroom and in the hyperloop itself, I had facial recognition, infrared scanners, and voice recognition software confirming your and your team's identities. Wanted you to know that we don't let just anybody in here, which is why Sergeant Calles is still in the anteroom being searched and investigated. Though we already have a detailed dossier on her, other than having her on the payroll, we don't know much more about her. You've all been scanned for smart dust and cleaned when you came into the first chamber. Any that you might have had on you has been neutralized. The point of the hyperloop entrance is to provide some standoff as we are screening newcomers."

I nodded as he punched some buttons on a sleek silver console. The wall to his front lit up with a jumbotron consuming all the wall space. A blurry picture of Mahegan's face projected onto the wall.

"Let's get right down to it. Not much time," Drewson said. "Jake Mahegan. We took this picture a minute ago. Very little information out there on you. Good job. Former Delta Force operator from the Outer Banks of North Carolina. Left the unit several years ago and now do freelance security work . . . when you're not grinding personal axes. Mother was murdered when you were fourteen. You killed three of the four men who had gang raped and killed her in Lumberton, North Carolina. Father died an alcoholic on the Lumbee reservation searching for his roots, which Jake found on Roanoke Island. Croatan. The Lost Colony."

I looked at Jake. He was clenching his jaw and flexing but he kept his cool, for the moment.

Hobart's scarred face now dominated the screen.

"Joe Hobart. Sergeant Major. US Army. The best sniper in the inventory, as they say, as if you're simply property of the government, which I guess you are. Or, at least, were. From Missouri. Ozark region. You have a wife, Zoey, and daughter, Syl, back home in North Carolina. Syl is actually Sally Sylvester Hobart and is named after Sally McCool, your former pilot, and Sylvester Morgan, Zoey's father, who was your former command sergeant major, both killed in action at the Eye of Africa fight."

"The fuck?" Hobart said.

Van Dreeves' picture appeared next.

"Randy Van Dreeves. Also, a sergeant major. Surfer boy from San Clemente, California. Technology and communications whiz and good enough with an aid bag most medical schools would be proud to have you. While all of you miss Sally, Randy and Sally were planning on marriage after returning from Africa, but that wasn't meant to be."

Van Dreeves looked away and then at me.

"Is this necessary?" he asked me.

"What's the point of this?" I asked Drewson. "We're here because Jake brought us here, I presume at your request."

Drewson nodded and said, "You're here because I created the conditions for you to be here. Quid pro quo. I did the quid. You now get to do the quo." Then he continued.

"And Lieutenant General Garrett Sinclair. The man of the hour. Saved an inauguration of his friend, President Kim Campbell, and led the fight at the Eye of Africa to stop Chinese hypersonic glide nukes from being delivered to precise locations in the United States. Wife Melissa, dead, presumably to cancer. I have some more information on that, by the way, which I'll save for later. Your father was a general. Your grandfather was a general. All West Pointers. Ring knockers. But you have a unique reputation, General, as a cowboy. Like to get your boots muddy, shall we say? Instead of lifting a pinky and sipping tea while watching the troops duke it out on the big screen you get right in the middle of the fight. Grandfather, Garret I, known by friends and family as 'Coop,' was a legit World War Two hero."

Drewson paused, held up a gunmetal-gray dog tag and said, "More about this later."

Then he continued, "The Coop nickname came from a fully restored 1935 Cadillac LaSalle Series 50 Coupe he dragged from a Raleigh junkyard and rebuilt in the summers while attending West Point. He climbed the cliffs of Pointe du Hoc and fought his way across Europe as one of the very first army Rangers. Garrett the second was a Vietnam War hero, having led his Green Beret A Team to A Shau Valley to reinforce his brethren who were being overrun by the People's Army of Vietnam. Both your father and grandfather received the Distinguished Service Cross for their gallantry, second only to the Medal of Honor. And you, Garrett III, a general, received a prison sentence after a truly distinguished career. What do you make of that?"

"I'm not sure why we're here or why you're busting our chops," Hobart said.

"Not busting anything, Joe," Drewson said. "I'm telling you that I know who you are."

"Why diss the general?"

"On the contrary, I have tremendous respect for the general. The better question is, why did the country diss the general? Why did the secretary of defense do it? The chairman of the joint chiefs? The president, even?"

"Joe, I understand what Mr. Drewson is doing," I said. "He's pointing out that Coop and my dad were rewarded for their combat action, while I've been punished . . . we've been punished. He's making commentary on the condition of society. If my father could be rewarded even in a controversial conflict like Vietnam, for example, despite the social divisions, then the government must have been hanging together at the high concept level. Political divisions be damned, military sacrifice could still bridge those gaps. There was some semblance of cohesion at the highest levels of governmental decision making. Now, Mr. Drewson is claiming that the chasms in our country have penetrated up through all our institutions, and that we've been punished for doing our duty."

"The general gets a star," Drewson said. "Would that make four or one? It's hard to keep count these days."

"You're testing my patience, Drewson," I snapped. I didn't appreciate his condescension.

He sighed and ran his hand through his hair, then looked down. He lifted his hands and pushed out with his palms. A wry smile came across his face.

"The truth is, guys, I'm nervous. I know I'm awkward. The most elite military squad in the country is in my command center. I'm awestruck. So, this is how I burn energy. By knowing as much as possible about the topic, any topic. Right now, that topic is the Dagger team and its status, or lack thereof with the US government."

"Why don't we cut to the chase here, Mr. Drewson?" I said.

"Mitch. It's Mitch. Please call me Mitch. And yes, one more photo and I'll do exactly that. Cut to the proverbial chase."

On the screen was a man with black hair and a grayish white beard standing at a glass lectern giving a speech with a white foam microphone headset resting next to his mouth. He was tall and ropey but didn't give off an athletic vibe. His eyes were narrow, suspicious even. Feet were splayed at ninety degrees, like duck feet. His hands were large as if he cut wood with an ax. He might have been a rock climber or aficionado of some other hipster sport like kayaking. For some reason he looked familiar, but only vaguely. I couldn't place him.

"This is Aurelius Blanc. He was born in France near Caen. As a kid he tinkered with coding and developed several different software platforms that were first to market in their niche. If you've purchased anything online, you've probably used his software either directly or indirectly. Invented the drag-and-drop method of coding, for example. Instead of having to bang out millions of lines of code to establish a platform, he created the big chunks of preprogrammed code and put them in tiles so that programmers can lay the foundation. Just that is worth billions. The only thing better than his coding skills are his business skills. With every platform he developed, he made it reliant on the entire universe of his platforms. As each became ubiquitous, so did the others. Better facial recognition begat better biometrics, which begat better surveillance, which begat Blanc's epiphany that he really could have it all."

"'All' meaning what?" I asked.

"What any megalomaniac wants. Control. He sees the United States faltering economically and politically. He sees an opening for his global security state."

"But how?" I queried. "All this high concept stuff is easy to talk about but hard to do."

"By aligning his significant technology with all the enemies of the United States. Leverage their significant capabilities."

I nodded, thinking it through. I could see the concept of technofascism coupled with multiple governments. Strength in numbers and all that.

"Even so, I still don't understand what you or even Blanc want from us," I said.

"Blanc sees you as an impediment, I believe, to his plan. Likewise, he sees me and Project Optimus as competition. Have you ever met our common adversary, Aurelius Blanc?"

I thought about the Eye of Africa fight where I vaguely remembered seeing someone that looked like Blanc standing on the balcony of the castle at Dakhla Point. He had been in a shouting match with Chinese General Liang as Sanson the executioner had raised his sword above the heads of President Campbell and Evelyn Champollion. I couldn't be sure, but it was the only connection I could fathom.

"Maybe last year in Dakhla," I said.

"You saw him? Yes, he was there. That must be it. Perhaps now he is tying up loose ends. Our informant tells us that he ordered a hit on you in prison, true?"

"Maybe," I said.

Drewson pulled a dog tag from his pocket and held it in his hand, flipping it between his fingers like a magic trick. When he pinched it between his fingers for a brief moment, I could make out the stamped letters: S-I-N-C-L-A-I-R. I wondered if it was mine, but it looked dated. Perhaps it was Coop's?

"And then there's me," Drewson said. "I freed you so you could help protect my people as we counter Blanc's nefarious scheme. I need security, vision, planning, and operational capability to safely deploy my Web 3.0 technology, which by default will undermine Blanc's global security state. He knows that I've got you."

"You don't have me or us, at the moment, Drewson. Why would we even be interested in that?"

"The world will become a harsh place very quickly if we don't counter Blanc. Your children, Brad and Reagan, and Hobart's daughter, Syl, will grow up in an AI-dominated surveillance state that restricts the very freedoms you have fought for."

"The world is already harsh," I said.

"The people you love are here. Your team. You can make a difference. Blanc is after my team because we are an existential threat to Phalanx."

"After your team?" I asked.

"Blanc used his LanxPro platform of artificial intelligence, satellites, and GPS to find two of my developers, Emily Sedgewick and Blair Campbell, and an entire team managing my server farm in Grass Valley, California."

"Blair Campbell? The president's daughter?" I asked.

"Precisely," he replied.

"Where is Blair now?"

Blair Campbell, the president's daughter, was a friend of my daughter, Reagan. I knew Blair reasonably well, as we had interacted during family outings when Melissa and Kim made plans to go to dinner or the rare moments I could make a vacation on the coast of North Carolina. Blair and Misha had connected through Reagan, who'd had a crush on Mahegan at the time.

"We're trying to locate her. She was supposed to link up with Evelyn Champollion in Denver but didn't make the link-up point. My Zebra team is geolocating her and will feed the information to Misha. We're just getting the reports in now."

"Zebra team?"

"Geniuses that work for me in a separate wing of the tunnel system here," Drewson said.

I nodded, piecing it all together.

"If Blanc is out to destroy you using his technology and these assassin squads, as you claim, and this is an epic struggle between Optimus and Phalanx, who does Optimus have?"

"Just you," he said. "Dagger team."

I STARED AT DREWSON, whose light blue eyes sparkled with the anticipation of my response.

"You're talking about two tech giants covertly using military machinery and information dominance to fight a global war," I said. "Instead of the United States and China, it's Drewson versus Blanc. I pledged an oath to a constitution, not a tech mogul."

"No. I'm talking about stopping that," he replied, pointing his finger at me. "And you are out of prison precisely because this tech mogul got you out."

He pointed triumphantly at his chest, as if he had blown the hole in the side of the DB. "And I'm not asking for allegiance to me; I'm asking for allegiance to the people you served all your life. The American citizens you pledged to protect and defend. And more precisely, to appeal to your familial nobility, I'm asking you to help find Blair Campbell."

"Of course, but other than helping Blair, we're not interested in some grand struggle between you and another billionaire."

His face hardened. A cloud passed across his eyes before he paused and looked at a camera in the top right-hand corner of the room.

"Then we should get you briefed up on Blair. My operations lead will brief you," Drewson said. He handed me a smart tablet. "You'll need this."

I entered, the doors shut behind me, and then I saw Misha Constance.

Misha sat in a padded chair surrounded by her four large monitors on a table. At her feet were four high-powered computer stacks. Against the wall were rows of servers blinking red and green passing terabytes of information wherever Misha desired. The room was cool, in the mid-sixties, which kept the equipment functioning. Her chair had two pads the size of sofa cushions pressing against either shoulder, supporting her head. Her hands clicked away at the keyboard until she stopped and looked at me.

Her eyes were wide and blue behind a set of unique tri-colored glasses. Her blond hair hung loosely on her forehead. Her skin was almost porcelain. She wore jeans, a light yellow sweater, and Nike running shoes on her feet. She rocked forward, looked at a monitor on the wall that appeared with the text:

How may I help you, General? Can't you see I'm busy??

I smiled and held up the tablet, which I assumed was connected to Drewson's private server, and typed:

Too busy for me, ma'am?

Misha smiled, her teeth showing a set of white braces and pink rubber bands.

I'll make an exception for you ;)

I typed:

My lucky day

"But . . . talk to me. Don't type," she muttered.

I stepped back, then moved forward to hug her before she held up her hands, smiling.

Let's not get carried away, she typed.

I nodded. "Of course." Then, "You look beautiful, and all grown up."

"The glasses . . . help me understand . . . keep me calm," she said. Her words came in fits and starts, the rhythm like a car with a carburetor issue. Sometimes fast, sometimes sputtering.

Misha parlayed her autism into a superpower more than a disability. Several years ago, as an eleven-year-old, she had written a code that replicated swarming birds and schools of fish. The Iranian government hacked the code so they could swarm self-driving cars loaded with explosives to destroy high value targets like land-based cruise missiles. Misha had disabled the program through her backdoor program, which had prevented the Iranians from implementing their nefarious scheme until they kidnapped her, hoping torture would coerce her to patch the code. I had met her after Mahegan had saved her. Afterward, her father had built her the special glasses she was wearing today that modulated the sensory input and output as best they could. When I had seen her seven years ago, she was an awkward kid. Today, the glasses looked hip and modern, and her hair was a well-tended platinum blond. She spoke better than I remembered and her jumbotron communications platform seemed to give her control of her environment. Still, though, like many on the spectrum, hugging and physical contact was sometimes awkward.

"Monster saved you," she said.

She had nicknamed Mahegan "Monster" because of his size, especially when compared to her eleven-year-old self.

"Yes, he did," I replied, looking in her eyes.

"But . . . I showed him the way," she replied. She turned to the jumbotron on the wall, clicked a few keys until the tunnel system leading from the banks of the Missouri River into Fort Leavenworth was apparent. She had Mahegan's route into the tunnel mapped as well as the cell I escaped from pinpointed.

"You have me . . . to thank," she said. A wry smile formed on her lips as she huddled back into her padded chair, mildly embarrassed about taking credit for something. The cushions provided her a sense of security.

"Thank you, ma'am," I said.

It was good to see Misha, Mahegan, and the rest of my team. Too much of my life had been focused on mission accomplishment and not nearly enough on nurturing the relationships that revolved around me. My charges seemed to understand my task-oriented nature and treated me with kindness, respect, and even some good-natured ribbing, as Misha was prone to do. Leave it to a teenager to bring me to my senses.

"Where's Blair, Misha?"

She rocked back and forth for a moment. Her eyes went distant briefly, and her countenance migrated from welcoming to businesslike. She held up a slender, pale finger.

She was meeting Evelyn to work on the Phalanx Code, she typed.

"Phalanx Code?" I asked.

Blanc's plan. I found it in the dark web. Evelyn was helping me."

"So, what's Blanc's plan?"

We believe that Blanc's Phalanx Code has something to do with their goal of 100% global surveillance 100% of the time.

"Sounds bad but not all that different from today, like an evolution of where everything was already headed. Look at London. Cameras everywhere, but I'm listening."

She shook her head, turned to the jumbotron, and began typing.

Aurelius Blanc is evil. He is building a police state for total control. Mitch and his Optimus team have a technology that counters Blanc's cameras and other surveillance equipment that gets deployed with Web 3.0. We believe that the Phalanx Code corrupts the Project Optimus code.

"It's all Greek to me," I said. "But I understand you're trying to stop Blanc. That much I get." I did take notice of her use of Drewson's first name, Mitch.

Yes. Blanc is attacking and killing our development team. They even want to kill you!

"Who have they killed, and why do you think they want to kill me?"

She looked at me hard and then manipulated some keys that popped up a video display next to her chat box.

A massacre of our people happened in Grass Valley, California an hour ago.

The video showed four commandos dressed in black uniforms with a Phalanx patch, which was a small diamond shaped rhombus not unlike what Coop had drawn in his diary. The word "Phalanx" was printed in gold letters on the dark blue background. The commandos breached a mine shaft and began swarming through a server farm, killing at least ten people, who didn't stand a chance.

"This just happened?"

"Yes," she sputtered.

"How did we get the video?" I asked, suspicious.

Mitch's Zebra team hacked them. Zebra also gave me the video of Blanc's reaction to your escape inside his headquarters.

She clicked some buttons and images of people I didn't recognize appeared in the video box. She pointed at the large screen on the wall and said, "Watch . . . it's bad."

"Where is this Zebra team?" I asked, looking around.

Separate mine shaft wing. No one else is allowed in there. Not even I have met them. Now watch please. If you are going up against Blanc to find Blair, you need this intel.

She had a point. I looked at the screen.

Aurelius Blanc stared at his own jumbo monitor on the wall of what I presumed was his headquarters, wherever that might be. The screen showed the smoking hole of the Fort Leavenworth Disciplinary Barracks where Jake had helped me escape.

The hack had captured video and audio, though the video was blurred at times and often heads or bodies would distort or disappear for a moment. Blanc turned to a group of men and one woman dressed in dark tactical clothing. The men were large, and the woman was tall and fit.

"That's Tyger . . . Cyrilla," Misha said. "She leads . . . his commandos. Blanc makes them all wear body cams. He has cameras . . . everywhere."

The audio played.

"Team meeting now," Blanc said to his commandos.

Blanc wore his jet-black hair in a slanted pompadour. He had a large diamond in his left ear and bleached white stubble on his face. The contrast was stark. The winking diamond was the only disruption to his monochrome appearance. Blanc appeared lean and muscled. He wore a black designer T-shirt that highlighted his dyed white beard. White pants and black Pro-Ked sneakers completed the black-white-black cycle.

The woman, Cyrilla, looked into Blanc's gray eyes. She was as tall as he was, at what I guessed was my height at six foot two. She was dressed in a boxy gray top with black slacks. The shoulders on her jacket were triangles protruding outward, like a space uniform. Her nose had a slight bridge, and her lips were thin. She wore no makeup and had chopped her red hair just above her ears.

"Topic?" she asked.

"Jake Mahegan used brute force to breach the 'impenetrable' Fort Leavenworth Disciplinary Barracks," Blanc said, motioning with air quotes. "This makes retrieving the Phalanx Code all the more important."

"Sinclair is out? Not possible. We learned of the president's pardon. Smyth was handling it."

"Smyth failed spectacularly. Drewson either paid him off or hired a team to free him." Blanc's voice was baritone with a French accent. His aura was one of command. He stepped back and inhaled deeply before releasing his breath in a slow whisper, raising his arms as if performing a yoga pose.

"This was Drewson?" Cyrilla asked.

Blanc stared at Cyrilla then turned away to gather his composure. "You're supposed to be providing me information. Not the other way around, Commander. I want Sinclair, understand? He is the key to the stolen code. If they find out what is in the code, Phalanx is done forever, especially with Sinclair out of jail. But yes, who else could it be other than Mitch the Bitch."

Cyrilla pressed the small receiver in her ear and held up her hand.

"Okay, there was an attempt on Sinclair's life."

Blanc looked away and sighed. *"Tu m'étonnes." Tell me something I don't know.*

"Get me the information operations team and then get to Leavenworth with boots on the ground," he said, then turned and walked into a conference room kitted with a touch screen jumbotron and twenty glass lecterns facing the three-foot-high stage. Each lectern had a slim black microphone and a white foam cover, matching Blanc's hair/beard combo.

Before anyone else entered the conference room, Blanc looked at the camera and smiled.

"Papa, peux-tu me voir maintenant?"

Papa, can you see me now?

Misha stopped the video and typed:

He wants to kill you. Us. We must stop him.

"I didn't hear that, Misha. He wants to find me. He said nothing about killing you and the others. Obviously, he doesn't like Drewson, and he's concerned about you hacking the Phalanx Code." I looked at Misha as I spoke, then turned to the screen when she began typing.

Zebra team gave me part of the list of people Blanc is going after, which is embedded in the Phalanx Code, but they can't figure the rest out. Nor can Evelyn or I, but we're trying. It is quantum protected.

"Okay show me where Evelyn went, please."

Misha nodded at me and typed some more.

In Denver to meet Blair and see a demo on the new 3.0 microchip. She mentioned she had something to give you.

"What did she have?"

Something to do with your grandfather.

"Coop?" I asked.

Focus, she typed. *They want to kill all of us.*

"But why, Misha?" There was an edge in my voice I didn't intend.

Misha startled and then looked at the jumbotron as she typed:

1. *Blair is a voice for decentralized Wi-Fi, or DeWi, and crypto currency to empower individuals. She has a huge social media presence on Twitter, Facebook, Instagram, Mitch's Shoutter, and Blanc's LanxPro. 14 million followers. Her blog is named 3POINT0 and her tagline is "Big Tech Has Got to Go!"*

2. *Evelyn is the greatest cryptologist in the world.*

3. *And I'm just me (and scared).*

"That's understandable. Has Blair linked up with Evelyn yet? Where are they?" I asked.

Misha pressed some keys and nodded at the jumbotron. Her text box was now a small square next to a large black-and-white live video feed.

OMG! Blair's on the run.

An Optimus Earth globe spun until it zoomed in south and west of Denver, Colorado. A geo tag dialogue box indicated it was Blair Campbell that was running down a long sloping hill toward a wooded area along a river. She was looking over her shoulder into the sky as if she knew a drone was watching her. Misha toggled the camera lens and zoomed into a close shot. Blair's eyes were wide with fear yet determined. Her jaw was set as she pumped her arms and zigged and zagged into the wood line, ostensibly to avoid the sniper drone that was homing in on her position. Misha flipped the camera to thermal imaging, and we tracked Blair into the river where she disappeared.

"Lakota Hills . . . south and west . . . of Denver," Misha said.

The doors behind me hissed open. Drewson and my team walked in. This time, West and Matt Garrett were part of the group along with Patch Owens, Sean O'Malley, and Zion Black.

"We've got an alert that Blair and maybe Evelyn are in trouble," Drewson said. "We confirmed with a medevac drone that another developer named Emily Sedgewick, a friend of Blair's, is dead in Houston." He nodded at the screen. A young woman's body was splayed over a sofa, a dark stain inching its way across the white davenport.

I looked at Drewson but said nothing.

"You can see what I'm up against with Blanc. Can you and your men find Blair? Protect her? Bring her to this compound? We're talking about the president's daughter here. If not for me, then for her?"

The plaintive look on his face suggested compassion and concern. Crow's feet burst on either side of his eyes. His lips were downturned and set. He was pensive, contemplative, and alarmed.

I looked at my team. I saw in their eyes both defeat and anticipation. Not knowing what was happening to the world or who we worked for, we had always believed in the highest of all principles, duty to one another. The concept of America and our Constitution was the bedrock of our belief system. We had sworn a pledge to uphold and defend our Constitution and nation against all enemies, foreign and domestic.

And we would forever do so. Too many men and women had sacrificed too much, including Sally McCool, to falter in the face of adversity.

But here we were being handed a mission by a tech mogul to save the daughter of the president of the United States, who was being hunted by another tech mogul theoretically bent on global hegemony. We were nothing more than a few escaped prisoners and their enablers who were presumably no longer on active-duty status. It didn't get any more complicated than this if you layered in my thorny relationship with the president. Her debatable role in Melissa's death notwithstanding, I, as always, placed duty to the nation above self.

"Boss?" Hobart asked, pulling me back to the moment. "We have to do this."

"Why do you say that, Joe?" I asked while pointing at the screen. "It starts small. Saving Blair. Then grows and pits us against formidable odds. Haven't we had enough death and destruction?"

"We have an alert about Evelyn, too," Drewson interrupted, as if I needed reminding. I turned and looked at Misha's jumbotron again. Evelyn Champollion was arriving at Denver airport's private terminal. Behind her two black Suburban SUVs parked in front of the small terminal. Men with weapons stepped onto the sidewalk as Evelyn entered the building. A Hawker jet awaited on the apron.

"What's happening?" I asked.

"Blanc has gone full operational. He knows you're out. I set the conditions for the release of Hobart and Van Dreeves with my San Diego guy. Resourced Mahegan. Worked your discharges with the president. So, you can help me fight or you can watch, General. But I'm going to fight. Law enforcement is no help and as you know, some of our FBI leadership is corrupt."

He had a point. What was one last mission?

"What are they going to do, throw us in jail?" Van Dreeves quipped.

He, too, had a point.

I thought about Melissa and what she might want me to do with respect to her college roommate's daughter. She would want us to try to save Blair.

"Okay, we get the president's daughter and Evelyn. But then, we're done."

WE STOOD IN A giant cavern that reminded me of Batman's Batcave.

To my right were two MH-60 Special Operations Pave Hawk cargo helicopters. To the left was a Sherpa short take-off and landing cargo airplane. I liked the Black Hawk family of rotary wing aircraft because of their two T700 engines. They were powerful and relatively easy to maintain. The pilot could fly the aircraft on one engine, as McCool had done with us once when machine-gun fire had ignited a fire in our left engine. It was a durable airframe that could withstand serious punishment.

I should have inquired how and when Drewson came to own these state-of-the-art military airframes, but time was of the essence as it always seemed to be.

"Jeremy, you're with me, Hobart, and Van Dreeves. Matt, can you fly this other bird with Jake leading Patch and Zion?"

Matt Garrett shrugged and flashed a cocky grin. "Landing is just a controlled crash, General."

"Why you're taking the other team," I replied.

Matt was about six foot tall with dark brown hair showing some flecks of gray. Last I heard, he had helped his niece, Amanda, establish her medical company that catered to underserved regions of the world.

Matt grinned and nodded, saying, "Good to be back in the mix, General."

I nodded back at him, then turned to the small group gathered.

"No big speeches. Hobart, Van Dreeves, and I will get Blair while Matt and team go after Champollion. Jake, you have Sean and Patch. Our missions are to secure high-value personnel and return them to base. Intent is to kill as few people as possible in doing so, but don't let that be a deterrent. Remember, we know stuff that no one else does. To ninety-nine percent of the population, life is moving along normally, at least until it isn't. Cops don't know about some global conspiracy. They're punching a clock like everyone else. Some are on the take, some are cowards, but most are good, honest salt-of-the-earth men and women. They're not the enemy. Blanc's Phalanx team, on the other hand, is fair game."

"Hard to tell the difference between the good guys and the bad ones, boss," Van Dreeves said.

"That's why I pay you the big bucks," I said. "Make the right calls. Kill the right people. Secure the right targets. Save the president's daughter and Evelyn."

Jeremy led us to the MH-60 that was similarly kitted with state-of-the-art satellite communications, UHF, VHF, HF, lidar cameras, GPS, Kevlar, M134 miniguns in each crew porthole, and an internal communications suite. One of Drewson's guys fired up a Polaris all-terrain vehicle with a Y-shaped tow bar connected to the front wheels of the Hawk. As the aircraft moved forward, giant retracting doors opened, revealing the night sky with white-capped mountains across the valley. A small field with a short dirt runway jutted out from the wall of the mountain housing the hangar.

Soon, West had the blades turning and we were airborne. With the familiar sounds and vibrations of the Pave Hawk, I said, "Everything we do is in memory of Sally and why she died. She died for us and our country. Everything we do honors her memory."

Hobart nodded and Van Dreeves looked away through the windscreen then back at me.

"Roger that, boss. San Diego gave me some time to reflect on that. We're all going to die. We should all be so lucky to do so on a mission surrounded by those we trust the most. There's no honor in growing old, but we never really had time to process Sally or prison or our careers. Drewson says we're out and we're supposed to accept it just like that?"

"Well, technically we *are* out, and Drewson supposedly had something to do with that," I said. "And never discount that these are his helicopters and his communications systems." Drewson could be listening to us in real time or recording everything we said, or both.

"I get it, boss, but how do we know it's all real? He showed us those discharge papers, but it doesn't take a tech genius to fabricate something like that. Hell, even I could do that. Are we his personal mercenaries?" Van Dreeves asked. He held up the Opti-Sleeve smart devices that Drewson issued us. The slick technology looked exactly like an NFL quarterback's wrist-carried playbook when in fact it was Drewson's latest addition to the defense industry: a highly powered computer with touch screen and Velcro-tabbed protective cover. "Plus, these things are tracking devices more than anything else."

I looked Van Dreeves in the eyes. He either hadn't caught my meaning or didn't care what Drewson heard. I shrugged and asked, "Does any of that matter?"

He looked at Hobart and then back at me, locking eyes.

"I guess you're right, boss. Nothing matters, really. Except this right here. This is what we do," he said, waving his hand in a circle. "This is who we are."

"Yes, and the president's daughter is in danger," I said. "Our mission continues."

He took a deep breath, nodded, and then pointed at the touch screen on the small table situated between us.

"I've got some chatter that the Denver Police Department found two dead Secret Service agents about an hour ago inside her car. They were picking her up to take her to the airport to meet with Evelyn, supposedly. Based on what I'm hearing on police radio band, they were . . . executed," Van Dreeves said.

"Jesus. How did Blair escape?" I asked.

"Not sure, but she has weapons permits for a bunch of guns, including her Colt." Van Dreeves said.

"Roger that," I replied. "Let's find her."

Van Dreeves nodded. "This is our route to the area west of Denver where the drone last tracked Blair through the snow, here into this wooded area with a creek."

"No thermal on her?" I asked.

"None that we can find. I'm assuming Phalanx and the president also have teams out here looking for her."

"Flight time?"

"At two hundred knots, less than an hour. We will be pissing off all kinds of air traffic controllers," Van Dreeves said.

"Let me worry about that," West said from the cockpit.

West maneuvered the helicopter like a roller coaster through the valleys angling west to east off the front range of Colorado. Lights slipped beneath us, and small towns flashed as we studied the map where Blair had disappeared.

"That river has snow on either side," Hobart said. "Should be able to track her."

"Got a bogie in the same AO. About two miles from where Misha saw her an hour ago. Westland helicopter is setting down. No ping for friend or foe, which means they're foe," West said.

"Has to be Phalanx," I said. "What's the size of their usual hit squad?"

"Their commander is Tyger Cyrilla, and they have scout teams of three to four pax, like a mini A-team. Medic, comms guy, sniper, and leader," Van Dreeves said.

"Same as what Misha said," I said.

"I'm . . . here. Listening," Misha chimed in through our headsets.

"Thank you, ma'am," I replied. Then, "Time on target, Jeremy?"

"Seven mikes," he replied. In seven minutes, we would be over the last known location of Blair Campbell and perhaps facing off with a Phalanx team. After what seemed like an hour, West lowered the aircraft onto an open field. Our doors were open, and we sat on the edge of the cargo bay, legs dangling in the sky. The reassuring weight of the M4 carbine in my hands felt good after a year away from my chosen profession. I had always been a soldier, even as a kid. It was my duty to serve and lead. There had never been another option.

"Got movement up the ridge. Go, go, go. Taking fire," West said as he began hovering above a snow-covered hilltop. We were out of the helicopter in less than three seconds. The biting wind sliced across my face.

"Three up," Hobart said. He used the call sign Dagger Three because he was the operations lead for my team.

"Four up," Van Dreeves said. As the medic and communications lead, he used the suffix typically associated with logistics.

"Six up," I said. As the commander, I was Dagger Six.

"Six . . . this is command," Misha said through our earpieces. "I have . . . imagery. Opti-Sleeve."

"Roger, out."

We huddled and looked at our Opti-Sleeves. I lifted the camouflaged cover and stared at a dimly lit thermal projection of a hillside. Three figures were scrambling up the ridge toward a lone individual, who had to be Blair, edging along a narrow cliff. She leaped across a small defile and removed something from her backpack as she turned toward her pursuers.

"Can you get a shot on that, Joe?" I asked Hobart, who had charged his SR-75 sniper rifle with thermal sight and infrared aiming device.

"In about a minute when they will get to the ridge she was just on. It will have to be quick," he said.

Van Dreeves said, "I've got thermal on my SIG. You take the first two. I'll take third in line. They'll be strung out along that skinny ridge."

"Command confirm we are on target," I asked Misha.

"On . . . target," she replied. The stress of the situation was impacting her speech. She spat out the word "target" as if sprung from her vocal cords.

"Roger. Good copy."

"Shoot to kill?" Hobart asked.

"You know any other way to shoot?" I replied.

"Roger that," he said.

"These could be federal agents and not just some rogue hit squad for Phalanx and Blanc," Van Dreeves observed.

"Understood. They're still going after the president's daughter. We have no authority, but we also have no constraints. We execute our code to take care of each other and our duty to the country, which includes protecting the president's family. There are two dead Secret Service agents. All the proof I need we are doing the right thing for the country."

"Roger that," Van Dreeves said.

"Target," Hobart said.

My Opti-Sleeve showed two flashes coming from Blair's location, followed by thunderous booms.

She was shooting at them?

I recalled her love of marksmanship and firearms and infrequent trips with her and Reagan to the range at Fort Bragg. She asked about shotguns, pistols, rifles, and military hardware. Had me teach her to break them down and put them back together. Her sincere curiosity humored me. Reagan was interested but Blair was *into* guns.

Hobart squeezed off two shots in chorus with Van Dreeves' one shot. Van Dreeves followed with a second on his target.

"Two down," Hobart said.

"One down," Van Dreeves said.

"Command, do you have comms with Jackpot?"

There was a long pause and I wondered if Misha understood that "Jackpot" was the commonly used call sign for a high-value target we were rescuing.

"Standby," Misha said.

"Who's there?! Who's there!? This is Colt!"

Misha had connected us directly with Blair Campbell. The Secret Service had assigned her the call sign "Colt," given her love of firearms and the fact that she had a concealed-carry permit for her Colt Python .357 Magnum 3″ revolver.

"Blair, Garrett Sinclair here. We are close," I said.

"I shot them. I think. Wait. One is moving . . ."

Two more booms echoed along the valley. The drone video playing on my Opti-Sleeve showed Blair hunkered down behind the trunk of a large tree and three bodies littered on the ridge just twenty meters away from her. We had delivered an unplanned ambush upon the Phalanx team.

"We are coming to you. Hold your position," I said.

"Okay . . ." Her voice was hesitant.

"I know your mom. My wife was your mom's best friend," I said.

She paused, processing. She was Reagan's age and had an entire universe of life of which I was only a small part. It probably took her a few seconds to make the connection, especially because there was no face to go with my disembodied voice talking in her ear.

"Reagan's dad," she said. Not a question.

"And Brad's," I added for further confirmation.

"The general in jail," she said.

Not exactly the memory spark I had been hoping for, but it did have a certain ring to it. By now Van Dreeves and I were moving while Hobart remained in place to secure our pickup zone and cover our movement to Blair's location.

"Yes, that one," I said through rapid breaths as we crossed a small creek and climbed up a steep slope. We grabbed at rocks and tree roots on the icy incline. Eventually we were behind Blair's position and halted.

"Blair, we are behind you," I said.

"I see you," she replied. A flashlight blinked twice, maybe thirty meters in front of us. We moved toward Blair, who was trembling. Van Dreeves extracted a Gore-Tex jacket from a rescue bag he carried and slid it around her shoulders. She hugged him and then me.

"Thank you, General Sinclair," she said, likely shivering both from the cold and the intensity of the situation.

"Let's get you out of here." Then to Hobart, "Call West back in."

"Already inbound," West said in my earpiece.

While I held on to Blair, Van Dreeves navigated the ledge and inspected the bodies, securing equipment and hopefully identification. Soon, we were moving quickly along the trail we had blazed through the woods, across the creek and up onto the landing zone hilltop.

"Dagger Six coming in," I said.

"Tracking you," Hobart replied.

We clawed up the icy slope about the time helicopter blades sounded in the distance. Dirt spit into my face as I was cresting the hill.

"Taking fire," I said.

"Drone," Hobart replied.

"I see it with thermals," West replied.

Remembering the Dariush Parizad incident two years ago in our nation's capital during the inauguration and the recent drone shot on Emily

Sedgewick, we had secured two counter drone missiles from Drewson's Batcave. One was with Hobart and the other on West's helicopter.

"Acquired," Hobart said.

A *thunk* sounded nearby and a rocket streaked into the sky, deploying a net that wrapped up the drone and caused it to spin wildly until it smashed into the ground. On our way to the pickup zone, Van Dreeves secured the netted drone, disabled the weapon, and carried it by his side.

"PZ clear," I said.

"Thirty seconds," West replied.

He touched down, we hopped on, and he lifted away. Hobart sat on the edge of the cargo bay, knees in the breeze, while Van Dreeves used a snap hook to secure his outer tactical vest.

Placing my headset on, I said, "Who we got following us?"

"Just about the entire world," West replied.

By now, Blair had assessed her situation, donned Hobart's headset, and slid onto the bench next to Van Dreeves.

"This is Blanc," she said. "He's got these contract mercenaries working for him." She froze and looked at me, her eyes wide. "Oh my God, is Evelyn okay? Where is she? I was supposed to meet her when those guys started chasing me."

"Jake Mahegan and his team headed to Denver International to find her."

"Yes, that was where I was supposed to meet her," Blair said. "The private terminal there. She wanted to discuss the Phalanx Code with me."

I nodded and looked at her across the table in our command suite. "Blair, you need to know that—"

"Emily's dead. Oh my God. Misha told me. Oh my God."

She put her hand to her mouth and looked away. The helicopter banked hard, lifted, and sunk into a valley. West was doing his pilot stuff.

"I'm sorry about Emily, Blair," I said, reaching across and gripping her hand. She looked at me with her mother's upturned nose and wide blue eyes. Her blond hair was ratty and dark, askew between the headset earmuffs.

"We knew there was a chance of this when we joined Mitch's team, but it seemed so . . . remote."

"Nothing remote about death," I said, releasing her grip. Turning to Van Dreeves I asked, "Status on Jake and team?"

"Dry hole," Van Dreeves said.

"Already?" I asked.

"Just filtering in," Van Dreeves said.

"Dagger . . . Six . . . have update . . . when you arrive," Misha said from the command center.

"Roger that," I replied.

Shortly, West landed us on the ledge of Drewson's giant Batcave. We deplaned and hustled through the yawning cavernous doors. Two crew pulling an aircraft tug jogged past us. Inside the hangar, we walked to the far wall, maybe a hundred meters across, and knelt. Drewson came barreling from the door nearest us and scooped up Blair in his arms.

"Oh my God, I'm so happy to see you," he exclaimed. Drewson spun around holding Blair, who pushed away.

"Mitch. Come on. Emily's dead. Evelyn could be in trouble. The Phalanx kill list is still active. I mean, there's nothing to celebrate."

They separated. Drewson stared at her awkwardly for a moment, then composed himself.

"Yes, yes, of course," he said. He placed his hand on her shoulder, but she was quick to shrug it off. "I'm just so glad that you're alive."

"I know. I'm sorry. I just need some time to process," she replied.

"Mr. Drewson, first, we need a doctor to look at Blair. If you don't have one, Van Dreeves here can do it. Second, we've got some stuff that needs to be analyzed. I'm assuming you've got some folks that can go through phones and smartwatches?" I asked.

"Our doctor is on the way in the hyperloop and will be here momentarily. And yes, I have an equipment technician," Drewson said. "But as Blair said, there has a been a development with Evelyn."

"JAKE AND TEAM DIDN'T get Evelyn," he said. "Follow me."

As I thought about Evelyn Champollion and what she might be to Drewson and even Coop, we followed the billionaire along a labyrinth of mine shafts until we were in a brightly lit room with white ceilings and glassed walls. Inside the room were about ten tables where an assortment of men and women were dressed in the Drewson uniform of khaki pants and black shirts with *Optimus* stitched in italics on the left breast. *Optimus* was on a light blue background that faded to a starlit black night sky, as if humanity's possibilities were infinite.

"Hopefully something you found here can lead us to where they're taking Evelyn," Drewson said.

Van Dreeves spread three LanxPhones, three Zenith ZF-5 submachine guns, three communications headsets, and an assortment of ammunition, field dressings, and other tactical items such as knives, compasses, flex-cuffs, and night vision goggles. This was a tactical team. Van Dreeves spread his arms, as if to say, "It's all yours."

A slim, African American woman in her mid-thirties pushed inside the group. She was wearing a white lab coat, her thick black hair pulled into a ponytail, and nodded at Van Dreeves with serious eyes behind rimless spectacles.

"I'm Vanessa. Any pictures?" she asked.

Van Dreeves held up his OptiPhone and air dropped to Drewson's server three facial pictures he had taken on location. The images of two men and one woman appeared on the twenty-four-inch tilt monitor that was in the center of the table. Vanessa punched some buttons and used a scanning device like you might see in a grocery store checkout line to image the weapon serial numbers.

"I'll run these through Zebra team. Thank you," Vanessa said.

As Vanessa left the room, a woman carrying an aid bag with a stethoscope around her neck walked in. She appeared mid-thirties with reddish blond hair and green eyes. Her lab coat had the Optimus symbol on it.

"Patient?" she asked.

"Not very much," I responded.

She smirked and said, "Cute, General Sinclair. Now where is the patient?"

"Here. Blair Campbell. The president's daughter," I said pointing at Blair.

"Yes. Blair and I know each other, don't we?"

"Hi, Amanda," Blair said.

"What seems to be the problem? Chased by those guys?" Amanda said, pointing at the screen Vanessa had displayed.

There was something familiar about the doctor that I couldn't place just yet, but her golden hair and green eyes took me back ten years or so.

"Something like that. These guys came and got me," Blair said, pointing at us. Not rescued me. Not saved me. Came and got me, as if she was fine on her own, which she might have been, in retrospect.

"Where's Matt?" Amanda asked.

"Other mission to get Evelyn," Blair said. "Which didn't pan out."

Then it hit me. This was Doctor Amanda Garrett, Matt's niece.

"Amanda Garrett?" I asked.

She stared at me and smiled.

"Yes, General. Zach's daughter. Matt's niece. Small world that all your protégés are in this crazy mine shaft, isn't it?"

I looked at Drewson.

"Did you collect up *everyone* associated with me?"

"As many as possible." Drewson smiled. "If we are going to take on Phalanx and Blanc, then I need the best. It's our only chance at peace or harmony in the world."

Amanda took Blair into a side room, presumably to medically diagnose her, and we continued our sensitive site exploitation of the equipment that Van Dreeves had secured.

Taken aback by the presence of my closest operators, I said, "What's the endgame here, Drewson? You've gathered most of the people I've ever cared about in one location, save my two children and a few others."

"They all came willingly. In fact, it was mostly Misha's idea. And Brad and Reagan are welcome any time, as are Zoey and Syl." He turned to Hobart when he mentioned Zoey and their daughter Syl. "I encourage it, as a matter of fact. As you see with Emily Sedgwick and Blair's Secret Service agents, Blanc will stop at nothing."

Vanessa reentered the room and interrupted the conversation.

"I've got something here that might be of interest," Vanessa said. "The Zebra team's analysis of the technology the Phalanx assassins carried is notable."

"Please," I responded. We huddled around a white table that was backlit so that the items Van Dreeves had collected stood in stark relief on the top.

"These wireless earbuds and communications packs that Randy took from Blair's pursuers use advanced frequency hopping to avoid detection by anyone trying to hack the communications. I'm able to track the signal back to a communications site in northeast Colorado."

"Colorado?" I asked.

"Yes. Zebra believes it is one of Blanc's command posts. Could be a combo Chinese government and Phalanx operation."

"Why do you say that?"

"These guys," she said pointing at the images on the monitor. "There's overlap between the geolocation and what we know to be Chinese–owned land."

China and Phalanx, just like the Eye of Africa operation.

Everyone in the lab stopped their respective tasks. Heads turned in our direction. Drewson looked at Amanda and Blair as they exited the exam room and walked toward us.

"Other than trauma from Emily's death, she's fine," Amanda said.

"I'm ready to go to work," Blair said. "I need to finish what Emily and I had started. And we need Evelyn back here to help with breaking the code."

I didn't fully understand what was happening or why everyone was so committed to their purpose within the Project Optimus enterprise. I was not an expert on the next iteration of the internet or decentralized finance. I understood that more control in an individual's hands was generally a better thing. The genius of the framing documents was the balance of power, both within the federal government and between the states and the feds. Were ascendant technology companies strengthening one over the other, tilting the balance so that too much power was resident in the federal government? Probably, but that was a problem to be sorted within the system, not with violence.

Not with Dagger team.

"What's going on?" Amanda asked, stopping next to Drewson.

"The general isn't sure he wants in on the mission," Drewson said.

Blair looked at me and said, "How could you not? We came here *because* of you. You are the one we want to lead us to defeat Phalanx. Everyone has been talking about General Sinclair this and General Sinclair that. He's our best hope against the weaponized Big Tech and techno-fascism. You're walking away from the people you love? Who love you?"

"I've never walked away from anyone. I get it that you view this situation as good versus evil. And I understand the importance of your project Optimus, I think. It is a good thing to empower people with more control over their internet and financial environments. But how do we stop a monolith like Phalanx that is embedded like a tick in our own government, not to mention other governments around the world? China, North Korea, Iran? We're hiding in a mine shaft for crying out loud."

"You're the general," Blair said. "Think of something. We came here because Mitch said he was getting you out and that you would help us. Emily is dead. Evelyn has been kidnapped. I survived, barely. Others are at risk as we stand here. If you protect us and allow us to finish our rollout of Web 3.0, then all we need to do is decouple Phalanx from China and these other governments, maybe even our own government."

"We will not attack our own government."

"These are evil people, General!" Blair snapped.

"You don't get to tell me about evil, Blair," I shot back.

"Fine," Drewson interrupted. "Then cut the head off the snake and get Blanc. But understand that Phalanx's rogue government contractors are sucking up every communication in the world using LanxPro software and artificial intelligence and selling it to the Chinese. Combined, the algorithms triage information at unimaginable speeds. It is the nerve center of the global security state. I brought your team together because you are the one person that everyone believed they could count on to carry this torch, to defend the people of this country against the all-seeing eye of the security state and Phalanx's oppressive tactics."

By now, Mahegan, Matt Garrett, Patch Owens, Zion Black, and Jeremy West had walked in and were listening to the conversation. These were my protégés and they, as always, watched my every move and scrutinized my every word.

"As you see with this technology, General," Drewson said, sweeping his hand over the communications gear on the table. "Blanc and Phalanx are working with the Chinese to infiltrate the US government. It's the end of our country as we know it if they succeed."

"That's not news," I said. "The Chinese have been after us for decades. And Blanc wouldn't be the first company in the world to do business with China."

Drewson pointed at the monitor where a map of Wyoming, Utah, North Dakota, and Colorado suddenly appeared. There were three locations highlighted. One was the Utah Data Center just southwest of our location by 270 miles. Another was Warren Air Force Base in the southeast corner of Wyoming on the border with Colorado. The last was Grand Forks Air Force Base on the eastern edge of North Dakota, overlooking the Red River border with Minnesota.

"What do all three of these locations have in common, General? Any idea?"

"The DB prison library was a bit outdated, but I know enough about the nuclear and drone missions at Warren and Grand Forks," I said.

"China has bought thousands of acres next to all three," Van Dreeves said. "They're eavesdropping."

"Bingo. The navy brig must have been more current," Drewson replied.

"You're saying that the Chinese have built listening stations next to some of our most sensitive bases?" I asked. "To what end?"

"I'm saying Phalanx and China are partnering on data collection for the most nefarious scheme possible," Drewson replied.

"Which is?"

Drewson paused. "That's what the Phalanx Code is all about, but I'd prefer the president tell you."

8

DREWSON LED ME TO a room that had an eighty-six-inch high-definition monitor bracketed to the wall. I sat in a standard office chair behind a sleek white table. After a minute or two, the monitor blinked to life and President Kim Campbell's face filled the screen. Her normally perfectly coiffed blond hair was disheveled, but her sharp green eyes stared back at me. She was wearing a dark blazer, white blouse, and a red-and-white brooch shaped like a tiger. Her face was stoic and weary. The room was dimly lit and she spoke in a husky whisper.

"Garrett," she said.

"Madame President," I replied.

"Thank you for saving Blair. Though she and I may disagree on many things politically, she is still my daughter."

"She's a quite capable young woman," I said.

"But yet, here you are doing my bidding again," she said.

"We have a lot to catch up on. Why the FBI raided Figure Eight Island last year. Why you locked me up in prison. You know, small stuff."

She put her head in her hands and looked up at me.

"Garrett, I am talking to you on a burner smartphone that is connected to the Washington, D.C., Wi-Fi network from the balcony of my bedroom in the White House."

In the past, I had a burner phone myself that was point-to-point encrypted with her phone. We used it for communication about in extremis missions she needed Dagger team to execute. The FBI had my phone now and most likely knew what its purposes had been.

"Very well. Blair is fine. She's also . . . determined. She and some others believe that there's some epic struggle between good and evil happening here. And that you're, at least on the surface, part of the evil."

"Please. Every daughter hates her mother."

"That is between you and Blair. As for me, I'm evidently retired, and I'd like nothing else than to go live in the mountains of North Carolina or Virginia and be off the grid. Unless you can convince me otherwise, that's what I'm going to do."

"First, there is no more 'off the grid.' Blanc will find you in ten minutes. Just look at Blair's Secret Service team. We got the word they were killed about the time the head of Secret Service notified me she had been rescued. But those poor agents. Shot in the back of the head."

She paused. Her eyes were cast downward, mournful. I said nothing.

"Anyway, if you're helping Mitch, you're Blanc's enemy. And because you're you, the big bad Special Forces general, you're a threat to Blanc. Mitch, by the way, made a big play for you and your team to be free. Called in favors. I was happy to retire you, though I still need your services."

"Jake blew a ten-foot hole in the wall of the Fort Leavenworth DB. That's a favor?"

"Semantics," she said. She was a no bullshit woman who didn't get wrapped around the axle of the past. I had to give her that. "I ordered the SecDef to sign your discharge papers. Honorable discharge. Full pension. Keep your three-star rank. That was the best I could do. Randy and Joe same deal, except of course they are sergeant major rank and not generals. Lucky them."

"Thank you for at least honoring my team's service. I never expected a gold watch, but I also never expected to spend the last year of my career in jail—and for what? Serving my country?"

"I was protecting you, Garrett. So many rats in our government want you dead. The world is changing. There's little hope of coming back from this abyss. Maybe you're the last hope? I think that's what Mitch sees in you. If he can disable Blanc's grip on our government with this Web 3.0 stuff, we can fight back against the others."

"But why? From where I'm sitting, you're all in this together. One big monolith that shafts the little guy every chance possible."

"You know that's not me. Anyway, Blanc has moles in our government. Everyone but you and me seem to be on the take. In effect, our government is being run by unelected bureaucrats who sign deals with other countries that bind us in ways that have real impact."

"You're the president, fix it," I said.

"If only it were that easy. This task is geared more for a warrior like you than a politician like me," she said.

"And what task is that?"

"What Mitch needs you to do. Protect his people so that he can finish the Web 3.0 build-out without Blanc playing Whac-A-Mole and destroying everything Mitch does. Giving the power back to the masses with decentralized Wi-Fi that isn't controlled by big tech is the only hope we have of unifying the country. If you help Mitch finish his project, you in effect decouple the liaison between Blanc's government moles and our national security apparatus. You save the country, Garrett."

I hadn't thought of the situation as she just described it. On one hand, she knew there was nothing more appealing to me than defending our country. On the other, she knew me well enough to see that I could be understandably jaded about public service after the last year in jail. Legions of brave men and women had died defending the Constitution. If I could honor their sacrifice by helping to neuter big tech and shore up the foundations of our republic, then I was listening.

"I'm still here," I said.

"I thought you might be. We may not be the last patriots, but we're damned sure going to do everything we can to preserve this union."

"Yes, ma'am," I said. "True patriots."

"The first step is to find Evelyn," she said. "You need to get her. Mitch tells me that Blanc snatched her. Not sure why. For all the reasons we just discussed, I can't really have my intelligence team run this to ground so I need you to. Diplomatically, she is important to the solution in disabling Blanc's empire because she knows him. French circles and all that. Also, Mitch tells me there's a code or something she was trying to break."

The president was adept at plucking my strings, and she almost had me. Almost.

"Slow down," I said. "I hardly appreciate that you took away a year of my life. If Melissa were still alive, she would put her finger in your chest and tell you to get your shit together. Before you start barking orders, at least honor her memory and apologize to me."

"Melissa," she whispered. She looked away from the phone. I visualized her staring out of the window at the Washington Monument and the National Mall, perhaps missing her friend, perhaps wondering why she had played a role in her death, if she had done so.

I had met Melissa in our church in Fayetteville, North Carolina. We dated in high school and were married after I graduated from West Point. While I was at the military academy, Melissa had attended Meredith College, an all-women's liberal arts university. Melissa and Kim Campbell had been roommates and best friends when one of their classmates had died during a drinking game led by Campbell. My relationship with the president, through Melissa, presumably got me both thrown in jail and released from it. My suspicion was that Campbell believed that Melissa had told me about the murder investigation that the future president had been subject to after their classmate's death. I did know about it but, of course, would never have used the information to disrupt Campbell's presidential bid or for personal gain. I probably should have. Either strike first or be struck.

"Yes, Kim, try channeling Melissa and her belief that *Good Wins*. I had it engraved on her headstone in Vass. You should visit."

The video went black for a few moments, and I wondered if she had disconnected. It wasn't like me to demand an apology, but Melissa would have wanted the pain of the last year to resonate with her easily distracted, and sometimes dismissive, friend. The picture reappeared. She had moved and her face was shrouded in pixelated darkness.

"It's not like that, you know, Garrett. I loved Melissa. I love you. D.C. is filled with vermin. My husband is banging everything that moves, and you are the one true loyal friend I have."

"Had," I snapped.

She gasped. "I've tried so hard to balance personal and professional and serve the country."

"Try harder. The United States will be a subcontractor to China or to Blanc's Phalanx if you don't pull it together."

"Garrett, I promise you on Melissa's grave—"

"Don't you dare, Kim," I snapped. "Don't you invoke Melissa's name with any grand scheme that you might be designing. Melissa was about sacrifice. You're about serving yourself."

"That's not true!" she shot back. "I have sacrificed. I have led this country through the most horrible advancements in technology and political partisanship! You try doing it. Take it on the chin every single day from the bloodthirsty press or bloggers or tweeters or random people that just make shit up every single day!"

She had a point. While my pain had been mostly driven by personal loss, she was attacked from every side on an hourly basis every day. The relentless media pressure gave her such little respite that she most likely tuned everything out. I was exhausted just thinking about it and decided to change the subject.

"Okay, you win, Kim."

"We are in this together, Garrett. Think what you will of me, but I have always held our friendship dear. They wanted to kill you and prison was the safest place for you. Do you understand? I did that to save you and your men, whom I love dearly!"

A light sob escaped her breath. "God," she muttered.

I sat there in disbelief, though what she said was entirely plausible. A long moment passed between us. Cycling through my mind were moments back in college flipping quarters into plastic cups filled with beer, Melissa on one side and Kim on the other. Infectious laughter through the night as we bonded. Both seeing me off to West Point from the Raleigh-Durham airport, Kim there primarily to accompany Melissa back to their Meredith College dorm and provide solace. Then her rise through the state senate and governorship of North Carolina. Annual trips to Figure Eight Island that we could barely afford, but which Brad and Reagan greatly anticipated each year. Then the cryptic messages as she was campaigning for president, including visiting my troops after missions. No media. No press releases. Just heartfelt thanks and an attempt to understand. Then the requests for advice after my appointment as the joint Special Operations commander. That advice then translated into classified missions with a small portion of my team.

"Like a dagger," she had said before the very first mission. "In and out without leaving a mark."

And so, it had begun. From those heady days of being the razor's edge of American foreign policy to a musty prison cell in Fort Leavenworth's DB. There had to be some redemption out there for both of us.

The truth was that Kim and I were deeply connected, and we both simply missed Melissa, who had been our foundation. Ultimately, I decided to place my trust in Melissa's instinct to love Kim and hold on to her as her dearest friendship in her too-short life.

"Okay. I'm sorry. I understand. I'll help," I said.

She composed herself with a few brushes of her hands against her cheeks and eyes. Perhaps she had cycled through the same memories and come to the same conclusion.

"I, too, understand, Garrett. Never forget that I love you as my closest friendship, no matter what you think. As for Evelyn, ask Mitch. He has the details. And believe me when I say, I'm not on Blanc's team. *They* kidnapped me in Dakhla, remember? *They* were going to cut my head off on camera. Thankfully, you saved my ass. Again. Remember?"

I did remember. Henri Sanson, the French executioner, had his blade raised above her and Evelyn's heads before Van Dreeves and I had come barreling onto the castle balcony above the Sea of Dakhla.

"Yes. It seems you're always fifty-one to forty-nine percent on the margin of whatever is happening. And yes, Madame President, I love you, too."

"It's how you survive in politics, Garrett," she said. "Now go find Evelyn."

The president disconnected and the screen went blank. Drewson stepped into the room, no doubt having watched the entire conversation.

He reached out his hand and opened his palm. Inside was the dog tag he had been twirling between his fingers. It was one of my grandfather's from his Ranger unit. Typically, there were two, with both hanging loosely around the neck. One stayed with the body if the soldier was killed in combat, and the other was issued to the officer who had the unwelcome duty of burying the deceased.

LIEUTENANT COLONEL
GARRETT SINCLAIR
2ND RANGER BATTALION
FAYETTEVILLE, NC

"Evelyn wanted to discuss this with you. Your grandfather has a role here, I believe, but I'm not sure what it is. She wouldn't tell me."

I took the silver piece of metal and looped the chain around my neck.

"Where did she get this?" I asked.

He shrugged. "She told me to give it to you. No other explanation."

"Where is she?"

He pressed some buttons, and a map replaced the president's video chat screen. Drewson continued.

"You saw the video. A Phalanx team scooped her up in Denver. The flight plan says Biarritz. This dog tag should help you find her. We can track her."

"Smart dust?" I asked.

"Something like that," he replied.

"Can you get me to France?" I asked.

"I can," he said. "But I don't think your team will appreciate being excluded if you're considering doing this alone."

"If Misha has a chance of being on that list because of her capabilities, I want Jake to stay here to protect her. If Hobart and Van Dreeves want to stay and pull shifts with him, that's fine. Jeremy, Matt, and the rest should go home. The war is over for them."

Drewson stroked his chin with a long finger, a look of bemusement crossing his face. His intelligent eyes remained fixed on mine.

"Was it prison or something else?" he asked.

I shrugged. I knew what he was asking. How had I gone from being an all-in selfless military leader commanding thousands of soldiers in defense of our nation, to becoming a broken man sapped of spirit and hope? I didn't have the strength to argue with him and acknowledged the truth.

"It's everything, Mitch. The loss. Destruction. Callousness. You name it."

"I never visualized you as someone who would feel sorry for himself."

He was attempting to pluck a chord in me, I knew, but I clapped back at him.

"I don't feel sorry for myself, Mitch. I feel nothing for me personally. My emptiness is that it's quite possible it has all been for nothing. The sadness I feel is for everyone on the other side of that door. The people I love. What might their futures hold if we don't find a path to unifying the country? Very few men or women have fought and sacrificed so much for so little only to have an ungrateful political class bastardize our constitutional moorings to achieve their shallow, contemporary power grabs. I don't care about political parties or philosophies. I care about results, and if anything, I'm energized to save our nation."

"I think we are closer in heart and mind than you think."

"It never occurred to me to consider any alignment between us because I simply don't care about you. I will, however, fight to the death to protect those close to me and for the ideal of America."

"Very well then. That's essentially what this is about. We should get you moving. I'm afraid that Evelyn's skills are needed posthaste."

I nodded. "With Phalanx looking for me, I'll need some sort of diversion or disguise. I can't just buy a plane ticket to Paris. I'll never make it."

"Leave that part to me, General. I am a billionaire."

"All right, call my team in here," I said. "I'll deliver the news."

They came filing in, Mahegan, Hobart, and Van Dreeves leading the way.

"I'm going alone," I said.

"No way, sir," Van Dreeves said.

"It's the only way," I replied. I had expected pushback, but I wasn't going to waver.

"Look at that map," he said, pointing at the display on the wall.

The map showed several blinking red icons scattered across the United States and world, including Denver, Houston, and Biarritz.

"Those are known locations of Phalanx squads based upon LanxPro intercepts that this Zebra team gave Misha," Hobart said. "You're toast if you go anywhere alone."

I turned to Jake and said, "I need you to stay here and protect Misha. The others can stay if they want. I can go find Evelyn and bring her back. Mitch is resourcing me with a plane and other essential equipment," I said.

Jake nodded. The rest of my team glared at me.

I thought about Evelyn, my grandfather's dog tag, and why I really wanted to go find her. I wasn't sure. More than my father, "Coop" had been my mentor and role model. My father wasn't a bad man, he just didn't possess my grandfather's wit and wisdom, and we never connected in the way Coop and I had. I still had his black and red 1935 Cadillac LaSalle Coupe that he had dragged out of a junkyard in Raleigh and over the years fully restored. It was one of my greatest memories of him, working on the car and me handing him tools. It was a lifelong project. He was always replacing a mirror or the seats or anything to make it .01 percent better than it was before. He was a perfectionist, and so it was fitting that when Cat and I were born, we were instructed to call him "Coop." Not gramps or pop-pop or any other cute nickname. His soldier friends had nicknamed him Coop, and that's what everyone called him. In turn, Coop had nicknamed me Trip, short for Triple, for being the third in the Sinclair lineage. Absolutely no one, other than him, called me Trip.

"This place is more secure than Fort Knox," Van Dreeves said. "What happened to the team, boss? Don't need us anymore?"

"I need you more than you could ever know, Randy. You can stay with Jake to pull shifts to protect Misha and the others if you want. But I'd prefer that everyone just go home. Joe, you go home to Zoey and Syl. Randy, I need you to fill that giant hole in your heart left by Sally." I turned to Misha and said, "I need you to take care of your father." Then to Matt and Amanda I said, "Go home to Virginia and live your lives. Go to your farm in Greene County and get off the grid." To Jeremy, I said, "Go to your wife and four kids in Arkansas."

I turned and faced Mahegan. "Jake, protect Misha, like you did before. We are all we have left. It's time to live your lives and quit sacrificing for an uncaring bureaucracy that only takes and never gives."

Then to the collective group, I said, "I love all of you. In addition to Brad and Reagan, you're the only family I have left. And my decision is that you stand down and go home to love the people you have while you still can." For me, it would be my children. I could no longer say the same about my parents. Though still alive, I hadn't heard from them since I was sent to prison, and our relationship was marginal before that.

After a pregnant pause, I added, "Until Valhalla."

They were silent a moment, perhaps caught off guard by the Valhalla comment. A cloud crossed Mahegan's eyes, then he said, "Roger that, boss."

I walked out of the room, leaving them dumbfounded. I hadn't thought out a big speech and that was about all I had in the fuel tank. Something broke inside me, a last reed perhaps, as I stepped through the chamber into the hyperloop where Drewson was waiting for me like a chauffeur.

"All set?" he asked.

I nodded. The doors hissed shut and we rocketed somewhere underground for a couple of minutes. When the doors opened, we stepped through another chamber and then walked through a door into the crisp air inside of a sleek hangar. A nondescript white Hawker jet had its passenger steps open. Two pilots were twisting knobs inside and preparing for flight.

"This is a brand-new Hawker with a supplemental type certificate approved for an extended range fuel tank addition that gets you from Colorado to Biarritz without needing to refuel. These are my personal pilots. Inside are two duffels filled with everything you requested."

I turned to Drewson and put my finger in his chest, which caught him off guard.

"If you fuck with my people, I will come back and deliver you straight to hell. Understand?"

He stepped back, held his hands up, and said, "I got them out of jail, remember? I brought all of you together. I appreciate your loyalty, but your anger is misdirected at me when you're really pissed off at the world. I'm your only resource. Your government if you will."

"You're not my government," I snapped back.

9

I TURNED AND WALKED up the steps of the luxury jet. He was mostly right. I *was* pissed off at the world. We taxied out of the hangar and drilled into the early morning sky whereupon I lifted Coop's dog tag from my chest and stared at it.

I remembered the way Coop had affectionately called me "Trip" to distinguish me from my father. I always suspected that Coop had been disappointed in my dad, though I didn't know why. My dad had retired as a three-star general and was living the good life in South Florida now with my mother. They had transitioned to Naples, and the years had scratched away the father-son linkages. I couldn't remember the last time I had spoken with him.

As a kid, I would help Coop most days in the summer when I wasn't playing baseball. He was always tooling around his garage workshop behind their home on the outskirts of Fayetteville. He would turn wrenches while I held a fender or bumper in place or some other menial, low-risk task where a kid could do no harm to his prized Cadillac. Even in the sweltering heat of a North Carolina summer, Coop typically wore long-sleeve shirts. I remembered watching him roll up his sleeves, where I caught a glimpse of a dark blue elongated diamond shape no bigger than a dime.

"What's that, Coop?" I asked one hot summer morning when he had absently rolled up his sleeves.

He looked at me and said, "My business." He never later explained, and I had forgotten about the moment until now. My mind spiraled into much needed sleep after almost forty-eight hours of continuous operations.

THE GARAGE WAS *dank and musty, which was the way he liked it.*

"Like a German pillbox," he said. "We got in several of those concrete pillboxes and killed every last son of a bitch. Started with Normandy and we fought our way across France, into Holland and then Germany. By the end there were less than ten of us left. Lost ninety percent of my men. Damn fine men."

"Was it worth it, Coop?" I asked. I was twelve years old and more interested in playing shortstop than going to war at the time. It was hard to calculate the staggering losses and the psychological pain he must have endured. As he turned the wrench, a small black tattoo on the inside of his wrist that looked like a baseball diamond peeked from beneath his shirtsleeve. Even as a kid, I understood this symbol to be the World War II Ranger battalion insignia.

"My only regret," he said, "is that I didn't go with them. I tried, Trip. I got in the face of every Nazi I could find and charged full speed ahead. After every fight, I sobbed because I hadn't been killed."

"You were lucky . . . and good," I said.

"No luck in living, Trip," he said.

"What else is there?" I naively asked him.

"Just about everything. Pride, honor, dignity, shared sacrifice, defeating evil, comrades, family, country."

I was flipping a Rawlings leather baseball in my hand as we talked. The red stitched seams were worn from use, and the once-white cover was pocked with bat bruises and dirt stains from the infield.

"No, sir, young man. No luck in living, at all."

The plane hit some turbulence, and I rolled onto my side, sliding back into the dream.

Now, Coop and I were standing in the middle of the village of Sainte-Mère-Eglise surrounded by American paratroopers landing from the sky all around us. Silk parachutes fluttered. The "oomph" of wind leaving the diaphragm accompanied the soft thud of jump boots twisting into the cobblestones. German soldiers and French civilians ran in every direction. Gunfire popped all around us, though we were impervious to the bullets, perhaps just as a young, twenty-five-year-old Major Sinclair had been leading his Rangers. Coop clasped my hand, and we moved swiftly through the melee into the outer reaches of the village. Three gray-uniformed German soldiers piled into a small home from which female screams pierced the sky.

My grandfather suddenly had an M1 Garand in his hands, as did I. I was no longer a kid but my adult self. Flames engulfed the house as we burst through the heavy oak door. Three women were huddled in the corner, the Germans clawing at them to use as human shields.

Coop fired, killing one. I shot a second man, felling him. A third ripped my grandfather's dog tags from his neck as he held two girls, a knife in his hand. The girls were blond and no more than eight or nine years old.

A bullet hole appeared in the German's forehead but neither of us had pulled the trigger. I looked over my shoulder and saw Evelyn Champollion standing there, holding a modern sniper rifle and shouting, "Leave my family alone!"

I SNAPPED AWAKE, a light turbulence rattling the airplane again. Last year, in the Eye of Africa, Evelyn had referred to Coop having some connection with her family. I had read in his combat diary that he had called France his "new home and family." What memory or fated hand had guided that dream? The presence of the dog tag could have spurred the visions, but was there more to it?

I looked at the small monitor on the bulkhead in front of me. We were crossing the United Kingdom with another two hours to Biarritz Airport. I needed to call my children and let them know I was okay. I was conflicted, though, because I knew every communication would be monitored, but I missed my kids, and I needed a favor.

While in prison, Brad, Reagan, and I did the old trope of leaving draft emails in a jointly accessed account. Reagan was more active than Brad, but they both sent me almost daily missives expressing their love for me. I looked at prison as just another deployment, being somewhere I didn't care to be, though sent there by "my country." There was a greater than 90 percent chance that Warden Smyth and his minions had been reading the drafts, and now I suspected Aurelius Blanc and the Phalanx team may have read them, too, but we had always been a close family and I wasn't going to abandon my children.

I dialed from a satellite phone that was part of my equipment request to Drewson. On the third ring a sleepy Reagan answered.

"Who is this?" she asked.

"Hey baby girl," I said.

After a long pause, which I imagined included her checking the windows of her apartment in Charlottesville to see if she was being watched or if any listening vans were present, she said, "Dad?"

"Just wanted to let you know I am not where I was," I said.

"The papers are saying you were moved. That there was an accident at the prison. Brad and I have been worried," she said. I recognized the sound of soft sobs that she was trying to suppress. She was a tough girl, an athlete and beautiful woman, but a daddy's girl at heart. So that was the story Phalanx had run to disguise their botched hit? Or had Drewson run it to give me cover? Either way, I didn't want to endanger my children, so I remained vague.

"I'm okay. Just wanted to let you know. Can you loop Brad in?"

"Yeah, sure, but Dad, what's going on?"

"Loop Brad in. I don't have long," I said.

After a long pause I heard Brad's voice, "What's going on, Reags? I'm in between sets."

Brad played lead guitar in a rock band that toured the East Coast college campuses. It wasn't my first choice for my William & Mary College–educated son, but I was proud of him for pursuing his dream. He had named the band Napoleon's Corporal, after he and Reagan spent a couple of weeks in Paris, Normandy, and the southwest coast of France not far from Biarritz at a place called Hossegor. A French exchange student in Brad's high school class, Laurent Ballantine, had briefly been the lead singer of their band until he had to return home to attend the Sorbonne. Brad liked the addition because the kid looked like he had just walked off the cover of *GQ*, at six foot four, with his Elvis smile and eyes, lean, muscled frame, and lyrical voice. The college girls loved him, and by extension, Napoleon's Corporal. His family summered in Hossegor, a beach resort and surfing mecca twenty kilometers north of Biarritz. Laurent had worked as a manager at the campground nearby while he studied for a master's degree in tourism. Whether he, or anyone for that matter, would be at the rustic cabins in the lashing winds of February on the Atlantic Coast was doubtful.

"Brad, shut up," Reagan said.

"Hey Brad," I said. "I only have a minute, but I wanted to tell you both that I love you."

"Dad? WTF? Where are you? We've been going crazy. There was an explosion at the prison. Oh my God. Where are you?" Brad wasn't typically an emotional person, but I could hear that they both had been worried. As a father, it bothered me that I had caused them concern but also plucked a chord of love and comfort within me to know that despite my troubles, my kids still loved me.

"Just remember, guys, that good wins," I said.

They stopped arguing enough to listen to me when I used their mother's refrain.

"Dad, oh my God, what kind of trouble are you in?" Reagan gasped.

I didn't reply, because I knew they were smart kids and would understand what I had just said.

"Tell Laurent hello for me and that I might need to build a bonfire," I said and hung up the phone.

For a few minutes, images of Brad, Reagan, and Melissa flipped through my mind like a slide show. I loved my life. Beautiful, smart wife. Two amazing children. Loyal black lab named Scout, who resided with Brad now, though Reagan would steal him occasionally and sneak him into her UVA dorm. I had everything I ever wanted in life until it was taken from me, and I continued to power on because it was the only alternative. The only way out of the ambush, as they say, is through it. If you don't move, you assuredly die in the beaten zone of enemy fire.

I imagined that they stayed on the phone trying to decipher what I had said and what they should do. Brad would understand that I couldn't stay on the phone for any length of time because of intercept programs both foreign and domestic, but it would be Reagan who would get the Laurent comment. As a sixteen-year-old girl, she had been smitten with Laurent, who had managed the campground just south of the Adour River in the Pignada Forest on the bluffs east of Biarritz. She and some of her friends had spent a week at the camp with Brad, Laurent, and some mutual friends. They had built bonfires on the beach, surfed, and spearfished.

My destination was one of the cabins at the site. The surveillance state we lived in today necessitated me being off the grid as much as possible while still being able to conduct reconnaissance on Evelyn's location. It would be the best I could do on short notice. I used the remainder of the time to dig through the kit bags Drewson had scrambled for me. He had assembled an assortment of gear that would be useful regardless of what I found. After an hour, I had checked the equipment, applied the disfiguring makeup and contact lenses, and prepared for night movement to wherever Evelyn might be.

The satellite phone buzzed next to my captain's chair. I answered and Drewson shouted into the phone.

"My sources are telling me that Blanc is on his way to interrogate Evelyn at the Hôtel du Palais. It would be best if you got there first," he said.

I hung up without responding to him, free of the burden of answering to anyone or, quite frankly, of being responsible for my team going once again into the fray. This time it was just me, and I preferred it that way. The only loss I could cause would be my own, or so I thought.

As Coop had said, "There's no luck in living."

It was 1:00 A.M. local time when we landed and pulled into Drewson's private hangar in Biarritz. On the descent, the Atlantic Ocean's white breakers were etched across the Grand Plage between Côte des Basques and the Phare de Biarritz, marked by the spinning lighthouse lamp casting strobes of yellow beams across the roiling black sea.

The steps dropped, and I descended with a backpack slung over one shoulder. I had condensed what equipment I needed into one small ruck, leaving everything else on the plane. Having done my best to check for tracking devices, I was still concerned Drewson had placed trackers somewhere in the gear. If there was such a thing as smart dust, anything was possible these days. While it was most likely that Drewson was tracking me via something he put on Coop's dog tag, it was Blanc that I needed to elude.

A man wearing a gray herringbone driver's cap and a matching overcoat approached from a door, hands stuffed in his pockets. He looked left and right, assessing potential threats, I presumed, and then locked eyes with me. The turbines whined as they wound down. The air was frigid inside the hangar.

"Monsieur, pour vous," he said, placing a set of keys in my hand.

"Merci," I replied, and walked past him, through the door that he had entered, through a nondescript hallway and into the cold night. A small blue Peugeot 208 was parked in the lot. I quickly used a Spy-Hawk GPS detector to scan the outside and inside of the vehicle. Satisfied there were no overt explosive or tracking devices, other than the actual GPS of the car, I unplugged that device and left the cord hanging by my feet. The car started promptly at the push of a button, and I followed D260 to D810 for a couple kilometers around the airport. I pulled into a Best Western Hotel parking lot and parked the car at the far, unoccupied end. Disabling the dome light, I slipped into the night with my backpack strapped across my shoulders.

Walking through an adjacent neighborhood, I tugged a ball cap low over my forehead and eased along the quiet streets. These were mostly summer homes owned by wealthy Parisians, like Martha's Vineyard or the Hamptons in the United States. Very few houses showed any signs of life here in the biting February winds. Few had any lights switched on, and the manicured rows of twenty-foot boxwoods provided me concealment as I hustled along Avenue du Braou past the Olympic training facilities. These neighborhoods, too, had security cameras and sometimes actual guards, or at the very least house sitters.

Two cars crept toward the town of Anglet, three kilometers to my north, as I swiftly crossed Avenue de Biarritz. One of the cars braked as I continued north toward the Forêt du Pignada. I switched streets so that I was now on a smaller road as the vehicles traveled on the street perpendicular to this one. It wouldn't surprise me if Phalanx knew that I was in Biarritz looking for Evelyn, either through eavesdropping devices inside Drewson's headquarters or via their massive surveillance operation connected to every camera in the world, whether it be a security camera or ring doorbell. Phalanx had created a virtual web cast around the globe.

I was surprised I had made it this far.

A light buzzing above me had me blending into a densely forested front yard to my left. I knelt next to a large hardwood tree and held my night vision goggles up to my eyes. A tethered drone swept the expansive front yard of the mansion across the street. Assuredly passively connected to Phalanx, the drone's cameras clicked and whirred as it traveled the forty-meter arc. I waited until it began scanning the side yard to continue my progress toward my destination. Another car approached me from behind, so I cut through the campus of the Lycée Stella Maris. Angling from there across a golf course, I was able to enter the heavily wooded Pignada Forest from the south.

By now it was nearly 4:00 A.M. Part of the mature forest had acres of charred husks of tree trunks, the victims of a fire no doubt. The southern end of the park, however, was filled with towering hardwoods and untrodden tanglefoot. After navigating through the trails, I found the Pignada Campground. A few of the buildings were dilapidated, but others seemed reasonably fit. Thunder rolled in the distance, and before long, wet slaps of cold rain were hammering my back and face. I slid inside one of the buildings and heard movement. When I shined my flashlight, there were two raccoons seeking shelter, also. They stared at me with their burglars' eyes and went about their business. Once the rain subsided, I continued my inspection of the summer grounds.

As expected, the area was totally vacant. I picked up the glint of small metal in the dense tanglefoot. Upon inspection, it was a bicycle of relatively new origin. The tires were warm despite the cold rain. Someone was here, and I was hoping I knew who it was. I walked across a gravel driveway, rain coming down in sheets now, lashing at me as if to warn me to stay away. I stepped onto the stoop of the headquarters building, which seemed to be in decent shape. I picked the lock in the back and stepped inside only to be confronted by a man and a weapon.

"Monsieur?!"

"Laurent," I said, quickly, placing my hand on the long-barreled shotgun he was nervously holding in his hands.

"Général?" The word came out, *gen-eh-ral,* with his smooth inflections.

"Oui," I said. "Were you followed?"

"Non," he said, shaking his head. "Reagan said to meet you here. I took all precautions. But you look . . . different."

He was trembling as I removed the shotgun from his hands.

"We won't be needing this," I said. "And yes, I've been trying to be incognito for a bit."

"It was all my parents had in the cottage," he said.

Their "cottage" was a four-thousand-square-foot beach home overlooking the high sand dunes and Atlantic Ocean in Hossegor, some twenty kilometers north of here.

"Where is your car?"

"I rode my bike," he said. "It is laid flat in some bushes."

No one else was here for the moment, then, but I didn't trust that would last long.

"Okay, thank you for meeting me," I said.

"Please, General, have a seat."

We sat in two chairs, and he opened a brown paper bag with a six-pack of Kronenbourg's 1664 beer, handed one to me, and said, "General, looks like you could use this. Remember we drank these and talked about Normandy and your grandfather Coop?"

"Stop calling me 'general,'" I said. "And yes, I remember. That's why I had Reagan reach out. How's your business doing?"

Laurent had a company called Alpes et Océans, with the tagline *"Et Tout le Reste."* From the Alps to the Oceans . . . And Everything in Between. Once, we had shared a six-pack of Kro's when I had visited their home in Hossegor a few years ago with my two children. Though just twenty-five years old now, Laurent was an old soul. While Brad, Reagan, and their friends had hung out on the beach, Laurent and I sat on the patio overlooking the ocean while we drank beer and discussed his budding tourism start-up business. Conversely, he had asked me about American Special Forces and mentioned that the French DGSE were recruiting him because of his family connections and the fact that he was literate in multiple languages. While he eagerly pursued his business, there was a light in his eyes when he spoke of the spy world. That connection and pursuit of intrigue might have explained why he made the effort to be here tonight.

He shrugged. "Business is good. Many Americans traveling after COVID. Everyone was cooped up for two years. Now they want to get out and see the world." He changed the subject and asked, "How are Reagan? Brad?"

"They're okay. Their old man was in jail for a year, so it's been tough on them."

He looked through the window at the rain hammering on the glass. It was the most miserable type of weather. Not cold enough to snow but still freezing. He had a small propane burner providing useless heat and some light. His face glowed orange in the pulsating flame.

"I can't imagine," he said. "The things you have done for your country. The world. It's ludicrous what governments are doing to their people, including mine."

I tasted the beer. It was cold and bitter, just how I liked it.

"Yes, that's why I need your help, Laurent. I'm reluctant to involve you but cameras are everywhere, and I know you own a tourist business."

He nodded and smiled. "That's correct." Then he frowned. "Is this concerning Aurelius Blanc and his Phalanx squads? Can I help?"

I wondered how much he knew about Blanc. Was it coincidence that he latched onto Blanc's Phalanx teams when I mentioned the cameras?

To 99 percent of the population, Blanc was a good Samaritan tech mogul making the world a better place through technology.

"Perhaps. What do you know about him?"

"He's French. Everyone here knows him. Like Elon Musk or Mark Zuckerberg in your country," he said, mostly dodging my question about Blanc.

I paused and nodded. "Of course you know who Blanc is. Do you use Phalanx social media apps?"

"Yes of course. Like Facebook or Amazon, they are everywhere. I have a LanxPro profile for my business. It generates a lot of income for me. They use artificial intelligence to scan people's phones or listen to their conversations. I pay for the premium service, which provides me leads for people considering vacations in Europe. LanxPro then drops an advertisement for my services in their social media feeds. They can geolocate at high-end resorts and do discrete messaging. Blanc may be bad, but LanxPro is good for business."

"That's the dilemma, isn't it?"

"It seems so," he said.

"His company is the fulcrum of everything that is happening."

"How so?"

"Think about what you just told me. They are listening to everything we do. Watching every step we take. They have infested many governments and intelligence agencies," I said.

"Probably our DGSE, for sure," he added. I agreed. France's foreign intelligence agency was no more immune from skullduggery than ours.

"Speaking of which, this person I need to find can be helpful. I can't do it alone, though. I need you to do some observation."

"*Mon général,* I get to do double top-secret spy things with you?"

"I just need you to talk to people in the Napoleon hotel and ask if they've seen someone."

"The Hôtel du Palais?" He chuckled. "This I can do. It is my business. What would you like for me to do?"

I liked Laurent and had vetted him prior to Brad and Reagan visiting him. All indicators were that he was a normal French kid that liked girls and Formula 1 racing. His LanxPro profile, which I retrieved during the flight, included lots of pictures of him and beautiful young women at scenic resort spots around Europe. A striking blonde at the Tower of London. And the same woman again, on Corsica. And later in Dubrovnik, Croatia. It was my good fortune that he was not similarly indisposed with his girlfriend tonight. Perhaps I had caught him before a ski trip to Garmisch, Germany. Regardless, I was glad he was here. And the chances of him owning his own tourist business and not being an undercover DGSE agent were near zero. The only question was, whose side was he on, Blanc's or Drewson's, because there really was nothing else today. My guess was Drewson because I was still alive.

"Be yourself," I said.

"Beautiful ladies in Biarritz. I am always happy to go there," he said. "Even this time of year, the spa is a destination."

"I need you to ask around about this woman," I said. I handed him a picture of Evelyn Champollion. Her hair was a mix of brunette and blond, eyes crystal blue, and full lips slightly spread enough in a smile to see a glimpse of teeth. The slightest crow's feet pinched around her eyes. She was forty-seven years old and an international enigma who supposedly possessed the key to dismantling Aurelius Blanc's authoritarian grip on the world.

In the picture she was standing at the Eye of Africa a few days before I met her over a year ago. With one foot propped up on a rock, she was holding a sweat-stained olive Australian breezer hat in one hand and a claw hammer in the other. She was wearing khaki-colored pants with a matching multi-pocketed safari shirt. The sun was setting behind her, the orange hues subtly highlighting the blond hints in her hair.

Laurent smiled. "*Mon général* has a crush. She's beautiful, for sure, but wouldn't the general prefer a much younger woman?"

Laurent was amused.

"Not my style," I said more defensively than I intended. "She is important to solving a large problem for all of us."

He shrugged. "As you wish. I know many beautiful women who would die to be the wife of a general."

I didn't know if he was pimping or genuinely interested in finding me companionship. Either way, it was irrelevant.

"Thank you, Laurent. I appreciate the gesture, but this is mission related. I will pay you."

He pursed his lips and nodded. "There is compensation?"

"Of course," I said. I handed him two thousand in cash. I had asked Drewson for euros, but Laurent's eyes brightened at the thick wad of dollars, which I hadn't anticipated would be a problem.

"I am happy to do this as a friend," he said.

He wasn't pushing back hard enough for me to believe he didn't want the money.

"No. If you don't do it in a day, we're done, and you go home. I don't expect she will be there much longer."

"The hotel?"

"There is a rumor of a tunnel from the hotel to an escape hatch beneath the lighthouse. The lightkeeper supposedly lived in the old hotel before it burned down a hundred years ago. The tunnel remained and in fact became an escape route for several trapped by the fire."

Laurent nodded furiously.

"Yes. Yes. I know this story," he said. "Remember, General, I have a tourism degree and escort foreigners all over the country. It is my business. I have toured many times through the Hôtel du Palais. It has an iron gate across this tunnel. I've seen it many times if it is the same one you are looking for."

"Sounds like it," I said.

He opened his phone, snapped a photo of the photograph, then pinched and squeezed the picture on his phone until he had the face large enough. He added a filter and saved the image, handing me back the picture.

"I find this woman for you, whatever she means to you. I know you are a serious man, and I must ask the amount of danger I might face. As you must know, the internet makes the world a small place. I look up the news on you and one minute I learn of an explosion at a prison in Kansas and the next there is an article correcting the information."

"All of that is part of what I've been saying. The only thing worse than a fascist state is an interconnected fascist world where there is no refuge. Just by being here with me you are placing yourself in danger. If you can't do this, I understand. I appreciate the beers."

"I can do this," he said quickly. "If it is for you, I'm in. If it is for a good cause, I'm also in."

I opened another beer, and we tipped the bottles together.

"Thank you," I said.

I had a lot of experience working with indigenous forces in lands across the globe. As a private citizen, I had just hired my first insurgent.

WE TOOK TURNS SLEEPING for the remaining three hours of darkness using Nemo Disco ultra-light sleeping bags that Laurent had carried in his hiking backpack. I had my Beretta 9 mm pistol clutched in my right hand on my chest through the night.

When I woke, he was huddled over a small propane stove making coffee on what would be the check-in counter of the camp front office. I walked to the window and studied the landscape. The sun was cresting over the ridge, which meant last night's cold front had passed. The ocean and the bluffs were still shrouded in darkness. A light mist was rising off the damp floor of the forest.

"Warmer today," he said. "Still crisp but okay."

"Let's exchange phone contact information," I said.

Laurent took my phone, entered his information, then texted himself.

"This is my burner mobile," he said.

He handed me a cup of coffee. It was scalding hot on my lips but felt good going down after a bone-chilling night.

"Tell me, General, this woman is Evelyn Champollion, no? A direct descendent of Champollion *le jeune*?"

"Yes," I said.

"She is quite famous in France. Infamous in some circles."

I nodded.

"She has notoriety from the Eye of Africa fight," he said. Not a question.

"Perhaps," I replied.

"Why is it that everyone knows that war is a bad thing, but we never seem to stop fighting?"

"That's a question for another time. Right now, we're burning daylight," I said. "If you go into the hotel and see what you can find out, I'm going to recon the lighthouse and its perimeter."

"*Oui.* I only have one bike, which I'm happy to loan you."

"No, I'm going to be dressed in running clothes and pretending to be jogging," I said.

He looked at me with curious eyes and a smirk. "But won't you be actually jogging? Not pretending?"

"Just get to the hotel and pretend like you're planning for some Americans coming over," I said.

He smiled again and said, "Well then, I'm off. I'll text you if I see anything."

He slung his backpack over his shoulder, walked outside where mist escaped his mouth, and ambled into a white beam of sunshine cutting through the trees. With my first task accomplished, I changed into a long-sleeve T-shirt and running shorts with New Balance shoes. I slipped the Beretta into a clip-on holster and covered it with a light blue windbreaker. In the mirror, I checked my newly shaped ears and brown contact lenses, thanks to the disguise materials Drewson had provided. I tugged a wool skullcap over my head and low on my brow and slipped some Oakley sunglasses over my eyes.

A flash passed across the office window, an interruption in my periphery. It could have been Laurent zipping along on his bike, but the timing didn't compute. Drawing my pistol, I slid quietly against the wall, out of view of the windows. A tree branch scratched against the roof. The night before, I had assessed the security of the camp office. There was a locked back door that led to a room with two windows and four desks scattered with papers and old tower desktop computers. The passageway from the reception area where I had spoken with Laurent was to my left.

The glass on the far reception window crashed when a smoke grenade came tumbling through. I immediately slipped into the back office, remaining low and avoiding my attackers' line of sight through the window. Another smoke grenade came tumbling through the north window of the back office.

Because I had prior experience with aerosolized nerve agents and mind-altering drugs, I had added a small Avon M50 full-face respirator with dual filters to my shopping list. Retrieving it from my backpack, I fitted it onto my face and took up a position behind the counter where I had a line of sight to both doors.

My attackers' obvious strategy was to smoke me out and have me come through one of the doors or windows, where I was sure they were casually prepared to riddle me with bullets or attempt to capture me.

At my knee was Laurent's shotgun, which I checked. It was loaded with four shells of buckshot. Opting for my pistol, I remained motionless, listening to the hiss of the smoke canisters and muffled voices outside the cabin. Combat is sometimes like that old game we played as kids to see who could hold their breath the longest. The first to let go and breathe lost. The waiting game continued for another minute or so, and the smoke filled the entire office complex. Without my protective mask, I would be dead from smoke inhalation—which perhaps was what they were thinking when two men clad in black with balaclavas pulled over their faces opened each door. They stepped through the foggy haze of boiling smoke cannisters, moving long rifles smoothly in each direction. There were no Police Nationale markings on any of their clothing or equipment, not that it mattered to me. There was no difference in confronting the state or the technology company in today's technofascist world. If they were attacking me and those I cared about, they deserved to die.

With that thought, I watched as the smoke rose and obscured their vision, leaving me enough visibility to target their torsos and below. I was unsure if they were wearing body armor, so I aimed just above the first man's groin and snapped off two quick shots before spinning to the man approaching from the inner office and repeating the process. I was up and moving beyond them, expecting at least two more attackers outside. On my way I confiscated their Czech CZ-805-A2 assault rifles and radio earpieces.

One voice was saying, *"Statut! Statut!"* Status! Status!

"Tous est clair! Entrez!" I replied. All is clear. Come in.

Two men came barreling through each door. I waited until I had clear shots on them and used the 805 to kill the distant one entering through the back office and shoot the near intruder in the thigh. He doubled over at the waist, and I dragged him outside where I could remove my protective mask. I quickly gagged him with duct tape from my rucksack and used zip ties to bind his wrists and ankles.

"Fils de pute!" he muttered as I cinched the cloth tight on his mouth. Son of a bitch.

Leaving him there, I spent a minute circling the cabin, where I found Laurent similarly gagged and tied up with his hands behind his back next to his bike in the bushes. I took a moment to release him of his binds and said, "Get out of here. Continue the mission."

"Mon Dieu, Général!"

"Go," I said. "I told you there were some risks."

"There were four men. Be careful," he said. His eyes were wide with fear, but he jumped on his bike and cycled away as fast as he could. After completing a full recon of the area, I found four Voxan Wattman electric motorcycles, which would explain why we had never heard anything. These blue-and-gray machines were made in Monaco and clocked the fastest speeds of any motorcycle in the world at 455 miles per hour.

These guys had all the markings of one of Blanc's Phalanx assassin squads. I walked through the cabin, which now had a few growing fires creeping up the walls ignited by the grenade sparks, to ensure the three men I had shot were dead. They were. Returning to my wounded prisoner, I figured I had a couple of minutes before some good Samaritan, or the police, arrived to check out the smoke. I removed my prisoner's gag.

"Why come after me?" I asked him in English.

"Fuck you," he responded in the same language. He was fluent, I presumed.

I held the blade of my Blackhawk CQD Mark 1 spear-point knife to his throat.

"You saw me kill your friends. No problem in doing the same with you," I said, pressing the razor-sharp tip into his neck above his carotid.

"Attendez! Attendez!" Wait! Wait!

"No time, pal," I said, pushing the knife deeper.

"Blanc. We are with Blanc," he spat.

"Too late," I said, as the blade nicked his artery and blood began to course along his neck.

I dragged him into the cabin where the smaller fires had gathered and were beginning to engulf the entire building. A phone dropped from his pocket, but I was too busy grabbing a Beretta pistol and keys to one of the motorcycles from another attacker. As I reached for the phone, the ceiling collapsed sending embers in every direction. Unsuccessful, I escaped from the inferno to where the four blue-and-gray bikes lay on their sides about fifty meters away just off the trail. I put the pistol under the seat and tossed the Czech rifle, though it had treated me right. I grabbed two helmets and snapped the extra one to the seat frame.

The bike was easy enough to start and made no noise as I eased onto

Boulevard de la Plages which took me to Boulevard de Mer and onto Rue d'Haitzart, where I laid the bike down in the tall shrubs near a gulley running up from the beach north of the lighthouse. Across the street were large, gated mansions. These homes had unobstructed views of the Atlantic Ocean from their rockbound perch a hundred meters above the sea.

After cinching my backpack tight around my shoulders, I slid down the slick ravine and scoped out the paths, or lack thereof, before climbing back up. It was almost 8:00 A.M. now, and the sun was shining everywhere except on the sheer cliffs I was scaling. Once back on the road, I picked up a natural jogger's lope, as if I were casually bounding onto the West Point baseball field, and continued my reconnaissance.

I was reminded of the old army television commercial that had a young paratrooper completing a jump and firing some artillery in the early morning hours when the narrator said, "In the army, we do more before 9:00 A.M. than most people do all day." Already, I had killed four Phalanx operatives, burned down a cabin, and conducted route reconnaissance to find a kidnapped friend.

Indeed, the ad's narrator had a point.

There was no question that Blanc knew I was in France or that I was looking for Evelyn. I had lost the element of surprise if I had ever had it. I needed to find Evelyn quickly, and the only clues I possessed were Drewson's tip about a secret chamber beneath the lighthouse, which was connected to the Hôtel du Palais by a tunnel, and his odd emphasis on her having one of Coop's dog tags. Of course, I held the other one, which Drewson had given me prior to departing with a vague reference to "smart dust." I lifted the slender piece of metal from my chest as I walked across the street.

Sliding my hand across the surface, I felt a rougher texture than the shiny surfacel might otherwise produce. I thought about how Mahegan, Misha, and Drewson had all referenced smart dust in the last twenty-four hours.

Then it hit me.

I retrieved my phone, which Drewson had provided, and studied the few apps on the screen. One of them was a game called Damsel in Distress with a blond-haired cartoon character shouting from a lighthouse window. I looked up and saw the Phare de Biarritz a quarter mile away. The cartoon was an exact replica of the lighthouse, which was a forty-meter-tall white cylinder with a black cupola and beacon perched thirty meters above the ocean floor.

Clicking on the app, it connected to the local French Orange wireless phone network and a globe spun until it was showing me standing on the road in real time via an Optimus satellite. A blinking red dot appeared about three hundred meters to my ten o'clock.

Evelyn.

I pinched and pulled at the screen until it was large enough for me to see that her beacon was transmitting from the west side of the peninsula upon which the lighthouse sat. I studied the area for a moment. It was a crisp, sunny morning and by now several bundled-up locals were walking their dogs and exercising along the path to my front. Looking back at the screen, I registered in my head where she might be and then began a light jog across the street onto the asphalt path.

The firefight at Pignada Forest and the quick recce into the north ravine had consumed some energy. I was breaking a sweat as I casually trotted above the waves ripping across the rocky beach.

Approaching the lighthouse, I checked my phone and saw that I was relatively adjacent to the pulsating red dot on the screen. Pocketing the phone, I slipped over the lip of the trail and onto the steep rocky cliff, now on the opposite side of the ridge from where I had dumped the motorcycle. My map recon on the flight had indicated the midway point of the cliff showed some man-made anomalies. Using my best climbing skills again, I found the midpoint, which had a minor trail etched along the side. Crashing waves beneath me billowed with salty spray that stung my face. The distinctive two-tone wail of French police vehicles pierced the air above me. Hopefully they were headed to the fire and not yet looking for me. As the sirens faded, I grew more confident.

I followed the trail some twenty meters above the beach. The going was treacherous with the previous night's rain making everything extra slick. The running shoes helped me maintain my grip until the trail widened and I felt a distinctive flat wall instead of the rocky outcropping I had been traversing.

This was man-made, and I gained confidence that perhaps the rumors of an escape hatch were accurate. I felt my phone buzz in my pocket and answered it.

"*Mon général,* you are very well hidden, but I can see you and my sources tell me you're very close to her. You have maybe ten minutes before others come, though. Blanc's men are on high alert and have called in reserves. I have done my best at misdirection but must leave quickly. Keep going," Laurent said. "She's there."

I looked across the beach and saw him standing on the balcony of the Hôtel du Palais. He nodded, put his phone away, and turned to walk in the other direction.

I moved another twenty meters and found a crease in the wall. It was a padlocked door with rusted hinges. Two swipes of the pistol and I had the padlock busted. I used my knife to scrape open the seams and pry at the lip of the door. A thumping from inside told me that someone was in there. If not Evelyn, who?

I felt the door budge, as if pushed from the inside. The lip moved enough for me to get my fingertips on the side and pull outward. Over my shoulder I noticed some commotion on the Hôtel du Palais balcony. Four armed men came pouring from the far door. They were scanning the ridge and pointing in my direction. Voices atop the high ground above me were shouting in French, as if directing or commanding others.

A shot rang out. Dirt blew into my face. I put my shoulder into the door, and it flew open as rappel ropes dropped from the cliffs above.

Evelyn Champollion was staring at me. "Took you long enough, Sinclair."

11

I EMBRACED EVELYN TO pull her from Blanc's lair, but her wrists were bound with medieval shackles that were chained to an anchor bolt in the floor.

The voices above us grew closer, as did the gunshots from the Hôtel du Palais balcony. Shouting from inside Evelyn's chamber also joined the cacophony. We were trapped against the cliff with the only possible escape route into the ocean.

I fumbled with my rucksack as I removed a small UST ParaHatchet and landed two blows against the chains running through the cuffs.

They sparked and fell away as Evelyn scrambled through the door onto the ledge.

Two shots pinged against the stone wall behind us.

"I think I was safer before you got here," she said.

"Good to see you, too, Evelyn," I replied.

"Is the general getting sentimental on me?"

"Let's try to stay alive."

I grabbed Evelyn around her slender waist and leaped onto the beach as two men rappelled down from the street with MP5 machine guns. We landed in a sandy patch surrounded by high boulders, which protected us from the fusillade of gunfire. The only safe spot was north of the lighthouse, which was the direction in which we scrambled. I hadn't been sure about Evelyn's physical condition after she'd been detained, but she looked as fit and healthy as she had when I'd first met her, when she had run faster than me in the Sahara Desert as we liberated Zoey Morgan. I was confident she would at least keep up.

We were able to reach the point to the immediate west of the lighthouse, which was underwater until the tide ebbed for a moment, opening a narrow path before another wave crashed against the rocks. The hotel snipers were now out of range and the MP5-bearing rappellers were behind us on the beach.

With the terrain protecting us for the moment, I led Evelyn up the cliff along a trail that beachgoers used to sneak onto the private stretch of sand north of the lighthouse. It connected to the path I had scouted earlier. Hustling up the slippery incline, we grabbed vines and roots until we were atop the steep ravine. The motorcycle sparkled in the sunlight as we donned the helmets. I snapped my backpack onto the front handlebars as we simultaneously mounted the small, narrow racing seat. Her body was pressed tightly against mine, and she wrapped her wiry arms around my torso as we sped north toward Hossegor.

Police cars passed us in the opposite direction at high rates of speed. The fire from the Pignada Forest was now a gray plume of smoke as we throttled our way up A63 past Hossegor toward Bordeaux. It wasn't lost on me that Drewson could track our every move with Evelyn's locator and that Phalanx most likely knew the precise GPS locations of their motorcycle fleet.

"I know a guy in Bordeaux if we can make that far," Evelyn said through the microphones of our Neotec II flip-up helmets with built-in Bluetooth communications systems. Her voice was surprisingly calm for a person having just escaped captivity from the most powerful tech assassins in the world. Why Blanc had not killed her immediately, as he was trying to do to me, I didn't yet know. But I was eager to find out what Evelyn knew that the rest of us didn't.

The charge indicator on the motorcycle showed we had another thirty minutes of power remaining. I was ready to ditch the bike anyway and get somewhere safe with Evelyn. I wondered if I should hang on to the phone or the dog tags. The chances that Drewson had only one form of tracking device on either of us were low, so I didn't see the point. The motorcycle needed to go as soon as possible, though.

We zipped past rows of single and double échoppe homes, the staple of the middle class in the outer suburbs of Bordeaux, known for their workshops and stucco, brick, and timber construction. Evelyn told me to cross the Garonne River and take two lefts and a right, until we turned onto a dirt road that sliced between at least fifteen acres of vineyards climbing above the river. At the end of the drive stood an estate that looked a few hundred years old. Not a castle, but not a simple home, either. There was a courtyard and a circular drive around the fountain. It had arched windows and roofs with overlapping Spanish tiles diving at steep angles against the brown stucco façade.

I pulled the motorcycle to a stop and said, "This bike is probably being tracked by Phalanx. Anyone you care about here?"

"Just my brother," she quipped. "Sometimes I can do without him."

Ah yes, the Evelyn I came to know in the Sahara last year. Cool under fire with a quick wit.

An impossibly good-looking man stepped onto the porch, which was gray cement with at least fifteen beveled steps leading up to the landing. The man appeared to be in his mid-forties, well over six foot tall, with dark brown hair that was feathered behind his ears. His quizzical look transformed into a smile when Evelyn removed her helmet.

"Evey?" He pronounced it *Eh-vee*.

"*Oui,* Charles!"

He ran two steps at a time down to meet her. Two large black Labrador retrievers darted from the house and beat him to her. They had their massive paws on her lean frame and almost knocked her over when Charles came up to Evelyn and hugged her.

They rattled off a series of rapid-fire colloquial French that surpassed my basic skills, but the gist of it was: "My God, it's so good to see you. Are you okay? We've been so worried. Normally we talk every few days. And who is this guy?"

Evelyn turned to me as I was removing my helmet and leaning the motorcycle against the fountain that had a cherubic boy peeing into the pool. Perhaps the entire Champollion family were comedians.

"Garrett," Evelyn said. "This is my younger brother, Charles. He owns this vineyard and lives here most of the time. It's one of our family estates."

The dogs jumped up on me and began licking my face. Standing on their hind legs and with their paws on my chest, they were almost my height.

"Charles," I said, maneuvering around the labs until they responded to Charles' whistle and sat on either side of him. "Pleasure to meet you." We shook hands, and before he could continue with pleasantries, I said, "This motorcycle is stolen property and the owners aren't the nicest people. I'm sure it has GPS on it and so I'd like to take it somewhere unrelated to your family but it only has a few minutes charge remaining."

He studied me a moment, perhaps upset with me for sprinkling reality on his happy reunion with Evelyn. He nodded at me with serious brown eyes.

"*Oui*. I can have Philippe, our handyman, take it somewhere. He knows how to do such things," Charles said.

"I'm happy to do it if I can get a ride back," I replied.

"*Non*. You will go to the wrong place. Philippe will know where to dispose of this item."

Charles pulled out his cell phone and texted Philippe, who appeared a minute later.

He was short, maybe five foot five, pushing sixty years old, and wore a heavy brown corduroy blazer with a tan turtleneck sweater. His narrow eyes were partly hidden by the worn newsboy cap he had pulled low over his forehead. The earflaps covered his ears, and I thought about including the hat in my next disguise.

"Oui, monsieur?"

Charles rattled off some French that basically told him to ditch the bike somewhere on the other side of town and that he would meet him in the Bordeaux town center. I handed him the keys, retrieved my backpack from the front handlebars of the Voxan racing bike, removed the pistol from the seat well, and stepped back.

He muttered something in French; perhaps, "What is this?" referencing the electric motorcycle. I reached over and pushed the button that started the engine. He nodded and gunned it, the power surprising him and almost causing him to pop a wheelie and lose control. Nonetheless, he righted the ship and sped down the long driveway back to civilization.

I turned to Evelyn and her brother, who were watching Philippe navigate his way through the vineyard.

"The GPS track is going to show the bike coming here. If they don't already know, they'll know soon enough."

"I'm not worried about Blanc," Charles said.

"Blanc kidnapped your sister," I replied.

Evelyn and Charles exchanged a glance before Evelyn placed a hand on her brother's arm.

"Garrett, it's true that Blanc held me in that dreadful dungeon. Thank you for retrieving me and setting me free. I'm forever grateful, as is Charles and the rest of my family, I'm sure. We will use one of our family cars to continue to move so that none of my family is in danger."

"Yes, *merci, Général,*" Charles added.

"Your nobility is appreciated. Now, I think we have time for a quick meal and a shower before we head out. Game?"

I looked at Charles and then at Evelyn.

"I woke up to four armed assassins trying to kill me. They are dead. I endangered my children's friend in Hossegor. I avoided being killed and captured so that I could find you, as Mitch Drewson asked me to."

When I mentioned Drewson's name, Evelyn smirked and said, "Busy morning. I was wondering where you got the fancy motorcycle."

"My point, Evelyn, is that the Phalanx assassin squads could be flying in here any moment now. We have endangered your family and should leave."

"*Mon Dieu!*" Charles said. "You are like husband and wife!" He laughed. I can now say I've seen my sister in love!"

Perhaps we were arguing like a married couple, but I didn't see what he was talking about.

"You're blushing, General," Evelyn said. "By the way, how *did* you find me?"

"Not blushing. The wind is stiff, and the air is crisp," I said, defensively, and avoiding answering her question in front of her brother.

The truth was that I might have been embarrassed about my emotions toward the enchanting Evelyn Champollion. What was not to love? Standing here, she stared at me with ice-blue eyes, a cocksure grin, and a lithe frame that belied her mid-forties age. More to the point, my dear deceased wife, Melissa, had been gone for over two years now, and I hadn't even thought of another woman for fear of feeling unfaithful to her memory. But she had told me from her hospital room prior to my departure on the mission to kill Baghdadi, "Find love, Garrett. For yourself. For the children. And most importantly, for me. There will never be another love for you like we have, but you're the best man I know, and you deserve to feel everything you've given me."

I had replied, "Melissa, stop talking like this. You're going to make it.

The doctor said six more months and the experimental treatments might even lead to a breakthrough cure."

She had shaken her head softly.

"You and I both know that's a long shot. If I go before you get back, promise me that you'll find love. You know how I say that 'good wins?' Your finding love after I'm gone is 'good' winning."

When I had first met Evelyn in the Sahara Desert at the Eye of Africa archeological dig site, she had acted pretty much the same as she was acting now. Quick, smart, funny.

"Okay, the wind and the air it is," she said, smiling.

"It *is* a tad chilly. Let's go inside, shall we? I'll get you settled and then go pick up Philippe," Charles said.

We entered the mansion, which had two curling staircases on either side leading up to the second floor. Ornately decorated mirrors and picture frames donned the walls on either side, hanging against wallpaper lined with bold burgundy and white stripes, an homage to the grape business, I guessed.

"That's him," Evelyn said as we stepped onto the first step of the right-side staircase and came face-to-face with an oil painting of Jean-François Champollion, which looked like every other portrait done during the Neoclassical years in the wake of the French Revolution and Napoleon's wars. Champollion was universally known for breaking the Rosetta Stone code, which had led obviously to fame and wealth. He had a soft face with pink cheeks, wispy hair, and mutton chop sideburns. His white shirt had the collar popped up with a white bow tie beneath a black coat, in which Champollion had his left-hand stuffed à la Napoleon's traditional pose.

"Interesting," I said. "He broke codes, and you break codes. Perhaps a genetic gift?"

"*Mon général,* whatever do you speak of?" she said, smiling.

"I'm just surprised you're in such good spirits after your ordeal," I said.

She paused our climb to the landing and looked at me with her hand on the mahogany rail. She placed the other hand on my left biceps.

"You should know by now, General, that I handle stress differently than most people do. I go to a place that does not consume but gives me energy and comfort," she said.

I had a hard time holding her gaze. Her intellect coupled with her unbridled beauty and boundless wit captivated me. I would never forget Melissa, ever. On the contrary, I could feel Melissa's presence encouraging me to at least acknowledge the attraction.

"Your vulnerability is attractive," I said.

My smoothness must have been lost on her because she turned and continued to ascend until we reached the top of the steps. I followed her into what turned out to be a giant bedroom. Her brother called from the bottom of the stairs, "Heading to pick up Philippe!"

"Be safe!" she shouted through the door, which she then closed.

Evelyn turned to me and placed her hands on my cheeks, staring at me with a soulful look that stirred something in me that had been dormant for so long.

"Thank you for saving me, General," she said. She stretched up on her toes and leaned into me, kissing me on the lips, the first woman, other than Melissa, to do so in thirty-five years. Guilt, fear, and excitement coursed through me. Which emotion should I listen to, if any at all? I decided to apply her approach to challenges.

Go to a place that gives me energy and comfort . . .

And so, I did. I received her kiss, awkwardly at first. My inexperience showed as I fumbled with what to do with her petite frame. I didn't want to break her but remembered she was strong and fit. I clasped her head with my hands, which almost completely encompassed her face.

She pushed me toward the bed and removed her top. Between her breasts dangled Coop's second dog tag, presumably with Drewson's locator smart dust on it.

"I've kept you close to my heart for a long time," she said.

From there, it was all a blur. For all practical purposes, in those thirty minutes, I slayed too many demons to count. Or perhaps she slayed them, noticing my reticence. Regardless, as we lay in the aftermath on the crumpled sheets, I noticed a scar on her abdomen and asked her about its origin.

She leaned into me and kissed my forehead, Coop's dog tag dangling from her neck atop the one around mine.

"I love your protective instincts, General. I think we should get cleaned up and hit the road. I need to show you something," she said. As she was rolling out of bed, I caught the flash of a small black tattoo of an elongated baseball diamond inside of her wrist. A dime would cover it, but it reminded me of the larger tattoo Coop had in practically the same location.

"You're staring," she said.

"That," I said, pointing at her wrist.

"In due time, *mon général.* A girl can't reveal all her secrets at once," she replied.

I followed her into the shower but was distracted by thoughts of Coop. Was it a coincidence? What could it mean that both Coop and Evelyn had the same tattoo?

We showered and dressed in new clothes. I had a pair of tactical pants in my backpack. She gave me one of her brother's flannel shirts, which fit well enough over my prepacked polypro shirt. I switched into my boots and stowed the running shoes. We shared a toothbrush and went downstairs where two warm plates of venison and vegetables were covered in tinfoil with a bottle of Champollion wine on the table. The labs waited expectantly until I slid them both big chunks of deer meat, which produced sufficient tail wagging and made me miss my own lab, Scout.

We wolfed down the food and drank some of the wine. Evelyn penned a thank-you note to her brother and grabbed a set of keys from a dish in the large mudroom that transitioned to an enormous garage filled with ten cars. The dogs followed us until she kissed both on the nose and closed the door. We stepped into a brightly lit showroom, where on the floor were a light blue 1963 split-window Corvette Stingray, an assortment of vintage and late model Porsches, and a black Lamborghini Urus SUV.

Evelyn thumbed the key fob and the SUV lights blinked. She punched another button that elevated one of six garage doors that opened away from the front of the home. She tossed a bag in with some clothes and another with provisions in the back hatch. She threw me the keys, so I slid into the driver's seat. My pickup truck didn't have nearly the cockpit that this machine presented in a light blue neon-lit array worthy of a jet console.

"Lift this, push this, pull this, and then it's all the same once you get your mirrors right," Evelyn said.

I did as instructed and pulled forward through the open door. The winter sun was low over the river, shining an optimistic ray of muted orange across the leafless vines. The automobile was solid and handled smoothly. Evelyn punched some information into the dash and a woman's soft voice began speaking French, giving us directions.

"Two French women telling me what to do?" I asked.

"We do have a history of wanting to be in charge," she replied. "But after what just happened upstairs, I'm not taking anything away from you, General. Command away."

"That was . . . nice," I said.

"I know what you're trying to say, and I agree."

The truth was, I wasn't sure what I wanted to say. This was all very fresh. Should I open my heart to another person, allow her into my life, only to eventually lose her, like Melissa, Sly, and Sally? Loss was a part of life, but to lose my wife, my command sergeant major, and my command pilot in less than two years made me gun-shy about letting others into my emotional orbit.

I looked at the map and saw she had programmed a small airfield maybe ten minutes away. I navigated the roads and pulled up to a long building with a sign that read BORDEAUX AÉROCLUB.

"Pull into this hangar here on the left," she said. Evelyn punched a button on the fob and the hangar door slid open. Two Hawker 850XP jets and a King Air were parked inside. There was a man standing at the steps of one of the Hawkers, which was painted burgundy and white, much like the wallpaper in the family house where Charles resided, and I guessed that there might be some family crest with those colors, given the Champollion lineage. The man was dressed in a blue mechanic's jumpsuit and looked as if he'd just done an oil change. I parked the SUV along the wall of the hangar and popped the hatch, retrieving my backpack and Evelyn's two bags.

"She's ready for you, ma'am," the man said.

"Thank you, Claude," Evelyn said.

We climbed up the steps, Evelyn making an unexpected turn toward the cockpit. As I was leaning toward the cabin, she tugged on my sleeve and said, "I need a copilot."

I strapped the bags into a captain's chair, tugging the seatbelt through the straps to secure them. Climbing into the copilot's seat on the starboard side of the aircraft, I watched Evelyn as her hands flitted around the cockpit dashboard, pushing buttons and twisting dials as she had done in the SUV.

Soon, the aircraft's engines were spooled up, and we were taxiing along the runway as the sun had maybe another two hours of hang time in the western sky. She braked, powered up, and released, causing us to throttle along the runway and lift into the sky. She spoke into her headset, presumably with air traffic control in the region. Soon we were over the

Atlantic Ocean, bending north. I watched the waves crash on the shores of the French beaches as she smoothly guided the plane to twenty thousand feet.

"You're a pilot?" I quipped.

"Not especially, but I always wanted to give it a shot," she replied.

"So far, so good."

"These buttons do confuse me, though." She was smiling beneath her microphone and headset. Then her demeanor turned serious. "You may be wondering where we're going or why I didn't need to see a doctor after being in captivity."

"Other than what happened upstairs, those are two of the top things on my mind," I said.

"Well, what happened upstairs was a combination of mutual attraction, budding emotions, and sexual release based on adrenaline."

I nodded and said, "I imagine there are lots of studies about that stuff."

"Lots," she continued. "And we will put all that in context in due course. First, though, you need to understand why Mitch wanted you to find me."

"Your ancestral cryptology skills are needed to crack the Phalanx code," I said.

She looked at me.

"Yes, and I will do that. But the emphasis is on *you*. Why *you* specifically needed to rescue me."

I pondered what she was saying, thought about our northerly course, and replied, "My grandfather's dog tags? When we were in Africa, you mentioned my grandfather. I'm guessing there's more to the story."

"Not just more to the story, but Coop is, in some ways, *the* story," she said.

"How did you know his nickname?" I asked.

"In due time, *mon général,*" she said.

"I'm intrigued," I said. "I was very close to him. He was in many ways my inspiration for attending West Point, becoming an officer, and serving in the Rangers. Leading his men over Pointe du Hoc on D-Day made him a legend to me and so many others."

"You're a good man, Garrett Sinclair. Coop would be proud if he were with us today."

"I would like to think so, though the prison gig probably wouldn't have set well with him."

I turned away from the mesmerizing ocean waves and looked at her. She was fixated on the windscreen, which afforded no view. She was thinking of something else.

"I need to prepare you for something and I'm not sure how," she said.

"A rare moment of indecision from Miss Champollion? Say it isn't so," I said.

"Obviously, based on what happened upstairs, as you say, I have feelings for you. I have since I met you in the Eye of Africa. You're a powerful force, Garrett. Your wonderful marriage to and love for Melissa sheltered you from the repercussions of this inexplicable aura you generate. You were rightly focused inward and most likely didn't notice the swooning girls. On top of that, you're rugged, handsome, smart, and physical. Just the kind of man the world hates today, but *mon dieu,* I have fallen for you."

"I'm not sure how to respond to that," I said.

"See? Even that is the perfect response. You shouldn't know how to respond. You haven't stopped grieving over the people you love, but I digress."

I held up a finger and said, "In all fairness, before you continue, you're the first woman, Evelyn, I've even thought about since Melissa left us, much less . . . been with."

"I know that, Garrett. Thank you." She wiped something from her eyes. The sun was hanging low above the ocean on her side of the airplane. "None of that was the point, though I imagine it was a necessary start to making sense of this."

She took a deep breath and blew it out before continuing.

"The point is that I don't want to hurt you, not only because I care about you but also because of how I feel. It would cause me pain to tell you what I have to tell you. No, show you. The whole purpose of this excursion is to understand what we are dealing with before we confront Aurelius Blanc."

I nodded.

"So unlike you to be cryptic," I said with a hint of sarcasm.

"Is it really?"

"And again. Regardless, you've got me wondering what the hell you're going to tell me and where we're going."

She began banking the airplane and descending. She circled low along towering cliffs above an oval of sandy beach.

"See that right there," she said, pointing.

I looked to my right as she was cruising low along the shoreline about eye level with the towering cliff at which she was pointing. It all looked very familiar and for good reason.

"That's Pointe du Hoc."

EVELYN GREASED THE LANDING of the Hawker, as Colonel Jeremy West would say, at Caen-Carpiquet Airport, which was the equivalent of a regional airfield in the United States. It had a few large blue hangars, one of which Evelyn guided the aircraft into using the same precision with which she had flown the plane. The airfield was surrounded by pastures of cattle and sheep milling about on the windswept plain of the Cotentin Peninsula.

An elderly gentleman greeted us as we deplaned. He explained that there was a car waiting for us in the parking lot. The vehicle was a respectably kept olive-colored Land Rover. This time Evelyn drove because she apparently knew the way.

"My family is originally from Grenoble and Figeac in the mountainous part of the country. Over the years the fame and fortune had them migrating west toward Paris, the Sorbonne, the coast in Bordeaux and even a small village here on the peninsula called Sainte-Mère-Église. My father was a professor of linguistics, as one might expect a Champollion to be. My mother was an elementary school teacher. She taught both French and English and was the rock of the household. My parents eschewed the ancestral wealth at least for a bit, being the idealists they were, and moved to this town I'm going to show you and which I suspect you have read about in your history books."

After thirty minutes of driving, we passed through the towns of Bayeux and Carentan-les-Marais. The terrain was mostly farmland dotted with tan, two-story homes with trapezoid-shaped roofs. Evelyn followed the coastline, climbing through the dunes and bluffs until we were north of Carentan-les-Marais and passed a large building that appeared to be new. Dozens of cars were exiting and entering a large parking lot. A construction crane swiveled under bright lights. Workers came and went, as if it were a factory at shift change.

"I'll explain more about that later," Evelyn said.

"What is it?" I asked.

"As I said," she replied and continued staring straight ahead.

The mysteries were piling up. The tattoo. Her possession of Coop's dog tags. The plane flight. And now the building. I was along for the ride but was I being taken for one?

I studied the building. The elevation attempted to blend with the farmhouse countryside motif that was native to the peninsula. It had a light brown stucco exterior with wooden beams crossing at key support areas. But whatever concessions the designer had made to the local architecture was lost in the sheer size of the rectangular building. It had to be over 200,000 square feet, or 18,500 square meters as they would measure it here. Large flatbed trucks coughed diesel as they powered into the large parking lot from a separate lane than the personnel were using and parked near the loading dock. As we rounded the corner, an unfinished section of the building was visible, a skeleton under construction. The tall construction crane was bent at right angles, pivoting over the framed area, lowering a wooden crate into place. The further we drove, the more massive the facility seemed with one oddity now visible.

A two-story farm home with the same Normandy architecture sat about a hundred meters away but within the fence of the construction area. A sidewalk led from the back of the home to the facility. The upper floor had a balcony that looked over the peninsula and, I was sure, the beaches of Normandy, most likely Utah Beach, which was closest to this part of the old battlefield. A short airfield divided the property in half, running from north to south. Lights surrounded the facility as at a football stadium.

When we entered the town center of Sainte-Mère-Église, I forgot about the monstrous building when I saw the church where Eighty-Second Airborne Division paratrooper Private John Steele had pretended to be shot when his parachute snagged on the steeple the night before D-Day in 1944. Today, there was a dummy parachutist snagged and hanging in the very same spot as a tourist attraction.

I pointed at the steeple and said, "H-minus. 505th parachute infantry regiment. Private John Steele. There was a fire that night and the entire town was lit up and being ordered around by the Germans to deploy a bucket brigade and put the thing out. Instead of everyone being asleep at night for a silent parachute assault from the sky, the entire town was wide awake, including the German occupiers."

"You know your history. My family lived there," she said. "That's where I grew up. I was born long after World War Two, but your soldiers saved my mother and some other children. To be more precise, Coop saved my grandparents and my mother, who was just a frightened child. He was a twenty-five-year-old major in the Rangers, and they were advancing the day after Pointe du Hoc. My mother was eight and she was watching over our neighbor, Colette, who was six at the time. The Germans had rounded up the women and children while the men were on bucket brigade trying to put out the fire. I lost my grandfather in the battle, but thankfully my grandmother and mother survived."

She continued driving past the church and pointed out the airborne museum, shaped like a deployed parachute. Given its pivotal role on

D-Day and beyond, the town was a regular stop for tourists wanting to walk the battlefields of World War II. She slowed and turned on Le Vieux Chemin, then pulled into an asphalt driveway that cut through a fenced pasture and led to a large brick-and-stucco home with the same tan-and-brown trimmings around the rectangular windows and a steep, pitched roof. Cattle roamed aimlessly on either side of us as we approached. By the time we parked and I stepped out of the car, the galaxies swirled in the blackness above. With little ambient light, the resolution was stark. The north star was shining as if it were God's lantern. The brisk wind swept from the ocean and tumbled over this peninsula that nearly eighty years before had been the stage upon which human history had been altered. Just standing here I could sense the tens of thousands of troops scratching up the cliffs, crawling through the beaches below, fighting from house to house, and quite literally saving freedom.

Evelyn came over and looped her arm through mine, pulling me with her through the side yard and up onto a slight rise where someone had built a gondola.

"If you listen closely, you can hear them," Evelyn said.

The howling wind and crashing waves carried the faint echoes of the shouts and screams of the men on the beach. I felt Evelyn's arms embrace me from behind.

"Come, let's go inside," she said. "You can see where I was born and meet some people."

I had so completely let down my guard that I noticed for the first time two men carrying long rifles at the far corners of the property. I reached for my pistol, but Evelyn stopped me.

"Guards, Garrett," she said. "I told you. We are safe. My brother is a very good man."

"Speaking of which—"

"He and Philippe are safe. With our own capabilities, they saw two Phalanx squads in Bordeaux descending on the car lot where they took the motorcycle. Charles and Philippe picked up the dogs and are staying at another home for a few days. Such is life under Blanc."

As we were walking back, I asked, "Is Charles married? Girlfriend? Kids?"

"No, on all accounts. He's a lovely brother but nothing has stuck for him . . . or me, for that matter."

My windbreaker flapped in a gust as we ascended the back deck of the home. Evelyn inserted a key into the door and walked in. We were in a kitchen, then a living room where two elderly women sat. They were wearing long floral dresses. Both had gray hair, though the one who looked like Evelyn had blond highlights. The room was fitted with a sofa and two oversized chairs. A guard was standing at the door, and he remained focused outward beyond the glassed-in storm door, which given the security, I imagined was bulletproof.

Both stood as soon as they saw Evelyn and began blurting French in rapid fire, coupled with hugs and kisses. Then they were upon me with hugs and more French quickly transitioning to English.

"Garrett, this is my mother, Marguerite." She lowered her voice to speak in my ear. "She's almost ninety and hasn't lost a step," Evelyn said, smiling. She walked toward the other woman and embraced her. "And this is Colette, her best friend and a second mother to me."

"Oh, be quiet, child," Marguerite said. "Let me see this big strong man."

She placed her hands on me with a firm grip and assessed me as she might greet a future son-in-law.

"Mon Dieu," she said. She looked at Colette, who was motionless. When Colette placed her trembling hand to her mouth, Marguerite let go of me and embraced her friend.

Evelyn stood next to me and said, "Now the hard part."

The three women were looking from one to another, as if they were determining where to start.

"Hi Marguerite, I'm Garrett Sinclair," I said, shaking her hand and trying to remove some of the awkwardness.

She said, *"Je sais, je sais."* I know. I know.

"And Colette, it's a pleasure to meet you," I said.

"Mon dieu, il sonne comme lui quand-même." My God, he even sounds like him.

My basic understanding of French allowed me some interpretative skills that perhaps they didn't know I had, but that didn't mean I knew what they were talking about. To make sure they knew I had some language understanding I had used to good effect at the Eye of Africa, I said, *"Comme qui?"* Like who?

They were staring at one another now, clearly wanting someone else to talk first. As was her style, Evelyn took charge.

"Mama, Colette, let's speak in English. While Garrett has some understanding of French, I prefer he not miss anything. It's too important. And, where are your manners? We are all standing. Let's sit down."

We arranged some chairs facing the sofa with a mahogany coffee table separating Evelyn and me from Marguerite and Colette, who held hands in mutual support. Their eyes were, however, staring at the coffee table. They were looking at a stack of old-school photo albums. Then they looked up at me.

"Can I get anyone something to drink?" I asked. "I could use a glass of water." I was flying blind here. They obviously had something they wanted to discuss with me but were having a hard time articulating it. I stood and walked into the kitchen. No one stopped me. I retrieved four bottles of water from the refrigerator and sat down, passing them around. My brief absence seemed to allow them to reorganize after the initial shock of meeting me. Evelyn took charge again.

"Garrett," Evelyn began. "Remember I told you in the airplane that Colette and my mother were little girls when the paratroopers and Rangers came to Sainte-Mère-Église? About day three of the battle, the Germans were still holding women and children captive. The Eighty-Second Airborne Division was fighting hard but they were focused on blocking the German tanks from counterattacking onto the beachhead at Normandy just over the bluffs here." She pointed toward the backyard, where we had been standing before entering the house.

"As the paratroopers' mission carried them toward the tank units west of here, the Rangers that had scaled Pointe du Hoc came up the main road to assist. When the Germans felt the pressure from the paratroopers and the Rangers, they must have known their hours were numbered."

Evelyn paused. She was looking me in the eyes with the most soulful expression I could imagine. The pain she was muting in my defense was obvious. I just had no idea what it was.

"So, the Germans, being the bastards that they were, set the home on fire where they had trapped all of the women and children. A group of men braved the fire to rescue who they could. Your grandfather was the first into the building and he began carrying two children at a time through the smoke and flames. He made four trips before it was untenable."

Marguerite and Colette were openly sobbing now as Evelyn told what I presumed was their story. I recalled Coop's diary and pieced it with what Evelyn had told me.

"He saved us," Marguerite said through her tears. "He was the bravest man. A god to us. He almost died from the smoke. He saved fifteen children in four trips into the flames. He was badly burned. His comrades had done the same but not nearly as much as him. Many died, but more lived because of Garrett Sinclair. His story was in the museum."

Was in the museum.

"I'm listening," I said. So far, this was nothing but something I could be proud of, not an embarrassing tale that would besmirch Coop. I suspected there was more to the story, and I was right. I just didn't realize at the time how bad it could be.

Colette finally found the courage to speak.

"We were so frightened, thinking that this was it. We were going to die as little girls. The Germans were going to kill us. They poured gas throughout the house. We were in the basement and the back bedrooms. Scattered everywhere. Garrett shot the two German guards who had lit the fire and were outside the house watching us burn. Then he came running through the flames and just started grabbing children and yelling at the mothers, 'Run with me! Run with me!' We were scared because our two options were being shot or burning alive with our mothers and friends. But, *mon Dieu,* I can still see Garrett come through the smoke and flames in slow motion. He grabbed me and Marguerite under his strong arms. Our mothers followed him out. He put us down on the edge of the forest, checked us briefly to make sure we were alive, then went back in. Other soldiers came to our side, but Garrett went back in, each time coming out with four or five children, their mothers following. Finally, he didn't come out and we thought he had died. Other soldiers, the Rangers he commanded, went into the almost completely destroyed home and found him. I had gone back to the opening with Marguerite and saw the Rangers dragging him out. He was barely alive, coughing, but saying, 'There's more. Get them,' to his men. But as soon as his men dragged him beyond the foyer of the house, it collapsed, killing another twelve of our friends."

Marguerite and Colette both wiped tears from their eyes. The trauma they experienced as children was unimaginable. Colette opened a scrapbook and turned it to face me and Evelyn.

"The house before and after," she said. Black-and-white photos showed a two-story farmhouse similar to the one in which we were sitting. It was in perfect condition with its tan stucco and dark beams and shutters, looking almost Bavarian. Brickwork was five feet high around the foundation and footings. The after picture showed smoking embers and a barren piece of land. A German artillery piece sat in the distance in what would have been the backyard. The view looked similar to where Evelyn and I had been standing, and I got the distinct impression that we were on the very same piece of property.

She flipped a page, and it showed young girls in stained T-shirts and jeans huddled with army blankets around them sitting in a cluster of trees, eyes wide, and faces streaked with black soot from the fire. Some were holding canteen cups with butterfly handles filled with dark liquid, probably the precious coffee that the troops gave up to the girls and mothers. The images were heartbreaking black-and-white stills of innocence lost amidst the carnage of war and evil. Yet, there was something reassuring about seeing these young faces peering up at the camera. They had endured, and, indeed, some had lived full lives filled with happiness and, to be sure, sadness and loss.

Coop had saved many of the children in the picture, risking his own life to do so. He had always avoided discussing his combat time other than high-level concepts like "it was tough . . . there's no luck in living . . . the things I've seen." For my grandfather, this was an era he wanted to forget but would always remember.

She flipped another page, and there he was on one knee handing a chocolate bar to the same group of kids, who were now smiling. How he found the energy to do that having nearly died himself, I would never know. Perhaps he needed the purity of children to wash away the sins of what carnage he had already delivered on the Germans, or maybe he was just happy to see them alive, the result of his bravery.

Colette placed her hand on the album as I was about to flip the next page. She looked at Marguerite and then Evelyn.

"Garrett," Evelyn began. "This is where it gets difficult. You know as well as anyone the high regard in which the French on the Cotentin Peninsula hold the American soldiers, especially your grandfather. Every year many would come back for the reunions. These men here were all frequent returnees. We came to know many of them." She paused for a moment. "Your grandfather came often."

Evelyn nodded at Colette, who removed her hand from the scrapbook.

I flipped the page and there was a picture of Coop wearing his green-and-tan uniform with his combat infantryman's badge for action in World War II, Korea, and Vietnam. He had a gold star on his jump wings for a parachute assault with the Rakkasans in Korea. His chest was filled with medals that he had never shown me but that I knew he must have earned, including the Distinguished Service Cross. I had read about his exploits in history books and had stumbled across his diary after his funeral, but I had never seen these pictures of him.

The next page showed Coop when he was probably mid-fifties, thirty-plus years into his career. He was a three-star general in charge of the XVIIIth Airborne Corps, the nation's rapid deployment force consisting of the rival Eighty-Second and 101st Airborne Divisions. Coop had served in both, and there was no better leader to command our elite forces. He was smiling with his crooked grin, which I personally didn't see much, which made the photo a bit awkward. My memories were of a serious man, troubled by the losses of his men in combat. Or maybe I had just presumed that. He had never really told me.

Coop had his arm around a young woman, probably in her late twenties or early thirties. She had wavy blond hair and a giant smile. Perfect straight teeth were visible in her open mouth, as if she was laughing. The nose really gave it away, though. It was a slender ski slope that added intrigue and beauty to a remarkable face, and it took me a moment to realize it was Colette.

I looked up and she nodded. I suddenly didn't like where this was going.

"I loved him," Colette said calmly. "He saved my life, and I got to know him every year when he would come for a week during the D-Day reunion. He was always respectful. It wasn't until I was in my late twenties that it became romantic. I think it surprised him more than me. He was this larger-than-life character. He saved many of the people who still live here today. When we pray we call him 'Saint Sinclair.'"

I nodded and swallowed as I turned the next page and saw the happy couple, holding a baby.

"YOU HAD A CHILD with my grandfather?" I asked.

Colette nodded, and I felt Evelyn's hand on my back, but I didn't want that. I didn't want these people to destroy the image I had of my grandfather. Worse, it was entirely possible that they actually knew him better than I did. To me, he was an iconic figure. A World War II hero lauded by every general to come after him.

I flipped the next page in the scrapbook. I could feel my temperature rising. I rarely displayed a temper and never in the presence of women. There were pictures of Colette and Coop holding the infant, then the infant becoming a toddler and then an adolescent. I flipped more quickly, as if knowing the end would lessen the anger I was feeling. Betrayal. Evelyn had been right to worry about me.

I stood up and walked outside, climbed the hill with the observation pad, and listened to the wind carry the screams of the haunted souls that rested here from so many years ago. Only this time I heard children screaming as they were burning alive right here on this property. Children that couldn't be saved. I looked at the sky dotted with millions of stars in the blackness, tiny flames dancing in the void. To my left, I noticed a small cross toward the back fence where the land fell away to the ocean.

This was sacred ground.

But what was I to make of this information? What was this child to me? Was he an uncle? A half uncle? Who was he and where was he now, if he was still alive? I had so many questions that were clouded by the anger I felt; not only at myself for minimizing Evelyn's concerns, but also at my grandfather. His affair started while he was married to my grandmother, his wife. How could he have done this to her? And how could he have had a child that he never let me or Kat meet? What did this say about his character? Who was he, after all?

The door opened thirty meters behind me. The security personnel moved closer toward my location, either concerned about me or for me. Evelyn approached me from behind and this time didn't touch me.

"Garrett, I understand this is upsetting. This news however does nothing to diminish the accomplishments of a great man. So many people are alive today because of your grandfather. Not just here but all across Europe. He freed us. He was willing to die for us."

"That doesn't excuse a lapse in judgment," I said.

She scoffed. "Is that what you think this is? That Colette was just some fly-by-night hookup? *Mon Dieu,* I was worried about the wrong thing if that's what you think."

"Tell me, Evelyn, what should I think? This is my grandfather, one of the greatest of the greatest generation. A real hero, and you've just shown me he was no hero at all."

"How dare you say that," she spat. "That man risked his life for all of us in this village and beyond. You heard Colette. We call him Saint Sinclair! You may be disappointed in him but I expected more from you than to discharge his bravery so quickly."

"Bravery? Is it brave to have a child out of wedlock while he is married to another woman, my grandmother? Is it brave to leave a child fatherless for eleven months out of the year or however often he was involved or wasn't? I wouldn't know because I didn't know about this person. Was it brave to keep the fact that my sister and I had an uncle or a cousin or whatever nomenclature would apply to this situation? Is the child still alive?"

"I understand your questions. They are the right questions, and now is the time to answer them. Your grandfather was human. Colette is a beautiful woman. You can see that for yourself. They were soulmates. I saw them—"

"You saw them, but I didn't?" I shouted. My anger was all about being left out of this important part of Coop's life.

"I did, Garrett. This is my mother's best friend we are talking about. My second mother, if you were paying attention to me. A survivor of the war. A survivor of the very same Germans who killed millions of Jews. I never imagined you for someone who would so blithely toss away the high regard you have for a great man. If you cannot see the flaws in yourself, there is no way you can accept flaws in others. And I'm here to tell you, if that is true, then you are unprepared for the rest of this conversation."

"There's more? Twins?"

"Don't you dare, Garrett Sinclair. You pay proper respects to this man who on this very ground gave everything he had to save my people! I wouldn't be here right now if it weren't for him. So don't you damn dare on my land, in my house, in front of my family, dishonor the great man that I know your grandfather to be. Talk about bravery? Be brave enough to listen and process the information. Be brave enough to accept the truth as it is revealed to you."

She was angrier than I was, it seemed, and I started to understand.

Saint Sinclair.

He had saved the village, or most of it, anyway. There would be no Marguerite or Colette or Evelyn today if it weren't for Coop. The high regard I had always held for him was predicated mostly on the things he hadn't said, not what he had told me. My imagination had run wild with visions of him leading the charge across Europe as a conquering hero. And I wasn't far off. His courage was beyond comprehension, as it had been for so many of his peers from that generation.

But how was I supposed to reconcile his faults?

"He was a human being, Garrett," Evelyn said as if reading my mind. "True, we view him as a god, but he was human and everything that implies, from strengths and weaknesses to ego and humility."

She placed her hand lightly on my chest.

"He was every bit the hero you imagine him to be."

"But why keep this a secret?"

"You know the answer to that better than anyone. Look at how your army and your government treated you until the very end. Do you think that rumor of a French lover would have been good for his career? There was no doubt he loved Colette. And I'm sure he loved your grandmother, also."

"But did he love his son, who I guess would be my uncle?"

"I know in his heart he did but there were issues with the time and distance. Why don't we go back inside so that Colette can answer your questions more fully?"

I pulled her close to me and kissed her. I was angry but also felt an inexplicable bond to this woman who had just walked me back from the ledge.

"Thank you," I said.

She pulled away and shook her head.

"Don't thank me yet."

We walked back into the house where Marguerite and Colette were whispering in hushed voices. They looked up at me and then looked at Evelyn, who shrugged and said, "We expected this, no?"

The women nodded. Colette motioned to me to have a seat.

"How do you say the phrase 'to pull off the bandage?'" she asked.

"Rip the Band-Aid off. It's another way of saying, let's get it over with, yes," I replied.

"Yes, let's," she said, showing some steel that I hadn't noticed earlier.

She flipped a page, and there was Coop and his mistress, Colette, and their love child, whatever his name was. He was about five, I guessed, and had brown hair with a pageboy haircut and was wearing a blue-and-yellow AS Cherbourg football jersey, which must have been the team nearest to Sainte-Mère-Église. Perhaps it had been taken on one of his frequent business trips when he was consulting and speaking. As a legitimate World War II hero, Coop was in high demand in Europe and the United States to discuss leadership and team building, eventually branching into technology that could inform real-time battlefield decision making.

Regardless, in the photo Coop, Colette, and their son were standing on a field and the boy was holding a soccer ball tucked under his right arm. He had piercing eyes, even at that age. It struck me that my grandfather had traveled to see this boy play a game in the same fashion as he had attended dozens of my baseball games in high school and at West Point. A pang of jealousy shot through me, but I stifled it. My sense was that there was something more important here, and I was right.

She flipped another page without saying a word and now the picture was of my grandfather attending a graduation, perhaps high school or even university. The boy's hair had grown long, hanging around his ears and neck above the green-and-gold graduation gown he and the other students wore. Most of the pictures were from a distance but the next page showed more detail, and it was the Sorbonne, not high school, from which he was graduating. He looked way too young to be a college student, much less a graduate, unless he was a prodigy of some type. He appeared to be about fifteen years old in these pictures.

No one said a word.

She flipped another page.

The picture was of a young man who looked vaguely familiar to me. I had been in prison for a year and didn't follow Hollywood much, but my first thought was that he was some B-list actor that I might have seen in a low-budget film the DB showed on Thursday nights. I usually attended—it was something to do—but rarely paid attention.

I flipped another page and instantly recognized the man who these women claimed Coop had fathered. My jaw hung open. Evelyn's hand came onto my back again. This time I let it stay there because I would need all the strength I could muster to process this.

"Is this true?" I croaked.

The three women nodded. There was no denying it.

I looked at Evelyn and understood the caution she had exercised and the determination she had demonstrated in making sure we came to the source instead of just telling me. I looked at Colette.

"What is your maiden name?" I asked.

"To protect Garrett, I always kept my family name," she said.

"Which is?"

"Blanc," she whispered, looking away.

"Aurelius Blanc is my half uncle, if that's even a thing?"

"Yes," Evelyn said. "Which explains a lot of what's happening."

I glanced at the pictures of Evelyn and Aurelius Blanc, their arms around each other. The photo showed two teens, with the beach in the background. Both were smiling, though Blanc's grin was subdued, as if he was embarrassed. They appeared to be friends, not lovers. Blanc's head was cocked away from her, twisting his body in an attempt to separate himself. The next picture was of Blanc much older, maybe in his thirties, with the large red TED Talk logo behind him. He was wearing a sleek black microphone juxtaposed to his white beard and matching his black hair. He looked similar to the video Misha had shown me just a couple of days ago where he projected an alternating monochromatic presence.

Without warning, the hired guards rushed into the room, forming a tight protective diamond around us when gunfire sang out across the windswept bluffs of Normandy.

ONE OF THE BYPRODUCTS of World War II and the French Resistance had been a series of underground tunnels that led to typically safe escape routes. Evelyn's security team led us down a hatch into the basement, which led to a rectangular tunnel with sturdy four-by-four beams.

"This way," Evelyn said, taking the lead from the armed scout.

Because Colette was struggling to keep up, I cradled her in my arms and carried her, ducking my head to miss the crossbeams and swiveling Colette's to miss the side beams. Marguerite was more fit and maintained the pace as we hustled along the tunnel. Faded black rhombus symbols were visible on the cross beams—a path the French resistance had marked for the D-Day Rangers. The three men from the security team followed and provided protection to our rear to stop any threat from that direction.

The tunnel was musty and dark, but the high-powered flashlight Evelyn shined to the front helped light our way. After fifteen minutes of rapid movement, we turned in to a small cubby and climbed a ladder, which opened into the church rectory in the center of town.

The lead French guard assisted Marguerite, and then Colette as I lifted her through the hatch. The three rear guards assumed kneeling positions scanning in both directions as I exited. Evelyn led us through the rectory into a garage connected to the church. In it was a Land Rover Defender that we piled into. I buckled Marguerite and Colette into their seats, then jumped into the shotgun seat when I saw Evelyn was already cranking the engine and putting the vehicle into drive as the security huddled into the extended personnel carrier in the back. Evelyn shot out of the garage like a rocket as soon as the automatic door elevated high enough. She turned south toward Caen and muscled her way through the traffic, passing other cars at over one hundred miles per hour. The monstrosity eyesore of a manufacturing plant near Carentan-les-Marais loomed in the distance, its glowing floodlights burning as workers plied whatever trade was required. A crane swiveled and turned, lifting heavy crates of equipment or machines. Evelyn was weaving through heavy traffic. Her driving distracted me as something about what I had learned today scratched at my brain.

"Lots of precious cargo in here, Evelyn. It's going to be okay. You can slow down," I said.

She didn't respond but backed off the accelerator. Her mother and Colette were speaking in French. I understood most of their conversation though some of it was lost in the local Norman dialect. They weren't surprised by my reaction to the information about Blanc, evidently, and thought I handled the information better than they expected. That remained to be seen, but I was seasoned enough to be able to put aside personal angst to focus on mission accomplishment. The mission presently was to usher these women to safety, then find Blanc to stop his headlong drive to global hegemony.

"Who are these guys?" I asked, pointing at the men in the rear of the Defender.

"My security guys," she said, nodding toward the rear. "All part of the same thing. Even the ones in Bordeaux."

“How were you captured by Blanc if your security is so tight?” I asked.

“The threat in the US seemed remote. They stayed in Manhattan where I keep a place. And you know, General, even I shake my security at times. I was flying from the private terminal at the Denver airport. When Blair didn’t show, I decided to board, anyway. I realized too late that one of the Phalanx squads had already hijacked the airplane, and they took me to Biarritz where they held me in that god-awful chamber.”

That all tracked with what I knew and what Drewson and Misha had told me. Blanc had put a lot of effort into kidnapping her, but why? Also, I had rescued her rather easily. Not that I was itching for a bigger fight, but something didn’t ring true about the entire scenario. This action, though, had distracted me from the real issue at hand, which was that Blanc was my relative and he wanted me dead.

“What does Blanc want with me?”

“I’m not sure, Garrett. Honestly.”

“He must know that Drewson is trying to enlist me to stop Phalanx from achieving its global security state, at least more so than exists today,” I said.

“Maybe,” she replied. “But I think it’s more personal than that. According to Colette, he did feel lost without his father. She tried to explain the situation, but you know a child has no concept or understanding of why a parent can’t be there. Maybe since your grandfather has passed, you’re the only valid target. My efforts to reach Aurelius lately have been unsuccessful.”

Homes ticked by as the headlights punched into the night along dark stretches of poorly lit highway. Evelyn found the Caen airport and pulled to a stop at the private terminal building. Her Hawker jet was sitting on the ramp, stairway down and awaiting our arrival. We transitioned quickly to the plane with two of the security team members joining us and two remaining with the Defender. I buckled the ladies into their seats and joined Evelyn in the cockpit as one of the security team pulled the stairway up. Evelyn taxied the aircraft and spoke some technical French into the headset, and soon we lifted into the night. To the east, the lights of Paris shone bright as we banked over the ocean and drilled to the south.

I looked over my shoulder and saw Marguerite holding hands with Colette and conversing with her about Evelyn and Blanc, which made me think of Brad and Reagan. With Blanc pursuing me, it made sense he would come after my kids if I proved too elusive. Retrieving my phone, I called Jeremy West.

"Falcon Six here, boss," West said.

"Where are you?"

"Where you left me. Ain't none of us quitting on you, boss. That departure speech was a good act, though."

"Wasn't an act but it doesn't matter. Can you get one of Drewson's jets and fly to Charlottesville to pick up my kids? Blanc is turning up the heat, and I'm concerned he's going after them. Parizad went after Brad and put him in a suicide vest. I don't want a repeat of that." Two years ago the Iranian Quds Force commander had kidnapped my son and strapped a booby-trapped suicide bomber vest on him moments before he attempted to attack President Campbell's inauguration.

"Let me talk to the big guy. Might help if you called him."

"I'll merge him in right now."

I used my OptiPhone to put West on hold while I called Drewson.

"General. Great job on snatching Evelyn. The world is back in balance," he said when he answered.

"Nothing's in balance, Mitch. Blanc has turned up the heat and we are on the run."

"I have full confidence in both of you to evade that bastard. Kids okay?"

"That's why I'm calling. It's not us I'm worried about. It's my kids."

"How can I help?"

"I need an airplane. Jeremy can fly it."

"Nonsense. The one that flew you to France is sitting in a hangar at my factory in North Carolina. Pilots are doing crew rest and were preparing to head back to Wyoming in a few hours. They can be there in an hour."

"Send them. I'll call and get them moving."

"You got it, General," Drewson said.

"Stay safe, boss," West said.

"Roger that," I replied to both. I hung up and immediately dialed Reagan, who was the more reliable one to answer her phone, especially a call from me.

"Dad, you okay? Did Laurent ever make contact?" Reagan said.

"Yes, I'm okay, but I need you to find Brad and get to the airport. Something is going down and I don't want a repeat of the Parizad incident. Can you merge Brad in?"

"You're scaring me, Dad, but sure."

After a second, I heard Brad's grouchy voice on the phone.

"Reags what's going on?"

"Shut up, Brad. Dad's on the phone."

"Hey Brad, Reagan, I need to get you guys to Wyoming. Blair is there along with the Garretts and Jake, Joe, and Randy and the others."

"I've got gigs lined up for the next two months," Brad said. "I can't just leave my band."

"Napoleon's Corporal is going to have to wait," I said. "This is life-and-death serious."

"That's my income, Dad. And I have responsibilities to my team just like you have to yours," he said. "I didn't see you abandon them, ever."

"Brad, your safety is at play here. Phalanx Corporation is deploying hit squads to come after me and, I believe, us. There's a connection to Coop that makes things real bad."

"Papa Coop? How is he involved? He's dead," Reagan said.

My children had blended a traditional grandfather name, "Papa," with his military nickname to arrive at Papa Coop. It was cute when they were younger, and like most family monikers, it stuck.

"I will explain later. There's an airplane headed to Charlottesville right now. Where are you, Brad?"

"I'm in C-ville. We had a gig last night at the Rapture. Crashed with a buddy on Albemarle." The defiance in his voice was replaced with resignation. I imagine the Parizad episode might have triggered some post-traumatic stress. Having a suicide vest strapped to your torso will do that.

"Okay, go pick up your sister and get to the airport. If you have weapons, take them."

There was a chime in the background coming from one of their locations.

"Hang on, Dad, someone's at the door," Reagan said.

I thought of the video we had watched where Emily Sedgewick and Blair Campbell were attacked in their homes.

"Yeah, Theo has someone at his door, too. Weird."

"Don't answer it!" I shouted. "Reagan, get your gun and stay away from the windows. Brad, you, too."

My heart clenched as Reagan switched to FaceTime on her iPhone. She was running to her nightstand, pulling out her pistol and spinning just as the window shattered above her head. Brad switched to FaceTime, too. He reached into his guitar case and extracted a ZF-5 submachine gun I had purchased for him after his run-in with Parizad. He scrambled into Theo's bedroom. Theo was asleep and Brad pulled him to the floor with Theo saying, "Dude!" Feathers flew from the mattress as the windows shattered and bullets thudded into the bed.

Reagan stayed low and took up a shooter's pose from the prone position as her front door splintered. She had propped her phone against something and reversed the camera. Two men in black uniforms came into her apartment with long guns held at eye level. Reagan's hand was trembling. She shot the lead man, who doubled over, giving her a face shot on the trail man. She ran into the living room and shot both men in the head. More bullets shattered the living room window as Reagan dove onto the floor. She spun and fired at the drone hovering outside of her window, emptying her magazine.

Brad's predicament was equally tenuous. Not nearly as practiced as Reagan, Brad left his phone on the floor so all I could see was the ceiling and some shadows crossing the walls. But I could hear Brad say, "Bad guys. Stay down." Then the metallic clank of the ZF-5 not firing. "Fuck. Safety." He had forgotten to turn off the safety and the Phalanx Squad was inside the bedroom, shooting. I heard the ZF-5 rip and shouts from Brad.

"No! No! No!"

More gunfire. Then Brad's phone was picked up and FaceTime was dancing throughout the apartment.

"Dad! Got them, but Theo's hit. What do I do?"

"Check for other attackers first then come back to him," I said. "Reagan, status?"

"Drone down. Two dead in my condo."

"Okay, grab your go bag and get in your car. Pick up Brad and Theo and get to the airport like your life depends on it, because it does. Do you have an aid kit in your bag?"

"Yes, yes, moving."

The FaceTime continued with her running. She grabbed an aviator's kit bag filled with a packing list I made her keep beneath her bed. Meanwhile Brad's FaceTime continued to show the ceiling and provide audio of him breathing heavily.

"Calm down, Brad. You're doing great," I said.

Evelyn put her hand on my arm. The ladies in the back seats were quiet. Colette had placed her hand over her mouth in horror. Perhaps she was wondering how her own child could be trying to kill my children.

After a few minutes of indecipherable images from both phones, I heard Reagan's car starting. "On the way," she said. She tossed the phone in the passenger seat, and I could see the roof of her car. It was only a few minutes before she was stopped and running up to help Brad.

"Grab his legs," Brad said. I assumed his phone was in his pocket because the ceiling view had disappeared and I could only hear the grunting and mumbling of hurried movements. The hatch to Reagan's SUV shut, two car doors slammed, and Brad picked up Reagan's phone. His eyes were wide and his hand was trembling so much the phone barely captured his face.

"Headed to the airport, Dad," he said.

"Anyone following you?" I asked.

"Not that I can see," Reagan said.

"How's Theo?" I asked.

"In pain. Shot in the shoulder."

"Life-threatening?"

"Don't think so," Brad said.

"He looks okay, Dad," Reagan said.

"Okay, to be on the safe side, use your go bag burner phone to call an ambulance to be at the airport. Call 911 and tell them you've got a gunshot victim."

"Okay."

I stayed with them as they made the quick trip to the airport on the north side of town. Reagan made the call and Brad kept me on FaceTime. Fifteen minutes later they were at the airport.

"Pulling in now," Brad said.

I gave them the tail number that I recalled from my first flight over to France and said, "Park anywhere."

"There it is," Reagan said. "Hawker?"

"Yes. Ambulance?"

"Right there," Brad said. "Coming in hot about a mile away."

The ambulance's sirens blared in the background.

"Leave the tailgate up and the keys in the car. Get to the Hawker now."

Brad said, "You're going to be okay, buddy," to Theo, then they were running to the airplane through the private terminal. Someone yelled "Hey!" at them as they ran to the airplane, which had dropped its staircase. They were in the Hawker and taxiing.

"I'm watching the ambulance load Theo. Feel shitty about leaving him."

"You saved his life," I said. "You pulled him out of that bed before it got shot up. You called him an ambulance. He's going to be okay."

"Might write a song about this," he mumbled.

"Do that," I said. Then to Reagan, "You okay?"

"Yeah, Dad, but what's going on? We're wheels up, by the way."

"I'll tell you. We just went through the same thing."

"We?"

"Evelyn Champollion, her mother, and a woman named Colette, who you will meet. Ask the pilots where you're refueling and then call me from there."

Reagan paused. "Okay, Dad. I don't know what's going on and we're both really scared. I've never seen Brad like this."

"I'm writing something," Brad mumbled again.

"It's going to be okay, babe. All okay. Take care of each other. Send me an update on Theo when you get one, and when you get to Wyoming, you'll be with the entire Dagger team. You'll be safe there."

I think about those last words to my children every day now and wonder how I could have been so wrong.

EVELYN LOOKED AT ME as she banked south.

"Are they okay?" Evelyn asked.

"They're on one of Drewson's jets headed to Wyoming to hole up in his compound with the rest of my team," I said. "I can't think of a better place for them at the moment. Protected by Jake, Randy, Joe, and the others."

"Good. What about your parents?"

"Mom and dad are retired in Fort Myers, Florida. Dad is completely disengaged from everything in life, save a few boards and consulting gigs, which he calls 'free money.' Mom sends the occasional birthday card. Coop's wife, my grandmother, is in a memory care facility near them. I think they're fine but you're right, I should probably give them a heads-up."

She nodded as I used my OptiPhone's satellite feature to call my father. It was late afternoon on the East Coast and my dad answered, shouting into the phone.

"I don't want any more fucking spam calls!"

"Dad, it's Garrett," I said, trying to catch him before he hung up. I wasn't sure, though, he might rather take a spam call than one from me. For reasons I never understood, we weren't on the best terms.

"Garrett's in prison. Go fuck yourself, you scum sucking media douchebag."

"Seriously, it's me," I said. "It's about Coop."

He paused. It wasn't a well-advertised nickname for his father. I could hear wind blowing and the roar of motorized golf carts in the background.

"Okay fuckstick, tell me what Ranger battalion my father served in during the war," my father said.

"Dad, Coop served in Second Batt. He scaled Pointe du Hoc. I used to help him fix his Caddy, which is where he got his nickname."

After a long pause, he mumbled, "Just a sec, I gotta take this. Give me a par on this one." Then to me: "Where are you? Saw something about an explosion at the DB and then suddenly there's nothing on it?"

"Phalanx Corporation is attacking family members. Brad and Reagan were almost killed. They're on their way to a safe location. I'd offer the same to you, mom, and grandmother."

"What are you talking about? Is this some prison bullshit? Brad and Reagan were fine last time I talked to them a couple of months ago. You're locked up. What do you know?"

It had been more like a couple of years, but I wasn't going to quibble.

"They're fine now. My point is to warn you that Phalanx is attacking a list of people."

"A list? Who's on the list?"

I thought I heard him chuckle. The wind was blowing in the phone speaker so I couldn't be sure but it would have been on brand.

"I've got someone who's going to decipher all of that in the next twenty-four hours."

"Sounds like a bunch of bullshit to me. I don't see any of this on the news. There's no mention anywhere on the talk shows. I just traded in my iPhone for a LanxPro phone because it has a better international business suite for my consulting gigs. But thanks for the heads-up."

"Roger that, Dad."

"Hey, let me finish this putt. Might be a birdie after all," he said away from the phone. Then to me: "Anything else?"

"Negative," I said.

He hung up.

Evelyn, who had heard the conversation over the headset, said, "I'm sorry, but I'm glad that Brad and Reagan are okay."

I shrugged and shook it off. No matter the compartmentalization, it still stung that my dad didn't care about his grandkids. I had long ago reconciled his lack of empathy for me, but it was unforgivable the way he had cut out Brad and Reagan, who desired a relationship with their grandfather. His selfishness and self-serving nature were legendary in the army, leaving me to sweep up the broken glass of relationships he had damaged all the way up the chain. And today, he cared more about a putt he'd probably miss than the fact that his grandkids were in danger or, for that matter, that the world was about to spin out of control. He would argue that he'd done his duty and indeed he had. Do we ever give up responsibility to use our talents to make the world a better place for those we love? I didn't think so, and so here I was compartmentalizing and changing the topic so I could refocus on the tasks at hand.

"What about our rear seaters here? What are we doing with them?"

"Dropping Mama and Colette with Charles, and then we will make a decision about how best to continue," she said.

"Continue where?" I asked.

"You know where," she said.

I didn't know but I suspected what she wanted to do was confront Blanc, wherever he might be.

"So, if we're going to engage Blanc, do we know where he is?"

"My team has pinpointed Monsieur Blanc in his New York City flat," she said.

I nodded and said, "So the purpose is to confront him and say, 'Here he is, see, he's not such a bad dude'?"

She smiled. "Something like that." Then, "You should know that one of the pictures you saw, in which he and I were adolescents, was after I saved his life."

"If you saved his life, why would he want to capture you? Harm you?"

"I don't think he wants to harm me," she said. "Aurelius is a weird guy. Has this devout sense of loyalty and yet sometimes gets lost in his own genius and blocks everything out. When he's focused, he exclusively shuts out everything but the singular thing he is focused on. I can tell you more in due time, Garrett, but please be patient with me."

"Patient? One of his teams kidnapped you in Denver. Brought you to France under duress. Locked you in a dungeon," I said. It made no sense.

"Like I said, it requires some imagination to understand. Was I unhappy with what was transpiring? Yes. Was I ever concerned for my safety? I don't think so, but maybe. If he was going to kill me, he would have done it on the spot. One of my captors, who were all respectful, by the way, told me that Aurelius was coming to see me. You got there first, though, and I've learned my security team tracked the tail number of his airplane, which never took off from New York."

I paused for a moment, thinking about the insanity of what I just learned about Blanc and his connection to not only Evelyn, but me. Choosing reason over emotion, I proceeded.

"Two questions," I said. She banked the airplane over the coastline and began a descent toward Bordeaux. "What did you save him from and how much contact have you had with him since?"

"Fair questions. When we were kids, he used to like to go down the bluffs and onto Normandy Beach. He was never an athlete, certainly not a swimmer, and, well, I was always an athlete. I was running on the beach one afternoon after school training for a track meet and saw him playing around in the shore break. Normandy Beach has a mean riptide because of all the Allied equipment that sank in the ocean. The water funnels in and sucks out through these man-made canals. Sharp edges everywhere just below the surface from all the mangled and destroyed equipment. It's very dangerous. Aurelius got pulled out to sea and I jumped in—the water was freezing—and let the rip pull me out until I caught up with him. He was basically dead, limp, floating in the water doing the one thing you're not supposed to do, which is fight the rip."

"Yes, never fight the riptide," I said.

"In all matters, indeed."

She looked at me pointedly before continuing.

"Have you remained friends?" I asked.

She played with a few dials on the cockpit dashboard and then responded.

"Off and on but not lately," she said. "He's a bit of a recluse. I'm still puzzled by how Drewson's Zebra team found this kill list and neither Misha nor myself have been able to crack the rest of the code they gave us. Some of the people on the list are now dead. Others have been chased, like your daughter's friend, Blair Campbell. I find it hard to believe that Aurelius is having people killed, though. It seems . . . out of character for the Aurelius I know."

"Who are these Zebra people?"

"Mitch's skunk works people, is what I'm told. I've never actually met them."

"How can you be sure this code is real? That it was Blanc's guy or gal? Or even his stuff?"

"All coders have a fingerprint. They leave their mark. Some even leave calling cards, or Easter eggs, data packages. It's an ego thing, like when killers leave a calling card. An 'I was here' sort of statement. Among other things, the code said, 'We will execute the Web 3.0 developers if Optimus does not reveal the code in open source.' From what I can determine based on this limited information provided by the Zebra team, Aurelius wants Drewson to share the Project Optimus code so that all can have access to it. Drewson, of course, wants a monopoly on all Web 3.0 activity. Who wouldn't?"

"That doesn't explain the Easter bunny, or whatever," I said.

"Easter egg. From what I was shown, the coder, a woman named Ximena Alcaraz from El Salvador, created a unique 'X' that is like the crossed sabers in the Phalanx logo when she coded the word 'execute.' It's how she signs her name in the metaverse. It's as distinct as her own fingerprint. Subtle and hard to notice, but I saw it with my own eyes."

"You used your cryptological skills to do this?"

She smiled beneath her headset microphone.

"Yes, that I can confirm."

Changing the topic, I asked, "What was the big building we saw near your home?"

"Ah yes, very controversial. Aurelius is building a plant between Sainte-Mère-Église and Carentan-les-Marais that manufactures semiconductors. Many protested two years ago when it was built. Others cheered. It creates jobs for everyone in that part of France but is also in the middle of a very historic part of the world as you know. Other than the two nuclear plants on the south side of the peninsula, it is the largest facility in the region."

I thought about that for a second and asked her, "What does Drewson have in North Carolina that you were going to see?"

"Something very similar. He either makes the chips there or imports them," she said. "I never got there, as you know."

"Two of the biggest billionaires in the world are facing off on the world stage and creating their own means of semiconductor manufacturing?"

"Perhaps, but it doesn't seem all that odd to me. Mitch is working on Web 3.0 that needs chips for the Internet of Things, decentralized Wi-Fi, decentralized finance, and the like. Aurelius needs chips for his augmented and virtual reality, artificial intelligence, and lord knows whatever else he is working on. Why have someone else build the core of your business if you can do it yourself?"

"Are these two facilities connected in any way?" I asked.

"Why would they be? They're two different companies. They're competitors."

"Maybe there's a clue in the Phalanx Code. Maybe it's something beyond a simple kill list," I said, frustrated with the conversation. It seemed circular.

"Perhaps," she said.

"You have doubt in your voice," I replied.

"Is that what it is? Doubt?"

"You're not convinced."

"You'll understand if you ever meet Aurelius. He's . . . not a violent person. I have a hard time imagining him wreaking all this havoc on the world. He would go after one person, maybe if there was a good reason, but not on this grand scale that we seem to be witnessing."

The rhythm of the conversation and the fact that we were landing caused me to not focus like I should have on her last comment. The wheels rolled smoothly onto the airfield in Bordeaux, ostensibly one step ahead of the Phalanx teams hunting for me. Perhaps being with Evelyn made them more careful about who they killed. When we pulled into the garage, armed guards were standing at the four corners with long rifles and Charles was waiting for us next to an armored Cadillac Escalade. He pecked Evelyn on the cheek, hugged his mother and Colette, then looked at me and nodded before whisking us away in the SUV. The driver wound his way through the streets like any good graduate of a defensive driving course. We pulled into the garage and soon were in the Champollion family home. Charles had increased security to the point that I could see guards in the front and back yards as well as one winking sniper's scope on the roof.

Evelyn looked at me with tired eyes.

"I need some crew rest," she said.

"I think we're all a bit smoked," I said.

"Join me for a nightcap?"

I nodded. We said our good nights to everyone. Marguerite and Colette were already crawling into separate twin beds in the same room. Charles and his dogs were fast asleep. The security teams switched out. Evelyn and I sat in a small alcove of the large guest bedroom sipping Irish coffee she had concocted. The moonlight showed bare vineyards stretching into the horizon to the east. It was 3:00 A.M. local time, and I wondered about my children and Dagger team as Evelyn nuzzled her nose against my neck.

My OptiPhone buzzed in my pocket. It was Reagan.

"Rea, you guys okay? Refueling?"

"Yeah, Dad, just following orders here. We made it all the way to Jackson, and Joe and Randy met us at the airport. We're in an SUV headed somewhere."

I breathed a sigh of relief. My two most trusted operators were watching over my children. The world was righting itself just a bit.

"Okay, babe. Brad okay?"

"Yeah, he's been writing. Says he's pissed off he left his guitar in his car."

"Sniper fire will do that to you," I said.

She chuckled, and it was good to hear. "Dad, come on. This is super serious."

"Yes, I know. So serious that I've got two of the best soldiers in the world protecting you."

Evidently I was on speakerphone, and I heard Van Dreeves say, "Man, I'm telling Mahegan that shit. He isn't even on the list."

"Randy, you know what I meant."

"Sorry, boss."

"Okay, guys, you have some precious cargo in that vehicle. You have the conn," I said.

"We have the conn," Van Dreeves said.

"Love you, Dad."

"Love you guys, too, Reagan and Brad."

"But not us, boss?"

"Do push-ups," I replied, and hung up to the delightful sound of Reagan laughing.

I leaned back and closed my eyes, holding the phone in my hand.

"A quoi tu pense?" she asked.

I paused, wrapped my arm around Evelyn, and pulled her close. Her warmth felt good. On some level I had been hoping that the spark I had felt amidst the chaos in Africa last year was mutual.

"What am I thinking? Well, I can't tell you how happy that conversation makes me," I said. "My children and my team are all secure. And I'm thinking about how I left all of that to come find you."

She ran her hand along my chest.

"When I did leave Drewson's headquarters, I told them that there is nothing more important than them and that they should go home to their families. I'm glad they didn't, though."

"I imagine you mentioned that you are all one big family, no?"

"We are," I said.

"Then you can understand if they're confused about what they should do," she said.

I nodded even though she wasn't looking at me. "I know they are confused. The team is all they've ever known."

"And yet you left them to come get me."

"As a matter of national security."

"You know how to flatter a woman."

"You know what I mean."

"I do."

She kissed my neck and said, "Let's go to sleep. I put just enough whiskey in the coffee to knock us out. Tomorrow morning, we will do three things: call Mitch and get me connected with Misha so that I can get back into the Phalanx Code; let you talk to your team so you can get an update on their status; and have my team confirm the location of your half uncle. My hope is that he truly is in New York City. I hear *Le Prophète* is playing at Lincoln Center."

"We all have our motivations," I said.

"Indeed," she replied, standing.

Evelyn pulled me toward her and onto the bed.

16

THROUGHOUT THE NIGHT, I woke to the sound of a guard's footsteps on the roof or a dog barking in the distance, but mostly, I slept soundly with Evelyn's head on my chest.

I awoke the next morning to her body enmeshed with mine, and we took quick showers, scarfed down a breakfast made by their family chef, and transitioned to a basement where the family office was the equivalent of a crypto mining data center replete with liquid immersion cooling tanks holding their mini server farm. The tanks looked like large photocopiers from the outside but had coolant running through ducts that surrounded the red-hot servers and routers of the family compound.

"Saves on energy," Evelyn said. "When I'm cracking codes and doing my thing, I'm burning fuel, and I do care about the environment as much as I care about my wallet."

"From the looks of it, your wallet is just fine. Private airplane, vineyards, mansion, security, hired help. What am I missing?"

Evelyn looked up at me with her steady gaze.

"Our family's fame and fortune come with a price, Garrett. Deciphering the Rosetta Stone was only a small part of my ancestors' work. The trademarks and patents that followed have locked down a substantial amount of income so that we are financially independent. Being so, of course, allows me to focus on the things that matter most to me. You, for example. Helping Mitch and his Web 3.0 enterprise. Figuring out what in the world Aurelius is up to. When you have the two biggest tech moguls going up against each other, something's not right. I know them both, and as someone who makes a living solving puzzles, I'm stumped here. Why would Blanc want to dominate the world and hurt Drewson's people? Everyone is just trying to do the right thing, no?"

We sat at a small conference table and sipped coffee, this time with no alcohol. The lack of sunlight was compensated for by monitors on the walls that showed beaches and mountains, as if we were looking through windows. I sipped my coffee.

"We have a different worldview, I suppose. I've been confronting evil all my life. You've been solving puzzles."

"We're not so different," she said. "On the battlefield, you have many puzzles to solve. I simply translate."

"That's not true and you know it, Evelyn. Your mind is like a microchip."

She nodded, then turned to a large monitor at the end of the conference table which sat above a fireplace. Its natural gas flame flickered and produced welcome heat against the bitter cold outside.

"One of our priorities is to find Aurelius. My network places him in New York City, as I had hoped."

"Your network never ceases to amaze me," I said with a fair amount of sarcasm.

"If you must know, our family office owns a private security company that works closely with the French government in places such as Senegal, Mauritania, and all the other godforsaken places our leadership has attempted to conquer, colonize, or otherwise corrupt. The name of the firm is Pierre-Tranchante."

She laid a business card in front of me. It read SHARPSTONE.

The background was a dark blue rhombus, an elongated diamond turned on its southern point, like the original Second Ranger Battalion unit patch. The east and west points of the rhombus touched the left and right sides of the card. The north and south points touched the top and bottom sides. Sharpstone was indicated in a muted gray. There was something else gnawing at the back of my mind, but I couldn't place it at the moment.

"Yes. This is my company."

"These men outside are your employees, not hired help?" I asked.

"Again, yes. We pay them well. They win government contracts. They are no different than your Academy or Triple Canopy contractor companies. Or Wagner in Russia without the ethical vacuum. Governments hire former soldiers. We happen to have the best. I believe there is a pep in their step since they know that you are involved. Protecting the former Special Operations commander of the best military in the world. All of you have a bond, no?"

"I appreciate their efficiency. I'm assuming they have an intelligence-gathering network which is how you pinpointed Blanc?"

"Yes. We have a satellite that has an upgraded payload on it. We can go over two hundred gigapixel on imagery resolution, which is more than good enough for facial recognition. We have voice intercept so that we can get two layers of confirming intelligence before making decisions. Protection of the people I love is paramount, and in today's environment no one is safe. Case in point, my abduction from Denver."

"When do we leave for New York City?"

"After we talk to Drewson and your team," she said.

With that, she scooted next to me as she pulled up an Optimus private video-conferencing application that connected us with Drewson's Wyoming compound. Misha answered the call looking frazzled and tired.

Her typing scrolled across the screen:

Good to see Reagan!!! (And Bradley . . .) They're sleeping and it's midnight here. I see you found Evelyn. We need to finish the code. I've been trying but no luck . . . ;(.

Reagan had spent time with Misha after Jake had saved her from the Iranian assault force in Wilmington, North Carolina. Reagan was an empath who gained personal satisfaction from helping others, but no one should ever mistake her kindness for weakness. As she had just demonstrated, she was hardened and decisive. Eight years ago, we brought Misha and her father to the farm in Vass, North Carolina, so they could regroup and process. Reagan was only a few years older than Misha, and they had all bonded. Reagan said of Misha, "Dad, she's helping me more than I'm doing anything for her. She . . . teaches me."

"Misha, we've confirmed that Blanc is in New York City at his compound there. That's where we're going. We'd like you to transfer the Phalanx Code to me in the dark web. Whatever chat room you'd like. And then Garrett would like to talk to Jake," Evelyn said.

Monster is like my shadow. Mitch's Zebra Team already has the code ready for you. Check Optimus drive. We have level gazillion security on that.

Then more bubbling as her eyes got wide. She squinted at the camera. Perhaps Evelyn was sitting a bit too close to me.

Wait a minute. You guys look . . . different. Omg. No way.

"Go get Jake, please."

OMG!!!

"Please get Jake for the general, honey," Evelyn said.

Never underestimate the intuition of a teenage girl. We could see Misha's face. Her eyes were half-lidded behind her tri-colored glasses. Her blond hair was in a ponytail, a look I had never seen on her. She was smiling and showing off her braces. She wagged a finger at us as she stood and walked to the door. She disappeared from the screen for a moment, then reappeared with Mahegan.

"Boss," Mahegan said. He sat down in a chair next to Misha, who beamed at him like a doting daughter might to her father. Mahegan was wearing a black long-sleeve hoodie. His massive arms and chest pushed at all the seams. He laid an M4 carbine with a three-point sling on the conference table to his front.

"Jake. Just need a status report."

"We got word from the Sharpstone guys that you found Evelyn. Randy and Joe brought Brad and Reagan in. They're sleeping and secure."

"Thanks for taking care of my kids, Jake."

"Randy said I'm not on the list of the best operators in the world," Jake said. His voice was deadpan, and it was rare for him to joke, but here he was.

"You're in a class by yourself, Jake."

"Happy to wrestle him for the trophy," Jake said. Jake was a North Carolina state champion wrestler in the alternative school system. At fourteen years old, he had been freakishly big and had come home to find four men from a road crew raping his mother. He killed two on the spot and a third later. The fourth had died of his own accord, but Jake had been off-ramped into the dead-end public school alternative high school system, which he miraculously survived to become a loyal and dedicated operator. His mother had not survived that attack, and I gave Jake wide berth when he left the unit to go home to the Outer Banks of North Carolina.

"I don't want to see Randy in the hospital, Jake."

"We'll see."

I changed the subject. "What do you know about Sharpstone?"

"I've worked with them some on different ops. Quality. Mostly former Legion guys."

"I only hire the best, Jake," Evelyn added.

"Anything we need to be updated on there?" I asked.

"Drewson's freaking. All his employees were killed in the California data center raid. Our intel shows Phalanx moving on other Optimus 3.0

locations. Something big is happening in North Carolina near Camp Lejeune and Fort Bragg. Lots of people moving around in eastern NC."

"Kinston?" I asked.

"Yes, that's pretty specific, boss. What intel do you have?"

"Evelyn and Sharpstone have significant assets that I was unaware of until now. Satellite capability with comms and imagery payloads. Anyone go home as I requested? Or did everyone . . . stay?"

"No one left. Just the opposite. Joe has Zoey and Syl on the way. Amanda called her dad, Zach, who is bringing his wife, Riley Dwyer, the shrink. The four of them are linking up in Dallas today and should be coming in the next day or two. Blair Campbell is staying. The pilot, Patch, Sean, and the others are all here. The intel we're seeing from the Zebra team via Misha is that there is a target list, so we're preparing. I gave Drewson a specific catalog of equipment we needed if we're going to stop Blanc and protect the Optimus team."

I had mixed emotions about nearly the entire universe of people I cared about being in one location, but ultimately it was never a bad thing when family was together.

I looked at Evelyn, who seemed to know what I was thinking. She said, "I think it's a good thing you are all in one place together to support one another. Between the Phalanx teams and the government tactics, we are all high on the list of undesirables. We need to focus on finding Blanc and whatever it is that Mitch's intelligence operation is seeing."

"More on the Zebra intel, please," I said.

"Drewson's Zebra team has intel that shows dozens of four-person teams moving across the country doing exactly what happened with the massacre at the Grass Valley Optimus server farm and with Emily Sedgewick and almost with Blair, Brad, and Reagan. Assassin squads with a list. Misha says the list is in this code Zebra gave her. Until we break that, we won't know all the targets. Once we know the targets, we can defend against the threat."

I processed for a moment and said, "Okay Misha, Evelyn will stay here and help decipher the code. I'm going to go to New York to find Blanc and try to cut the head off this snake. Do we have an assessment of how centralized or decentralized this thing is?"

I was also thinking about this Zebra team. Who were they? What did they do? How come no one had ever met them?

"They get orders from Blanc in the dark web. That's also in the Phalanx Code. They carry out those orders and then move on to the next one. Note the simultaneity of action with Grass Valley, Emily Sedgewick, Blair Campbell, Evelyn, and even Brad and Reagan. Six teams all executing in near real time."

"What is the North Carolina operation all about?"

"We're told semiconductors, but there's a public-private government facility there with a million satellite dishes, a two-mile runway, a rail spur, and interstate access. It's a logistics hub with a recent significant upgrade to their communications infrastructure," Mahegan said.

"We may find ourselves there again," I said.

Mahegan said nothing.

"Okay, so that's the plan. Evelyn stays here. I go find Blanc. You and the team hunker down there. We stay in comms using only our Opti-Phones and check in daily," I said.

"Roger that, boss."

"Misha, are you okay?" I asked.

The screen bubbled and she typed: *Are you saying I look tired, General?? ;)*

"No, but I had to ask." I smiled and signed off by saying, "Until Valhalla."

Jake nodded and said, "Roger that. Valhalla."

The screen went blank, Evelyn looked at me and asked, "What's up with referencing a Nordic mythological heaven?"

"Just a thing from Dagger team when we were together. If we don't make it, we'll see each other on the other side."

My explanation wasn't entirely true, and I felt the slightest pluck of guilt lying to Evelyn, but my team was my family and my trust lay with them, not Evelyn, though she was growing on me, and I was smitten. The important thing was that Mahegan and my team understood what the signal "Valhalla" meant and the actions they were intended to take.

"And I presume you're Odin?" she mocked. Odin was the god who ruled over the Nordic heavens where honorable combat fatalities ascended after battle.

I shrugged. "I'm just a simple soldier, Evelyn."

"Remember, I'm a cryptologist. I break codes." She leaned over and kissed me. I checked to make sure the cameras were off, having never been comfortable in a conference room with microphones and cameras, much less a world brimming with them.

When she pulled away, I said, "I think I could get used to being around you."

"You already are," she replied.

Before I said anything more sophomoric, I reverted to operational mode.

"Jake is with Misha in Drewson's compound. You're going to be here breaking the Phalanx Code. And I'm going to head to New York City to confront Blanc before this gets out of control."

Her email dinged on cue.

"I like that plan. Misha just sent me the link from the Zebra geniuses. I'm diving in as soon as you leave."

On the television above the computer monitors, CNN went to breaking news. Evelyn punched up the volume as we watched President Campbell speak. She was sitting in the Oval Office behind the *Resolute* desk holding a thin stack of papers. Her blond hair was combed back, falling on her shoulders. She wore a navy-blue suit top with a white blouse and small American flag lapel pin that sat slightly askew from horizontal. She had flint in her eyes and steel in her voice.

"My purpose today is to make the American people aware our country's future hangs in the balance, that an existential threat to the United States is imminent, and to tell you what I intend to do about it. We face an unprecedented time of collusion between those developing life-altering technology and lethal military weapons and those that seek to consolidate power to one's own ends. As I speak, the Phalanx Corporation has unleashed secret squads of assassins around the country and globe. Phalanx owner Aurelius Blanc's unrivaled artificial intelligence monitors your online activity and identifies deviation from what they consider acceptable norms of behavior or speech. This is more than deplatforming or silencing someone by way of shaming them into submission; rather, you're threatened, kidnapped, or murdered. The more of a threat you pose to Blanc's orthodoxy, the higher on the response scale you will be. I have a plan, but let me first add some context.

"My daughter Blair is only one example, and I will start with her. She faced down a Phalanx assassin squad within the last forty-eight hours and survived. Unfortunately, those in the Project Optimus Grass Valley, California, facility did not survive, nor did young Emily Sedgewick, who had just started her teaching career in Houston. These attacks were planned military raids delivered by a tech conglomerate that has become more powerful than any nation-state in the world.

"I often enjoy walking across the street to the National Gallery of Art where I often study Thomas Cole's four paintings of his *Voyage of Life,* where in the first, a child emerges from a tunnel in a canoe on the river of life, innocent and protected. The second painting is of an adolescent floating peacefully in the river, joyous, aspirant, and hopeful. The third, titled *Manhood,* is of an adult in that same canoe approaching rapids with stormy skies above and demons below. And the last of the four titled *Old Age* shows our passenger peacefully floating into the cave from whence he came.

"The consistent theme in each of Cole's paintings is the presence of an angel, or spirit, guiding the way. If you will, a spiritual compass that has helped him navigate the sometimes calm and sometimes turbulent waters. Cole's painting was delivered at a significant cultural shift in our United States history called the Third Great Awakening in the late nineteenth and early twentieth centuries. Many believe that Cole was as gifted a philosopher as he was an artist. His metaphor was indeed a warning of what was to come without some type of spiritual compass guiding our way. Unchecked technological advancements and wealth are the demons to which we are surrendering our national spiritual moorings.

"Fellow Americans, we are in Cole's metaphorical rapids, and we have lost our spiritual compass. Our canoe is smashing against the boulders of hate and division. The darker sides of our nature are winning, and as a result, as a nation and as a people we are unraveling. The greatest example I can give you is that all our government agencies are runaway trains filled with immoral government bureaucrats that carry out their own agendas despite my executive orders and our Congress' legislation. Weaponization of our government has empowered career civil servants beyond anything that our Constitution granted and has exceeded the checks and balances it established. Our founders ensured the document was written to guard against the establishment of a powerful central government as they knew that the European experiment had gone awry. Yet, entrenched bureaucracies and mega moguls have created a technofascist state that is nullifying your participation in our government.

"Our nation has always been that shining beacon of light that draws all walks of life to her shores. We were the youthful nation in Cole's canoe filled with hopes and dreams about what the future could become. And we built a great nation, but now amidst the chaos, tech moguls wish to make you believe that our institutions are outdated, archaic, and no longer useful so that they can fill the very void in your souls that they hope to create. The combination of strengthened federal governments around the world and omnipotent technology companies has led to the

Great Global Security State, a technofascism, that is crushing dissent, free speech, religious worship, and so many other freedoms upon which our great nation was founded.

"There is no one person to blame. Our journey to this sordid moment has included President Bush's misguided and mislabeled Patriot Act, which laid the foundation for the penetration of our federal government into every single communication each of us has. His wasteful folly in Iraq disaffected an entire generation of men and women here at home and paved the way for greater instability in the Middle East. President Obama was no saint. His Internal Revenue Service was caught red-handed targeting political opponents and his Department of Justice and FBI were weaponized against hardworking Americans beyond even what the wildest conspiracy theories might imagine. You couple just those two examples, and it is no surprise that we are a badly broken nation, shipwrecked on the jagged shores of avarice.

"These abuses of power have given way to Aurelius Blanc and his nefarious Phalanx Corporation. Blanc has targeted each of the major military industrialized nations, China, Russia, France, Iran, North Korea, and our very own United States. His combination punch of first sowing discontent via his LanxPro social media platforms, and then swooping in with his algorithms to control speech, has proven lethal. Combining the capabilities of those nations with the global security apparatus that each nation has, freedom as we know it is diminishing. The Great Unraveling. The Fourth Turning. Secular Spiritual Stagnation. The rocky shoals of adulthood. Call it what you will.

"Today, I am labeling Phalanx Corporation a Terrorist Corporation and adding them to the terror watch list, because we have discovered a plan by Phalanx Corporation to violate the Constitution and penetrate every aspect of society. They intend to invade your privacy and control your lives. You. Your children. Your parents. Your spouse. Nothing will be safe from Blanc's prying eyes. You and the people you love will be held to their standard of accountability and live by their laws; be subject to the punishment they mete out by their own standards and by their own means. If you're lucky, you will only be humiliated beyond belief if you do not comply. Your federal government is involved, as are the governments of the other nations I mentioned. It is not an alliance as much as it is a hostile takeover by Phalanx Corporation. The nation-state is but a means to their end.

"On the same night of the raid in Grass Valley, California, that led to the murder of twelve Project Optimus employees, my daughter was targeted for assassination. Thankfully, she was saved by direct action from a team associated with Mitch Drewson and Project Optimus. Unfortunately, her best friend, Emily Sedgewick, was murdered the same day in Houston in a simultaneous action that smacked of a professional military operation. What did those three incidents have in common? They were working on the antidote to Blanc's LanxPro technology that enables his all-seeing eye and allows him to dispatch sniper drones and Phalanx squads to your front doorstep, or in Emily's case, through a rear window where she was shot in the back.

"These brave heroes were finalizing preparations for the deployment of Web 3.0, which empowers individuals to protect against Blanc's all-seeing eye. Mitch Drewson's Project Optimus that finalizes Web 3.0 deployment will provide an air gap, to use a technology term, between you and the government, between you and Blanc. Many features of LanxPro and other apps would be disabled because your data will be stored on your own devices and you control when you release your identity or financial information, as opposed to today where your information is stored on Phalanx servers around the globe. User agreements that we all blindly agree to every time we download an app allows for Phalanx to do as it wishes with your information, to include targeting you.

"The threat we face from Blanc has been developing for some time. In fact, a year ago, I ordered an investigation into the circumstances surrounding the battle at the Eye of Africa and who might have been involved in the conspiratorial efforts in Dakhla where much of this began. As you now know, international and corporate forces conspired to kidnap me and to take over the United States government. While that effort was thwarted, entrenched bureaucracies and the lucrative excesses of global hegemonic corporations have sustained the momentum secretly in governments around the world, including ours.

"My investigation alone resulted in my firing my National Security Advisor, Koby Bertrand, the head of the National Security Agency, General Roger Harper, the head of the Federal Bureau of Investigation, Allison Gray, the head of the Internal Revenue Service, Cletus Wohl, the Secretary of Defense, Angela Blankenship, the Secretary of State, Bryn McHenry, and the Chairman of the Joint Chiefs of Staff, General Julius Rolfing. To a person, they are now employed by Phalanx Corporation earning large salaries to help penetrate our government from the outside. They have been successful.

"Therefore, I have ordered their immediate arrest by my Secret Service. I am fighting this fire with fire. I am also requesting that Congress fund fortifying the Web 3.0 build-out. I believe this is a nation worth preserving and protecting against the nefarious aims of technofascism. I will not give in to the entrenched bureaucrats and tech billionaires who think the world is their science lab. My duty is to the American people and you alone—"

The camera jiggled some and two men in black uniforms raced into view of the lens. Gunshots sounded and both men fell. A team of four men in suits, perhaps her Secret Service detail, descended on President Campbell, and it was hard to determine what was happening. They formed a diamond around her and escorted her off camera, presumably to a safe location, but were they protecting her or apprehending her?

The camera went blank for a moment, then a wide-eyed Anderson Cooper began speaking.

"WHAT WAS THAT?" EVELYN asked.

"I think the president may have just played her entire hand. Either Drewson talked to her or she's just livid that Phalanx went after her daughter. Or both."

"I still don't believe Aurelius has the designs that are being ascribed to him. It's not in his nature. He's an ambassador emeritus with the French Ministry of Economic Diplomacy and Foreign Trade, for Christ's sake. He's one of the top three wealthiest men in the world. Why would he do this?"

"He also built a global tech company that overtook Facebook, Amazon, and Google. His LanxPro app has billions of downloads, and the only thing that rivals it is Elon Musk's X app. He didn't get all that by playing Mr. Nice Guy."

"Just because Blanc is a tough and shrewd businessman doesn't make him an evil tyrant," Evelyn said.

"So, you're in the camp of the guy who had you kidnapped? The guy who apparently just breached the White House during the president's speech?"

"I'm in nobody's camp." She held up a finger. "Check that. I'm in your camp." She pointed the slender finger in my chest. "Can't you see what I've led you to? I'm no longer close to Aurelius, but I do know his character. And if he's got any part of your grandfather in him, can you believe that he is this sinister mastermind?"

I didn't want to believe that, but it was the only logical answer. Plus, Coop turned out to be a different man than I had known. I was still processing the fact that he fathered a child in France and was a rare interloper in Blanc's life, not to mention Colette and what she must have endured as a single mother in Normandy.

"People change. You saved his life thirty years ago and he may want to protect you if that's what you're driving at, but I'm certain he's trying to kill me. And it all may be related to his hatred of Coop, but then how do you explain the Phalanx Squads doing all these surgical hits?"

"I can't explain it right now, which is why I will work from here to decipher the Phalanx Code. You go to New York and confront him. I'm happy to go with you, by the way. It's just that all the tools of my trade are right here," she said. Evelyn waved her hand around her office, the servers inside the immersion cooling tanks. Air conditioners were blowing chilled air on the monitors, keyboards, and towers.

"While I know you can hold your own, I'd prefer you provide me vector from afar instead of mixing it up with your friend. He might kidnap you again."

"I wouldn't call him a friend, Garrett. He might have been a friend at one time. I'm not sure what he is to me now. But I for certain know what he is to you."

"Where is his place in New York City?"

"Where all the wealthy people are," she said. She clicked a few keys and pulled up a satellite image of Manhattan, New York City, zeroing in on East Eighty-seventh Street and Fifth Avenue. "He's got the entire top floor of this building here on Museum Mile. He has gardens and such surrounding the living quarters, and I imagine it's not all aesthetics as I'm sure he has quite a few guards roaming the rooftop."

She was manipulating the image of a twenty-story-tall building that towered over Fifth Avenue and Central Park. The Metropolitan Museum was to the south and Jacqueline Kennedy Onassis Reservoir was directly west with a shallow line of trees separating Central Park from Fifth Avenue.

We spent a few more minutes studying the building when Evelyn said, "I'll download all this imagery for you and give you an iPad to use. My pilot will fly you to an airfield we use in New York called Stewart International Airport. You may know of it."

"I do. In my day, it was called Stewart-Anderson Air Force Base. Now there's a National Guard base there and I guess it does some private and commercial traffic."

"It does. I can have my driver pick you up and you can stay in our family place on the Upper West Side. It will give you an opportunity to contact Aurelius perhaps on neutral ground in Central Park."

"Your plane. Your car. Your pilot. Your driver. What am I missing here?"

"Nothing, General. My family has wealth. We're not rich. We're wealthy. We've built that over the years. We have a presence in all the right places to be able to influence the matters that are important to us. The displays at New York museums carry many of my family's interpretations and work. We have twelve homes around the world, two jets, a helicopter, and a yacht. I don't talk about it much unless I'm forced to, which seems to be the case here."

"I was making maybe a couple hundred grand a year as a general and feeling pretty good about that," I said.

"Woefully underpaid and underappreciated. Stick with me and you'll see improvements in both."

"Is that a job offer?"

"I'm only interested in you filling one position on my team, Garrett," she said. "While I know it makes you quite uncomfortable, this can all be part of your world."

"Seems it already is," I said. "Of all the things I expected when I came to find you, a marriage proposal wasn't on my pre-combat checklist."

She chuckled lightly. "I'm unaccustomed to being the aggressor in amorous pursuits, but you'll find that if you're my general, you will win any wars you choose to pursue."

After one more rendezvous upstairs and a good meal of grilled lamb prepared by the staff, she put me in the armored Benz with Philippe, and I was off to the airfield. I had repacked my rucksack and refreshed my battery supplies, and while the president's speech was gloomy, I oddly felt a glimmer of happiness perhaps for the first time since I could remember. With Brad and Reagan secure in Wyoming, and a budding relationship with Evelyn, I felt an unfamiliar peace. Images of Melissa, Brad, Reagan, and me danced in my mind. Brad's baseball games and band rehearsals. Reagan's soccer games. Movie night with Melissa holding my hand in the theater, her head on my shoulder. That kind of happiness. That kind of hope. That kind of erasure of guilt.

True, I had just learned that a madman was my grandfather's son by a French survivor of the battle of Sainte-Mère-Église in World War Two. But my charges were together and safely secured in a compound in Colorado where they could support one another. Challenges we confront in life always seem more solvable when partnered with the right person or team. My Dagger team days convinced me that the trust established amongst a tight inner circle was more powerful than a Hellfire missile or Abrams tank. Collectively, we focused on mission accomplishment and the sense of teamwork and camaraderie was a force multiplier.

As I left French airspace with the fluttering ascendent hope that a new teammate had made herself available to me in every respect: emotionally, physically, and intellectually, I began reading the dossier on Aurelius Blanc in preparation for meeting him.

As I was dozing off, my mind drifted with the thought of semiconductors and a new internet, both technologies and concepts with which I was only vaguely familiar. I couldn't understand the alarm bell ringing in my mind as I fell asleep from exhaustion.

THE PLANE CIRCLED ABOVE the Hudson River fifty miles north of New York City and landed smoothly. Evelyn's Sharpstone security team drove a black Lincoln SUV to the dropped stairway. Behind the SUV was a gunmetal-gray four-door Dodge Charger Hellcat chase car.

The man riding shotgun in the Lincoln stepped out and opened my door. He was easily six and a half feet tall. Shaved head, bulky neck, steel eyes, locked-on gaze, black-on-black shirt, pants, and outer tactical vest. A French F1 FAMAS was slung from a snap hook connected to his vest.

"I'm Maximillian. Most of my men won't be speaking to you. We are Sharpstone. I'm in charge." When he opened the door for me, his sleeve slipped up his forearm, revealing a small black rhombus tattoo inside his right wrist.

"Roger that," I replied, and slid into the back seat with my backpack.

As we wound our way around Storm King Mountain and past the gates of West Point, I recalled my days of drinking beer, playing baseball, and laughing with my friends. Today, I was alone in the back of a bulletproof SUV with six people securing me between the two vehicles. I didn't do a lot of musing about where I would be in thirty years when I was an eighteen-year-old cadet, but if I had, my current situation would not have been on the list.

We slowed to a crawl approaching the George Washington Memorial Bridge with the usual traffic snarl I remembered from the few times I visited the city as a cadet. The driver followed the cloverleaf, inching along until we were climbing the upper level of the bridge. A police car was in the distance, forcing four lanes to three and then to two. A typical day on the GW Bridge.

"Don't like it," the man to my left said into his earbud.

"Wasn't here on the way out," the driver said.

"Chase, deploy the drone," Maximillian said from the shotgun seat.

On the headrests were small display monitors where a real-time video feedback loop of the GW Bridge panned by. There was a single line of traffic squeezing out of the slowdown at the checkpoint. There was no accident that the chase car drone had imaged, yet. As it was making a westward pass, the feed showed flashing lights at the entrance to the bridge. When the operator zoomed the camera, it was obvious that these were not authorized police vehicles. They were basic sedans and SUVs with light racks on the top.

They were Phalanx squads, some of whom had dismounted and were running at us from both directions in traffic. Dressed in black uniforms with black outer tactical vests and Special Operations helmets, each member carried a long gun and was jogging at us from a hundred meters away east and west.

"Plan B," Maximillian said.

Within seconds, my door was open, and two Sharpstone security team members were ushering me toward the railing while another two were moving with weapons trained in each direction. They formed a protective diamond around me, two focused on getting me to safety and the other two deterring threats in both directions.

Lead pinged off the metal trusses, followed quickly by the muted report of silenced weapons firing at high rates of speed. My Sharpstone bodyguard bearhugged me as he wrapped a nylon rope around me and tied it off with a square knot. He hooked a carabiner into the knot and snapped it into his Swiss climbing seat built into his outer tactical vest.

"Hang on," he said.

He pulled me over the railing from two hundred feet above the Hudson River as if we were scuba divers going off the back of a dive boat in the ocean. We tumbled in the air, and he threw a parachute square-up like a base jumper. While I had conducted hundreds of freefall and static line parachute jumps, this was the very first tandem I had ever done. With double the body weight, the parachute marginally slowed our descent into the river.

As we hit the water, the *puck, puck, puck* of bullets burrowing into the murky Hudson surrounded us. We splashed, submerged, and then resurfaced beneath the bridge. The Sharpstone operator had turned the parachute to the north and managed to get us under the bridge where, within seconds, a Zodiac boat appeared.

The two security men in the rubber boat were holding long guns and scanning upward. The operator of the motor spun the bow toward us and tossed a line over, which I grabbed. He pulled us into the raft, and we sped north and east on the opposite side of the bridge from the Phalanx squads. Sirens blared and helicopters began screaming north along the Hudson, but by then we were making our way past the little red lighthouse at the base of the eastern portion of the bridge.

"I'm hit," my Sharpstone protector said. "Get to this address as fast as you can."

He handed me a piece of paper and I leaped onto the rocks, managed to climb over the mossy boulders, jogged past the lighthouse onto an asphalt greenway, and continued south. The wind was whipping, and the windchill was below freezing. My second dip in a frigid river in less than a week.

I jogged along the path for a couple of miles, only seeing a few hard-core workout fanatics doing a lunchtime cycle or run into the teeth of Canadian winds hawking down the Hudson. Thankfully, the wind was behind me, pushing me along, and the heat my body generated from running prevented hypothermia. On my right were the West Harlem Piers and I came upon an underpass on St. Clair Place, where I slid beneath the Hudson Parkway and exited the river trail and the biting winds. The path led me onto Broadway, which I followed as it sliced on a southeasterly path through Manhattan Island.

The city had the usual traffic and sounds. It smelled of grime and garbage. Full bags of trash lined the storefronts. Once I hit a street in the eighties, I cut east toward Central Park, huddled low in my soaking wet clothes. My outer Gore-Tex jacket had dried marginally, and my body was still producing heat. I cut right at Central Park West and crossed into Central Park where I wound my way into the wooded area, following a trail. The entire park seemed sparsely populated. Wisps of snow were built up in assorted areas, remnants of an incomplete thaw. The trail ended at a sundial-looking circular piece of artwork in the path. The word *Imagine* was in the center memorializing John Lennon's assassination as he returned to the Dakota apartment building at Seventy-second Street and Central Park West.

Two homeless men were huddled in sleeping bags on the green benches on either side of the path. Given the freezing weather, there were no tourists loitering around the landmark. It was late afternoon, and the sun was already blocked by the twin-spired Dakota, my ultimate destination, to the west. I moved to the low stone wall that separated the park from the road, which had moderate traffic. For an hour, I studied patterns of life, moving from one observation location to the next, mostly to avoid detection but also to get moving. The wet cold was settling in, and I needed to get warm.

Kneeling between two leafless dogwood trees next to a Canadian fir that still held its protective cover, I stood as the SUV that had been carrying me and the Dodge Charger chase car turned left off of Seventy-second Street into an alley behind the Dakota, next to the archway where Lennon had been gunned down in 1980.

I hustled across the street and followed the path of the Sharpstone cars where I saw them carrying two of their teammates into a side door. Two men were standing guard in the darkened alley. One raised his rifle at me, studied me for a long moment, and then beckoned me forward with the turn of his chin. I jogged past him and into the flow of the team members loading their wounded onto a service elevator. I joined them as the doors snapped shut and it rocketed to the top floor.

The Sharpstone team members were stoic, speechless, as they had been for nearly the entire time. I imagined that they were worried about their wounded teammates and potentially about failure of their mission, particularly if that mission was to get me safely here.

"Bon travail," one finally said. It was Maximillian, the big guy in the shotgun seat of the Lincoln SUV.

Good job.

The elevator opened to a foyer with two doors. A Sharpstone member held open the door on the left and said, *"Blesse."*

Wounded.

As I moved with the flow, one of the Sharpstone operators nudged me into the door on the right, as the injured were hustled into the adjacent condo.

"Vêtements chauds," he said to me.

Warm clothes.

He allowed me to enter and then closed the door behind me. I was alone in a penthouse condominium that had floor-to-ceiling windows with towering three-hundred-sixty-degree views of Central Park, the Hudson River, Midtown Manhattan, and Harlem farther north. The furnishings were modern with low sofas in white or silver colors in the sunken den, which opened to a terrace that overlooked Central Park. The kitchen was large and seemed equipped with every modern appliance. Walking through the hallway toward the bedrooms, I glanced at the modern art decorating the walls. There was nothing I recognized, but it was tastefully done and smacked of Evelyn's class. Off the main aisle were two guest bedrooms with full baths and made beds that would make a West Point tactical officer proud. The master bedroom in the rear was at least a thousand square feet including a large bathroom with two showers and a jet tub. Tucked behind the bedroom was an office that replicated Evelyn's workspace in her Bordeaux mansion.

As I walked in, the screen came to life, perhaps motion induced, perhaps a coincidence. Either way, Evelyn's face appeared on the screen. She was in her office in Bordeaux looking harried.

"Garrett, you had me worried to death. My men told me about what happened," she said.

"All in a day's work. It's obvious my uncle wants me dead or maybe even alive, which, come to think of the effort he's putting into this, might be worse than dead," I said.

"You're in my Manhattan crash pad. Shower and change. I had the team stock clothes for you in the closet on the right," she said. "Then let's chat. I want to go over a target folder I've built for you, and I have some more headway on the Phalanx Code."

"Some crash pad," I said.

I entered the large walk-in closet, and there was a section of men's clothing still in the hanging bags from Nordstrom. There were Zegna and Canali suits, spread-collar Nordstrom brand white and blue dress shirts, jeans, pullovers, hoodies, loafers, dress shoes, running shoes, work boots, and the expected assortment of T-shirts, underwear, socks, and ties. I spent ten minutes stripping off my wet clothes and showered for fifteen minutes with the pressurized rainfall showerhead blasting the grime off me. I looked at Coop's dog tag on my chest as I pulled on a hoodie sweat-shirt and black jeans with running shoes. I had to admit that the shower felt good, and I was more intrigued about Coop's secret life. A French lover. Another child. An entire business, perhaps?

When I entered the office, I found a woman dressed in chef's clothing removing a steel dome from a plate that contained a ribeye steak, baked potato, and broccoli. A giant bottle of San Pellegrino sparkling water was sweating on the tray next to the plate. The large screen to my front jumped to life as Evelyn reappeared from her Bordeaux home office.

"Have a seat and eat something, Garrett," Evelyn said.

"Fattening me up for the kill? Last meal?" I asked.

"I told you, if you go to war with me, you will win," she replied. "Now eat while I show you two things, and then we'll talk about the Phalanx Code. First, Blanc is on his balcony less than a mile from you right now."

I nodded, picked up the knife and fork, and began to eat.

The eighty-inch monitor to my front went to a split screen with Evelyn on the right and a satellite or drone shot of Blanc on the left. Blanc was standing on the penthouse terrace of his condo in what appeared to be a heated argument with three men and a woman, all wearing tactical gear. There were no long guns in the picture, but they were all wearing holsters with pistols. They were young in appearance and physically fit, wearing layers of dark clothing to keep them warm from the biting February winds as the sun hung low in the southwest.

"That's Cyrilla, his security commander," I said. "And her main squad."

"How do you know this? I've never met his US-based team," Evelyn asked.

"Misha showed me the video of their reaction to my escape," I replied.

She paused, thinking. A doubtful look with furrowed brows followed, as if she didn't understand something, but she remained silent.

"Any audio?" I said between bites, keeping the conversation going.

"Unfortunately, no. Our presumption is that these are the commandos that were in charge of killing or capturing you. They of course failed . . . so far . . . and my lip-reading algorithm is picking up snippets. He keeps moving around so it's hard to capture full sentences."

The left side of the screen split into two halves with Blanc and his four commanders on the top and a closed captioning system printing out on the bottom.

. . . no fail mission . . . want him . . . can't let this happen . . . dead or alive . . . only thing I care about . . . Drewson after Sinclair . . . find him . . . stop him.

Blanc turned in anger and the software presumably couldn't read the lips if the video couldn't see them. He turned back into view and pointed at his commanders and said: *. . . twenty-four hours . . . no fail mission . . . find him . . . everybody . . .*

Then he stormed from the rooftop and into the glassed sunroom, where he paced back and forth between a long bar and a set of high-top tables with bar stools. He walked behind the bar and poured himself a drink and sat down at a large piano, which was perhaps a Steinway that matched the decor. The amber liquor in the glass sat on an end table as he plucked at the keys, picked up some rhythm, swayed his body with the flow of whatever song he was playing, and sang soundlessly to us. He started bouncing his shoulders as the beat picked up and he grimaced.

The lip-reading software, however, began interpreting:

But I grew up quick and I grew up mean . . . My fist got hard and my wits got keener.

"Do you know this song, Garrett?" Evelyn asked.

"Sure. It's Johnny Cash's 'A Boy Named Sue,'" I said. "About a son who hates his father but ultimately grows to respect him in an odd way."

"I don't understand," she said. "Wouldn't it be 'A Girl Named Sue'?"

"The ballad talks about Cash's dad leaving his mother and him but naming him Sue before he did so. A boy named Sue would be bullied and so on, so the song's narrative is that he set out to find his father and kill him for giving him a girl's name. When he finds him, they fight, and as Cash has a gun ready to kill his father, the father says, essentially, that Cash should thank him for naming him Sue because it made him tough and prepared him to deal with a tough world."

"Does he kill the father?"

"Not in the song," I replied. "They hug and make up, but I wouldn't read too much into that. Maybe he just likes Johnny Cash songs."

"He's playing another," she said.

Got a wife and kids in Baltimore, Jack . . . he went out for a ride, and he never came back . . .

"This one?" she asked.

"Bruce Springsteen. Same theme. Dad leaves the kid. 'Hungry Heart' is the song, but Springsteen sings it in the first person," I said. While I was answering her question, the thought going through my mind was that this was Blanc's way of processing the pain he felt from Coop's absence in his life.

"So, Aurelius changed it to third person?" she asked.

"It appears so if the software is doing its job," I said.

Blanc finished the song and tossed the drink into the sink. He stared at his commanders, who were still standing on the rooftop talking, shook his head, and then walked back into the condo.

"You said you had a target folder?"

"Yes. I've shared it to the computer for you to study on your own time. It's got the blueprint of the building he lives in and the one next to it. There's an interesting set of scaffolding on the neighboring building that goes to one level below Aurelius' level. The gap is only about ten feet between the scaffolding and the ledge onto Blanc's balcony where he just was. There is security there, however," Evelyn said.

"My read on the conversation, if taken on face value, is that Blanc is ordering all hands on deck to find me. They have to know I'm in the city, perhaps even less than a mile away in your crash pad."

"Perhaps, but my Sharpstone men are good. All former Legionnaires. I hope you've seen that by now."

"They're good," I said. "What is Blanc's routine with respect to the balcony?"

"Every morning he has his coffee in the sunroom, which it appears has ballistic windows, and every evening he watches the sun set, provided there is one."

"Even if it's freezing outside?"

"That's the pattern we've seen. Our satellite has been over him for some time now," Evelyn said.

"The president's speech," I said. "Why is the FBI not raiding his place right now?"

She chuckled. "Remember, he's an official French diplomat and has all the protections thereof. But do you really think this president would be so brazen as to do that? Not everything is a simple black and white, go or no-go decision, Garrett. Especially in diplomatic affairs."

She was right, of course. Washington, D.C. and Paris worked in their own ways, I imagined, and were quite different from the direct action to which I was accustomed. Sometimes it was about the performance, not the results or action.

"I have a thought about how to do this," I said. "But you said you wanted to discuss the Phalanx code."

"Before I get into that, I want to say I would prefer it that you don't kill Aurelius."

"Have you told him not to kill me?" I shot back.

"I haven't spoken with him. He's a recluse hidden behind heavily guarded palaces and compounds. But, yes, I would prefer if you don't die, either, Garrett. If you can get to him, perhaps I can talk to him through video chat."

The imagery on the monitor showed two guards remaining on the patio and another two entering the condominium. Moments later, the satellite showed Cyrilla and her partner enter an SUV and drive south on Fifth Avenue.

"I'll have the satellite track that vehicle, but I need to show you something, Garrett," Evelyn said.

A picture of a young woman with black hair and brown eyes appeared on the monitor. She had teardrop tattoos coming out of both eyes and a small hoop in her nose. She appeared to be in her mid-twenties, and I guessed from my travels that she might be Central American.

"This is Ximena Alcaraz, the coder that Zebra team claims wrote the Phalanx Code. It's her signature 'X' with crossed sabers. Oddly, she sent a distress signal in a dark web chat room my Sharpstone cyber team monitors. She is a longtime Phalanx employee, which with today's younger generation is a relative term. She's been there maybe two years, maximum."

I studied the photograph. I struggled to find the right adjective to capture what I was sensing from this frontal black-and-white shot taken from a security camera.

"She looks . . . irritated," I said. "Maybe not angry. Maybe not upset, but bothered. What does the distress signal mean?"

"She's in New York City as we speak. My Sharpstone reconnaissance team lost her trail somewhere around Columbus Circle when everything unraveled on the GW Bridge."

"What do you need her for? Torture her to finish breaking the code?"

"Sometimes you can lack nuance, Garrett. But if we're going to be blunt, I'd like to know why she wants to contact you."

"Contact me?"

"She left a coded message on Tor, 'the dark web' as they call it, in a chat room that discusses the Phalanx and Optimus duel, saying she needed to speak with you, it seems."

"Me? Why?"

"Only you can find out," she said. "I don't think she's violent, but the progress I've made on her coding is minimal. Misha and I keep winding up in blind alleys where we think we've broken through and suddenly we're blocked. If we had Ximena on our team, we could use some finesse to stop Aurelius, instead of brute force."

"Maybe she realizes what she has set in motion with the kill lists and is having second thoughts. She looks about the same age as Emily Sedgewick. That can weigh on a young mind," I said.

"Or even an old one," she replied.

"Touché," I said.

"I love it when you speak French. Now, why don't you use this number she left in Tor to contact Ximena, and I'll tell Maximillian to have a security team for you to use as you see fit?"

"Okay," I said.

But I had a different plan.

19

EVELYN GAVE ME THE number that Ximena had left in the dark web chat room as I finished my meal.

I changed into more appropriate tactical clothing for nighttime surveillance, and then retrieved the pistol, night vision goggles, and a flashlight from the kit bag prepared for me. I tucked the OptiPhone in my pocket as I studied the wall behind the large monitor. There was a seam on one side but not the other, likely indicating a safe room or even an exit out of the condo, should she need it.

When I had first met her in the Sahara Desert, I had no idea the extent to which Evelyn was connected globally nor did I comprehend the vast wealth she maintained. It made sense, though, when I thought about it. Her family had deciphered the Rosetta Stone, a pivotal contribution to world history. From that, it appeared that wealth had built generationally to the point that she had her own air fleet, security force, and intelligence apparatus. She had lent her skills to Mitch Drewson and Project Optimus in a philanthropic effort intended to help individuals square off against oppressive and controlling governments and corporations. Anyone who threatened the technofascist global security state being ossified by Phalanx would be a threat. Perhaps only Evelyn's relationship with Blanc had saved her.

The wall gave way to a dark, musty passage that led to another door, which was cool to the touch. I turned the knob and found a cement stairwell that spiraled down. I took the steps until I was at the bottom and pushed through a door with a spring-loaded bar handle. I nudged the door open and studied the dark alley. The entrance the Sharpstone team had used to ferry in their wounded was to my left about fifty meters away. The Lincoln SUV and Charger were still parked there, which told me that the entire crew was still occupied upstairs.

To the right was a long dark alley that looked like it emptied to a parallel street to the north. I chose that direction. As I walked, I retrieved my cell phone and texted Ximena's number.

Where r u?

She responded immediately.

Who is this?

You're looking for me.

General?

Y

Meet in the small park across from Lincoln Center.

Kk

I tucked the phone, turned left onto Columbus, and hustled several blocks until I saw a P.J. Clarke's restaurant across from the brightly lit Lincoln Center, which was teeming with people attending an event. Perhaps it was Evelyn's *Le Prophète*? There was a small green space in a triangle that separated Columbus and Broadway where I saw Ximena for the first time. She was pacing, looking at the ground, unaware of her surroundings, and not the least bit concerned about her security. I assumed she wanted to meet in this relatively public spot because she didn't want to be alone with a Special Forces general in the darkened and expansive recesses of Central Park, which would have been a far more secure place to have a conversation. Then again, perhaps Phalanx was watching her from multiple angles and wanted her to be secure.

But if she weren't rogue from Phalanx, why would she be talking to me?

As I approached, I scanned in every direction and did not notice anything that would indicate this was a baited ambush. Cars came and went through stoplights. People huddled in overcoats against the February winds that funneled down the Hudson Valley and accelerated through the canyons of high-rises.

I walked on the Lincoln Center side of the triangle, which put me behind Ximena. Looping around P.J. Clarke's and turning back north at a Duane Reade drugstore, I approached her from south to north, having thoroughly cased the area.

Approaching her, I said, "Ximena?"

She looked up, startled. I kept my eyes trained on her hands, which were still stuffed in her pockets.

"General?"

"Call me Garrett," I said.

Her eyes were wide. She was scared. Nervous. The teardrop tattoos made her look mournful. She had black hair and brown eyes. Her lips were full, and she possessed a youthful beauty despite her obvious deep concern. When the wind blew her hair, a small eagle tattoo was visible as if it was flying up the back of her neck. Her nose ring was a small pewter loop in her left nostril.

"Okay . . . Garrett."

"Why are you meeting with me? You work for Blanc," I said.

"The full stack developer community is very small, Garrett. I had several friends killed in the Grass Valley massacre. I'm scared. I accessed the

Project Optimus files to find out why they would have been killed and didn't like what I saw," she said.

"Optimus files? But the killing is being done by Phalanx," I said.

She was distracted, looking nervously over her shoulder and snapped her head back to look at me. "What?" she said.

"Let's walk. It's cold and walking will keep us warm," I said. But what I was really thinking is that it was harder for a sniper to hit a moving target.

"It's not safe," she said.

"All the more reason to walk. Loop your arm through mine and stay close."

She removed her right hand from her coat pocket and slid it between my left elbow and torso. She was not wearing gloves, which I assumed explained why she had her hands stuffed in her pockets. We crossed Broadway toward Lincoln Center and began walking north toward West Sixty-sixth Street.

"I found a package that I must give you," she said. "But I'm confused by what you just said."

"A package?" I asked, and immediately thought of Smyth telling me Coop's dead lawyer had left a package for me and then Calles giving me a small flash drive. "You're holding nothing."

She lifted a triangular pendant at the end of simple chain necklace and said, "Not that kind of package. It's blockchain based. I'm told you have the other half?"

"That?" I said, pointing at the necklace. "We've got Blanc's Phalanx assassin squads everywhere rounding up defectors, and you've got a necklace you want to give me?"

She stopped walking and looked at me.

"That's not true about the assassin squads. What are you talking about?"

"What are *you* talking about? Blanc and his Phalanx squads have been rounding up all of Mitch Drewson's Project Optimus. They killed your friends in Grass Valley. I assumed you had the plan because you wrote the Phalanx Code."

She stared at me with a bewildered look on her face. She pushed her hair behind her ears, the eagle's beak showing below her right lobe. Her eyes looked away, fixating internally. A piece of logic fell into place, and something made sense to her. She nodded.

We were standing in front of the brightly lit courtyard of Lincoln Center. Her puffy winter coat was open, showing a lanyard with credentials hung around her neck beneath the necklace. She held up her hands and separated them to add emphasis to her words. With her left hand, she lifted the triangular necklace and pinched it between her thumb and forefinger. She looked in both directions before speaking.

"I didn't write that code. Somebody copied my signature X. It was done by a team of people in Wyoming," she said.

I thought of Drewson's mysterious Zebra team. They had provided Misha and Evelyn with everything. The video. The Phalanx Code. The intelligence about the Chinese in Wyoming, Colorado, Utah, and North Dakota. What was happening?

"We should get moving," I said. It was never a good idea to remain stationary for too long.

She lifted the necklace to my eye level. She wanted me to notice it, so I did. The pendant bulged in the middle, as if it carried something. Maybe Phalanx members had to carry cyanide pills. She placed her right hand on my arm to stop me and reiterate her point, while holding up her left hand showing me the pendant.

"You have the other half, correct?"

Then it hit me. The triangular device Calles had given me. As I reached into my boot and fumbled with the small package, she said, "And you're wrong about Drewson and Blanc. It's the other way around."

When I lifted the cellophane-wrapped device that Calles had given me, she snatched it quickly from my hand and detached half of her necklace.

She snapped the device Calles had provided me into the half of her necklace, creating a new rhombus. A slight buzz emanated and she nodded, as if satisfied that something worked. When married together, the two pieces resembled the Ranger insignia's rhombus shape.

"Here. This has everything you need to know."

"This?"

"Yes. When your grandfather created Phalanx, he was way ahead of his time—"

The wash of the bullet whipped past me before I heard the unmistakable sound of a silenced weapon firing from close range. Ximena slumped into my arms, blood draining from her temple and onto my coat. To others, she most likely appeared to be a daughter hugging her father, but it was clear she died instantly as she fell into my arms. A black jacket flashed in my periphery about a hundred meters away. The shooter.

"Ximena!" I said, holding her. She was unresponsive, so I cradled her and began moving swiftly just to avoid a second sniper shot, but none came. I called 911 using her cell phone and laid her on a bench near the West Sixty-sixth Street subway entrance. No one stopped. No one offered to help. No one seemed to care that this young lady had just been murdered, if they knew at all.

I felt for a pulse, but there was none. Her wide brown eyes were open, staring at me, telling me something. I clasped the necklace and the credentials, snatching them from her neck and pocketing them. I closed her eyes, the teardrop tattoos weeping down her cheeks. As I heard the ambulance arriving, a young man dressed in a hoodie and jeans and smelling of weed came up to me and said, "Dude, is she okay?"

"This ambulance is for her. Can you make sure she gets on it?" I asked.

"Whoa, dude."

"Thanks, man," I said. I put a one-hundred-dollar bill in his palm, which seemed to ease his concerns as the ambulance braked in front of us. I joined the flow of the crowd, saying a silent prayer for Ximena's soul.

As I began to walk back toward the Dakota, I made an on-the-spot decision to confront Blanc tonight, without hesitation. But first, I took a left on West Sixty-sixth Street and walked through the lobby of the Phillips Club, an upscale fractional or timeshare that ebbed and flowed with traffic. I walked in like I owned the place and passed the busy front desk. The doorman even held the door for me. I patted my pockets as if I was looking for my room key and, once past the front desk, hooked a left at the hallway that led to a library with a bank of three computers with monitors. I twisted open the rhombus shaped pendant and found a flash drive, which I plugged into the tower and played with the mouse until the external drive icon showed. I clicked on that and opened a file that oddly was not encrypted.

Ximena had included a diagram of Blanc's condominium with arrows pointing at an access point. I printed that out, folded the piece of paper, and put it in my pocket.

I clicked on a second link, labeled PHALANX DOCS.

There were multiple images of boxes with bowtie wrappers around them; the packages, I presumed. I scanned the titles, most were technical or commercial, relating to agreements, employees, and facilities. But near the bottom was one that was labeled GSI LAST WILL AND TESTAMENT/PC.

GSI? Garrett Sinclair I, I presumed. And PC for Phalanx Code?

As I was clicking on the package indicator to begin reading, two security men came into the lobby and moved to the front of the line. They were dressed in blue uniforms with yellow patches, but it was obvious to me that these were Phalanx operatives based upon their build and the weapons they were carrying.

I printed the file, ejected the flash drive and zipped it into a sleeve in my boot, then powered down the screen. Hustling through the back door of the lobby, I jogged past the washing machines and dryers, and emptied into the street. Sprinting along West Sixty-seventh Street, I crossed Broadway, dodging traffic, found Columbus, and then leaped over the low retaining wall separating Central Park from the sidewalk. Tumbling through a series of shrubs and down a hill, I righted myself and set out on a northeast azimuth toward Blanc's condo.

I avoided the major roads and trails as night fell on the park. A disheveled man began to approach and then avoided me as I likely appeared menacing with my pistol, knife, and night vision goggles. I carried the full interpretation of the Phalanx Code in my pocket, not that I'd had time to make sense of it yet. Why Ximena had provided it to me, I could only guess. Perhaps, as Evelyn had posited, she was driven by guilt about the killings by the Phalanx squads. I reached the Metropolitan Museum, angled behind it and along the Onassis Reservoir, where I found a covered and concealed location adjacent to Blanc's building.

I was surrounded by granite rocks jutting from the ground like fangs and towering oak trees. I lifted the goggles to my eyes and studied the terrain. The elevation of the building prevented me from seeing Blanc's penthouse condo or its rooftop garden, but I studied the security around the structure. There was a doorman and inside the lobby were two Phalanx guards dressed similarly to those who had appeared at the Phillips Club. Looking at the map that Ximena had produced for me, the entry to Blanc's building was through the rear exit of a men's clothing store on East Eighty-second Street.

I then took a moment to read through what I had printed, but it was mostly coded gibberish, so I burned the papers using a lighter. As I was building a plan in my mind to follow the path found on Ximena's flash drive, my phone buzzed in my pocket. It was a Wyoming number. I had texted Mahegan my new contact information.

"Sinclair," I said.

"Boss, it's Jake," Mahegan said. "You're whispering."

"I'm conducting recon of Blanc's place. Everything okay?"

"Actually . . . I'm getting a weird vibe here," Mahegan said.

"Weird how?"

"Drewson made some big announcement that we were all to gather in another facility for a team meeting. We had to get on the hyperloop with the whole crew. Joe, Randy, Matt, Misha, Amanda, Brad, Reagan, Blair, and the others. Even that prison guard, Calles, is here and came with us. She's turned out to be useful. Zoey and Syl are with Zach and Riley in Dallas. They were getting ready to leave to come here, but I told them to squat hold there for a bit."

The term "squat hold" was airborne parlance for "stop what you're doing."

"What was the announcement?"

A spider of fear began crawling up my spine.

"That's just it," Mahegan said. "Drewson is almost an hour late and we're in this hyperloop pod waiting to go somewhere."

"Get out of there. Take everyone and just get outside and go to Jackson or get Jeremy to get one of Drewson's airplanes."

"We can't open the pod. It's locked," Mahegan said.

THE PEOPLE I LOVED the most in the world were all together in one place deep inside a billionaire's mine shaft because they had followed the clarion call to help save the world from technofascism at the hands of billionaire Aurelius Blanc.

My only assumption could be that Blanc's men had infiltrated the Wyoming compound and seized control, maybe through deepfake videos or technology that could remotely unlock and lock Drewson's compound, control his hyperloop systems, and operate his video. But why hadn't Drewson or Evelyn contacted me with distress signals? My entire world was inside that mine shaft.

And what should I make of Ximena's comment regarding me being wrong about Blanc *and* Drewson?

Whatever the answers might be, I was now more motivated than ever to confront Blanc and force him to acquiesce, to release my people and find some path to settle the score between the two billionaires. I waited about thirty minutes until it was close to 11:00 P.M. in New York City. The activity in the city that never sleeps at least begins to ebb around this time.

I crossed Fifth Avenue and found the men's clothing store drawn on Ximena's map. At this hour it was locked, and the security cameras hummed with each robotic swivel. After two passes from either side of the road, the alley in between the men's store and an adjacent apartment building seemed like the best option. I waited for a few cars to crawl past, then shot across the road into the alley, which was filled with trash bags stacked high from a restaurant in the bottom of the neighboring apartment building. Rats the size of small house cats scrambled as I plowed through the alley and climbed a fire escape ladder. The second story of the men's shop had a narrow set of living quarters above it. Perhaps the owner's residence?

Standing on the landing of the fire escape, an empty bedroom, den, and kitchen were all visible. No lights on and no signs of life, save the rats below. I used my elbow to smash a windowpane in the wooden side door, one of four rectangular windowpanes, reached in and turned the lock, slowly turned the knob, and stepped into the apartment. Moving through the upstairs, I found a spiral staircase that fed into the store's back office area. Using the flashlight on the rail of my pistol, I swept it in every direction looking for cameras and trip wires. Holding my goggles to my eyes, I searched for infrared beams that could trigger a camera or alarm and found two.

Stepping into the circular stairway, a boot crunched the gravel and tar of the roof above me. Shadows moved across the window of the door through which I had entered. I braced against the handrails and slid to the first floor, rolling against a rack of suits yet to be put on display. Thuds sounded against the roof and the upstairs door opened. Something flashed across the front door window as I moved toward the rear of the office.

Having memorized the diagram that Ximena had provided me on the flash drive, I saw a China hutch where the door was drawn on the map. As someone scrambled down the stairwell, I leaned into the hutch and slid it fractionally until I could see the outline of a door. Pushing through the crease in the wall, I found a locking bar on the opposite side and flipped it down. Using the flashlight on my pistol, I navigated a dank tunnel that led generally northwest in the direction of Blanc's condo building. Someone pounded on the door behind me and fired shots into the steel locking bar, to no avail. I imagined that this was an escape route for Blanc, and I was using it in the opposite purpose and direction for which it was intended.

The route hit a dead end into a cinder block wall. A loud bang signaled that my pursuers had somehow breached the door that was now maybe a hundred meters to my rear. My flashlight found a metal ladder, which I ascended until I hit a circular hatch, like a manhole cover. For a moment I wondered if I was beneath Fifth Avenue. The distance was about right.

Pushing up on the round metal plate, I found it gave way until I was able to roll onto an enclosed concrete slab. I slid the manhole cover until it was fitted back into the rim. I flipped a locking bar over the manhole cover and slipped hard plastic flex-cuffs from my pocket into the U-rings to secure the bar and hold off pursuers. Not perfect, but the best I had for the moment.

I ascended the switchback staircase that beckoned to my left, which matched the diagram that Ximena had provided me. Taking the steps three at a time, I lunged forward propelled in part by the subtle urgency of Mahegan's call. Jake had been in difficult situations throughout our collective careers and only a few times had he asked for help. Even then, his requests were mostly logistical. Weapons, phones, cameras, data processing, information.

I couldn't recall a time that he sent up the distress signal that he might be in a situation that he couldn't personally resolve. While my children and closest relationships were in Drewson's facility, so were my best operators. Hobart, Van Dreeves, and Mahegan, along with the teammates with whom they had served their entire professional lives. These were men and women that I had mentored and developed over the past three decades. Other than what I felt for my children, I had no greater love for anyone than everyone locked in that hyperloop right now. They were all that mattered to me.

I slowed my ascension as I approached the top landing.

They were all that mattered to me.

Drewson had collected us all into one location to help him with his nerdy project of delivering Web 3.0 to the masses.

As I put my back against the wall, these thoughts circled through my mind like birds of prey on the hunt. What was really happening?

Blanc was the richest man in the world and my half uncle, and he was terrorizing his enemies with assassin squads. Drewson, the second richest man in the world, juiced up Jake to break me out of prison, and asked me to find Evelyn. And Evelyn was an enigmatic elite living off generational wealth, or so it seemed, who had introduced me to the concept that my grandfather, Coop, had sired the monster Aurelius Blanc.

Where did I fit into this mix? I was a recently retired three-star general who mattered little in the grand scheme of things outside of my mostly clandestine world. Sure, I had led well and served my country as so many other good citizens had done, but what placed me at the center of this struggle between two titans of global power?

I felt the door to my left. It was cold to the touch, meaning it most likely led outside somewhere. Twisting the handle down, I pushed through the opening and rolled low onto an AstroTurf landing surrounded by designer planters the size of boulders. Lights shined onto the surrounding area, causing me a moment of vision adjustment. Spinning to one knee and raising my pistol, I saw a man with black hair and a white beard dressed in a black silk robe standing in the middle of the platform, his back turned to me. He was wearing black Pro-Ked tennis shoes and white athletic socks.

The usual melodies of New York City traffic sang upward with honks, shouts, and revving car engines even though it was near midnight. From my relatively protected position behind the planters, I sensed motion from all four directions. Shadows moved toward me even though the man in the robe remained motionless.

I lifted my pistol and raised above the shrubs in the planters when a shot rang out, striking me in the chest.

The last words I remember hearing were, "So good to finally meet you, nephew."

I AWOKE IN A haze feeling like I had a couple of bruised ribs, which on the surface seemed a whole lot better than being dead.

That might have been a misjudgment.

Generously put, after being shot with a nonlethal stun gun, someone had secured me to a bed. Nylon strapping was cinched tightly across my chest and legs, though I had freedom of movement of my arms. The room was dark save ambient light leaking through drawn curtains. Soft linens and a heavy blanket covered me. I was still dressed in the same clothes, but my boots were not on my feet.

The rhombus flash drive in my boot was my first thought.

Across from me sat Aurelius Blanc with his awkward black hair and bleached white beard. Beyond that, though, were not the eyes of a madman but those of someone searching for answers. Though looks could be deceiving, he appeared inquisitive, not necessarily hateful. He lifted a remote and elevated the bed so that I was at a forty-five-degree angle and able to look him in the eyes.

"Comfortable?" he asked.

I said nothing.

"Garrett, we shot you with the stun gun because, as you certainly know, you are a most dangerous man," Blanc said.

I said nothing. He continued.

"I'm not sure what Mitch Drewson may have told you, but I can also assure you that he has lied to you on a grand scale."

I said nothing.

"My company, Phalanx, is the one that is attempting to unify the world, its people, by bringing peace and harmony. If you think about the term, Phalanx, it's a noun that embodies the spirit of protection, of strength in numbers. My vision has always been to extend power to the people."

He paused. I looked at an unopened bottle of water on the nightstand next to me.

"Pardon my manners," he said.

He leaned over and with one hand released the top nylon strap with a pop. He freed my torso, extending the bottle of water to me with the other hand. I took it from him and unscrewed the top, never breaking contact with his eyes. He stared at me a second longer and then popped open the other strap. My legs were free.

"My men take extra precautions," he said. "I don't want to kill you or even harm you. On the contrary, I've been waiting all my life to meet you."

I sucked down the bottle of water and screwed the top back on, then leaned my head into the pillow, thinking. Drewson, Blanc, and Champollion. What did they all have in common? What made them different?

The honest answer was that Blanc was related to me. His motivation would be the purest, whether fueled by hate or love. There would be little middle ground for Blanc. Where was Evelyn in this? She was a childhood friend of Blanc. Did she truly love me or was she part of the manipulation? Unless she was an Oscar-winning actress, her actions felt like love to me, but then again, I had known only one true love in my life, Melissa. Finally, there was Drewson and his eagerness to help me and my team. Misha's presence with Drewson had disarmed me, as had the presence of my team and friends. Did I still assess Drewson through objective eyes or even at all? Mahegan's troubled call gave me pause, but then again, maybe Drewson had just been running late. Or maybe their confinement in the hyperloop was a protective measure against Blanc's forces attacking the Wyoming compound.

"Have it all figured out?" he asked, studying me. He uncrossed and recrossed his legs. His black hair and white beard were stark contrasts in the dim light.

"Why the monochrome?" I asked.

He chuckled.

"It's grayscale. Everything is digital. Thank you for noticing."

His voice was masculine and pleasant. He was at ease with himself and the situation. He was calm as opposed to when I met Drewson, who had seemed overcaffeinated. Blanc's confidence seemed firm.

"What do you remember of Coop?" I asked him. I wanted to see how he reacted to this question without preamble.

He smiled gently and said, "I loved him. He was a great man and he treated us very well. I just wish . . . I had more of him."

There was no hesitation or indication of untruthfulness. This was a son speaking admirably of a father.

"I was there, you know," he said.

"Where?"

"Arlington. For his funeral. My mother and I."

"Why didn't I see you?"

"We waited in the car. A black limousine that was parked maybe fifty meters from you. You looked directly at us. At me. But the windows were blackened, and I doubt you could have noticed. I waved, held my hand up against the window, leaving little steam fingerprints like a kid even though it was just a few years ago."

I remembered the car but still didn't believe him. It was five years ago. I had just been promoted to brigadier general. Melissa was still alive and dressed in black, her red hair lying softly on her collar and her gloved hands laced through my arm. I was wearing my dress blue uniform with saucer cap and star on the sleeves. My new uniform pants fit precisely with a military crease just above the ankle. I was shaken to my core and was focused on my family, not an unknown interloper. My guard was down, and I was not in my usual scan mode looking for anomalies.

I nodded.

"I don't blame you, Garrett, and I'm not mad at your Coop, or as I called him, Papa. Sometimes as a child when I saw him more frequently, it was 'Papa the Parachutist.' I used to run around Sainte-Mère-Église and shout that when I was three or four years old. My mother would laugh, and Papa seemed happy. I was proud of him. *My father,* the paratrooper who saved our village. Saved my mother. Made my entrance into this world possible."

His eyes were brimming with the joy of memories. These were true stories in which he seemed grounded. Hearing Coop referred to as "Papa" in such an endearing term made me wonder if my own father loved Coop as much as Blanc seemed to.

"And yet, you have your Phalanx squads wreaking havoc around the globe trying to move the world to an authoritarian state."

He sat back in his chair, the light of childhood memories gone from his eyes.

"We will discuss that shortly because we need to. But the matter of Evelyn Champollion is a higher priority at the moment."

"There is no higher priority than the safety of my people. Are you attacking Drewson's Wyoming compound?" My voice was firm, unwavering.

He cocked his head at me and slowly turned it from side to side.

"As important as Evelyn is to me," he said, "I can agree that this matter must be cleared up."

"Then answer my question," I demanded.

"Come with me," he said.

As I began to slide out of the bed, there was a movement from the far corner of the expansive room.

"It's okay, Max," Blanc said.

I looked at Max, and it was the same Maximillian who was the leader of the Sharpstone security team that had picked me up at Stewart Airfield in Newburgh yesterday. I looked back at Blanc, who nodded that he understood my confusion. Were Evelyn and Blanc working together? Why was Evelyn's security team inside Blanc's compound? Where were Cyrilla and her team? What could be more important than protecting their boss, Blanc?

"All is not as it seems, Garrett. I want to show you more."

I stood and leaned against the bed, stretching my back and feeling the pain from the rubber bullet that struck me. My mind was woozy, and I asked Blanc, "Did you drug me?"

"Technically, I did not, but Max did. You are, after all, the former commander of the American Special Forces. It would have been unwise for us to attempt to reason with you up front when you have been fed so much disinformation."

I walked toward the edge of the bed. The door was behind Blanc, who was to my left. Maximillian was to my distant right, still in the shadows of the corner. I was still wearing the same clothes but had been stripped of my weapons and had Ximena's blood on my hoodie. I wasn't sure I wanted or needed the weapons, but, like good friends, they were always nice to have close at hand. Someone had neatly placed my boots side by side at the foot of the bed. I leaned down and pulled them on my feet, feeling the zipper pocket inside the boot. The rhombus flash drive was still there.

"That's the problem with disinformation," I said, feeling still a bit groggy. "Nothing is true anymore today. The world is just one big spin machine with LanxPro gobbling up a gazillion petabytes of data out there and spitting it back at us."

"That would be a yottabyte and you're not wrong, Garrett," he said. I continued moving around the bed as he held out his hand showing me the way. Another security guard stood in the doorway. Black cargo pants. Black polypro, long-sleeved shirt. Black outer tactical vest. AR-15 with its sling clipped into a snap hook. Sheathed K-bar knife horizontal across his vest. "But think about this. The articles about you. Do you see them anymore?"

"I'm not really an internet guy, so I wouldn't know."

"We removed them from the BackInTime Machine, which I created and own. It captures every single utterance on the Web. Tweets, Optimus, LanxPro, Shoutter, Facebook, Instagram. It's all there archived every second of every day. Artificial intelligence and machine learning catalogue it so it's easy to reference. LanxPro software can reverse engineer and follow the path of the data, perhaps a newspaper article, and we can erase it forever from the internet. Everywhere."

"A lot of power," I said.

He nodded. "It's all that matters now. We are moving to a society in which everyone either has an online avatar or someone makes one for you. It's getting harder to control your persona even if you engage every day, as I do. But when you actually own what's on the internet and can remove it, that's a kind of power that is hard to comprehend."

"What does this have to do with me?"

"Even though I am younger than you, I'm your uncle. As I've told you, family is everything to me. I removed anything and everything from the internet about you to protect your reputation."

"I saw you at Dakhla last year. I know the intelligence on you," I said. He had been on the balcony watching as Sanson the Executioner was about to behead Evelyn and President Campbell on livestream television. It was some sort of symbolic gesture from China and their US Partnership to cede sovereignty to a higher global structure of governance being billed as a "first step."

"It's true, I was there because my technology had been watching over Evelyn. When she told me she was going to the Richat Structure, I begged her not to go into the Eye of Africa. I knew what China and our two countries were doing. I was there to save her. I had nothing to do with those negotiations. I was arguing with General Liang when you and your team arrived in the nick of time."

That wasn't how I remembered it, but admittedly I was focused on Sanson and his giant saber hanging above the president's head.

"What is your relationship with Evelyn?" I asked.

"I owe her my life. She saved me from drowning on Normandy Beach. I'm a big strong man now, but I was a scrawny kid then. The riptide pulled me out between a few sunken landing craft." He looked away as we continued walking into a large living room with sofas and televisions. There were guards in each of the corners dressed in tactical gear and holding long rifles.

"Then why were you keeping her in a cell in Biarritz?" I asked.

"That was all performative art by your friend Mitch Drewson. He had her housed there. We have a bit of a technology battle going on, and he's figured out how to block some of my intelligence capabilities such as smart dust and the like. I lost the trail of Evelyn once she entered Drewson's compound, which has three layers of jamming. Next thing I know, you're on the way to Biarritz."

"The motorcycle hit squad at Pignada?" I asked.

"Drewson's guys. Just as it was his guys that killed Emily Sedgewick and his entire team in Grass Valley, California, at their server farm."

"Why would he do that? Kill his own people?"

"Drewson is a power-hungry madman. He's everything that he's told you that I am, only worse. He's trying to destroy me and use you to help him do so."

While Blanc appeared to be truthful, I had a hard time believing that Drewson had co-opted Blanc's persona and was wreaking havoc on the world.

"But why?"

"How else could he destroy me? He's tried everything else," Blanc said. He looked wistfully out the window into the eerie blackness of Central Park.

"The person I'm closest to in this world is Evelyn Champollion, for reasons I've already disclosed. Drewson knows this. He also knows that you and Evelyn . . . connected in Africa. She speaks very highly of you, and I believe has fallen in love with you. She was the perfect honeytrap for you."

"Evelyn's no honeytrap," I said.

"On the contrary. She's the best kind. Neither of you know it and the affection is genuinely mutual based upon what I've learned."

"But why? To what end?"

"As I said, Garrett, family is everything to me, as I believe it is to you. Drewson and I compete on a global stage vying to be the wealthiest man in the world, or the first to invent something, or to build a space station on the moon to mine Helium 3. You name the competitive arena, and he and I are slugging it out. And he never wins."

"And so, come after Evelyn and me? For what?"

He paused.

"Where are your children? Misha? Your team? At this very moment?"

I looked at Blanc's face. His eyes were sad, his face drawn.

"In Drewson's compound," I responded.

"While we just met, you are my family. He knows that I have sought a relationship with you."

A shiver of fear ran down my spine. The one burden I believed retirement and refusing to engage with Drewson had freed me from was the weight of responsibility for the lives of my team and, by extension, my children.

"What are you saying?"

"Mitch is a monster, Garrett. He will stop at nothing to destroy me. If he can destroy you, using my tools, my technology, and your people such as Misha, that would be devastating to me. To lose my closest living relative aside from my mother would be the end of it."

I stood up and paced the room realizing what he was saying.

"Drewson is holding everyone you love hostage," he said. "And by extension, he's holding you, me, and Evelyn hostage, as well."

"What does he want in return?" I asked.

"My empire. My company. My technology," Blanc said.

"I don't believe this," I replied. "I don't believe you." There was anger in my voice. The men in the corners stook steps forward.

"The Phalanx Code? Mitch teased you with that, correct? Misha has been trying to break it?"

"Yes. Written by your girl, Ximena. Evelyn saw the trademark 'X' with crossed sabers."

"Ximena is dead. I sent her to find you. She was trying to tell you this, but Drewson's men, not mine, killed her. All these assassin squads work for Drewson. He's a wolf in sheep's clothing."

"That can't be true," I said, but my voice didn't carry any authenticity with it. I was thinking about Ximena's comment about Coop and his relation to Phalanx. My grandfather *founded* Phalanx?

"I'll show it to you. The Phalanx Code, such as it is, was a compilation of letters I wrote to Evelyn about finding you. You were the hardest person in the world to contact. There was no access to Fort Bragg and certainly not to Fort Leavenworth."

"Misha showed me a video of you, inside your command center trying to find me," I said.

"I have been trying to find you, yes. But that was a deepfake video. Drewson has a secret team of coders, his Zebra team, who create misinformation for whatever politician is happy to pay his price. He connects social media to any of the corrupt journalists, which is most of them, to Wikipedia, and then the proverbial chicken or egg is in place. The fake story is in the Wiki and can't be disputed. He has trackers on the Wiki to keep the page locked down from accurate changes. It's real. It happens. And Drewson is the master at this. My team running the BackInTime Machine are in constant battle with Drewson's information operations. We are the vanguard of truth."

"Seriously?" There was a bite of sarcasm to my reply.

"I have no reason to manipulate public opinion. I'm taking a beating in the media and your president even named me and my organization a terrorist organization. Who do you think got her to do that? She's taking huge donations from Drewson and is publicly promoting his Project Optimus."

I thought about that. The duplicity was stark. I remembered the distortions around the edges of the people shown in the video. Was that all done on a green screen somewhere? As if reading my mind, Blanc continued.

"I do not have a command center in the United States that can fly to Fort Leavenworth in an hour or so. I have a presence in Washington, D.C., as all companies nowadays must have to bribe the politicians. And we've got the usual presence of recruiters and coders in Palo Alto, California. I have no commando teams other than Sharpstone, which Evelyn and I jointly own and use primarily for our mutual protection. It was her company initially, and she owns the lion's share, but my family office bought a stake in it. That's it. The rest of my team are in other countries. There's no Phalanx conspiracy."

"Let me see the code," I demanded. "And why couldn't Evelyn hack it if you're business partners? Why would she even need to?"

"Certainly, you can see it. But first, it's not like Evelyn and I talk every day. Maybe once every few months. She has her part of the business. I have mine. With that, Misha and Evelyn are the best cryptologists in the world, among other things. They can hack anything, but Drewson put a layer of quantum security on it, and it seems impossible. For every two steps forward, they take one maybe two back."

"But the names? The kill list?"

"The names are not a kill list. They are list of everyone I want to bring into my fold, my universe. I want you and your Dagger team as part of my team. I sent these suggestions to Evelyn in my letters, which in reality were digital communications by way of the dark web. Drewson's people, his 'Zebra team' to be precise, intercepted the letters and rearranged the information into a fake 'code' suggesting I had created a kill list to justify their own nefarious actions. They are protesting, and projecting, too much, as the saying goes. Anyway, Evelyn went to Drewson's lair to meet you about the time I sent that, and now they have successfully implicated me in a conspiracy."

He used air quotes around the term "conspiracy." He played with his phone for a second and a printer behind me whirred as it spit out sheets of paper. Blanc grabbed the stack of paper and evened it out on the table by bouncing it along its long and short edges. He handed it to me.

"The 'code,' such as it is, with a translation beneath it, is a simple letter to Evelyn outlining my desire to meet you and offer you and your team onboarding to my company to help support the decentralization of finance, internet, and power in general."

"That's what Drewson said his mission was," I replied.

He nodded and lifted his hand to emphasize his point. "Mitch is a con artist. He had a hand in the FTX debacle, if you remember that crypto meltdown. He's a multi-billionaire because he wisely bought Bitcoin aggressively in 2012 and sold all of it in 2020 at the peak. Other than one lucky stroke, everything he touches fails. This Project Optimus is a scam just like Sam Bankman-Fried and FTX were scams, or Bernie Madoff, or you name the carnival barker that evangelized in pursuit of other people's money, which is the fuel that drives these charlatans."

I held the paper and read.

> *Dearest Evelyn, I hope this note finds you well. I miss our chats and visits. These are extraordinary times. The most devoted engineers, developers, and coders are in grave danger. Project Optimus has chosen war with Phalanx Corporation to steal our LanxPro technology and stop our pursuits of improving mankind by empowering individuals by giving them control of their digital identities. They have a devious plan to create a global security state that provides them ultimate power through complete privacy penetration. Our intercepts show these are the names of the people on the Optimus kill list: Emily Sedgewick, Blair Campbell, Evelyn Champollion . . .*

The list continued with about fifty other names, presumably of those killed in Grass Valley and elsewhere. I continued reading.

> *More than anything I want to connect with Garrett Sinclair for three reasons. First, if you are on this list, you need protection and Sinclair can join forces with Sharpstone to do so. Second, other than my dear mother, he is the only family I have. While I understand that the situation may be uncomfortable for him, I would like to get to know him personally and begin a relationship with him. I know that the two of you met in the Eye of Africa, and he saved you from the hands of that bastard Sanson. I've been in talks with his friend, President Kim Campbell, to both try to recruit her daughter, Blair, to our global cause and to release Garrett from prison. I'm not sure why he's there, anyway. You were there when the FBI came*

after him. Maybe you have some answers? I wish I could talk some sense into my former colleague, Mitch Drewson, but he has gone off the rails. C'est la vie. Now is the time to fight to protect humanity. I want Misha Constance on the Phalanx team, also. I've looked at her code and there is no one better at developing other than perhaps you. She may be the best in the world. Somehow Blanc got his hooks in her and is using her naivete for his own purposes. The definition of evil.

The third reason I would like to speak with Garrett is that he and his Dagger team would be a great leadership structure for your Sharpstone Private Security enterprise. Perhaps a Sharpstone America? We could be a global security juggernaut that protects the downtrodden while we pursue our lofty digital goals, as well. My analysis of Garrett from afar is that he would be the perfect executive to run this enterprise.

Safe travels as you try to negotiate with Mitch.

Love and respect, Aurelius

I looked at Blanc. My mind was buzzing.

"Evelyn had this before she met with Drewson?"

"No, as I said, she was on her way to meet with him when it was intercepted, but this is the original. We are reacting to the information as we receive it, but Evelyn is ever the peacemaker. She's tough and brilliant, and she wants the best for humanity, believing that laudable efforts triumph over the diligent labors of evil even when there is no reason for optimism."

I thought of Melissa's maxim, "Good wins." Maybe that was my connection to Evelyn. They had similar hearts.

Blanc continued.

"As you might imagine, running a global multinational business with a presence in every country in the world keeps me busy. When I need to communicate with Evelyn I do so in a chat room in the dark web. Ximena was my personal coder. She wasn't as good as Misha, but she was good. She lived in El Salvador and would translate my text from our corporate Slack account. Someone apparently breached what Ximena did and put a real-time code editor into the document. Maybe Drewson himself. That's one thing he knows how to do. He could make it so that when Misha or Evelyn try to hack the document, all the words legitimately in the text rearrange to say something entirely different when someone opens the document. Just like he made that deepfake video, this is the text version of that. Every time you breach the security of the code, it rearranges into my supposed kill list."

I knew enough about the cyber domain of warfare to understand that what he was saying was possible, but that still didn't make it true. As a military officer, I was trained to be loyal and do my duty, assuming that everyone else in that institution did the same. I built a false sense of security around me and my team because I believed that most people would do the same, and if they didn't, the system would surely expel them in due time. It wasn't naivete; rather, it was training, and choosing to believe in a system filled with rules and checks and balances, not unlike our government. Removing the worry of internal sabotage from my daily command responsibilities was paramount to focusing on the mission at hand so that I could lead my men and women into combat in support of vital national security interests.

But now, after being imprisoned for a year and having stopped an insider threat at the strategic levels not once but twice, I had no illusions. Many, if not most, people with any semblance of real power were angling to increase that power by whatever means possible. This reasoning didn't exclude Aurelius Blanc, who was standing in front of me with a sincere, earnest look on his face. I was in the rare position of not knowing who to trust in a world filled with deceitful charlatans. Were they both lying, manipulative assholes or was it only one of them? They both had slithered their way through corporate backstabbing and accumulated unimaginable sums of money and power, which accounted for something. If Drewson was the one-hit wonder with Bitcoin that Blanc painted him as, that would make Blanc the more successful, and therefore palatable, of the two.

"A franc for your thoughts?" he said with a grim smile.

"That's a lot more than a penny," I replied.

"Yes, well, inflation and all that. Plus, I intend to compensate you well if you do me the favor of joining our team."

Two job offers in the last week since Mahegan blew a hole in the Disciplinary Barracks. The brief spat of news stories that followed were something that both Drewson and Blanc claim to have eradicated from the internet. It was mind-boggling.

"Honestly, I don't know who to believe, Mr. Blanc."

"There's a difference, General, between serving your government and serving the people of your country," he said. "Your country, any country, is but a grouping of bureaucracies filled with people mostly concerned about their own aggrandizement. You will come to appreciate my frankness and by extension my honesty. I have no reason to lie or play games. My chief interest here, as I said, is twofold: first, to get to know you better, and second, should we click, to offer you an executive role in Phalanx, an organization that I started with the help of your grandfather, my father."

"What role did Coop play in starting Phalanx and Sharpstone?" The Ranger patch–shaped rhombus tattoos, business cards, and flash drive weren't a coincidence.

"As you must know, Papa was an international consultant to many militaries around the globe. He spoke about leadership and strategy to forums in most of the Western nations. Much like you, your Coop was a champion for peace, having seen the carnage of war. It was his idea for Evelyn and I to team up. He was the first investor in Phalanx and Evelyn's security company, Sharpstone."

The first investor? Coop led an entire double life, it seemed. His long absences made sense now.

"For now, Max runs the Sharpstone business, but he is a tactician, not an executive. Phalanx, as I'm sure you're aware, is thriving. With Sharpstone, though, we obviously need to grow our capabilities that have heretofore been focused on personal protection of Evelyn after the Eye of Africa incident, and now of me, as well. But Papa believed that with my computer science training and her cryptological and linguistic skills, we would be a formidable team. I think adding you would be the third leg of the stool. Especially since you're family. You could carry out Coop's legacy."

Coop's legacy? Who was this interloper to tell me about Coop?

I remembered Coop being gone a lot when I was younger. He was a famous general, but I was just a kid proud that he was my grandfather. I didn't realize the business opportunities open to retired flag officers and even today hadn't given it much thought. When your life was consumed with leading men and women to defend your nation there wasn't much bandwidth left to consider alternative opportunities. Intellectual energy and passion were somewhat of a zero-sum process. At least that was the case for me.

"On your previous point, I've always served a constitution, which happens to begin with, 'We the People,'" I replied. "I understand the distinction. My government imprisoned me for doing nothing wrong. I led a small fraction of the fabric of our nation, and I led them well, but I don't understand what role I could play in Phalanx when much of the world believes Phalanx is killing innocent civilians. On your assertion that Coop is a plank holder in Sharpstone, I'd need to see some evidence of that. There's no record of this anywhere in any of his affairs," I said.

"Really? Do you think your father living the good life down in Florida is all on his own accord?"

"He's got a good pension," I replied.

"He owns a two-million-dollar house on the Gulf of Mexico and plays golf every day," Blanc said.

"Are you saying that my father knows about you?"

Blanc chuckled. "Knows about me? He was very upset at the reading of Papa's will. He not only knows about me because Papa extended to me all his overseas portfolio upon his passing, but he has aligned himself with Drewson."

"What are you talking about?"

"When was the last time you spoke with your father?"

"Just yesterday to warn him about you," I said. What Blanc was implying was beyond believable.

"Yes, well, how did that work out?"

"He was playing golf. He didn't care."

"Precisely my point. He has Drewson's assassin squads all around him for protection," Blanc said.

"I don't believe you," I replied. But somewhere deep inside me, I did. I had been unable to find any other explanation for my father's alienation of me and my children. I recalled Coop's funeral and my father's subsequent anger and dissociation from all of us, including my mother and grandmother. I assumed that he was genuinely upset about his father's death, and he was handling it the only way he knew how, which was to withdraw. Could he have been upset about Coop's will? Finding out about Blanc? Splitting Coop's fortune, whatever it was, with this gatecrasher who descended out of nowhere to claim half the stake?

"Do you have any proof of these allegations you're making against my father?" I asked. My tone was defensive, and I wasn't sure why. The man had never even reached out to me when I was in prison. Sometimes we blindly defend our family even when there is no worthwhile defense.

"Why don't I conference Evelyn in, and we can walk you through what we know?"

My phone buzzed.

"Jake, what's going on?"

"Boss, we have a problem."

VALHALLA IS THE NORDIC concept of Heaven for warriors, simply put.

It also was a code I had established within our team to be ready to fight, like a safe word. When I had left Mahegan and the team, I had done so with the hope that Drewson and company were authentic, but I had not been convinced. My handshake and mention of "Valhalla" was the first signal of alarm to my team that they were to always be armed and never leave any one team member alone; not that they needed reminding, but I wanted them to know I was concerned.

Even though the presence of Misha had dulled my normally sharp instincts, I had remained wary. And now I had two angels, one on each shoulder, chirping in my ear about saving humanity and bettering the world. Were they both dark angels, or were Blanc and Drewson representative of the classic showdown between good and evil? It wasn't clear to me who might be telling the truth. Now, perhaps too late, I didn't discount that Evelyn could be deceiving me. Was she to Blanc as Misha was to Drewson? Her apparent purpose being to filter my view?

My time with Evelyn had seemed genuine and sincere. There was nothing fraudulent about it. Right?

I looked at the phone in my hand.

"What's going on?" I asked Mahegan.

"Yeah, that earlier call? My gut was right. I've got Joe and Randy trying to open what looks like a hatch in this pod. Drewson's got something planned and it isn't good."

"Where are Brad, Reagan, and Misha?"

They were the only ones in the group who didn't have combat experience. A few years before, even Amanda Garrett had fended off Rwandan and French commandos to protect her orphan boys and the medical cure that they had developed.

"They're with us," he said. "No issues there. I'm telling you, though, that we might have to take direct action here from inside the compound."

"I believe you, but why? What are you seeing?"

"In the bench seats of this pod are some of the uniforms and equipment that we found on those Phalanx guys we killed near Denver," he said.

"Could it have been from them?"

"No, sir. These are new. Never been worn. Stacks of them that say 'Phalanx' on them."

This was not a promising discovery.

"Does Drewson know you've found it?"

"To the extent that he's not monitoring this call, no, but no guarantees there. We've got your entire world right here, so I decided to violate protocol and call you without encryption."

He was right about that.

"What's your plan?" I asked.

"Find a way out of this pod and then find some high ground," he said.

"Do that. I'll be inbound shortly. Stay up on comms," I said.

"Roger," Jake replied and hung up.

My mind was spinning. Everyone I cared about was locked inside Drewson's Wyoming hyperloop? Drewson was deploying the assassin squads? If he could kill his own people, then what would he do to mine? And my father? How did he factor into this and what was his role? I felt I needed to call him, but if he was truly on the side of evil here, something I had a hard time believing, then did I want to tip my hand?

I turned to Blanc and said, "We need to move fast to help my team. Show me what you've got."

He nodded and said, "Of course. I'm dialing Evelyn right now."

The large monitor to my front clicked on and Evelyn's face filled the screen. Sunlight was pouring in through the den window and the brown husks of tangled grapevines wound their way into the horizon.

"You left out some key information," I said to her. For the moment, I wasn't telling anyone about Ximena's rhombus flash drive.

"Yes, well, Garrett, some things are better discovered by oneself than lectured by another. You know the old saying, 'Show, don't tell.'"

"Did you know about my father?" I asked.

"I just learned that he has become Mitch's senior military advisor for global affairs."

"He has an official role?"

"It seems that way," Evelyn said.

She showed an engagement letter signed by Drewson and my father, with Drewson compensating him at a hundred thousand a month to be his strategic advisor. Over a million dollars a year to help him develop strategies to do what? Take over the world? My dad was a good soldier and general, but he was no strategic genius.

"Last year, he signed on with Optimus in a private deal. After Aurelius' dark web letter to me got hacked by Drewson's team, Ximena started digging back through their servers and found Drewson Enterprise's data room full of contracts and other business documents. She was vetting you and searched Garrett Sinclair and found this."

The document looked authentic, but I didn't know what information I could trust anymore. In the digital age anyone could create a fake video and make it look real, much less a fake document.

"When last year?" I asked.

Blanc paused, thought about it, pursed his lips, and said, "It was about thirteen months ago, to be precise."

I had never heard from my father after the Eye of Africa fight. At first, I rationalized his absence in my life as not knowing how to approach me in prison, or simple embarrassment at his son's fall from grace. Could it have been something more? Contrary to Coop, Dad was always focused on the money. Flag officer friends on the Theranos board of directors convinced the company to offer him a million-dollar private placement in 2012, all of which he lost in 2018 when the company dissolved. He scraped together some money and had built a decent savings, which he invested in the stock market. He sold his portfolio in early 2020 before the Covid outbreak based on a tip from his contacts in the intelligence community, which preserved his capital. Then he unwisely invested at the peak of the Covid rebound and held on to his portfolio, getting crushed. I only knew this because he was calling me screaming that he was broke and asking his son for consulting contracts when I was an active-duty general. I didn't need any consulting and, of course, ethically would not hire my own father.

I had never understood his anger toward me or my kids. Was the answer at hand?

"Do you have a copy of Coop's will?" I asked. "I didn't think twice about it. I was deployed immediately after the funeral. He always lived in a modest home in Fayetteville. Never seemed to live outside his means. Sure, he traveled a lot . . . for now-obvious reasons, but I have no idea what he was worth and, frankly, until now, didn't care."

I still wasn't saying anything about the file on the flash drive. I wanted to hear what Blanc had to say. Because Blanc had not mentioned it, I assumed that Ximena was a lone operator and that Blanc did not know about the flash drive.

"Yes, I have a copy," Blanc said.

"Aurelius, should you do this?" Evelyn asked.

"Evelyn, I have to," he said.

Split screen with Evelyn's face on the monitor was a legal document that had all the usual markings of a will with Garrett Sinclair I, aka "Coop." Blanc scrolled down to the meat of the language, which was all formal legal text.

"Cut to the chase," I said. "My team is in danger and you're throwing me hundred-mile-per-hour curveballs right now. Get to it."

"Bottom line, Garrett, is that Coop left everything to you and me, save a small sum of one hundred thousand to your father."

It still didn't register with me. A hundred thousand was a lot of money and maybe a large part of Coop's estate. I shrugged. "Seems reasonable."

"Five years ago, when he died, Papa's estate was worth close to twenty million. In Papa's will, the lawyer was forbidden from telling you anything about me or Sharpstone, or the sizable inheritance. I believe Papa wanted you to focus on your career and, of course, the revelation of a bastard child in the bloodline could have tarnished your image, not to mention what the allure of unknown riches might have done to your motivation to remain in the military."

I stared at him in disbelief but remained silent.

"Your father, on the other hand, was informed that he received less than one percent of papa's estate. By contrast, upon your retirement, you are set to receive close to five million. Papa put two point five million each in trust accounts for Brad and Reagan upon their graduation from college and upon the one-year anniversary of starting their first job. Whether Brad's band counts as a job, I think is up to you. Once the lawyers are done, you're the executor, along with the attorneys of record, of that decision. That leaves five million for you, with the only stipulation that you are honorably discharged from the military upon your retirement. Seems that has occurred. My portion of the will is simply giving me his investment in Sharpstone, which does about fifty million in revenue annually, clearing about ten million in profit, which accounts for the other half of the money. I must give fifty percent of that to my mother, which I will gladly do, once it is settled. Your father is gumming things up a bit. Also, there is a clause that I must offer you right of first refusal to lead Sharpstone, which I would do even without the clause."

"If what you say is true, I'm sure my father has contested this," I said.

"He has and he lost. He appealed and he lost again," Blanc said. He scrolled to the bottom page where several attorney signatures were affixed. "He had an entire legal team, to include representation in France, sign the document. The document is indisputable. The probate is about to order disbursement any day now."

"Is there any scenario where he gets the ten million set aside for me and my children?" I asked.

Blanc paused. Evelyn said, "Aurelius."

"He needs to hear this from us, Evelyn," Blanc said.

"There is an arcane law that affords your father a path to your share if you, Melissa, Brad, and Reagan are . . . deceased."

I turned away and looked out the window into the blackness. Lights burned in the distance, but I saw only my reflection. My jaw was set. My eyes were ablaze. My mind spun with the calculations. Coop died five years ago. Melissa died three years ago but was diagnosed closer to four years ago. My commander's mind analyzed every possible scenario. Was it all a coincidence? Was my father an evil monster willing to kill off his son, daughter-in-law, and grandchildren to get at ten million? Financially destitute people have done stranger things. Was there some middle-ground explanation where he contested the will because he never knew he had a half brother in Aurelius Blanc? Maybe he figured with Blanc's wealth, Blanc wouldn't want the money, but wealthy people didn't get wealthy by giving away large sums of money, especially when they were growing a business.

"But why?" I croaked.

"Papa brought your father to Normandy to meet me a year or so before he passed. I think Papa knew he was not well and wanted to right some wrongs, one being isolating me from the rest of your family. He told me that if he could do it all over again, he would have immediately made everyone aware of the situation. But he didn't, and of course we get no do-overs in life. Your father didn't handle it well and made a demand to Papa that he write me out of the will. As well as you know your Coop and I know my Papa, your father's lack of acceptance and outright greed compelled Papa to do just the opposite, which was leave his entire estate elsewhere. To take care of the people he loved and the people who genuinely loved him."

After a long pause, I said, "I don't care about the money, Blanc. I care about my people. Whatever Coop's will says is what I'll do. I'm trusting you and Evelyn. My children and my team are inside Drewson's maze of tunnels in Wyoming. I can't even fathom my father's role in this, if any. Regardless, it's irrelevant to the tactical situation and the need to move quickly. There is nothing I can do about my father now, but I *can* get moving to save my people. I have questions. For one, Evelyn, why you didn't at least hint to me that you were closer to Aurelius than you initially let on? Your involvement with Sharpstone? So many questions that I frankly don't have time to deal with right now."

Evelyn said, "Drewson was jamming our communications so that Aurelius and I couldn't talk. Now that he's got everything in place, I imagine we'll be hearing from him soon. We've been played. Your father is an unknown entity in the grander scheme. Being pissed off about a will is one thing. Killing your family is another. We'll deal with that as time permits."

"I think, Evelyn, we can get some of our Sharpstone troops moving in that direction immediately," Blanc said. He turned to me and said, "General, would you like the use of some of my commandos to go and secure your family and friends?"

"I'll need somebody. Drewson's compound is a defender's dream. If you can have a team ready at the nearest airport, I'm ready in five minutes," I said.

"Absolutely," he said.

"Godspeed, Garrett. I'll be available to assist as necessary," Evelyn said.

Less than an hour later, I was at Teterboro Airport boarding a Dassault Falcon 10X, a medium-sized business jet with nineteen seats and a top speed of almost Mach one, over seven hundred miles per hour. Most of the seats were filled, and my quick count told me I had twelve commandos, two pilots, two crew, and a communications operator sitting in the back. The front cabin was left open for me. Someone had placed a kit bag filled with weapons, goggles, ammunition, radios, and other means of war on the bench seat across from the facing captain's chairs. A box with a sandwich and two bottles of water was next to the kit bag. We taxied and were airborne within ten minutes of my arrival.

The only thing that mattered now was saving the people I loved.

23

ONCE WE WERE AIRBORNE, I used the time to meet the team that would be assisting me in securing the safety of my people, should they not be able to do so themselves. This new team and I had no real plan, were unaccustomed to operating together, and knew little about the facility we had to infiltrate other than my limited time spent in the compound.

I walked into the rows of comfortably spaced seats. Some of the troops were sleeping. I counted ten men and two women. All were dressed in black or olive tactical clothing with outer tactical vests filled with ammunition, medical kits, and communications gear. A few of the men eyed me warily while the others nodded off with their mouths hung open. I approached Maximillian, who had led the team that met me upon my arrival at Stewart and protected me during our movement to Evelyn's Upper West Side condo in the Dakota building. Sitting on the chair in the opposite row, I leaned forward and held out my hand.

"Bon soir," I said. "Garrett Sinclair."

He looked at me, then my outstretched hand, nodded, and we shook.

"Maximillian Pelletier," he replied. Then added, "You are a lot of trouble, you know that, right, General?"

Maximillian's grip was ironclad. He had a shaved head and a scarred face that bore the remnants of hand-to-hand combat. A couple of his front teeth were chipped. He was wearing a black T-shirt that was filled out by his muscular frame. On his arms were two dagger tattoos running along the top of each forearm with the tips pointing toward his wrists. Each one had blood dripping from the edge. The handle was elaborate and familiar to me, though I couldn't place where I knew it from. On the blade of the right arm were hieroglyphics and on the blade of the left arm were the words PIERRE TRANCHANTE: Sharp Stone. Above the daggers on each biceps was an open parachute with the number 2 inscribed on the canopy.

"Second para?" I asked.

He nodded. The French Foreign Legion had one parachute regiment, which was based in Corsica. It was the most elite unit of the Legion.

"I commanded it and then got an offer I couldn't refuse from Blanc," he said.

"How are the wounded Sharpstone men from the bridge?" I asked.

"Edgar is fine. The doctor's still working on Louis, but he should be okay. He's been through Iraq, Afghanistan, Senegal, DRC. Nothing will stop him. He was the one who took you over the railing," he said.

"I appreciate your team's sacrifice."

He shrugged. "It is their job."

"Why didn't you just take me to meet with Blanc straight from the airport?"

"I work for Ms. Champollion. She insisted that we go to her place to make sure Optimus did not follow us or plant trackers on you. She has a de-digitization chamber that we never got a chance to run you through with the chaos and your . . . departure. They would like nothing better than to get to Blanc in our draft. We were to transfer you the next day to meet with Mr. Blanc," he said.

"But why not just tell me that?" I asked.

He smiled. "You of all people should know that information remains compartmented for as long as necessary. Our survival depends on deception, among other things. Optimus has copied us in every way. They use our uniforms to kill their own people. It's a false flag operation. Drewson wants to destroy Blanc more than anything in the world. He has convinced your president that we are the enemy, not him."

"But why would Drewson want this?" I asked.

He smiled a gap-toothed leer at me and said, "Why does anyone want power? Fucking ego trip."

I met a few of the other men and women who weren't sleeping. There was a group toward the back of the airplane that looked away when I strolled through the aisle. Some soldiers didn't take to generals or leadership of any sort. Most were at least curious, but these men, all with shaved heads and tattoo sleeves, were distant.

I turned around and walked toward the front and stopped when a young woman looked up at me.

"Hello, sir, Barbara Ruddy," she said, holding out her hand.

I shook it and she proceeded to tell me that she was a British ex-pat. She was a petite blonde with wide gray eyes that sheltered what I imagined was a sharp intellect. Her hair was knotted into a ponytail that ended between her shoulder blades. She reminded me a bit of Lieutenant Colonel Sally McCool, my former pilot who was killed at the Eye of Africa battle.

"What's your mission?" I asked her.

"I'm the intelligence analyst for these cretins, sir," she said. "Without me, they'd just be banging their heads against the wall."

"What happened on the bridge?"

"They didn't listen to me, that's what happened." Her cheeks reddened. "Told them it was a danger area and to cross the Tappan Zee and come down through Harlem into Manhattan proper."

"You were right," I said. "So, what are we facing here?"

She lifted her tablet and pointed at the split screen showing a blueprint of the mine shafts and an external satellite image of Drewson's Wyoming compound.

"An impossible situation," she said. "Only three entrances that I can see. An improbably complicated series of mine shafts that lead to God knows where. The ventilation system has the capability to carry chemicals to render personnel unconscious or something . . . worse. The most defensible terrain I've ever seen from the outside. There are antennae and cameras everywhere, not to mention the assured linkage to the Optimus satellite constellation, giving Drewson a wholistic intelligence picture the likes of which I've never seen."

She looked up at me and shrugged, the glimmer of a smile on her lips.

"Trying to boost my morale?"

She pursed her lips, smiled, and said, "Cheeky one, aren't you? In a way, yes. It is dire, but I do have an idea."

"Talk to me," I said.

"Sit down, sir, if you don't mind. It's rather intimidating having an infamous general staring over me like some god," she said.

I moved from my position propped against the armrest and slid into the seat next to her.

"Infamous?"

She nudged me with her shoulder. "At least you're not boring."

"Doing some research on me?"

"Naturally," she quipped. "Need to determine how hard I'm going to work."

"Have you made up your mind?"

She blushed. "We're going to get your people out, sir."

"Thank you."

"What's up with the rogues in the back?" I asked.

"They're a new lot, as far as I know. Everything is pretty compartmented in Sharpstone. Could be snipers or something like that."

I nodded and looked at her tablet.

"Now here's what I'm thinking," she said.

She showed me, and it wasn't a bad idea at all.

24

AFTER SPEAKING WITH A few more of the Sharpstone troops, I checked my gear and ran through Ruddy's idea in my mind. It could work, but everything was priced to perfection. One mistake and everything unraveled.

Gnawing at the back of my mind, though, was my father. Garrett Sinclair II was a good soldier, if not a mostly absent and average father. As a child I'd had no real issues with his travels because he had deployed to combat in Vietnam and the Persian Gulf. Always living in the shadow of Coop, he had struggled to carve out his own name. He earned a reputation as somewhat of a career climber, which I always attributed to his efforts to break free of Coop's legacy. Instead of embracing it and emulating the traits that made my grandfather an icon in the military, Dad chose an alternate path where he sought out the most prestigious assignments in the Pentagon instead of repeated commands in the field with troops. While he did command at every level, the book on Dad was that he was mostly drafting on Coop's reputation. Plus, many of the leaders in the army were Coop's protégés and felt obligated to choose Dad over some other deserving candidate for promotion. Legacies existed in the military as well as in universities and business.

Running through every scenario in my mind, despite his emotional distance from me as a father, I couldn't reconcile his role as my father with the idea that he would be so bitter and angry as to attack me, much less my children. But if the contract that Blanc had shown me was true and accurate, Drewson was paying him a cool million-two to help him carry out his plan. Or, thinking generously, perhaps Dad was advising Drewson how to defend against Blanc's assassin squads, if indeed both Blanc and Evelyn were playing me. Because there was no reliable source of information anywhere in the world anymore, I couldn't know the truth. So, I kept coming back to the one thing I did know for sure: I loved my children and my team, and they meant everything to me.

My father knew this, as did Drewson and Blanc, and of course Evelyn. Drewson holding them hostage to achieve some pyrrhic victory over Blanc was the only scenario that made sense. Coop used to tell me, "Do something, even if it's wrong." His point being, don't be indecisive. Commit to something and move forward.

I chose to believe that Blanc and Evelyn were telling the truth, that Drewson was holding hostage my precious cargo. And that my father, despite his motivations, was irrelevant. I looked out of the window as we were descending through a snowstorm into Wyoming. If I met my current self in a dark alley, I would bet on the guy in the reflection.

We landed in a raging snowstorm at Central Wyoming Regional Airport three hours later. The pilots maneuvered the state-of-the-art aircraft through mountain passes with skill. Waiting on us were five black Humvees with electronic gear installed to jam roadside bomb signals, relay internal communications, and see in the dark via infrared and thermal imaging to avoid ambushes and safely arrive at the objective area.

Sharpstone was equipped with the most advanced gear in the business.

It seemed that Blanc and Evelyn spared no expense when it came to their troops.

We wound through mountain passes and down icy roads, approaching the compound from the northeast. The snow was coming down in sheets, and Maximillian had ensured there was winter gear for everyone stocked in the SUVs, including softshell white-and-tan digitized jackets, skis, and snowshoes.

Ruddy's plan called for all the above.

The SUV train followed an off-road path until the lead vehicle arrived at an area they called their forward command post. We pulled into a circular gravel or dirt lot that was covered in snow. Two trailers sat on elevated slab foundations with wooden steps leading up to the doors. A log cabin was farther up a path with smoke pouring from the chimney.

Maximillian said, "We organize here and get the plan set."

During the drive, I had tried to reach Mahegan, Van Dreeves, and Hobart several times. I had called Reagan and Brad with no success. Worry clawed at my stomach. Once we were inside the cabin, I asked Maximillian, "Is there a video communication link I can use?"

"LanxPro right there on the big screen," he said pointing at an eighty-inch television monitor hanging above a fireplace that was roaring with a wood fire. He used the remote to switch it on as I sat down at the dining room table.

"Can you mimic a number?"

"Have to get Ruddy in here for that," he said.

A minute later intelligence and communications specialist Barbara Ruddy came in and said in her British accent, "How may be of assistance, sir?"

"I want to make a call that could lead the receiver to believe that he's receiving a call from Drewson," I said.

"Easy enough," she replied. Retrieving a tablet from her rucksack, she plugged a wire into the control panel for the video conference equipment. After typing some commands and moving her finger across the touch screen, she pushed the control panel across the table, looked at me, and said, "Go ahead and dial your target's number."

I used the control pad to dial the number I wanted and let it ring. The camera above the television blinked from red to green when my father answered his phone.

"Drewson?" he barked.

Jesus. My father broke the first rule of operational security.

"No, but you need to understand your alliance with Mitch Drewson has put your grandchildren in danger. My questions are: did you do that on purpose, and can you talk Drewson off the ledge?"

He didn't respond for a long moment. Maximillian and Ruddy watched me. They both flinched when my father started laughing.

"What the hell are you talking about?" he said. "I've done nothing of the sort. I'm sure they're just fine up in Virginia. Reagan doing her college thing and Brad wasting his education on that stupid band Napoleon something or other."

The tinny voice was a few octaves off from his normal baritone, which was the tell, but I wanted more confirmation he was lying.

"Push that button on your OptiPhone, Dad. The one that says, 'OptiFace.'"

A few seconds later his forehead appeared on the monitor.

"Now look into the phone and talk to me," I said.

"Who are you to tell me what to do, son?"

"I'll be your worst fucking nightmare if you're lying to me," I said.

Ruddy smiled and turned away, covering a laugh.

"Well, well, prison didn't do a thing for you, did it?"

"Just another deployment," I said.

Finally, he was looking into the phone. His normally hard edges had softened. His neck was a bit fuller and his cheeks puffier. During his prime he had been trim and fit. He had brown eyes and graying hair that appeared dyed a darker color. He hadn't shaved in at least a day. He was sitting in his home office. A bottle of bourbon sat on his desk and a tumbler was filled with the amber liquid. In the background were dozens of plaques and pictures, all the marks of a storied military career tacked onto the wall as a reminder of prior greatness. The "I-love-me" wall was a relatively standard practice. Soldiers were rightly proud of their service and most tastefully displayed a few of their most grand achievements. Van Dreeves had once said there was an inverse relationship between the size of a man's I-love-me wall and his manhood. If that were true, my father had serious problems. From my one visit a few years ago to their new home, I knew that the pictures wrapped around all the walls of his office and bled into the hallway, but my mother had stopped it there.

"I've got stuff to do, Garrett. Wherever you are and whatever you're doing, I want nothing to do with. You brought shame to this family and to our lineage. Coop, of all people, would be ashamed of you."

"Before you dismiss me so quickly, Father, Aurelius Blanc asked me to say hello."

His face turned bright red, and he looked away. His hands fidgeted with something I couldn't see on the desk. He turned and knocked over his glass of whiskey, the booze spreading across a series of papers stacked on his desk. He muttered a series of expletives and stood up, brushing at his pants.

"Look what you've done!" he shouted.

"What are you doing for Drewson?"

He stopped, turned, and looked at the camera.

"Drewson is trying to help the world, Garrett. Something you wouldn't know about. All your bullshit with Parizad and killing the secretary of state and getting your sergeant major killed. You're a disgrace!"

"I may be, but I've never turned on my family," I said.

"Your family?" He walked toward the camera so that his face filled the screen. "Your family?! What have you ever done for your family? For me? Your mother? This past year has been hell on us. The embarrassment. The ridicule. Social media everywhere. People mistaking me for you, of all things."

"Yes, well, speaking of family, have you spoken with your half brother lately?"

"God damn you! He's provided no proof of anything. He's . . . he's an interloper. A fraud!" He visibly calmed himself, taking a different tack. "Son, listen to me. You don't even know. There's an encrypted file they conveniently can't locate, and if you knew what was on it you'd be singing a different tune."

The encrypted file was at least true, I thought. It was in my boot. His attorneys must have hired a forensic digital expert to comb through Coop's documents and will.

"If I were you, I'd be cozying up to him. He's got bucks," I said.

"So does Drewson, you dimwit," he snapped.

And there it was. The contract was real.

"So, what are you having to do to earn your one-point-two million a year?"

"Where are you getting your information, Garrett?"

"That's not important. What's important is that my team and your grandchildren are being held by Drewson locked in a tunnel somewhere in a mine shaft in Wyoming. What do you know about that?"

Again, my smash cut with the information stopped him cold.

"That's a lie," he croaked after a moment. His eyes went distant as he looked into the night through the window. Perhaps it was the first reflection of doubt. While I knew he was angry at me for a variety of what I considered unfounded reasons, he could have no substantive motive to be upset with Brad or Reagan other than that they were my offspring.

"It's not a lie. Jake Mahegan is with them—"

"Mahegan. The Indian?"

"Jake is an American, Dad, but yes, he's Native American from the Outer Banks of North Carolina, a state you know well from our years there. He is with them and has told me there's trouble. Now I can't reach him. So, I need you to call Drewson and tell him to knock off the bullshit."

His countenance softened, as if reflecting the reality that his grandchildren *could* be in trouble.

"I know nothing about this. Drewson offered me a big contract to help him with global strategy. It's what I do. Help companies understand the geopolitical environment in which they are operating."

"Even better," I said. "Then just call him and give him your best strategic advice to free my kids and my team." I was one level below shouting and growling into the microphone. If I could have reached through the monitor and grabbed his neck, I would have. He looked away again.

"He wants Blanc, not you," he said.

"I don't care what he wants. Call him and tell him to stand down."

"Okay, he also wanted your team. I didn't know about the kids," he said.

"So, you helped him plan luring my team into his compound so he could hold them hostage and blackmail Blanc?"

He never looked back at the camera. He might have imperceptibly nodded his head before dropping his chin on his chest. My father was a self-serving man and had spent much of his career putting his boots onto the backs of many good soldiers whom he saw as competitors. But I didn't believe him to be a depraved soulless grifter who would sacrifice his grandchildren at the altar of his greed. I was outraged enough that he had apparently helped Drewson plan the coalescence of my team into Wyoming to be used as fodder.

"So, it was your idea? The whole thing?"

He didn't respond, which was response enough.

"Call Drewson now or I will," I said. "I'm sure he won't take my call. Your path to redemption may lie in unscrewing this. Maybe."

He looked at the camera and nodded. Picking up his phone, he disappeared for a moment and then the monitor filled with a split screen of my father and Mitch Drewson.

"What is this, Garrett?" Drewson said to my father.

"Let my people go," I said.

Drewson apparently had not been warned he was going to be merged with me. Score one for Dad.

After a pause, Drewson smiled and said, "Not sure what you're talking about. They're here of their own volition."

"I know about your plan," I said. "Whatever you need from Blanc doesn't involve me, my team, and certainly not my children."

"On the contrary. It's all about you, Garrett the third, or should I call you 'Trip'?"

"Let them go," my father said.

Drewson smirked and said, "The million two isn't enough to keep your loyalty?"

"This wasn't part of the deal," he said.

"But you gave me the idea of getting them all here. The kids are just a bonus!"

"Let them go," he said again.

"You've obviously violated your mutual NDA with me, so would you prefer I do the same and tell your son about you and his beloved Melissa?"

Melissa?

"There's nothing to tell, Drewson, now let them go."

The screen went blank. Because my father controlled the three-way video feed, having patched in Drewson, he was able to terminate the entire call. I immediately tried both my father and Drewson's numbers. Neither answered after multiple attempts.

"Damn it!"

I walked toward the fireplace and stared. Drewson had mentioned something about Melissa when I first met him. Now again? The flame danced in front of me, licking my face with heat.

"General?" Ruddy said, pulling me back to the moment. Nothing was bringing Melissa back, and she would want me focused on saving our children, so that's what I did.

"Yes, Barbara?"

"We've got three drones working Drewson's compound. He's got counter drone technology in the air, but our tech is beating his tech right now," she said.

"What do we know?" I asked, as if Ruddy and I had been working together for years. She leaned forward, tapped some keys, and the large monitor was now filled with three drone feeds. They were grainy and obscured by cloud cover amidst the snowstorm, but using the thermal cameras, she was able to walk me through her assessment.

"Sir, drone one in the top left-hand corner is showing the heat signature from a large underground structure, perhaps a cavern. There are multiple heat signatures beyond the door, which appears to be a hangar. The outlines appear to be airplanes and helicopters," she said. Zooming the camera in, she was able to show the glowing orange thermal reflection of two helicopters.

"I was there," I said.

"Very well," she replied. "Camera two shows the trails from the southeast up to what appears to be an entryway. There's a flat surface here that runs maybe a hundred meters. It's gentle and sloping, providing for helicopter access. It's maybe four miles from the hangar. In between is a labyrinth of mines."

"I was there, too," I said.

"Well, then, maybe you should be briefing yourself?"

I looked at her and nodded. "You're doing great. Thank you."

"On the very north side, about five miles from the helicopter entrance and another six or so from the hangar, here at the apex, you've got a thermal anomaly. There's a large house on the hilltop here, and our ground penetrating radar shows a network of tunnels that lead to this building. We can't see into the building or beneath it. Maybe there's concrete and lead lining, like an underground nuclear shelter. Whatever it is, there appears to be a connection to all three of the locations."

She overlaid a rough drawing that looked like a peace sign.

"Here in the middle is the mountain top. The line terminating in the north is our unknown house. The line terminating in the west is the hangar. And the line terminating in the east is the helicopter landing zone."

"I see that," I said. My mind was churning. I was attempting to bleed out all the emotions I was feeling from having my kids locked in a tunnel to having my team in that same location to learning that Blanc was my half uncle and now knowing that this was all my father's idea. The only thing that mattered now was my ability to see the battlefield geometry that Ruddy was showing me.

"Here," she said, pointing at a ravine that bisected the path to the north building. "This is a possible point of entry. Our drone has imaged a possible weak point there. Some explosives. Block to the south. Move north. This is what I was telling you earlier."

"Yes. Your plan in the plane was a high concept of this," I said. "And you've confirmed it with the drones. Do you know what's in there?"

"I know enough that they are hyperloops. Trains that levitate on magnets and travel the speed of sound using suction and other physics. If we get in there, the possibility exists that we could be run over in a nanosecond. Even if he's not using it to move people or equipment, he could use it as a weapon. Breaching the tube could cause a change in pressure like when an airplane is at altitude and a section rips off. You know, like in the movies."

I thought about Ruddy's comments. I needed an engineer. But first I asked her, "Is there a way to disable the entire system? Depressurize it? Make it so the train can't move?"

"I think that's our next task. Figure that out."

I turned to Maximillian, who had been silently watching and listening, and said, "Sketch out a diagram so that we can do a team rock drill and go through the motions. We will need drone coverage, explosives, an overwatch team, an assault team, and a breaching team. Do we have an engineer that knows about hyperloops?"

"Is that all?" Maximillian quipped.

"Probably not, but it's a start," I said. "Sometimes saving the world requires saving your world first. If Drewson is doing everything he is accusing Blanc of, and he has access to the president, then he could potentially create the global security state he has been warning about."

"Save your people first, General, and the ship will right itself, correct?"

"Exactly. By the way. Who are the guys in the back with the shaved heads?"

Maximillian shrugged. "We were low on personnel. Monsieur Blanc recommended them. They are a new addition. Highly trained, though, I'm told."

I nodded, something scratching at the back of my mind.

"I studied engineering in university, sir," Ruddy said, picking up where we left off. "I know what a hyperloop is. It's a train that operates friction free. It uses magnets to propel the train forward at speeds up to eleven hundred kilometers per hour, or in American English, that's seven hundred miles per hour. Force equals mass times acceleration and all that good stuff. The air pressure is lowered to decrease friction, and sometimes there's a ducted turbine fan. If that's the case, if we disable one of the magnets, there should be no ability to pull from one end to the other."

"Where are the magnets?"

"On the rail and on the train. They pull the train forward. The entire thing is vacuum sealed. No wind resistance. No friction. Just go Mach one pulled by suction and magnets."

"How does it stop?" I asked.

"Everything that makes it go, makes it slow down and stop. It's magnetic levitation technology in a tube, like the high-speed rail in Japan, but with no friction and no wind resistance. That's all it is."

"With a vacuum, I'm assuming the car has an oxygen flow. We didn't seem to have any problem when we were in it briefly," I said.

"Yes. Oxygen tanks, so that's a vulnerability to anyone riding in it. If we're dealing with the hostages trapped in one of the rail pods, that could be an issue."

"That's what it sounds like," I said, recalling my conversation with Mahegan.

"I've focused the drone on this spot right here about a half mile from the building on the north apex of the triangle," Ruddy said.

"Thermal is showing more resolution there," I said.

"Two reasons, I believe. First, it's an exposed portion of the hyperloop vacuum tube, but it's disguised to look as if it is underground. My guess is that the straight line that this thing must take necessitated a short external span. See the pylons here and here," Ruddy said. She used a laser pointer to draw little red circles around two areas that upon close inspection were circular support beams.

"The thermal gets past the thin superstructure Drewson built over this to make it blend in with the terrain."

"What's the second thing?" I asked.

"This dark spot right here?" She moved the pointer to the right to a section of the rail tube in between the exposed area she just highlighted and the building she mentioned earlier. "Thermal is picking up a lot of heat. As if a lot of bodies might be tightly packed in there."

I nodded, understanding the predicament.

"The vacuum creates a seal and if the tube is punctured, it's like getting sucked out of an airplane. The pressure pulls you."

"Exactly," Ruddy replied. "And the shockwave of air barrels through the tube at Mach one until the atmospheric pressure is normalized inside the tube."

"If he doesn't blow them up, Drewson can shut down their oxygen and leave them there to die," I said.

"To use them as bargaining chips with Blanc seems to be his play, sir," she said. "If they die, they're no good to him. But, yes, he could do that."

Her frank assessment startled me, but she was right.

"What's the solution?" I asked.

"Best commanders modify the plan based upon new intelligence. We didn't know this coming in. The question is, what happens if we intentionally depressurize the system? Land the plane so to speak. At altitude, the pressure around the plane is fatal. On the ground, it's equalized. How do we get the equivalent of the tube and pod being on the ground? If we can do that, I think the car just stays where it is and Drewson loses control."

"Makes sense. There has to be some engineering in there that modulates pressure."

"We're looking for that," Maximillian said. "The control room. Seems there is one at each apex."

"So if we focus somewhere other than the north apex to depressurize the system, that could also serve as a ruse or feint."

"I like it," Maximillian said.

I turned to Ruddy and asked, "What communications infrastructure do we see on the north apex?"

She moved the laser pointer to a series of antennae that were poking up from a mountain ridge, lights blinking in the darkness.

"This is the cell tower that Mahegan last called you from. I'm thinking he had a few seconds of reception as Drewson's engineer slowed the pod to be positioned where we believe it to be."

"That would be a second indicator that my people are where you believe they are, the first being the thermal signature."

"Precisely, sir. You're pretty good at this, if I might say so," Ruddy remarked.

"Talk to me about good when we've got everyone safely out of the tube," I said.

"Very well. So, what's the plan?"

I turned to Maximillian. I wasn't his commander nor was he mine. I had lived by the leadership maxim, though, that when there was an opportunity to be in charge, then do so.

"I think that's it. Break into two teams. One goes to the southeast apex and attempts to depressurize the tube. One goes to the north apex to get into the tube or breach it after it's been depressurized."

"Better than what we had going in," Maximillian said.

"Can we get Blanc and Evelyn on the video?" I asked.

After a minute of Ruddy punching buttons with her fingers, a split screen showed Blanc in New York and Evelyn on an airplane."

"Do we have a plan?" Blanc asked.

"I think so," I said.

"I've put some thought into this, Garrett. I can cede much of my ecosystem to Drewson if he agrees to let everyone go."

"I think if you can do that, you should. How many billions do you need?" I asked.

"My point exactly. It's not really the money, but the technology and the ability to shape the future of mankind. That's what this is all about. Drewson has been rather unsuccessful other than that one Bitcoin bet, and everything else he has tried hasn't gotten traction. So, I recommend a two-pronged strategy: I'll negotiate with Drewson and you . . . do what muddy boots generals do. You've got our best with Sharpstone. What other resources do you need?"

"We need an engineer to tell us how to breach the hyperloop. Mahegan said all my people are in the hyperloop pod trapped in the tube."

Blanc winced. "Breaching the hyperloop is quite impossible."

"Our plan is to depressurize the system and then breach the tube."

"That's a very complicated process. I'm an engineer. I've designed these things. I have teams of engineers working on projects in Dubai and Mumbai."

"Can you get one of your geniuses to walk us through how to do this?"

"I'm the best genius you've got," Blanc said. "In addition to computer science, I have degrees in advanced thermofluidic dynamics as well as physics and space studies. I'll be your guide, but I have to tell you, if you breach without depressurizing the entire vacuum, the entire tube will implode with a destructive force beyond comprehension. A wall of air the weight of an elephant will barrel through the tube at Mach one. Everything and everyone in the tube will be crushed beyond recognition. There is no margin for error."

I swallowed hard, nodding.

"No margin," I said. Then, "Last question. Can you jam Drewson's intelligence collection operation?"

"We can try. He's pretty good but we have been sparring with his satellites in space."

"If you can block his eyes and ears, we can get into the control room and depressurize the system. Then it's a simple breaching operation and jackpot retrieval."

"No margin, but you have all the jamming support you need from me," Blanc said. "Meanwhile, I'm calling Drewson to negotiate this thing."

"Garrett," Evelyn said. "Be careful."

The worry in the lines etched around her eyes was well founded.

25

WE MOVED FROM THE cabin several miles from the north apex building in two teams. Maximillian led the south apex team that was to take over the control station and slowly depressurize the system. I led the north apex team. Our mission was to breach the tube once depressurized and retrieve everyone.

By my side in the back of the Land Rover was Jacques Desmond, who asked me to call him "JD." He was a six-and-a-half-foot-tall Nigerian who looked like he spent the bulk of his time in the free weight section of the gym.

"Legion?" I asked him.

"Seven years," he replied, looking through his window to the left.

"Combat?"

He smirked.

"*Mon général,* Max would not give you an inexperienced team leader. He reports directly to Ms. Champollion. We can't have you dying on us."

He looked at me and smiled, then nodded.

"I'll do my best to make you guys look good," I said.

"From what I hear, you won't have to try too hard."

I nodded and he looked away.

Because I had not been able to reach any of my people on the phone, I assumed by the heat signatures Ruddy had shown me that they were all in one place in the pod still stuck in the tube.

The question no one had asked was, did the hyperloop malfunction, making the stoppage a legitimate issue, meaning Drewson wasn't doing anything untoward to my charges? I didn't have the time to fully examine that question, but as we bounced across the frozen trails, I saw my phone light up with the number from which Drewson had called before.

If Blanc was jamming communications, somehow Drewson had found a workaround.

I had debated shutting off my phone and going in blind, but on the possibility that Mahegan or Reagan might call me, I'd kept it on with the full knowledge that, because he knew I was coming for him, Drewson most likely would be able to geolocate me. I let the call go through to a voicemail box that wasn't established. Thoughts circled through my mind, though. Had Mahegan, Hobart, or Van Dreeves overtaken Drewson and used his phone to call? Had Misha hacked into Drewson's phone and was she trying to contact me? There were so many possibilities. I had a hard time believing that any of my team had been sitting passively waiting for something to happen.

That was the real variable that could create a dynamic situation at the objective. No doubt if they were locked in the pod within the pressurized tube, they knew the consequences of breaking the seal.

Instant death.

The temperature was in the low twenties and the wind blew snow sideways across our windshield. At my urging, Ruddy had chosen to stay in the command center and relay communications despite her desire to be on the objective. We reached our primary position about two kilometers from where we suspected the pod was and pulled to a three-vehicle herringbone on either side of the road. We were in a swale with a dry riverbed to our front, high ground behind us and on both sides, but the land to our front was lower than our position, so we had good visibility of the north apex building.

Through the thermal goggles, the chimney glowed hot with a smoking wood fire. Ruddy radioed from the basecamp.

"Dagger Six, this is Sharp Base," she said. I had never told her my call sign but it probably wasn't a challenge to figure it out.

"Go," I said.

"South team on station. Eyes tell us there is movement on the ridge above them. We also have movement at north apex house. Two SUVs arrived. Eight commandos. Big guys. Long guns."

"Air support?" I asked.

"Two drones in orbit at your command," she replied.

"Roger. Anything identifiable?"

"Negative," she said.

While I knew that it was unlikely that Mahegan, Hobart, Van Dreeves, Matt Garrett, Jeremy West, Zion Black, and Patch Owens were in those SUVs, I couldn't discount the possibility. The video feeds were intelligence through a soda straw, giving the viewer a grainy image where they could count people and see weapons, but that was about it. More than likely, this was an Optimus team moving to secure the north end of the hyperloop.

"Taking fire," JD said.

"Roger," I replied. He knew what to do and didn't need any direction from me.

The crack of machine-gun fire sang through the valley. Ruddy shared the drone video to my tablet, so I was able to watch the ten-man squad take cover. I didn't recognize any of the people at the north apex house, but still. Erring on the side of caution, I didn't give the order to fire.

"Let's move on foot to the house and work our way down the tube from there. Maybe there's a control room at that end, as well. In fact, I'll be surprised if there isn't."

"Oui," JD said. He was poised at the prospect of attacking into the teeth of a heavily defended area.

We moved from the vehicles and were a six-man group picking our way through the icy cliffs of this rugged terrain. After ten minutes of walking, Maximillian's voice coughed into our earpieces.

"South secure!"

"Roger. Charlie Mike," I said.

"You've got two vehicles approaching south apex," Ruddy said. "Shoot?"

"Are we positive it isn't my people?" I asked.

"Negative. No positive identity," she replied.

"No fire," I replied.

Like so many times in combat, the decision to shoot was complex. Without having positive identification, I couldn't order to engage the vehicles. What if it were my children and colleagues? In my gut, I knew it wasn't. But still.

"Understand. Do not engage until positive ID," Ruddy said.

We took a knee about two hundred meters from the north apex station. JD did an excellent job of managing the flow of the team.

"High ground," he whispered into his throat microphone.

"Roger."

We moved to the north about a hundred meters from the trail the two vehicles had used to move to what was clearly a lodge. Lying behind a large piece of granite, I studied the objective. It was an alpine chalet with steep roof angles and cedar planks. Large rectangular windows ran floor to ceiling, though I imagined the glass was bulletproof. The entire valley fell away behind the chalet and then rose again where Drewson's main operation seemed to be located.

Was this Drewson's living quarters? Had we stumbled onto his hideout?

Was his Zebra team holed up here? If the hyperloop could get from here to the other side of the mountain twenty miles away in five minutes, any of those options were possible.

"Status of south apex?" I asked.

"In control room. Bogies coming. Need to act fast," Maximillian said.

"Roger," I replied. "Any intel on friendlies?"

"One pod at north end. Video shows people. Looks like your people. Four women, ten males. They have rifles and weapons but are enclosed in the pod. Ruddy called it right."

"Roger," I said.

My gut clenched. My entire world was encapsulated in a pod inside a vacuum-sealed tube pressurized ten times over a Boeing 747 flying at thirty thousand feet. There was no escape unless Maximillian and team could release the pressure.

"Another pod in the tube seems to be loaded with explosives," he said quickly. "Pardon, but we're just getting the intel here. Looking at cameras. Our engineer is studying the pressurization."

I knelt and looked at the tablet JD was holding in his gloved hands. Blanc's face appeared on the screen. The wind whistled along the valley and over the hilltop. It was biting cold.

"Blanc here. What's the psi in the tube?"

"Fifteen X is what it says," Maximillian said.

"That's fully pressurized. There are two courses of action here, and we probably need to do both. First, each section of the tube has shutoff valves that can stop or minimize the air blast from one end to the other. Find those," Blanc said. I noticed someone had activated the "record" function of the video call. Why would Blanc want a record of this call? Maybe to cover his ass later, but it was risky, as we were breaking and entering the Drewson compound and Drewson could simply claim it was an innocent malfunction that had locked my friends and family in the pod. Which, it still could be.

"Pressure sections?"

"Sounds right," Blanc said.

Gunfire pinged in the background.

"We're taking fire. I've got two snipers on the ridge holding them off. Not sure how long they can do it."

"Attack drones?" I asked.

"On station," Ruddy said.

"Bring them in," Maximillian said.

"Go," I said.

The sound of miniguns is an unforgettable noise, the burping whir they make while spitting out hundreds of rounds of high-explosive ammunition in seconds. The echo of reverberations up the valley was reassuring, especially knowing it might buy some time for Maximillian and his team to depressurize the tube. Distant combat noises on a cold night brought back many memories from Afghanistan, Iraq, Syria, and other locations. The pang of guilt and worry tried to emerge, but I held both at bay, hoping they would be supplanted by joy and relief. But I knew better than to open myself to hopeful thoughts, so I remained focused on the task at hand.

"Movement," JD said. He kept the video on and attached the tablet to a small plate in his outer tactical vest with the camera facing outward.

"Engage," I said. "We have positive ID that they are Optimus."

"Roger. Engage," he repeated.

Four men were walking from the chalet to the SUVs parked in front. All four dropped dead to the ground. JD's fire control was impressive. Four shooters, four dead.

"Prepare," JD said.

Two men came running out, looked down, looked up, and caught bullets in the face.

I thought, *six down and four to go*. As far as we knew.

The double oak doors slammed shut while two men attempted to slide to our flank by moving from the back of the chalet into the low ground. The left side security team exchanged fire and quickly silenced them. Our element of surprise had worked to our advantage, but now we were six attackers against at least two defenders, which were textbook odds: 3–1 was what all the manuals told us.

But actual door-to-door combat was much more challenging. There were always the one or two crafty commandos who were driven to win at all costs or go down trying. It was our moment to move, and our math told us that at least two commandos remained.

Sensing this window, JD said, "Close from the flanks. Middle will move once in place."

The flanks were two teams of two. JD and I were the middle team. In my goggles I saw two dark shapes scramble to the east side of the chalet. They were hunched over and running, staying low to stay alive. On my right, two more figures appeared and crawled to the west side of the chalet. Both teams of two stacked against the cedar planks on the side, weapons at the ready.

"Alpha in position."

"Bravo in position."

"Moving," JD said.

We jogged to the rear of the lead SUV. Kneeling, I watched as two men appeared behind the west team and fired into their backs.

Weapon up, I returned fire, though they were quickly out of sight.

"Bravo, status?" JD asked.

No response. I felt JD's body stiffen. We were shoulder to shoulder, protecting each other while attempting to coordinate a complex operation.

"Alpha, Bravo may be down. Two bogies. Watch your flanks."

A prolonged exchange of gunfire from the east interrupted the conversation.

"Alpha. Sitrep, over."

No response.

"Alpha, sitrep, over," JD asked again.

No response from Maximillian or his six-man team.

My phone buzzed in my pocket again. I didn't have time for histrionics or Drewson's bullshit. I didn't answer it as it continuously buzzed against my hip. Hanging up and calling back. Hanging up and calling back.

"Alpha hit," the team leader croaked into the microphone. "Got one."

If he was correct, that left one rogue vigilante somewhere roaming the terrain for us. We had no security, save ourselves.

"Back to back," I said to JD, since it was just him and me now. "Move to the door."

"Roger."

JD and I pressed our backs together and held our weapons at eye level as we spun and walked toward the door. A head popped up to my two o'clock and I unloaded five rounds into the vicinity, suppressing him if not killing him.

We made it to the heavy doors where we felt the concussive impact of multiple rounds of ammunition hitting the door from the opposite side. The lone survivor inside? Drewson?

"South apex taking fire again," Maximillian said. "We've shut down five sections of the tube, but someone is at another control station slowing our progress."

"Roger," I said. "Five minutes, we should be at the controls."

JD counted to three, and on two was barreling into the front door, weapon raised. I followed him as if I was a private in a battle drill to enter a building and clear a room. He spun left with his weapon raised and I slid to the right. The smell of gunpowder hung in the air. The front doors were splintered and pockmarked on the inside. A dim light shone from a stairwell that went below the main floor. The chalet was finely appointed with dark leather and mahogany wood, which told me we were in Drewson's man cave, if not primary residence here in Wyoming.

"Stairs," I said.

JD led the way, and we moved down the stairs until we were on a brightly lit landing. It was a white tiled room exactly like the one I had seen in the east and west apex stations twenty miles away. Next to the sliding hydraulic doors was a control room with monitors and keyboards. On the monitors I could see my team and my children in the pod stuck in the middle of the tube. Mahegan was staring into the camera. Hobart and Van Dreeves were wrapping their shirts around Reagan and Misha. They were taking care of one another in the direst circumstances. Misha was crying, surely knowing by now that she had made a mistake by trusting Drewson. Reagan was staring into space while Brad was scribbling something on the back of a piece of paper. Matt Garrett was inspecting the pod with his hands running along the seams. Jeremy West was playing with some kind of panel at the front, as if he was hoping it would fly and he could control it. Amanda Garrett was on one knee in front of Zion Black, who was injured in some fashion.

Standing in front of the control panel in the chalet was Mitch Drewson.

"It's not what you think," Drewson said. He sounded like a husband who had been caught cheating by his wife. *It's not what it looks like.*

"Let them go," I said.

"I'm trying," he said. "Blanc has jammed up my system. Trapped your team down here. I was bringing them up here for protection from Blanc's assassins."

While I knew what he was saying was false, it gave me pause.

"He's lying," Blanc said into our earpieces. I assumed he was listening and hearing through JD's tablet.

JD's weapon was trained on Drewson's tall figure. Drewson's signature blond shaggy hair was askew. He looked harried, as if he actually had been trying to help Dagger team and my kids out of trouble.

But his people had killed Sharpstone commandos, and all the evidence pointed at Drewson deliberately blackmailing Blanc.

"Do whatever you must to get that pod here and release them," I demanded.

"I'm trying, General. You must believe me." The look on his face was believable, but I had negotiated with the best of the Afghan warlords, the Serbian henchmen, and the Iraqi tribal leaders. They all had one thing in common: great theatrics. Like some of our own politicians, their pretensions of innocence were worthy of Academy Awards. Here was Drewson, standing in the control room of the hyperloop looking like the befuddled Wizard of Oz. All he needed was a curtain to pull across the opening so that he could return to his work.

JD and I were still back to back. He was covering the stairwell. I had barely lowered my rifle to speak with Drewson.

"I don't care what your beef is with Blanc. I told you that if you mess with my people, I was coming for you," I said.

His countenance changed and he smiled an "aw shucks" grin. "Yes, General, that's what I was counting on."

From two side doors sprang four commandos with their weapons up. They were wearing black tactical clothing and carrying SIG Sauer long rifles with flashlights and scopes. One of them shot JD, who fell to the ground at my feet.

They descended on me before I could fire a shot, then wrestled me to the ground. One of them placed an electric prod against my neck, but I prevented him from pulling the trigger. JD must have been only wounded because he shot two of the commandos in the back while I retrieved my Beretta and fired two shots into the gut of the prod wielder. The last man standing leaped onto me as I flipped the blade on my knife into position.

"Stop!" Drewson shouted.

"Second pod levitating," Maximillian said. His voice was nervous. Shaking.

My knife had nicked the femoral artery of the fourth commando, who was bleeding out next to me. Drewson awkwardly held a pistol in my general direction. I gave him 50–50 odds of hitting me, but I had made it this far and didn't want to risk it anymore. I felt like there was a path to success here.

Looking at JD, I saw he was gut shot, but hanging in there.

"Your people, Garrett Sinclair, are all right there," Drewson said, pointing at the monitor. "Twenty-five miles away on the other side of the mountain is a pod filled with explosives, not that they're needed."

His hand hovered over a button on the panel.

"If I press this button, this pod will travel at Mach one and in less than a minute hit the pod your team and children are in, and they will die instantly. The force will be tantamount to the World Trade Center collapsing onto them. It's not survivable."

"I thought you said this was all Blanc," I replied, stalling. "Why would you be doing this?"

I was staring at the monitor. Mahegan was pushing at something on the ceiling of the pod.

"System shutdown in process," Maximillian said into my earpiece. "Five chambers closed. Now six."

"No," Drewson said. "What's going on at south station? Come in," he said to no one in particular.

"West station here. All clear," someone said.

"South station come in," Drewson said again.

"What's going on?" I asked Drewson. I knew exactly what was happening but wanted him to keep thinking and talking, anything to keep him from pressing that button. The more sealed hatches Maximillian got in place, the safer I assumed my people would be. Instead of a bullet train car filled with explosives hurtling at Mach one directly into the pod, the pod would have to punch through multiple steel plates, presumably losing energy and explosive power. The unknown was what would happen to the section of the tube that my team was in? I didn't know nor did I think Blanc actually knew. I was sure they had run tests and experiments on pressurized sections of hyperloop tubing, but in real life, there was always a variable. What Maximillian was doing to section off the tubes with circular reinforced steel plates was crucial to the survivability of my team.

"Seven shut; four to go. It appears there is one steel plate every two miles or so," Maximillian said.

I remained stoic, not wanting Drewson to know that someone was talking in my ear.

"Team closing on south station now," a voice said over the command center.

"Let them go," I said to Drewson.

He looked at me with a drawn face. Gone was the cocksure billionaire. The energized control freak. What I saw now was someone who was genuinely scared. His scheme had not gone according to plan. There appeared to be no backup strategy, so sure was he of succeeding by holding my people hostage as a simple blackmail scheme.

"Get Blanc on the video," I said. "Let's work this out. I just want my people safe."

Anything to buy time.

"You don't understand. What your guy is doing in the south station is going to kill your people. By shutting down the sections of the tube, there's no way into or out of the remaining section without imploding it."

"Blanc said there's a way," I said. "He said this was the strategy. Protect the pod by sealing it off from a potential weaponized pod."

Drewson chuckled. "Yes, he would say that."

Drewson's hand hovered over the button to send the bullet pod into the steel plates. I was done wasting time. I imperceptibly pressed the detent button on my microphone.

"Can you bleed the pressure from the system? Make it so they can get out."

Simultaneously, Maximillian said, "Yes, trying. Taking instructions from Blanc," and Drewson, who thought I was talking to him, said, "No, it's not possible. What the people are doing at the south station is not helpful."

Suddenly, Blanc's face appeared on the screen above Drewson's.

"You know that's not true, Mitch," Blanc said. "Tell me what you want."

Drewson was nonplussed by Blanc's sudden appearance in the control room. The video on the monitor also showed that it was recording.

Maximillian spoke into my ear, "It will take twenty-seven minutes to depressurize the tube fully and safely. Oxygen indicator on the pod is only showing nineteen minutes. With so many bodies in the pod, they're consuming oxygen at a much higher rate than it is programmed for."

No one could live for eight minutes without oxygen. The tube was a vacuum, hence no oxygen. The pod was supplied by a tank that was running on empty. I looked at the monitor that showed my people in the pod. Misha was hyperventilating. Her special tri-colored glasses had slid down her nose. Mahegan was on one knee rubbing her back. His cheeks were bulging, as if he was holding his breath. Hobart was next to Brad and Van Dreeves was on one knee next to Reagan. They were all holding their breath, but I noticed something else, also.

Amanda Garrett was walking from her uncle Matt toward Reagan. She was carrying a small medical bag with a thin clear tube and a mask extending from the pouch. I couldn't be certain, but it looked like she had an oxygen supply she was sharing. She confirmed this when she turned her back to the camera and slipped a mask over her mouth and then shielded Reagan from the camera and gave her a pull, then Van Dreeves took a quick pull and she moved to Misha. Calles was in the corner, passed out. Amanda moved to her and shook her, but she didn't respond. She gave Calles some oxygen and she moved her head slightly. My team was in bad condition. I needed to act now.

For his part, Drewson was too focused on Blanc's image to notice the oxygen sharing. Little good it would do if we couldn't get in there to rescue them.

"It's a moot issue now, Aurelius. They're dead. There's no escape," Drewson said. "They'll be out of oxygen in ten minutes."

My neck was tighter than steel tension wires. My breathing began to elevate as the clock ticked down.

"Nothing is moot, Mitch. You can have it. I don't care," Blanc said. "We can't let innocent people die. It defeats the entire purpose of what we have separately been trying to do. If I need to tilt my king forward to the board, I'll do it," Blanc said.

Drewson looked at me and said, "You understand what's happening, right?"

I believed I did, and it wasn't what Blanc was hoping I'd think. I'd come to the realization that Blanc needed me and my kids dead so that he could inherit Coop's fortunes, which included Sharpstone. Everything had been a deception, using the layperson's general lack of understanding of difficult concepts such as blockchain and Web 3.0 to disguise a simple plot to gain and maintain power.

"Sadly, for you, I do," I said. My rage was simmering but I had to maintain my cool to keep my people alive.

"I've enjoyed the chat, Aurelius, truly. And I understand that what you and the general here have been doing is to buy time to somehow save the miscreants in the pod. You always underestimated me, didn't you? Well, this is warfare today, is it not, in which all things are fair? I hold hostage the team of your long-lost nephew in an effort to outmaneuver you on the battlefield, such as it is. My Optimus teams have been successful in portraying you and your company as evil. Meanwhile, we put a code bot on your much discussed Phalanx Code to keep everyone laboring away while we got the one thing you value in the world more than your precious Phalanx Corporation."

Drewson paused, looked at the weapon in my hand, and then continued.

"Your father's legacy. We kill the general and his seed and you have nothing left except yourself, and of course, that healthy inheritance, right, Aurelius?"

I tried to put it all together. Blanc wanting the inheritance, perhaps enlisting Drewson to help? Those thoughts fluttered away like bats from a cave because my primary concern, my only concern, were my children and my team.

"And I know exactly where you are. So, while we've been killing time here, so to speak, I've been stalling of my own accord. Your best squads are here, some dead, some alive. If you look around you, I'd say you're rather unprotected, wouldn't you?"

My finger on the trigger tightened. I didn't want to kill him before I better understood how to safely retrieve the pod.

Drewson looked at me and smiled. "Oscar worthy, don't you think?"

Then he pressed the button. On the opposite screen from Blanc's face, the weaponized pod located at the south apex station rocketed forward along the tube, smashing through the first steel door like an improvised explosive device, which was exactly what it was.

I began to squeeze the trigger on my rifle when the floor opened beneath Drewson, and he vanished.

26

DREWSON'S DISAPPEARANCE WAS THE least of my concerns as I watched the pod smash through the steel doors. The tube buckled and shook but so far held steady.

"Can you do anything to control the pod?" I asked Maximillian.

"We're under fire," he shouted into his microphone. As he spoke, I heard the *tap tap tap* of rifle fire.

Stepping around the cylindrical escape hatch that had consumed Drewson, I quickly studied the control panel. I flipped the communications switch and said, "Jake, Joe, Randy, can you guys hear me?"

Their heads jerked up. They studied the camera with hopeful eyes. I frantically searched the dashboard for anything that might move their pod toward us. There had to be a way.

"Yes!" they shouted. Mahegan, Van Dreeves, and Hobart all held their hands out, a symbol to be careful about consuming too much oxygen. By my count they were close to being out. Amanda shed her game of hiding the oxygen tank and was overtly passing the mouth cup to Misha, Reagan, and Brad.

"There's a train barreling down on you in about a minute. I'm going to try and move you. Buckle everyone up."

Blanc's screen had gone blank but Evelyn appeared.

"Garrett, Aurelius is under attack. If you toggle the joystick there in front of you, it might move the pod toward you."

In the center of the dashboard was a control bar with arrows pointing left and right. I moved the bar to the left and nothing happened. Blinking lights winked rhythmically. One for each pod. I pressed Pod One and tried the joystick again.

The pod shot forward, throwing Mahegan, Hobart, and Van Dreeves against the back wall. It slammed to a halt seconds later beneath us. I pressed the button that sent current to the demolition pod and pushed the joystick to the right, attempting to slow or reverse its course, but nothing was stopping it.

Loud banging thudded beneath our feet where Drewson had disappeared. I stepped to the side and pushed the same button he had pressed. Cylindrical metal covers retracted into the floor. I looked into the space and saw what Drewson had done.

There was a fireman's pole that had a levitating platform just a few feet beneath the surface of the floor. He had ridden that down and then most likely picked his way through some unseen escape route that led into the mountain redoubt. To the right was the pod with the chamber sealed behind it. Presumably my friends and kids were safe from the pressurized vacuum, but not from the speeding improvised pod that would impact in a few seconds.

I left the command station and dragged one of the dead guards into the hole where Drewson had escaped. I dropped the dead guard and slid down the pole like a fireman might, descending into the north station terminal. It looked much like the south and west apex stations with its bright lights, white walls, and blinking cameras. Lifting the dead man, I opened his eyelids and stood him in front of the scanner. Mahegan was shouting something at me through the glass. The hydraulics finally hissed, and the door opened. My team was prepared.

"You have maybe ten seconds," I said. "Get them away from here."

Mahegan was carrying Misha and Reagan like they were firewood. Hobart had Brad draped over his shoulder monkey-back as he jogged from the doors. Jeremy West, Matt Garrett, Blair Campbell, and Amanda Garrett were dragging Patch Owens and Zion Black, who were unconscious. Calles had managed to rally and move under her own accord.

"Go! Go! Go!" I shouted.

I inspected the pod, and other than random weapons and bags, there was nothing we needed. I followed my team into a large elevator that JD had found deep in the bowels of the hyperloop station.

We were all inside. The doors shut. JD, wounded though he was, used his bloody hand to press the button to go up. The gears engaged. The elevator lifted. The cable squealed under the weight. The ground shook with the pod snapping through steel plates at Mach one. When we were halfway up the elevator shaft, an enormous explosion thudded into the north apex station. There was heat below us. Heat above us. Flames cooked the metal elevator car.

The elevator stopped.

We were trapped inside a mountain as the explosion boiled through the compound. The flames receded as quickly as they had appeared.

Once we shook to a halt, I climbed the ladder on the elevator cabin wall and unscrewed the circular hatch. It squeaked on its hinges and rocks and dirt fell into the car. But it still opened. Dim light seeped in from above. The elevator shaft was still smoking from the explosion, gray wisps lifting upward like ascendant ghosts.

Van Dreeves and Mahegan climbed up after me, and I shined my flashlight on the granite walls of the shaft. The cable led another fifty meters up to a metal plate the shape and size of a sheet of plywood.

"I'll shimmy up this and figure a way out," Van Dreeves said.

"We've got rope," Mahegan said.

"Randy, you go up. Jake and I will feed everyone up. Let's get moving," I said.

"Roger," Van Dreeves said. He took the hundred-and-twenty-foot nylon rope and slung it across his torso. He proceeded to climb the steel cable pulling up with his hands and cinching with his feet. Pull. Cinch. Pull. Cinch. He did this until he got near the top and shouted.

"Cable frayed. We need to move fast!"

On cue, the elevator car shifted slightly. If we were fifty meters from the top and the shaft went two hundred meters deep into the mountain, the car would fall a hundred and fifty meters.

It rocked again.

"Cable's going out," Van Dreeves said. "There are climbing pegs on the side of the shaft."

Jake was lifting the team onto the top of the elevator car. The rock walls that had protected us from the blast might very well become our tomb if we didn't hurry. Van Dreeves adroitly maneuvered at the top of the shaft, swinging as if he was traversing monkey bars.

The car shifted again, this time tilting at a thirty-degree angle. We held on to one another with Misha, Brad, and Reagan clinging to me. Misha was hyperventilating still, but less so than in the pod. Amanda Garrett was kneeling next to her giving her what oxygen remained in her aid bag. Matt Garrett was tending to JD, Patch Owens, and Zion Black, all of whom were not faring well from injuries and lack of oxygen. Jeremy West was the last to climb on top.

"This is a soup sandwich, General," he said.

Van Dreeves shouted, "Rope coming down!"

He fed it down until Mahegan grabbed it. He quickly tied slipknots in it and ran rappel seats around those who were not wearing them. From his rucksack he retrieved snap hooks and began clicking those onto the rappel seats.

"Brad, Reagan, you two first. Get up there and see how you can help Randy," Mahegan said, snapping them into the rope. "Amanda, you take Misha with you next."

Like we were doing a SPIES extraction beneath a helicopter, they were snapped into the knots Mahegan had tied in the rope and somehow were ascending rapidly to the top.

After a long minute, the rope fed back down. The elevator car tilted another ten degrees. The cable was unwinding and going to snap momentarily. We had readied JD, Patch Owens, and Blair Campbell. Up they went. Then Sergeant Calles lashed in with Zion Black for the next lift. We snapped them in, and the rope moved faster this time, with more people to pull on the rope using the pulley Van Dreeves had found at the top of the elevator shaft. Then went Matt and Jeremy West.

Remaining on the top of the creaking elevator car were me, Mahegan, and Hobart. We had been warriors together for many years.

Just before the elevator car snapped away from the cable, I said, "Men, we did some good."

THE SHOUTS OF MY children and team echoed down the cavernous elevator shaft as we tumbled.

Because the fraying cable had tilted the car and the width of the shaft was marginally broader than the width of the elevator, the car was, for the moment, wedged precariously beneath the north and south walls of the shaft. A square peg and in a square hole, but tilted. The top lip of the elevator was squealing as it strained against the granite wall. It wouldn't hold out much longer.

Hobart and Mahegan had snapped their rappel seats into U-bolts on top of the elevator car, which had prevented them from sliding into the shaft below. They needed to unsnap and get to the ladder on the walls of the shaft before the car rocketed to the bottom. I had fallen against the wall and found one of the metal rungs that Van Dreeves had mentioned. Because the car had fallen some distance before stopping, the rope dangled teasingly out of reach.

"Everybody okay?" I asked

"Roger," Mahegan and Hobart said in unison.

"Okay, follow me," I said.

I began climbing the metal rungs, which were spaced far enough apart to make the climb far more challenging than I believed it would be. I loosened my rappel seat and fed enough rope to be able to reach up, snap into the next rung, stand on my toes, and leap up to grab the rung. There must have been no scientific design when the engineer had developed the plan for this elevator shaft. The rungs were about eight feet apart. Maybe they had run out or most likely thought that no one would ever need them. Maybe it was a government regulation that they place the rungs in the shaft and Drewson's team had done the bare minimum.

I was wondering where Drewson might have gone when a banshee wail of metal against rock filled my ears. The elevator car had finally given way. Mahegan had been the last and he was dangling by one arm from a metal rung as the elevator careened to the bottom of the shaft some quarter mile below.

The mangling of metal and rock was deafening. Cables whipsawed though the shaft like angry snakes, barely missing us. Dust and debris billowed up in a cloud resembling a small nuclear burst.

"All okay?" I shouted below.

"Hobart up."

"Mahegan up."

Mahegan had steadied himself and had gotten into the rhythm of snapping, climbing, unsnapping, and snapping again. He was six and a half feet tall, so the going was a tad easier on him than on Hobart and me.

As we got close to the top, Van Dreeves had managed to move the rope to our side of the shaft as a precaution.

"Looking good, boss," he said as I slid onto the top of the foyer where the elevator would have opened. I turned around and helped Hobart up and then Mahegan.

We were back inside of Drewson's house at the eastern end. Perhaps this was the path Drewson had taken out. There were two tunnels, one to the east and one to the west. There was no way of telling. Smoke hung in the air from the explosion below. One of the walls was charred. Debris littered the floor.

All that mattered for the moment was that my children and team were still alive. Misha was huddled over her MacBook with Brad and Reagan by the fireplace, while Amanda Garrett continued to talk to each of them, making sure they were okay. Calles was sitting against the wall, arms around her legs, forehead against her knees. Patch Owens and Zion Black were lying next to them, semiconscious, and Amanda had given them each an IV bag of fluids. My team never rested. They took care of one another and knew what to do without being told.

It made me proud.

I checked on them and knelt in front of my kids, who nodded that they were okay. Then I shifted toward Misha, who was trembling and focused, perhaps doing what made her feel best, getting lost in her computer propped on her lap. I handed her the flash drive from my boot and said, "Tell me what's on this, please."

Misha looked up, startled. Perhaps still in shock, she said nothing. Ever retreating inward during trauma, her savant mind cycling through thousands of outcome permutations as a method to shield her from the external chaos. After a moment of staring at my hand, she grabbed the flash drive and plugged it into the USB port and then retreated back into her world.

Jeremy West was standing near the door that exited to the garage, weapon in hand prepared to engage if necessary. I walked over to Van Dreeves, Mahegan, and Hobart, who were standing guard.

"Good job, Randy," I said.

His face was drawn, realizing how close we had come to perishing in the shaft.

"This pulley was a lifesaver," he said. He had threaded the rope through a basic block and winch pulley built into the interior of the shaft, perhaps as a safety feature, perhaps as a leftover from the mine shaft days. Regardless, it was a blessing and had saved our lives.

"Where's Drewson?" I asked.

"No clue, boss," Van Dreeves said. "But knowing this guy like we do now, we should probably un-ass the AO."

Van Dreeves' euphemism for leaving the area of operations, or AO, quickly was aptly put as sniper fire hit the window in the main foyer.

"What about Maximillian and the south apex team?"

Hobart was staring at the control panel that showed the south apex foyer.

"I don't see anyone alive there," he said. "Don't know if they're good guys or bad guys, but a lot of dead bodies."

"In the garage are two armored SUVs," West said. He had moved from the foyer to the garage. "Keys in them."

"Load up," I said. "We will establish comms on the way. We leave no one behind."

The rifle fire became more sustained as we hustled to move everyone to the SUVs. Jake and Hobart had Patch Owens, O'Malley, Blair Campbell, Matt Garrett, and Amanda, who tended to the wounded JD. I rode shotgun while Van Dreeves drove with Brad, Reagan, Misha, Zion Black, Calles, and West in the back. We had lost many of the weapons we had started with but still maintained a few pistols and long rifles.

Mahegan and Van Dreeves looked at each other as the garage's retracting steel plates opened. The night sky poured in. Orange tracers rained down on the compound. Mahegan went first and bolted the SUV from the garage. Van Dreeves followed. Soon the orange tracers arced from the house toward the vehicles.

We were without any support. No unmanned aerial vehicles for counterattack or intelligence. No air support to suppress the enemy fire. No artillery to call in to mask our movement. Our two SUVs, easily identifiable by whoever was trying to kill us, snaked along icy roads built for ambushes. Rock walls reached to the sky like jagged spires on the left. Sheer cliffs fell away into infinity on the right. Pounding enfilade fire raked and sparked along the egress route. Rocket-propelled grenades smoked and exploded all around us.

Slow is smooth; smooth is fast.

We teach that refrain to soldiers stacking with backs against the wall about to enter a building and clear the first of many rooms. We were in that zone.

Slow is smooth; smooth is fast.

We were all silent and focused. Scanning. Bracing for impact.

The more we drove, though, the less accurate the fire became. The roads were slippery with black ice, and twice we careened into the rock wall. Mahegan and Van Dreeves had both taken tactical driving courses, and their skills were being put through the PhD level exam tonight.

After thirty minutes of silent driving and maneuvering, we approached a tunnel and reached a sign that read: LEAVING DREWSON ENTERPRISES PROPERTY. ENTERING FREMONT COUNTY, WYOMING.

Mahegan pulled the lead vehicle into the tunnel that bore through a mountain pass just beyond Drewson's property. Van Dreeves stopped a safe distance behind. I met Mahegan in the middle. Hobart and Van Dreeves joined us. Then West and Matt Garrett appeared. Then O'Malley and Owens.

"Established comms with Maximillian," Mahegan said. "He's wounded. They are meeting us here in the next hour."

"Okay. How are our casualties?" I asked. People first, always.

"Amanda's done some good work on Patch and Zion," Matt said. "Misha's still a little freaked out."

"Is she scared or is she mad at herself for believing in Drewson?" I asked.

"Probably the latter, knowing her," Mahegan said.

"Fuel status?" I asked.

"Half tank in each. About twenty miles from Jackson Hole Airport."

"Let's get somewhere safe, regroup, and figure out a plan," I said.

"Get us to Jackson and I can have a plane meet us there," West said.

"Okay, and then we go to where we do best," I said. "My farm in North Carolina. Plenty of weapons and ammo. Chow. You name it."

In the car's headlights, Misha's long shadow approached us like an apparition in the dark, cold tunnel. Her blond hair was matted and disheveled. Her desensitizing glasses were cracked and askew on her face. Her mouth contorted downward, as if angry, which she very well might have been.

"Misha?" I asked.

Everyone turned and watched as she approached us.

She pulled from her rucksack the MacBook with the flash drive stuck in it and showed it to us, the blue light brighter in the black tunnel and, importantly, destroying our natural night vision.

She spoke clearly and fluently. There was no stutter in her words, as if the trauma of the last several hours had shocked her vagus nerve and shook her for a moment off the autism spectrum.

"I found the real Phalanx Code. It's the original version of your grandfather's will."

HEADLIGHTS APPROACHED FROM THE south. The proverbial light at the end of the tunnel coming at us from the direction we had entered. We were standing in a nontactical gaggle, our eyes whited out from staring at Misha's screen.

"The blockchain shows I am the first . . . to see it since your grandfather had it built," Misha said. Her words were clear, but her speech was beginning to stutter again.

"Just a second, Misha," I said, wanting to engage on the import of her discovery, but with more pressing tactical concerns.

Turning to Mahegan, I asked, "Is this Maximillian?"

"Standby," he said.

Erring on the side of caution, I said, "Everyone back into the cars. Now. Move."

Mahegan, Van Dreeves, Hobart, Matt Garrett, and I ushered everyone back into the vehicles. Blair, Brad, Reagan, Misha, Amanda, Calles scrambled into the SUVs, looking over their shoulders at the headlights racing toward us. Mahegan stepped back and began speaking into his throat microphone as he walked with Matt to the opposite side of the SUV I had been riding in. Hobart, Van Dreeves, and I assumed tactical positions on the other side.

The approaching vehicle fishtailed and spun on black ice as it caromed into the side of the tunnel and rolled, coming to a stop on its roof, spinning like a slow top. We raced to the smoking car, its engine ticking like a bomb. The radiator hissed. The air filled with the acrid smell of radiator fluid and burning rubber. Inside were four of Maximillian's team members, all injured, some perhaps dead. Same uniforms. Same weapons. Some I thought I recognized, but I couldn't be sure with all the blood. I didn't see Maximillian, however, and tried to radio Barbara Ruddy but got no reception inside the tunnel.

Amanda leaped from my SUV filled with Misha and my children. She began pulling bodies from the crash. With the help of Matt Garrett, Mahegan lifted the rear of the mangled car and slid three wounded men into the opposite lane to get them away from the smoking sedan. Jake and Matt loaded them into the hatch of my SUV as Amanda tended the injured men. As I jogged around the nose of the crumpled hood, the driver was crawling from the shattered windshield. Blood coursed down his face and over his scalp as he crawled onto the pavement where I knelt next to him.

"Where's Maximillian?" I asked.

"He's coming," he said. "Need to move."

I lifted him, cradling him in my arms, then walked the thirty meters to Mahegan's lead SUV where I slid him into the open rear hatch. Amanda stayed with the three wounded in our Defender while Matt tended to the driver I had just placed in the lead vehicle. A new set of distant headlights pierced the night to our south.

"Let's load up and get moving," I said. I didn't know if the approaching vehicle was Maximillian or Drewson's commandos. I decided to getting a rolling start instead of defending from the tunnel.

"Getting kind of sporty, boss," Van Dreeves said.

"Let's go," I said, pressing the detent button on my throat microphone.

Van Dreeves cranked the vehicle and started driving. Mahegan was already rolling ahead of us.

Misha leaned forward between the seats and started speaking rapidly before I told her to put her seat belt on. Van Dreeves gunned the SUV forward, following Mahegan.

"They're in this . . . together," Misha said. "Drewson. Blanc."

She handed me her MacBook, which had a message typed on the screen.

Drewson and Blanc. The Phalanx Code is a bogus program that both Blanc and Drewson created. What Ximena gave you is the truth. The Phalanx Code was a deception tactic to fool Evelyn and me as the Zebra team tried to break and maybe change Coop's will.

"Is Evelyn in on it?" I asked. I wasn't sure why that was my first question, but there it was.

"Not that . . . I can tell," she said. Less sure, but better than I expected.

"What's the real Phalanx Code say?"

We continued rocketing forward along the tunnel. She retrieved her MacBook and typed.

You own Phalanx. Your grandfather left it to you. The will is still being contested by your own father.

"I *own* Phalanx?" I asked.

Van Dreeves swerved as he looked over his shoulder driving ninety miles per hour.

"Say that again? You mean Sharpstone right?" I asked.

Frustrated, she grabbed her MacBook again and typed quickly.

Phalanx is worth $500 billion and you're the owner. Ximena's flash drive you gave me shows the will encrypted in blockchain. The will is the Phalanx Code. The Phalanx Code is the will. This blockchain was protected. The entire document was never read. The lawyer who was killed a week ago? Blanc did that. Your grandfather Coop was something of a techie for his generation and a successful investor. He gave seed capital to Blanc to start an intelligence *software system and a small private security company. That system became Phalanx and the security company became Sharpstone. He wanted you to have Phalanx and Sharpstone for your second career, but only after you finished the military. That's what the real Phalanx Code says. The other "codes" and letters are all part of a game Blanc and Drewson are playing. Upon your retirement, control shifts to you. You own Phalanx. If you're dead, then your children do. If they're dead, Blanc gets it all.*

I remembered Warden Smyth mentioning to me that Coop's lawyer had died. It had seemed inconsequential to me standing in his office just a few days ago, but now it was the primary clue in the entire mystery of the last week.

"Then why all the bullshit? Why not just kill me?"

Misha looked over her shoulder.

"The slayer rule. If he kills you, he loses it all," Misha said.

"Blanc and Drewson teamed up on this?" I asked.

"Yes," she replied.

I thought about the man in the lead vehicle and the three wounded in the back of our vehicle. The ones Blanc had added last minute to the team. Had he really checked them out thoroughly? Had we just now? Were they even Sharpstone employees?

"Sharpstone?"

Misha looked over her shoulder again and shook her head. "Sharpstone is . . . infiltrated."

"All this over a will?" I asked.

"Five hundred billion dollars is some serious coin, boss," Van Dreeves said.

"Amanda?" I said into my throat microphone.

A French voice spoke back to me as I heard a yelp from the rear.

"Too late, *monsieur.*"

Van Dreeves looked in the rearview mirror as three men came crawling over the back seat of the Defender, one wiping blood from his knife.

I rapid fired my pistol past Misha's head as I used my left arm to sweep her torso to the left, away from the arc of the knife. Misha screamed and put her hands over her ears. Brad, Reagan, and Blair dove to the floor-boards, though Blair came up firing with a pistol. Van Dreeves remained fixed on the road as Amanda, perhaps in her last act, shot two of the men in the back of the head.

"Insider threat!" I shouted, hoping Mahegan would hear me in the lead vehicle before it was too late. One of the men tumbled over Misha and slammed into Van Dreeves, causing him to swerve. He righted the runaway Defender and sped up to pull alongside Mahegan's vehicle. The injured driver we had placed in the hatch was crawling over the back seat, pistol in hand. The bulletproof windows prevented me from shooting him, but Matt Garrett intercepted him before he reached Mahegan.

Were these the equivalent of suicide bombers sent by Blanc to kill me, my children, and my team so he could own Phalanx outright and not have any threat to his empire? As all cowards do, they have others fight for them. Where were Blanc and Drewson? Why wouldn't they square off with me? What was Drewson's incentive from Blanc for helping kill me and my family? A promise to own a piece of Phalanx?

As we approached the tunnel's exit, two helicopters hovered in the distance. Rockets smoked toward us. Mahegan slammed on the brakes and fishtailed. Van Dreeves did the same. The mouth to the tunnel lit up like fireworks. Some of the rockets skipped on the pavement and ricocheted the full length out the south end. Boulders tumbled down to our front, blocking our exit.

Vehicles approached from the south. There was no escape.

"Dismount now," I directed over my throat microphone.

With the vehicles stopped, I led my children and Blair from the Defender. Brad and Reagan were in shock, speechless, doing exactly as told. Reagan held Misha close to her. Blair scanned with her pistol. I lifted Amanda Garrett from the back of the Defender. Calles was still in the back.

"I'm okay, General," she said.

"You're bleeding."

"He missed the big stuff," she said. "Plus, I blew two of their heads off."

That was good enough for me.

Zion Black, Patch Owens, and Sergeant Calles moved under their own power and grabbed weapons from our attackers. Even JD assumed a defensive position from the lead SUV. We joined Mahegan's team to the front. The Defenders formed a "V" and we gathered in the protective space in between. Brad, Reagan, and Misha in the middle. Machine-gun fire raked the bulletproof vehicles. Rockets exploded all around us.

We held our fire, unclear on the intent of the approaching vehicles or who was in them.

"Daddy," Reagan whispered. I felt her tugging at my back.

"Yes, baby," I said, eyes focused on the approaching vehicles.

"I think I'm hurt."

I snapped my head around and saw her holding her rib cage, blood oozing between her fingers.

This was not happening. Not my child.

I pulled up her shirt and saw a knife wound. The sweep had missed Misha but caught Reagan.

"Amanda?" I asked. "Can you take a look here?"

Doctor Amanda Garrett limped over to Reagan as she finished bandaging herself. She carried a small olive rucksack with a faint black cross on it. Bullets and rockets rained around us. I felt myself escape to a place I had never been. My mind disassociated from reality. I let out a primordial scream as headlights slammed into our SUV formation.

Then all hell broke loose as the mouth of the cave collapsed.

I KNELT NEXT TO my bleeding daughter. Her eyes were wide with fear. Her hair was matted against her forehead. She looked innocent and afraid.

"Am I going to die, Daddy?" she asked me.

"No, baby, you're going to be fine," I said. But I had no idea what the truth was. Amanda Garrett was moving her hands faster than a Vegas magician, ripping clothes, pressing ribs, sewing skin, clenching scissors in her teeth, all while she was severely wounded.

The one blessing of the collapsing tunnel was that the helicopter rocket fire no longer chewed at our meager defensive position, offering us minor respite. That sliver of fortune was entirely dwarfed by Reagan's predicament.

Amanda looked up at me with worried eyes.

"We need to get her somewhere fast, or we need to get her some blood. What's her blood type?"

"She's AB and so am I," Blair said.

"Okay, roll up your sleeve. I need to do this fast," Amanda said.

They went to work. I held Reagan's hand.

"I'm scared, Daddy. I don't want to die. Not yet, anyway."

"You're going to be fine, baby girl."

My insides were coming apart. I couldn't lose Reagan. I would stand in front of a hail of bullets to stop anyone from harming my children. Blanc and Drewson had teamed up to kill me and my kids.

"Two pints, three, okay. That's enough."

She checked the wound and hooked up an IV bag.

"I think I've got it. Blair, you're going to be lightheaded for a bit. Drink some Coke or something if we've got any. General, we need to get her stable. Any disruption can reopen the wound."

"Roger that."

"Hurts, Daddy," Reagan said.

I could tell she was both in shock and frightened. She used "Daddy" only when she reverted to the deep emotional bond that we held for each other. Otherwise, it was usually "Dad" or "hey you."

Mahegan, Hobart, and Van Dreeves came from the wreckage with Maximillian and two of the apparently actual Sharpstone employees. Maximillian was scarred and bleeding from his scalp.

"Blanc gave us traitors," Maximillian said.

I leveled my pistol at Maximillian. "Tell me something that will stop me from killing you right now."

"Oui. Je comprend."

He held up his right hand and showed me his inner wrist. Beneath the blood and scarring was a rhombus-shaped tattoo.

"In his later years, I was Coop's bodyguard. Why do you think I've been hanging around as old as I am. I have one job and that is to see that you get Phalanx. He made me promise."

"I don't have time to not trust you," I said.

"Your daughter?" he asked.

"Yes," I said, looking at a pale, weak-eyed Reagan. Brad was sitting close to her, holding her hand. They loved each other and had endured too many deployments together. While I had missed much of their childhood to serve our country, I knew that they had supported each other during my absence and their mother's illness. A famous Cherokee saying is that our life is but the mist of a buffalo's breath. Short and insignificant, evaporating quickly into the ether. But that one life was what we were offered, and I was defending it for my children and myself with everything I had. My children deserved the fullest lives I could provide for them.

My first task was to get Reagan to safety. Next was to kill Blanc and Drewson.

"Boss," Mahegan said. "Randy found explosives daisy-chained along the tunnel. I don't think we have much time. This was a baited ambush right at the edge of Drewson's property. Only way out is by land. If there is a way out."

Hobart shouted, "Got something!" I looked over and he had scaled the wall on the opposite side of the tunnel. We were in the northbound lane, and he had crossed into the southbound lane, ascending a small concrete staircase with a door.

"Let's go, team. Everybody grab a Dagger buddy and follow Joe Hobart. Jake, you take Misha. Randy, Amanda, and I will carry Reagan."

"Got a hammock right here, boss," Van Dreeves said. He laid a rectangular sleeping pad inside a mesh hammock and created a makeshift litter.

"Blair," Amanda said. "Come with us in case we need more blood."

"I'm with you," Blair said.

"My blood is AB, too," Calles said. "In case you need more."

"Stay close," I replied.

My team began moving out toward Hobart. Jake Mahegan was carrying Misha in his arms, cradling her gently with her face stuffed in his chest. Her thin arms were bundled up, hands clasped as if in prayer. Seeing Reagan wounded and the trauma from the attack in the back seat had fully overloaded Misha's senses.

Luckily, so far, Reagan was still lucid. Amanda held an IV bag above her as Van Dreeves and I carried her in the hammock, doing our best to not disturb Amanda's field-expedient suture work. Matt Garrett corralled JD, Maximillian and the other legit Sharpstone commandos, leading them along Hobart's path. Jeremy West pulled together Patch Owens, Zion Black, and Sergeant Calles, who had effortlessly meshed with the team. Maybe she would have made a good Ranger, after all.

We moved single file through the door that Hobart had wrenched open. It led to a musty concrete staircase. At the top of the steps, Hobart pushed open a metal plate hatch and began helping everyone up onto the rocky slope of the tunnel exterior.

We maneuvered Reagan's medical litter through the gap, everyone carefully passing her along as Amanda held the IV bag high and Blair remained close by. The cold wind blasting us in the face diminished as we descended into a rocky crevice to the side of the tunnel. We had everyone leave their phones and communications devices at the hatch with West.

As West was pulling Owens and Black through the hatch, the first of the explosions began. Loud and thunderous, the detonation cratered the south end of the tunnel. Once Black was out, West tossed the lot of the communications devices, save his own unused burner phone, into the tunnel, slammed the hatch shut, and slid a piece of rebar through the locking mechanism.

The remainder of the explosives detonated in rapid succession, causing the entire tunnel to fall in on itself. I imagined that the vehicles inside were crushed and the bodies of the Sharpstone traitors we had killed were entombed.

We snaked our way through a cavernous overhang that led through the opposite side of the ridge. We trudged along the frozen shale beneath the protective cover, shielded from view of Drewson's and Blanc's joint drone efforts to confirm the success of their mission. With that thought in mind, I told West what I wanted him to do, and he nodded.

Holding Reagan's hand, I gripped her tight and said, "We're going to be okay, baby girl."

"I know, Daddy. Thank you."

Beneath us was a valley with a road cutting through it. West came back alongside me and said, "That's Route 28. My guys have taken off from Jackson in an unmarked STOL that can land on the road. Link-up is in about two miles. Can Reagan make it?" STOL was military parlance for "short takeoff and landing." Most likely it was a Casa or Sherpa turboprop that could carry up to twenty personnel.

"I can make it," Reagan said.

My heart was bursting with fear and pride, but I didn't want to get ahead of ourselves.

"Can they have a medical team on board for Reagan and the others? My guys? The Sharpstone guys?"

"From what I understand, we're all your guys. But yes, I've already told them to bring all the docs and class-eight equipment they need." Class eight was the military logistics designation for medical supplies.

"Roger that," I said.

Once we emerged from the rocky overhang, we stayed low in a wadi. We had traveled maybe two miles and had about two hundred meters of open terrain to traverse before reaching the link-up point. The propellers from the STOL buzzed lightly as it cut through the quiet night air in the valley west of Drewson's compound.

"Now," I said. We all started jogging as best we could. I carried the front of Reagan's litter while Van Dreeves carried the rear. Amanda jogged alongside holding an IV bag above her torso and Blair, with Brad by her side, held on to the opposite side. We kept her steady given the relative unevenness of the terrain. Hobart popped onto the road first as the aircraft stopped and dropped its back ramp.

My charges entered the back of the airplane, and we hoisted Reagan up. Two men grabbed the litter and slid her onto a fixed litter that had been snapped into the side of the aircraft. They belted her in, careful to avoid the area where Amanda had performed her magic.

Mahegan, Hobart, and Van Dreeves counted heads, checked the exterior of the aircraft, and gave the load master a thumbs-up, whereupon the helmeted figure raised the ramp, and the pilots revved the turbines and released the brakes, shooting low into the sky.

The doctors gave Amanda a headlamp as they conferred with her. I stood close by but not too close to get in the way. Misha was across the way looking at Reagan, probably blaming herself. Brad and Blair were standing near Reagan's head. Because of the noise, I couldn't hear much of the conversation as one of the doctors began undressing the wound. He added some stitches and nodded at Blair.

They needed another unit of blood and Blair gladly complied. Calles stood by.

"That's really all she can give," Amanda said. "She's down four units."

"I'm good. Whatever she needs," Blair said.

"I'm ready," Calles said.

They tapped into Calles' arm and fed more blood to Reagan. The doctors did more work in the wound area, perhaps stitching something inside. They remained focused on Reagan with serious affect and concerned eyes.

Amanda said to me, "I did the best I could, General." She looked worried.

"You did great, Amanda."

She nodded, not convinced. Reagan reached for my hand and gripped it tight. The doctors continued to work. The airplane made mild banks to the left and right. Through the window I could see we were low in the valley, staying below radar and avoiding drones.

"We've got a facility near Craig, Colorado. Maybe another thirty minutes. I've called ahead and their medical team is ready. Best combat surgeons in the world," West said.

I nodded.

The doctors said, "One more bag."

Amanda said, "Blair can't risk it."

Calles held out her arm, clenching and unclenching her fist as she fed another pint of blood to my daughter.

Amanda went to the front of the airplane and found a six-pack of Cokes in a cooler.

"Drink up, you two," she said. "Otherwise, you'll pass out." Then she stuck a fresh IV bag in both to keep their electrolyte levels up.

The airplane touched down. The ramp dropped. A blacked-out ambulance parked ten meters behind the ramp. Two doctors came aboard. The two on the airplane and the two new ones unlatched Reagan's litter and put her in the ambulance. Amanda, Blair, Brad, and I jumped in an SUV that followed the ambulance, which pulled into an aircraft hangar that looked like an underground bunker or ammunition storage facility.

They unloaded Reagan and placed her on a surgical table. They sat Blair next to her just in case. A lab tech rolled a cooler full of blood units next to the table. The four doctors scrubbed and masked up.

Then they went to work on my beautiful daughter.

Night turned to morning. I didn't sleep. I stood alongside Reagan, holding her hand. Brad was on the other side. Blair stayed right there.

My team cycled through to check on her and me. Hobart, Van Dreeves, Mahegan, West, Owens, O'Malley, Matt Garrett, and of course, Amanda. Maximillian and his men, along with Owens and Black, had all received medical care from another medical team at this contracted black site that West in part managed. They all took turns sleeping, but everyone was restless.

A flurry of action picked up. Reagan's heart monitor raced and then settled. They had gone through another eight units of blood. It was obvious that Amanda, Blair, and Calles had saved Reagan's life. Was it possible to keep her with us, though? These doctors were giving it their all. I tried to remain focused and positive. The doctors took turns inspecting the wound. They grafted some veins from her leg and then came back to the wound, working their magic. Throughout the night they went back and forth between the leg and the abdomen.

Finally, one of the doctors turned to me and said, "Major artery was cut. We've had to reconstruct it. So far, so good. Not out of the woods but at the edge of the forest. Need to keep her from going back in."

Another hour. I never left Reagan's side. Held her hand. Kissed her forehead. Wept silently. How could I have done this to my children?

"General, our repairs are holding. We've done a major reconstruction. Right now, it's super fragile, but the last two hours have been encouraging. She's not bleeding and the bypass should keep her alive until it fully heals. She can't be moved for a few days, if not longer. Our team can watch her."

"I'm not leaving her," I said.

"Your call," he said.

"Thank you, Doctor. All of you. Thank you," I said.

I turned to Amanda, who was openly weeping and sobbing holding Blair, who was doing the same. Amanda's blond hair was entangled with Blair's brunette, both of their faces hidden in each other's shoulders.

"Oh my God I thought we lost her. Oh my God," Amanda said.

I hugged them both. Brad joined us.

The rest of my team came into the operating room to see what the commotion was. They all joined in. Grown men crying and hugging after the most important mission of our lives.

Saving each other.

30

I SPENT THE REST of the day by Reagan's side as she slept, listening to the wonderful music of her heart monitor as it played each joyous note with rhythmic regularity. I wiped her forehead every time I noticed a bead of sweat. I used a cloth with soap to clean the blood from her face. Slowly, color returned to her cheeks, though she was still pale.

The doctors routinely came into the unit to check on her. Their visits decreased as the day wore on. I took that as a good sign, and it was. Eventually, Brad, Blair, and Amanda came into the operating room on one of their many visits.

"General," Amanda said. "They want you in the ops room. The three of us will sit with Reagan."

She smiled sweetly at me, but I shook my head.

"Nothing more important than right here," I said.

"We know that, but there's something that is a close second they want to brief you on."

"Dad, come on. We've got her. She's in good hands," Brad said. He had three folded pieces of paper sticking from his jeans pocket. Songs he was writing, I imagined.

Blair stepped toward me and said, "General, the guys really want you in there. It's important."

"I'm not leaving Reagan," I said.

"We all get that, but they need a general in there to make some general-like decisions. Reagan's improving. The doctors briefed us several times. Every time they came in here to check, they came out and gave us the update. Each time, better. Your team needs you. I've watched you and how these people respond to you. It's really . . . unbelievable. You're here for Reagan and Brad. You'll be fifty feet away on the other side of the wall," Blair said.

I looked at the bloodstained towel in my hand and then at Reagan's face.

"Go, Dad. You get credit," Reagan said. She smiled weakly. Her mother's green eyes were half lidded. "We've got this."

I dropped my head, tears streaming down my face. My emotions were out of control. I was absolutely in no position to make decisions about whatever my team wanted to discuss with me.

Blair, Brad, and Amanda stood next to me and placed their hands on my slumping shoulders.

Amanda said, "You're here for Reagan. For all of us. You always have been. We're your family. We love you, Garrett. You're our north star, and we need your leadership. Please pull yourself together and go listen to the team. This is a black ops site monitoring some heavy-duty stuff."

Amanda knelt next to me and rested her head on my shoulder.

"We'll be right by her side," she said.

I realized I was still holding Reagan's hand when she squeezed it with more strength than I had felt from her since she was wounded.

"Go, Dad. I love you," she said. "I'll be here when you get back."

I squeezed her hand and said, "I love you, too."

My knees popped when I stood from the plastic chair. Amanda slid behind me and seamlessly took Reagan's hand from mine with no break in contact. Blair ushered me to the door as Brad pulled a chair next to the operating table, which had become Reagan's bed.

I walked into the Joint Operations Center, or JOC, of the contracted black site in northern Colorado. Standing before a series of monitors with maps and drone feeds were Mahegan, Hobart, Van Dreeves, West, JD, and Maximillian. Misha was seated in a wheelchair with some sofa cushions on either side of her. A tray table tilted to her front with a large keyboard. Her fingers worked furiously across the letters, numbers, and symbols. She was coding. What she was coding, I had no idea, but ones and zeroes clicked across the screen to her front in rapid-fire procession.

I saw Calles seated next to the door holding a rifle in her lap with one arm in a sling. She had a bandage on her neck and looked pale. She'd fought well.

"Good job out there, Ranger," I said.

She looked up, nodded, and said, "Sorry about the baton, but I had to keep my cover. Drewson paid me but I didn't know his plan."

"Roger that," I said and kept walking until I was standing next to Mahegan.

"Boss," Mahegan said. "We're glad Reagan's good to go."

"Roger that," Van Dreeves and Hobart said in unison. The rest chimed in also.

"Thanks for everyone's support," I said. "Team effort." Then to Mahegan, "She okay?" I tilted my chin toward Misha, who was beyond focused, tunneling into her algorithmic world.

"She's good," Mahegan said. He didn't elaborate.

"Okay, what do we have?" I asked.

"This is Black Site X-Ray," Hobart said. He typically briefed our operations, so it wasn't surprising to me that he took the lead. "Guys, no one is supposed to know this, but X-Ray has been monitoring Chinese activity around the nuclear bases. The mission here is to assess and report and then provide direct action if directed in the southwest up to Wyoming. Lots of chip plants. Lots of nukes. New Mexico. Arizona. Wyoming."

"Who's doing the directing?" I asked. I remembered Drewson's comment about the Chinese spying on the military installations in the Midwest and Southwest. His words about countering those efforts at the time seemed altruistic. Now, I knew they were lies and misdirection.

"Supposedly the CIA, but these guys are kind of on autopilot," Hobart said.

I nodded. "They must be talking to someone. STOL airplanes. Doctors. A full up JOC. Drones and satellites. I would imagine there's a healthy arms room somewhere nearby."

"All of that," Hobart said. "Let's just accept at face value that this is a highly compartmented operation with little oversight, if any. Wouldn't be the first time. Won't be the last time. Title Thirty-two. Title Twenty-eight. All that stuff factors in somehow, but this isn't the important part."

"Okay, accepted," I said. "What's the important part?"

I felt my emotions recede some, replaced by exhaustion primarily but also more objective thinking. Command and leadership are mostly about asking the right questions and then making the best decisions.

"The team here has signals intercept. They're tracking comms between Blanc and Drewson and also a company called Zeus Micron, which is nearby."

I became very interested, the emotions circling back with some adrenaline to keep me awake.

"Go ahead," I said. My jaw set, my eyes focused on the monitor that showed a drone circling around the collapsed tunnel we had escaped. I saw the route we had taken beneath the overhanging cliff, keeping us off the thermal radars that were surely watching.

"First, Drewson and Blanc think we're dead," Hobart said.

I nodded.

"And they're sending teams to confirm. Their engineer assessment thinks it will take two to three days to dig out the debris."

"And figure out that we're not dead," I said.

Hobart nodded. "Roger that."

"Where are they?"

"Blanc is in New York City. Drewson is on his way to Washington, D.C. to meet with the president. That's what we know," Hobart said.

"Where are they meeting?"

But I already knew.

"That's what Misha is doing. She's intercepting and deciphering their communications in real time. They're using encrypted text messaging. She was able to get inside their messaging system, maintain the access, and develop her own pattern-recognition algorithm so that she stays in front of the rapidly changing quantum security codes without being detected. If you ever want to see a severely pissed-off teenager with the capability of advanced revenge coding, just snap a picture of that," Hobart said.

I looked at Misha. She was a million percent focused, her hands clicking and typing trying to keep up with that brilliant mind of hers.

Misha snapped her head in my direction, directing a laser focus at me. Then she smiled showing off the pink rubber bands in her braces and nodded at her monitor.

General, their plan is to meet at the facility in Normandy. They're investing in something secretive there. The intel shows that they're hiding Chinese involvement in a chip plant that is connected to Sainte-Mère-Église, where Evelyn and Blanc are from. The Phalanx Code, like I said, is your grandfather's will, and in it is a document that makes two acres of French land become American territory owned by Coop. Just like the Normandy cemeteries are sovereign US soil. Blanc has built a headquarters there and used it to apply for and get approved a US chip-manufacturing permit. Drewson is his partner in the deal, but the property is yours.

"How is the American president involved, Misha?"

Unclear. She may believe Drewson's lies, or she may know they're lies and not care. Doesn't matter. The chip plant is a huge Chinese spy operation enabled by Blanc and Drewson, preventing the US from gaining control of its security apparatus while enabling its own. It's supposed to be a US–built chip plant so that there's no Chinese spyware on chips that are on EVERYTHING we use and do now. The only major chip manufacturers in the world are Taiwan Semiconductor, Samsung, and Intel. We have a single point of failure. China is inside all three followed only by Israel, Vietnam, and Malaysia. Intel is supposed to be building a new plant in Ohio that is sealed off from foreign influence, but construction delays have slowed that project considerably. Drewson and Blanc are skirting the intent of the law by using Coop's land. Your land. We need to stop that, find Blanc and Drewson, and then do whatever you do to those kinds of people.

"That's pretty much the mission, boss," Mahegan said. "Misha thinks she can remotely disable the machinery in the chip plant and just gum it up so bad that they never get to where they need to be. The real issue is to find Blanc and Drewson, together. It would make our job much easier."

"Resources?"

"Everything we need. What these guys are seeing here is China remotely intercepting nuclear communications, reverse engineering that, and designing a chip that provides them twenty-four/seven real time access to the most sensitive assets the United States has. Nukes. Jets. Aircraft carriers. They pass that to Drewson and Blanc, who make sure the spyware is in every chip they produce," Van Dreeves said. He was the logistics guy and had a handle on the equipment and transportation I would need. I took a full minute before speaking.

Misha typed:

One batch of the new chips has already shipped to Zeus Micron in Boulder, Colorado. They refurbish nuclear warheads and are upgrading the guidance systems with the new chips that Blanc delivered.

"How do we know this?" I asked.

I'm in Blanc's files. A shipping log shows they shipped a week ago. The CRM tool they use shows "delivered and installed." When I get into Zeus' records, they show "installed and prepping to move to Minot." When I get into the Air Force records at Minot Air Force Base, they show delivery of tomorrow. Obvs really bad if those warheads get put in a silo. Who knows what Blanc has done to the targeting.

"Is it really that easy to hack all these people?" I asked.

She quit typing for a brief moment and turned her head toward me, dropping her chin on her chest and leveling her eyes through the tri-colored glasses. It was a classic "you're kidding, right?" look. I questioned her no more.

"Okay, Randy and Joe, you two figure this side out. Wherever those warheads are, we need to stop them. I've got Blanc and Drewson," I said.

Naturally, they didn't like it one bit.

JAKE MAHEGAN, JEREMY WEST, and I took off at midnight in an unmarked MD-83 freighter operated by World Atlantic Airlines, which flew for all the three-letter agencies.

We left the rest of the team at Colorado Site X-Ray to disrupt the Zeus supply chain to Minot Air Force Base, to protect one another, and above all else, to be with Reagan as she healed. Not until Mahegan and I had eradicated the threat from Blanc and Drewson would my people be safe.

While there was strength in numbers, I was firm about not putting any more of my people at risk. The Zeus Micron mission seemed lower risk than the Blanc and Drewson mission, and therefore I assumed that task.

Importantly, by the time we took off, Reagan was alert and talkative, but still supine. The doctors assured me that she was on the path to recovery. They had clamped her femoral artery on one end and her external iliac artery as it entered her abdomen and conducted a peripheral arterial bypass. The Sharpstone traitor's knife entered her pelvic area and nicked the artery. Amanda had sewed it shut as best she could with what she had, assuredly saving her life. Blair's and Calles' blood transfusions kept my daughter alive, as well.

As we were flying no more than a quarter mile off the deck, I looked at Mahegan. He had ripped his cold weather gear off his torso and was pulling a T-shirt over his head. His barbed-wire tattoo that encircled his right biceps expanded as he maneuvered the shirt. It sat just below the tattooed word TEAMMATES as if he were protecting them with the barbed wire and his massive strength. On his left shoulder was a grotesque eight-inch scar beneath his black-and-gold Ranger tab tattoo.

I had selected Jake to accompany me on this mission for several reasons. First, he was the biggest guy we had other than Zion Black, who was injured, but recovering. Second, he grew up swimming the vicious currents of the Outer Banks, and we would be operating next to the Atlantic Ocean. Third, I trusted him as much as I did Hobart and Van Dreeves. And, finally, like me, he knew he was expendable. We all are expendable to a certain degree, but Mahegan and I were kindred spirits in that regard and always had been. I didn't want any harm to come to any of us, but he and I could in good conscience give everything we have to defend the people we love. As the Croatan saying went, it was better to die a warrior than grow old.

Teammates.

It was right there on his arm. It was all that mattered.

He lay on the floor of the airplane, rolled a couple of shirts beneath his head, closed his eyes, and fell asleep. The two most basic rules of being a Special Operations soldier were: sleep when you can and eat when you can.

I looked at West, whom I had selected for one reason: he could fly anything that had wings. He nodded at me and then leaned back against a pallet of ammunition and went to sleep.

I laid on the red webbing of the seats along the inside of the aircraft and fell asleep myself. My mind quickly spiraled into blackness.

I awoke hours later, and Mahegan was doing push-ups on the floor of the airplane while West watched and shook his head. "You army guys," he muttered.

I rolled off the webbing and did some stretching. Feeling guilty, I popped out a few push-ups and sit-ups, feeling more tired than I should have. The reality was that the continuous operations often precluded military or physical training and sometimes those skills atrophied.

"Thirty minutes, boss," Mahegan said. He sat with his arms wrapped around his knees as he rotated his neck.

West said, "Roger. Refuel, change crews, and keep going."

The pilots landed in the early morning hours at a private airfield at the old Dare County Bombing Range in the Outer Banks. Ten years ago, Mahegan had run into some ghost prisoners from Afghanistan there and gotten into a few fights over some found gold and devilish plans to attack the Hampton Roads military complex in Virginia. He had stopped all that from happening. We refueled there using some of X-Ray's classified fixed-based operator guys and kept going.

We stopped in Dare County because it gave us another chance to assess the intelligence. Misha confirmed that Drewson was meeting Blanc in France at the Carentan-les-Marais facility, where they would continue their collusion to steal my inheritance and use it to destroy all I had worked to protect over the years. The Global TransPark in Kinston, North Carolina, was most likely a sister facility for Blanc, who perhaps had used Drewson's US citizenship as a bargaining chip with the bureaucrats. Having two facilities would give them the flexibility to avoid the scrutiny of the US and French law enforcement communities as he built out his global security state, which included China, Russia, and Iran. They would all have visibility into Blanc's operations with little enforcement from the United States, ensuring they had access to the most sensitive technologies in the country.

A weaker America made for a stronger Phalanx Corporation.

West had coordinated with Maximillian and the Black Site X-Ray team to provide us two refueling locations, one in North Carolina and one in Norfolk County, England. Maximillian had assured us that his contact in England was not connected to the Sharpstone traitors and had the right kit we needed to execute our mission. As planned, the World Atlantic team shifted crews, all of whom were sworn to secrecy and none of whom said a word that would betray the plan.

We rested, exercised, and planned some more as we flew the remaining leg into England. Traveling nine time zones, we had already burned twenty-four hours of our predicted forty-eight strategic surprise window. Knowing Drewson, he would have teams working overtime to confirm our deaths in the tunnel. The pilots landed at Coltishall Airfield, a former World War II landing strip in moderate use today. We taxied into a nondescript hangar and parked next to a Casa 212 Aviocar aircraft that had its ramp down showing crates of ammo, guns, food, water, and other necessary supplies. Two freefall parachutes and two rucksacks were positioned next to the gear. Maximillian, West, and Van Dreeves had coordinated the logistics well, it seemed.

A tall man wearing an olive sweater and gray pants over Doc Martens boots introduced himself as James Bond, which I presumed wasn't his actual name, but matched the name we had been told to expect. Bond showed us to our gear and then to a small indoor shooting range at the opposite side of the hangar. This was obviously an SAS facility.

Mahegan and I inspected our gear and shot the weapons in the narrow shooting alley. An ultra-compact individual weapon (UCIW), which was a stubby version of the M4 used by the SAS, and SIG Sauer P226 for each of us with plenty of ammunition. We also had Blackhawk knives attached by Velcro to our outer tactical vests. We used Misha's satellite maps to rehearse several permutations of what we intended to do and what might happen, all the while using phones provided by West and the X-Ray team to speak with Misha, Hobart, and Van Dreeves, who were digging through intelligence on their side of the operation at Black Site X-Ray. Misha told me that Blanc had departed in his Dassault private jet from Teterboro, New Jersey, six hours ago and was headed "home" to the Normandy peninsula.

Misha's intercept of his call to Drewson had been a cryptic, *"Je vais voir ma mère. Elle aimerait vous voir."* I'm going to see my mother. She would love to see you.

Discussing Blanc's moves with Misha over the secure Black Site X-Ray communications suite using AtomBeam Quantum Protection made me want to contact Evelyn, but that, too, presented an assortment of problems that could ruin our strategic surprise.

Misha had done well, digging up open-source intelligence about the Normandy facility. The building was indeed a chip-manufacturing plant, and Blanc had used the land grant from France to my grandfather as his "headquarters," so that he could claim the facility was being constructed on US soil. Misha said that Drewson leveraged his relationship with the president to get the approvals needed for the deal. Meanwhile, Misha indicated that Blanc railroaded the permit process through the French system, promising high-paying jobs and an increased standard of living for those on the peninsula.

And thinking of mothers, the president was probably distraught over not hearing from Blair, but Blair, more than anyone, knew better than to communicate with her mother. Letting her think she was dead for a few days might be good penance for her, anyway, Misha had told me.

Misha's intelligence had tracked Drewson to the Normandy peninsula, following the tail number of his Hawker jet. Other than Maximillian's SAS friend who had coordinated the logistics here in Coltishall, we had stopped communication with anyone from Sharpstone headquarters, which was unfortunate because Barbara Ruddy could have been a big help with her analytical skills. While I trusted her, I didn't want to risk intercept of phone calls, emails, text messages, or radio transmissions. We had no way to determine who the other Sharpstone traitors might be. And we had to stay dead in the minds of Blanc and Drewson.

Misha had provided a satellite image of the facility near Sainte-Mère-Église, France, that I had seen when Evelyn had flown me to the peninsula. To the north were farms and homes with a small private jet runway just to the south, near where Utah Beach was located. The planes, I presumed, could land north to south or vice versa given the predominant winds on the peninsula.

The fresh satellite image showed a five-hundred-thousand-square-foot chip-manufacturing plant nearly completed, at least from the outside. We had some intelligence about the state of the interior based upon Misha's hack of the surrounding video systems at the facility and in nearby French towns. The cameras showed a steady stream of flatbed trucks carrying heavy material and dozens of cars arriving and departing every day. Workers. Likewise, the rail spur showed daily rail activity. Flight logs showed hourly deliveries of heavy equipment to the airfield in Caen, with trucks ferrying the machinery to the facility.

Once we departed Coltishall, we would be on listening silence, so it was important that we knew what each one of us was going to do. China's drive to insidiously plant spyware on every chip manufactured by the United States would undermine US national security beyond anyone's wildest imagination. Despite the weaponization of the American government bureaucracy, I would defend my country, the Constitution, and her people until my last breath. I equally cared about bringing Blanc and Drewson to justice. And, of course, I wanted personal vengeance for what they had done to Reagan.

Misha had provided satellite imagery of the collapsed tunnel. It appeared that Drewson was sparing no expense in digging out the rubble. Helicopters were buzzing above two cranes that were lifting boulders and moving them off the pile. They appeared to be making better progress than perhaps we had anticipated, which meant that we had no more than twenty-four hours before we lost the element of surprise.

At midnight, nearly twenty-four hours after escaping a baited ambush in a tunnel rigged with explosives, Mahegan and I were in the back of the Casa airplane, having packed our rucksacks and strapped into our parachutes. West climbed the aircraft to twenty thousand feet, flying over the English Channel, as our brethren from the Eighty-Second and 101st Airborne Divisions had done seventy years ago. The winds buffeted the airplane the entire flight. Rain lashed at the windscreen, but West bore through the night, as I knew he would. We stood when West began lowering the ramp. He talked into our headset.

"Heavy winds, guys. Out of the rain, but winds are twenty knots. Be careful."

"Roger, thanks, Jeremy," I said.

Mahegan nodded. We walked to the ramp, and I gave Mahegan the warrior hand to forearm shake and nodded. There wasn't anything to be said. We knew the mission.

The green light flickered, and we both stepped from the plane into the night, opening our parachutes immediately so that we could steer to our objectives. We had jumped several miles offset to the north to avoid the radar warnings and other tracking devices that Blanc and Drewson surely employed. Again, though, we assumed their defenses were down, believing that we were buried beneath the collapsed tunnel.

I watched Mahegan drift away to the south toward Omaha Beach as I steered to the west in the direction of Utah Beach. The cold air was rushing against my face, stinging my eyes despite the rubberized goggles I was wearing. The wind howled, causing my jumpsuit to flap loudly as I descended toward the northern edge near the facility. Before I landed, I flipped my night vision goggles down when I heard the whine of jet engines about a mile to my east. The Atlantic Ocean glimmered below me.

I toggled hard right until I missed my landing zone south of the town of Sainte-Mère-Église, close to Evelyn's home, and slammed hard into the bluff to the east. I slid down and tumbled onto the beach. The wind caught my parachute and began dragging me across the rocky shore into the crashing waves. I unsnapped my quick release assemblies to break free of the drag, but the parachute twisted around me when a wave pounded me into the rocks. I was nearly in a straitjacket until I was able to use my knife to slice my way out of the suffocating material.

"Not my best landing," I muttered to myself, realizing I was standing on Utah Beach where so many men perished saving the free world from Nazi Germany. I checked my gear and miraculously still had everything I needed: rifle, pistol, knife, and night vision goggles. Climbing over the rocks, I scaled the cliff using a ravine cut into the side that offered me an agreeable incline and sufficient hand- and footholds to go the fifty meters without falling back onto the rocky shoals.

Once on the plain, the wind howled, but the rain stayed out at sea. I leaned against a jagged rock and caught a breath on one knee. I trusted that Mahegan had a much better go of it than I had as I assessed the physical damage to my body. A few fractured ribs to go with those bruised by Blanc's stun gun. Twisted ankle. Bruised shoulder. Unbuckling the Future Assault Shell Technology Helmet, my finger pressed into a huge gash in the shell, which had probably saved my life. I stood and lifted my night vision goggles to my eyes.

A small jet wobbled as it landed in the wind shear on the adjacent runway to the chip-manufacturing plant. Its engines cycled hard in reverse and the airplane's running lights winked in the green haze of the night vision goggles. Despite my troubles, we were on time, just before 11:00 P.M. local time, the time the flight plan indicated Blanc's jet would touch down. The time was also important because Black Site X-Ray was to use its satellite capabilities to jam communications inside the facility at the top of the hour, freezing the cameras and perimeter sensing devices so that we could cut a hole in the fence and slide through unnoticed. It was scheduled to be a one-minute freeze, the kind of thing where the security guard uses his index finger to flick the screen, saying, "Come on."

Retrieving the bolt cutters, I waited until the second hand tripped my watch to 11:00 P.M. I then snipped a three-foot section of the fence, which I peeled back, slid through, and then replaced using metal twist ties to make the aberration invisible to the naked eye. As I was manipulating the ties, my ribs bit back at me with sharp pain. Definitely broken. In the distance, the chip plant shimmered with heat. At the far south end, the jet that landed pulled into yawning hangar doors, which began closing as soon as the tail cleared the opening.

There were two guards on the east end of the hangar, the direction from which Mahegan should be arriving. I moved along a drainage gulley that ran parallel to the runway and angled to the southwest. Following this terrain feature for about a quarter mile put me a hundred meters away from the side entrance, where a metal staircase switched back and forth the entire five stories of the facility.

Misha had found a blueprint that Blanc had submitted for approval to the appropriate French mayors and prefectures. The Phalanx construction permit application, the *demande de permis de construire,* was sufficiently vague with primarily exterior dimensions, size of the slab, drainage areas, electric and plumbing requirements, dimensions of the private airfield, and a host of other technical construction data. Importantly, it was scheduled to create five hundred jobs, which was most likely what got this behemoth passed on what once was considered sacred ground. The application had been submitted shortly after Coop passed away.

Regardless, based upon what our review of the blueprints showed, we were targeting a large conference room on the top floor that connected the runway hangar and the factory.

The private jet passenger airfield next to the manufacturing facility made sense provided these were true and accurate drawings. The Chinese, Iranian, North Korean, and Russian intelligence operatives could come in unnoticed and ensure that they were inputting the requisite software and codes into the chips that would be shipped all over the world as US-compliant chips. Blanc could fly whatever he wanted from his Normandy semiconductor plant into his Kinston, North Carolina, free trade zone. Then he could distribute the semiconductors to his Department of

Defense customers, who would believe they were receiving pure, made-in-the-USA chips for installment on the most sensitive military technologies. Blanc and Drewson themselves would want to hide within the secure confines of the facility, perhaps the house across the airfield with the wood-burning fireplace.

I stared at my target, the metal staircase and the guard standing on the top landing. A similar staircase was on Mahegan's side of the building. The Black Site X-Ray satellites were to warn us of any rooftop snipers or guards, and for the moment there were just the two guards, one on each landing. Any deviation and we would be getting a call from Colorado, but so far, we'd had no break of the listening silence. I trained my goggles on the open construction areas, noticing stacks of lumber and plates of steel next to dozens of pallets of drywall throughout the bays. High-tech machinery was hidden in wooden crates as far as the eye could see. The construction crane swiveled and turned, bright lights highlighting the work below.

I processed what I was seeing as we waited until midnight, which was the coordinated time for Mahegan and I to simultaneously approach the opposing stairwells and disable the guards.

Lots of things happened at the top or bottom of the hour, such as shift changes, conference calls, and meetings, which we were counting on. Dozens of cars were coming and going, workers pulling the graveyard shift from midnight to 8:00 A.M. Renaults, Peugeots, and Citroëns funneled in and funneled out. This was a serious effort if Blanc and Drewson were running three shifts. A light flicked on in the transition area of the building. My instinct was that whoever had landed was now upstairs, presumably Blanc and Drewson.

I looked to my far right and the two-story farmhouse had smoke curling from the chimney. I wondered if that was where Blanc and Drewson would be meeting. Or would they be in the business area that we were targeting? To our knowledge, no one had crossed the airfield to the house.

The guard at the top of the landing looked familiar. He was one of the large men from the video that Misha had shown me, which told me that Mahegan would have similar resistance on his side of the complex and that there would be at least two more inside the building.

At midnight, we had coordinated another camera and sensor freeze from the Black Site X-Ray satellite, this time for five minutes, giving us time to approach, ascend, and enter the building. About a minute before midnight, the guard stepped inside the hallway.

Top of the hour. Bottom of the hour. Things always happened.

As the clock read midnight, I stayed low and jogged with a limp to the stairwell, rapidly climbing without slowing down. My feet were like pillows on the grated metal steps. Using my hands on the rails to lighten my footfalls, I was standing outside the exit door, which had a vertical rectangular wire mesh window, like you might see at an elementary school.

As I tested the door to the interior, it opened. I used my knife to jab the guard in the neck as I covered his mouth. He was a big man and fought my grip, but I was filled with rage. Whoever got in my way would be an unfortunate pawn taken off the board. Blanc and Drewson would pay for harming my daughter, and I would fight to my last breath seeking vengeance. He threw a couple of elbows into my bruised and broken ribs, but he weakened quickly as he bled out. Holding the knife in place as blood oozed across my tactical gloves, I dragged the body to the landing and laid him there. Beyond the man dying at my feet, I assumed I was undetected, and that we had the element of strategic surprise, the rumors of our deaths being slightly exaggerated and still working to our advantage.

The wind howled. Metal banged on metal. The crane swung as it lifted heavy crates. The lock clicked open, and I pulled the door partially ajar, sliding my body through the gap as quietly as possible. The hallway reeked of new paint, wood, and drywall. All of this was a work in progress.

Men were talking loudly in an open door room near the middle of the hall, which was a long, straight, and brightly lit corridor. Mahegan appeared at the opposite end, as if we were dueling from fifty meters away. I imagined he had an encounter similar to mine. He stood there in all his bulk looking like the monster that Misha believed him to be. His face was painted black. His hands flexed in and out like two beating hearts. His eyes were focused on victory.

I lifted my rifle and began moving toward the conference room. Mahegan did the same. We braced with our backs to the conference room and listened to the conversation.

"Why on earth did you put me in the Hôtel du Palais, Aurelius? It was dreadful," Evelyn said.

"Drewson here did that. Quit stalling, Evelyn. Modify the code. Now," Blanc demanded.

"I'll do no such thing," Evelyn sniffed. "Garrett gets Phalanx and Sharpstone. It's as simple as that. Most important, it is what your father wanted."

"It is *my* company. I built it! All of it." His voice rose and he was angry.

"You can't change your father's will, Aurelius. The code is the code. He had it written in blockchain, being the techie that he turned out to be."

"You're the greatest cryptologist in the world. You can fix it for me."

"I'll do no such thing. Misha has it secured in a crypto vault. I couldn't change it if I wanted to."

A hand slammed down on a table or a wall.

"Fix it now!"

"No. The only way you could get the entire company would be to kill Garrett Sinclair, and even you aren't that depraved."

There was a long moment of silence. I looked at Mahegan across the glassed doors. We locked eyes. I shook my head slowly as if to say, "No, not yet."

"Tell me you didn't kill Garrett Sinclair," Evelyn said.

"It was a terrible accident. You must believe me when I tell you that I didn't mean to, Evelyn," Blanc said. "Mitch here can confirm that, can't you?"

"Coop left the company to Garrett, to inherit his fifty-one percent when he retired. And you've built this . . . this monstrosity on Coop's land. Garrett's land. France's gift to America as a thank-you for saving our country. And now you've killed him?"

"Well, that's irrelevant now," Drewson said. "As I get Sinclair's forty-nine percent."

"Shut up, Mitch. I didn't kill Sinclair. There was an accident, but it appears that he is dead."

"You can't be serious!" Evelyn spat.

Neither man said anything.

"Unbelievable. Well, then, his children will inherit all of this. Phalanx. Sharpstone. Whatever it is that you're doing here. Everything. From what I understand Reagan is quite intelligent and enterprising," she said.

There was another long pause.

"Oh no. No," Evelyn said. "You killed his children, too?"

"The accident killed his entire team," Drewson said. "Including Brad and Reagan. Very sad. They're exhuming the bodies as we speak."

"You bastard!" Evelyn spat.

Blanc chuckled. "Yeah, you got the bastard part right." After a pause, he shouted, "Now fix the code!"

"You had Drewson do this so that you could avoid the slayer rule? I noticed you recorded that call with this imbecile. That's why. So you had proof you were helping Garrett. Showing Drewson as a competitor helped you portray him as someone to whom you aren't closely tied. Unbelievable. I thought better of you, Aurelius." Evelyn paused and said, "And now that I know this, you'll have to kill me. I really did think better of you."

"You were wrong to do so," Blanc said.

A phone rang inside the conference room. Drewson answered.

"That's not possible," he said. "Keep looking!"

"What?" Blanc asked.

"The excavation team found a bag of cell phones by the exit," Blanc said, breathlessly. "And except for our guys, no bodies."

I NODDED AT MAHEGAN, and we spun into the conference room to find Blanc with a pistol aimed at Evelyn.

There was a MacBook open on the conference room table. The large monitor on the wall showed a black screen with a series of commands beneath a phrase.

The Phalanx Code.

"Fix it now!" Blanc shouted before he had noticed us.

She was standing, hands loosely bound to her front so that she could work the keyboard.

"Drop the pistol, Blanc," I said, but I was focused on the left corner. Mahegan had the right corner. We had entered the room low using a standard battle drill with sectors of fire, executing a "friend or foe" drill knowing that there would be more security inside the conference room. It was a good thing we did.

Stepping from the corner was the tall woman named Cyrilla that Misha had shown me in the video and who I had seen on Blanc's New York City rooftop. She was holding a French assault rifle at eye level. I didn't expect her to hesitate, which she didn't. The rifle spat automatic fire, which stitched the door above us as we dove. Another guard appeared from the opposite corner, and we were caught in an ambush. Because we had come in low and focused on the corners, our first shots were at the guards, who were wearing body armor. I emptied a magazine on Cyrilla, and it sounded like Mahegan did the same on her counterpart in the opposite corner. In a fluid movement I dropped the empty magazine on the floor and snapped another fully loaded one into place. Neither Cyrilla nor the other sentry were moving, so I shifted my focus to Blanc and Drewson.

Blanc was slack-jawed and wide-eyed, motionless, as if in shock. Drewson, who had no weapon, lunged to the floor. Evelyn used the back of her bound hands and this moment of chaos to slap Blanc's pistol away from her face. Still, he regained his composure and moved behind Evelyn, aiming the pistol now at us. Blanc began backing away with Evelyn, snapping rounds in our direction. Mahegan fired on Drewson as the billionaire went for the guard's gun nearest him, causing Drewson to scramble in the opposite direction.

As we clambered to our feet, Blanc hauled Evelyn through an exit, followed by Drewson, whom I tackled as his leg got caught in the door. Mahegan was trying to get past us, but it was impossible. I flipped open the bloody Blackhawk knife from my outer tactical vest and stabbed the tip into the side of Drewson's neck much as I had just done to the guard on the landing. The blood spray convinced me that I had severed the carotid artery and I wasted no more time on him.

I then ran down the steps with Jake Mahegan behind me. Blanc had locked the metal door to the chip plant behind him. Through the large Plexiglas window I could see he was holding Evelyn against his body as he backed into the center of the factory, half of which was operational. There were dozens of large silver machines the size of shipping containers with complex wiring and tubing, glassed-in bubbles, and high-velocity water nozzles. Fifty or so machinists and scientists were operating the machines, some holding clipboards, others inspecting the gear. Above them were large vats of solvents, fifty-gallon drums of chemicals, and other liquids with FLAMMABLE written in red letters on the sides.

The door was locked. Mahegan put a boot through the weaker wooden doorjamb, once, twice, and it buckled and splintered a third time before spinning open. We pushed through as Blanc fired his pistol at us as we spilled onto the factory floor. The sparking bullets reminded me of the many highly combustible materials mixed in with the machinery, which was operating at high temperatures.

Some of the employees dove to the concrete flooring while others were oblivious to the gunshots, which could have sounded like a hammer or piston on one of the shaper, grinder, or prober machines. Mahegan was taking aim on Blanc, but there was no shot without endangering Evelyn. Blanc snapped off a few more rounds, each one sparking until finally a blue flame ran along a set of piping above us and enveloped one of the wafer dicing machines. Because the solvents were pyrophoric, once they mixed with oxygen, the chain reaction of fires leaped from one machine to the next.

Soon, a ring of fire enveloped us as Blanc dragged Evelyn through a door that led to the unfinished part of the building. Opening the door and allowing the howling wind into the manufacturing area spread the fire to the point that everything was ablaze. The employees were trapped inside the circle of fire while Mahegan and I had an exit back into the transition area and the conference room. Smoke billowed. The chemicals were so thick, it was difficult to breathe.

"Let's go," I said to Mahegan as I donned a protective mask from my small rucksack.

Mahegan did the same as we waded into the group of huddled employees and began directing them into the metal staircase beyond the double doors and into the airplane hangar. Some followed under their own power, while others were already unconscious from the fumes and needed to be carried. We made several trips, but the smoke became so thick, by the third venture into the chaos I couldn't see Mahegan anymore. I frantically searched through the chemical fog until I tripped over two people crawling to stay low. I helped them to the hangar and went back in for Mahegan but couldn't find him. My mask was melting from the heat, but I made one more trip into the inferno, bringing with me two women who were screaming because their lab coats were on fire. They had been hugging each other in terror as they rolled on the floor trying to extinguish the flames, not realizing the floor was a blue flame of combusted solvents. My gloves and mask were smoking and unusable. When I removed my protective mask, the air smelled of burnt flesh and hair.

In the hangar, I bent over and took several deep breaths, then elevated and counted twenty-eight people either unconscious or milling around aimlessly.

None were Jake Mahegan.

Some were burned beyond recognition but still alive and wailing at the top of their scorched lungs.

A man ran into the hangar shouting something unintelligible. I grabbed him by his lab coat and said, *"Appellez les ambulances et médecins!"* Call the ambulances and doctors!

"Oui! Oui!" he said. Grasping his face in his hands, he said, *"Je suis le contremaître."* I am the foreman.

I looked frantically for Mahegan. The entire facility was an inferno now and the able-bodied employees were dragging the burn victims from the hangar onto the taxiway as police and ambulances began to arrive. Standing on the apron of the airfield, I watched the four-story semiconductor facility fold in on itself and collapse as the fire engulfed everything.

I walked the line of incapacitated bodies, some covered with sheets, looking for Jake and praying he had found a way to survive. Back and forth. No one was his size. I didn't see him beneath any of the sheets. I began shouting, *"Le grand homme?! Le grand homme?!"*

No one had seen the big man. The fire spat up a mushroom cloud like a nuclear explosion and in my fog of a mind I wondered if it was Jake's spirit.

Across the runway at the two-story farmhouse, Blanc was limping next to a four-door pickup truck after shutting the rear driver's-side door. I darted across the asphalt airfield, sprinting as fast as I could. At the last moment, I dove into the open bed of the truck. He peeled out, perhaps not realizing I was an unwelcome passenger.

I stayed low in the truck bed as he barreled along narrow, winding roads. The first drops of rain began to fall, and I had lost all communications. Everything except my outer tactical vest had either fallen off my gear or melted in the melee. I slid to the back of the cab and risked a peek into the vehicle. Inside were Blanc, who was driving, and Evelyn, who was in the back with her wrists and ankles bound with rope.

He swerved hard and I slid into the side of the pickup with a loud thud. The wind was still screaming across the plain and intensified as Blanc dipped into the low ground spanning the Carentan canals and then rose onto the coastal road high above the Atlantic Ocean. I saw a sign for Grandcamp-Maisy slip by as the rain began lashing down in sheets.

Police cars and ambulances raced toward the fire at the semiconductor plant and had blocked off the major arteries so the medical personnel could get to the mass casualty scene. Blanc kept turning left at police roadblocks until he passed through Grandcamp-Maisy, a coastal town overlooking the Atlantic Ocean. Flashing lights beckoned in the distance on this road, also, forcing Blanc to make another turn until he came to an abrupt, skidding halt, tossing me into the rails of the pickup bed.

I rolled over the edge on the passenger side, landing softly on the ground, as Blanc opened the back door behind the driver's seat and shouted, "Evelyn!" He dragged her onto the asphalt of what appeared to be a parking lot with painted lines, though in the rain it was difficult to tell. My ribs bit at me as I limped to the back of the truck. Red and blue lights flashed in the distance. Engines whined and roared.

To the left was a large ellipse and concrete bunker. Across the bed of the pickup, I could see Blanc dragging a bound Evelyn Champollion onto the grass. I retrieved my SIG Sauer from its holster on my hip and jogged into the wall of water raining down from the angry clouds rolling over the bluffs. I passed a marker dedicated to the Second Ranger Battalion and realized we were at Pointe du Hoc.

Blanc was standing on the bluff wrestling with Evelyn, who had managed to free her binds from her legs. She had dropped to the ground and was kicking him. Blanc lunged onto her and shouted, *"Réparez le code!"* Fix the code!

"Go to hell, Aurelius," Evelyn shouted. "You have destroyed everything that was given to you!"

"Phalanx is mine! I built it all! It is mine!"

I aimed but again couldn't shoot without endangering Evelyn, so I sprinted in their direction from about twenty meters away. Blanc stood her up and shoved a pistol under her chin, shouting, *"Réparez. Le. Code!"*

She was pressed against him, her wrists bound, as if in prayer. One of Blanc's arms was locked around her torso, the other had the gun cocked under her chin.

I angled my charge so that I would be tackling them away from the cliff, but best laid plans often unravel quickly. Blanc noticed me and spun toward the cliff, eliminating my angle. I collided with Blanc and Evelyn simultaneously. Evelyn slid toward the cliff, and I snagged the rope binding her wrists, pulling her onto the concrete slab that had at one time been a German pillbox. She rolled onto the cement as Blanc shot me. The bullet hit my left shoulder like a full swing from a Hank Aaron baseball bat. It spun me around to one knee.

Blanc, ever confident, walked up to where I was kneeling and reflexively holding my shoulder with my gun hand. Rain pelted down. My shoulder oozed blood. I locked eyes with my half uncle.

As he raised the pistol, an engine whined, sounding like a chain saw. A bright light shined on us. The rain poured down our faces. Blanc's eyelids were nearly shut, shielding his eyes from the rain and the spotlight.

His pistol continued to rise. I swept my right arm against his, backhanding him in the face. His pistol fired. His hand bucked with the recoil. The bullet whipped past my face and the flame from the barrel singed my right cheek. I reared back instinctively, leaving an opening for Blanc to land a roundhouse kick into my wounded shoulder and push me to the edge of the cliff.

I fell, my face slapping into the wet concrete, water sluicing onto me as it coursed over the bluff. I was wounded worse than I thought. My mind swooned, but I rose to one knee and cupped Blanc's ankle, picking it up and causing him to spin backward. He collapsed toward me, and I punched him with a weak right jab. I fumbled with my knife, opening the blade just in time to slice Blanc's face.

He rolled away and I followed, but we were out of land. The sensation of falling swirled in my mind as I thought of Reagan almost dying at the whims of this madman, related or not. I thought of Coop's prestige and wisdom in what he had done by helping a child he could hardly be there for and helping a grandson he nourished and raised. And I thought of Coop climbing in this very spot behind his commander, Lieutenant Colonel James Rudder. Their courage and bravery in the face of certain death.

There's no luck in living, Garrett.

Indeed.

Coop's gift would pass on to Reagan and Brad, and as I plummeted, that gave me great peace. I thought of Mahegan and Hobart and Van Dreeves and Sally McCool and all of the Dagger team.

And I thought of Melissa. As the Allman Brothers song went, "Lord, in his deepest dreams, the gypsy flies with Sweet Melissa . . ."

I was flying with my sweet Melissa after living a gypsy life of constant travel and deployments, but it had been a good life, filled with meaning and purpose. I had done the best I could.

And then I thought of nothing.

JAKE MAHEGAN

ALL OF US ON Dagger team believed the boss was immortal, that he would live forever, but I got there too late.

Better to die a warrior than grow old.

In the smoke and haze of the massive chemical fire near Sainte-Mère-Église, I had dragged about fifteen people out of the building and into the hangar. The general had done the same until we couldn't see each other. The smoke was toxic, and the heat was unbearable.

We had saved as many as we could. I didn't think we got them all, but there was no way to tell.

I went back in looking for the boss but got lost in the soup and exited through the wrong door. I had to wind my way around the back side of the hangar to get to where the bodies were. By that time, I saw the general across the runway diving into the back of a pickup truck and knew he had to be after Blanc. It was just like him to go headfirst into everything that mattered.

There were two motorcycles parked side by side in the employee parking lot. It took me a minute to find the keys on one of the survivors. He had removed his leather riding jacket to show tattoo sleeves running up both arms. He was wearing steel-toed riding boots that might have saved his life inside the factory, or at least his feet. Clearly in shock, he stared at me with confused eyes when I asked for his keys, which he handed to me.

I cranked the Yamaha MT-07 to full throttle and spun out of the parking lot, chasing the distant lights of the pickup truck, which quickly vanished.

The rain picked up and made it impossible to see anything except the flashing red and blue lights coming at me from the south. Police cars, ambulances, and fire trucks. I leaned over the handlebars and spun the throttle so that I was going over two hundred kilometers per hour, a hundred and twenty-five miles per hour, though a blockade almost made me ditch the bike.

I slowed, slid hard to the left, and kept turning left until I saw the crashing waves of the Atlantic Ocean. Having grown up on the water, I knew a northeast storm when I saw one, but had no idea what they were called over here in France. Storms were storms and the ocean was unpredictable.

I followed the coast road, the only way I could go without breaching police barricades. Slowing to pass through Grandcamp-Maisy, I saw taillights brake about a half mile up the coast. The headlights cut left toward the bluff. I raced the engine again. The streets were empty here as the weather and the hour, midnight, were not agreeable to anyone just ambling pointlessly about.

Having visited Pointe du Hoc on a terrain walk exercise with Dagger team in the past, I immediately recognized the pillboxes, artillery bunkers, and machine-gun nests that the Germans had emplaced. General Sinclair had taken us through the entire D-Day experience from the infantryman's viewpoint on the beach to the Rangers climbing the sheer cliffs of Pointe du Hoc to the paratroopers raining down on the Cotentin Peninsula of the Normandy region.

"Insurmountable odds," he had said as we stood on the beach some ten years before. We had taken an unusual detour from a mission we had conducted in Croatia to kill or capture an Al Qaeda member who had taken up residence in Dubrovnik. After a quicker-than-expected successful outcome, the boss had rerouted us to Normandy. Joe Hobart, Randy Van Dreeves, Sally McCool, Patch Owens, Sean O'Malley, and I had stood there on the beach as we climbed the rocky point using a rope ladder like the ones the Rangers had used until we had reached the casemate that the Germans built to defend against Allied invasion. We did all this at night and at high tide where the water was up to our waists. The boss never made anything easy, and we were glad for it. The practice was usually harder than the real mission. Climbing the ladder, I remembered steel pitons jutting from the face of the cliff, a guide for the rope ladder and something I'm sure the insurance company for the park required.

Of course, no one was supposed to be on this historic piece of property. Park officials back then, and I presumed today, were worried about beach erosion and damage to the famed decisive point of the battle to establish a lodgment on Omaha Beach. Millions of people reenacting the climb would chip away at the rock and shale until it didn't resemble the World War II obstacle that had to be surmounted.

But I did recognize everything tonight, including Evelyn Champollion crawling on her elbows, saying, "Help. Help. He's got Garrett."

I dumped the bike and, in stride, retrieved my knife, hurdling over an old chunk of concrete that was poking through the ground like modern art. Sliding on the wet dirt, I clasped Ms. Champollion's wrists and sliced through her ropes.

"Where's the general?" I shouted.

She came to one knee and pointed at the bluff.

"It's Blanc," she said.

The trail was maybe ten meters long before it disappeared. I saw two men locked in hand-to-hand combat against the black backdrop of a roiling ocean that reminded me of the graveyard of the Atlantic just off Hatteras Island. A pistol fired, and I drew my sidearm as I ran, but I couldn't shoot without knowing for certain which one was Blanc. The waves sprayed salt water into the air and the rain came down in buckets. My lungs burned from inhaling toxic chemicals, and I flexed every muscle in my body, shouting, "Valhalla!"

I was blind with rage. As I approached, the general fell over the cliff, pulling with him Blanc, whose eyes were wide with fear as he tumbled headfirst onto the rocky shoal beneath. I found the mock rope ladder, which was swaying with the crazy winds and slippery from the pelting rain. Climbing down, down, down as fast as I could, I reached the bottom where I was chest deep in freezing ocean water.

A riptide tried to pull me out to sea, like a sneering demon, but I stared at the beast, and having swam the treacherous currents of the Graveyard of the Atlantic off Cape Hatteras, I thought: *I've seen better than you.* I thrashed around in the ocean shouting, "General Sinclair! General Sinclair!"

I feared he was wounded. Rocks poked up through the high tide as a reminder that jagged teeth lay just beneath the surface.

Then I found a body floating facedown in the water, bobbing between two rocks, arms splayed outward as if in surrender. My chest tightened as I held emotions in check. I looked up at the impossible climb the Rangers had made in 1944 and had a brief moment of reconciliation. There was symmetry in Garrett Sinclair I climbing to a new life here and perhaps Garrett Sinclair III falling to his death in the exact same spot.

I was a man of few words and even fewer emotions. Ever since my mother had been brutally murdered in North Carolina, I have been nothing short of a wrecking ball. General Sinclair shaped me and molded me into something worthwhile, aiming my anger and aggression at the appropriate targets, always telling me, "Front toward enemy, Jake."

As the water sloshed around me, I pulled at the inert body. As I dragged it free of its rockbound moorings, a riptide swirled and sucked it out to sea without giving me the chance to positively identify the remains. The body darted past the tanks and landing craft that made the bay here so treacherous.

And it was gone.

I shouted, losing all control. "Nooo!"

Then a voice called me, perhaps from the beyond, "Jake." With the wind and rain, it was difficult to tell if it was real: Ms. Champollion calling from above, or the wind talking to me.

I looked at the spinning sky, wondering how this could happen. But I knew how it happened. Good people died doing the right thing, often for the wrong people and reasons. All we have in this world are the people we care about and who care about us. We do everything we can to protect them and then we leave. That's the warrior code, the Dagger code.

The ocean tugged at me, and for a moment I thought about letting it have me. To take me from this world of pain and anguish, of losing the people we care about. But then I thought of Randy and Joe and Patch and Sean and Misha and even Reagan and Brad. Each one of them was a reason not to release myself to the tugging demons whose icy claws were pulling me outward.

"Jake."

By now a high-powered flashlight was shining from the bluff onto my location. I turned and saw a body hanging from a steel piton maybe twenty feet above the high tide. His outer tactical vest had snagged on the beveled edge of the piton. His feet dangled above beckoning razor-sharp boulders that bared their edges with every ebb of the ocean.

"Jake."

I moved toward the body just as a rogue wave barreled in, slammed me against the headwall, and pulled the body free from the piton, sucking it past me before I could get there. In the seafoam and colliding swells, the body was an indecipherable black mass.

I released myself into the riptide and rode the surge outward into the bay. My leg hit something, and I felt a burn, perhaps a gash, on my calf. The underwater debris field was massive here, and it would make sense if a gun turret had nearly ripped my leg off.

Spinning in the vortex of swirling ocean was a body. The rip current had spat it out to the north side of the bay. Unfortunately, the rip spun me to the south. The separation was about fifty meters. The body was floating and spinning. My core temperature was lowering quickly in the freezing water.

I dove under the water, like duck-diving a surfboard, and struggled against the rip. I found a tank gun tube and pulled with my hands and then pushed with my feet, propelling me back into the rip. I tumbled with it and fought, which is rule number one not to do. I pulled and tugged and found another turret or tank tube. I pulled with my hands and then pushed with my feet fighting through the water sucking out to sea until I was mercifully on the other side.

I came out of the water, gasping for air, grabbed the body, and found a swell surging inland. I stumbled through the rocks and dragged the water-soaked, leaden body onto a sliver of beach not affected by high tide.

I rolled him over and said to myself, "Oh my God."

EPILOGUE

JAKE MAHEGAN SAVED MY life.

There on the beaches of Normandy, he entered the fray and pulled me to safety. I had lost so much blood that I was unconscious. The cold salt water, though, served a purpose in both slowing the blood flow and keeping my wounds clean.

I was jacked up in a hospital bed with Evelyn Champollion and Misha on either side of me. Evelyn had been hospitalized for a few days and released. She had her pilots fly the Dagger and Sharpstone teams from Colorado Site X-Ray here to the American Hospital in Paris on Victor Hugo Boulevard.

The doctors were excellent, and they were learning to not enforce visiting hours, which my family and team didn't care about.

Evelyn was holding my hand, stroking it lightly.

"We almost lost you," she whispered.

"And you," I replied.

A monitor on the wall to my front lit up with letters scrolling across the screen.

General is tough but monster is tougher!!! ;););)

I imagined that Misha dealt with fear like many young adults her age, with a thin veneer of humor. I slowly turned my head and looked at her huddled in her chair. Tears streamed down her face.

"It's okay, Misha," I said.

"But . . . it was me," she muttered.

"Drewson fooled all of us," I said. "Everyone."

"That's right, Misha. Both Mitch and Aurelius were nothing but charlatans. I imagine that's the case with most people," Evelyn added.

The screen lit up again.

Not with us!! Not with Dagger team and Sharpstone!!

"No, you're right, Misha. We have to figure out what Sharpstone is and who it belongs to, but you're right. This team is all we've got. Each other. That's all that matters," I said.

Let me review, General! Sharpstone is yours. Phalanx is yours. The Phalanx Code is a smart contract done in a digital ledger by your genius grandfather. Blanc wanted Evelyn to change it, giving Drewson your half. Then they were selling microchip access to the Chinese and others to allow enemies to spy on the United States. The kill list was just a fake code. A deception. I have it all stored in a vault. The will leaves you Phalanx and Sharpstone. It's yours.

"Not sure I want any of that," I said. Honestly, I didn't understand any of it, but I trusted Misha and Evelyn knew the facts.

"She's right, Garrett," Evelyn said.

Brad came hustling in, pushing Reagan in a wheelchair.

"Oh my God, you're awake," Reagan said.

"Dad, you gotta see these songs I've written," Brad blurted. Never once had he asked me to see anything he had created, and he usually cringed at the thought of me watching him play guitar in his band, Napoleon's Corporal. He handed me a stack of papers.

"I look forward to reading them, but would prefer you play them for me," I said.

"Seriously?!" he shouted. "I thought you hated what I do." He looked away.

"I love that you do something you're passionate about, son," I said. "And I hear you guys rock."

"Look at Dad trying to be cool," Reagan said. "By the way, they do 'rock,'" she said, dramatizing with air quotes. They both looked at Evelyn's hand still holding mine. I had worried about how they might feel about my involvement with someone other than their mother.

"OMG. No way. Brad and I were saying. OMG. I totally told you, Brad," Reagan said, stumbling over her words.

"Based," Brad said.

"I'm assuming you approve," I said, not understanding any of their lingo.

"More importantly, Mom would approve," Reagan said. "Evelyn's beautiful and famous and stuff."

"I'm right here, honey," Evelyn said, waving her hand at Reagan.

"Oh my God, I'm so sorry. I know. Dad's alive. Everybody's alive. I'm alive," Reagan said.

Mahegan, Hobart, and Van Dreeves came into the hospital room despite the best efforts of a diminutive nurse in a white lab coat to keep them at bay. They looked like three bouncers or MMA fighters or, well, Special Operations soldiers with their slightly too long hair, tight-fitting shirts, four-day growth, and humorless affects.

"Boss," they all mumbled in some fashion or another.

"Team," I said. Looking at Mahegan, I said, "Thanks, Jake."

Mahegan nodded.

"No problem," Jake said.

"The nukes? Zeus Micron?"

"Got the shipment from Boulder, but there's one batch unaccounted for," Mahegan said.

"Another time," Evelyn said.

"Yes," I replied, looking at my family. "Another time."

Evelyn gripped my hand tightly. Reagan wept. And instead of thinking of the missing semiconductors, I read Brad's songs about family, faith, and freedom.

ACKNOWLEDGMENTS

I'M GRATEFUL TO so many people for so many aspects of my life.

Within my writing universe, I'm thankful for my editor, Marc Resnick, and his superb assistant editor, Lily Cronig. The entire leadership and staff at St. Martin's Press has been fabulous and a million percent supportive of me and my writing.

I'm also thankful to the team at Kensington Books who brought Jake Mahegan to life over six novels. Steven Zacharius, Gary Goldstein, and Lynn Cully all supported me in the creation of the Mahegan universe, which makes a comeback in *The Phalanx Code*.

My agent, Scott Miller, and the team at Trident Media agency have been extremely supportive during my career as an author.

Likewise, I appreciate the support of my writing coach Kaitlin Murphy-Knudsen, who has been with me for all sixteen novels. Also, my fellow thriller authors have made it all worthwhile: Jack Carr, Simon Gervais, Mark Greaney, Brad Thor, Jeff Wilson, Brian Andrews, Ward Larsen, Brad Taylor, Jim Born, Joel Rosenberg, Bob Crais, Don Bentley, Marc

Cameron, Kim Howe, Daniel Palmer, Jon Land, Ben Coes, Eric Bishop, Jeff Ayers, Tosca Lee, and so many others.

Within my business life, as I've rebuilt my life after government service, so many people have surrounded me with support and opportunity: Thanks to Ben Carson, Jr., Nick Neonakis, Jeff Dudan, Pete Tocci, Marc Lopresti, Sara Sooy, Michael Weinberg, Jon Najarian and the Moneta team, Neil Greene and Jaboy Productions, Moner Attwa, Rickard Hedeby and the Intertec team, Mothusi Pahl and the Modern Hydrogen team, John Rogers, David Wertheimer, Phil McConkey and the Academy Securities team, Michelle Rhee, Chuck Schoninger and the USA Investco team, Sheila Driscoll, John and Greg Blevins, Don Cummins, and the B3 Bar team, Rick Geisel, James Bacon, Ezra Cohen, Heino Klinck, Ric Grennell, Paul Ney, Larisa Miller, DW Moffett and the Phoenix Global team, Jorge Suarez Menendez, Gabe Dymond, Chris Miller, Courtney Piemonte, Rick Connors, Wayne Danson, Mike Whitehouse, Keith Kellogg, John McEntee, David Crabtree, Rick French, Charles Yeomans, Ron Moeller, Henry Gayer, Gino Ramadi, Remy Szykier and Joxel Garcia, Michael and Sharon Cole, Greg and Kathy Fell, and so many others. The bookers, producers, and anchors of Fox News and Newsmax have been incredible to work with as we cover the evolving military and political landscape.

I appreciate the constant support of my lifelong friends Gary Austin, Larry Jeffries, Kevin Walck, Kevin Roomsburg, Amy Bowler, David and Sheila Bogart, Tom Speelman, Mike Sage, Mark and Marlene Creekmore, Tiny Barlow and the entire Coach Ray Barlow Believe in Yourself Foundation, Sheriff Donnie Harrison, Herb and Stephanie Wilson, Jim and Maryann Baldwin, Bert Austin, John Beaton, Tom Bosco, John McGrath, Bill Hein, Don Devine, Janet Petro, Mike Canavan, Tom Palmen, Rich Burns, Phil Volpe, and all the Scrauggs, and Linwood Todd, Brock Ayers, Bill Reagan, General (U.S. Army, Retired) Dick Cody, Lieutenant General (U.S. Army, Retired) Frank Helmick, Major General (U.S. Army, Retired) Ed Reeder, and so many others.

I am however most thankful for my family, who have been through the fire with me: Laura, Snowy, Bandit; Brooke, Peter, and Leo Anthony; Zach, Lindsey, and Allie Kate; Kendall Tata, Bob and Anne Ferrell Tata, along with Peyton, Rafe, Tinsley, and Lucy; Riley, Albert, and Charlotte Louise; Carter and Tad; and Lil' Robert; and Jamie and Carol Jones.

Special thanks to Barbara Ruddy, who donated $5,000 to the Vero Beach Veterans Memorial in exchange for becoming a character in *The Phalanx Code*.

There are so many more people to thank, but the theme is that my life's journey and especially the path in the last few years has been a team effort filled with supportive and loving people, for which I am most appreciative.